MARTIN MARTEN

BRIAN DOYLE

THOMAS DUNNE BOOKS
ST. MARTIN'S PRESS
NEW YORK

This is a work of fiction. All of the characters, organizations, and events portrayed in this novel are either products of the author's imagination or are used fictitiously.

THOMAS DUNNE BOOKS.
An imprint of St. Martin's Press.

MARTIN MARTEN. Copyright © 2015 by Brian Doyle. All rights reserved. Printed in the United States of America. For information, address St. Martin's Press, 175 Fifth Avenue, New York, N.Y. 10010.

www.thomasdunnebooks.com
www.stmartins.com

Interior illustrations by Katrina Van Dusen

Library of Congress Cataloging-in-Publication Data

Doyle, Brian, 1956–
    Martin Marten : a novel / Brian Doyle.—First edition.
        p. cm.
    ISBN 978-1-250-04520-1 (hardcover)
    ISBN 978-1-4668-4369-1 (e-book)
    1. Teenage boys—Fiction.   2. American marten—Fiction.   3. Martens—
Fiction.   4. Oregon—Fiction.   I. Title.
    PS3604.O9547M37 2015
    813'.6—dc23

                                                                2014040685

St. Martin's Press books may be purchased for educational, business, or promotional use. For information on bulk purchases, please contact the Macmillan Corporate and Premium Sales Department at 1-800-221-7945, extension 5442, or write to specialmarkets@macmillan.com.

First Edition: April 2015

10 9 8 7 6 5 4 3 2 1

For Mary

AUTHOR'S NOTE

The little crossroads hamlet called Zigzag in this book is *not* the actual little hamlet of the same name in Oregon in any way, shape, or form. I just love the name and borrowed it cheerfully thievingly. On the other hand, the Zigzag River in this book absolutely *is* the real Zigzag River on the holy mountain Wy'east, complete with tiny meadows and huge rocks and old cottonwoods and relentless burble and ice-cold pools clear as glass with young fish holding in them like tiny silver knives. My thanks to that brief but adamant river for allowing me to try to write down a bit of its story.

Beauty and grace are performed whether or not we will or sense them. The least we can do is try to be there.

—ANNIE DILLARD

We will never, we cannot, leave [animals] alone, even the tiniest one, ever, because we know we are one with them. Their blood is our blood. Their breath is our breath, their beginning our beginning, their fate our fate. Thus we deny them. Thus we yearn for them. They are among us and within us and of us, inextricably woven with the form and manner of our being, with our understanding and our imaginations. They are the grit and the salt and the lullaby of our language.

—PATTIANN ROGERS, "ANIMALS AND PEOPLE"

The unthinkable / is thinkable.

—WISŁAWA SZYMBORSKA

PART I

DAVE IS FOURTEEN YEARS OLD. He is neither tall nor short. He is probably thinner than he should be, all things considered, according to his mom, who is deeply and continually amazed that a boy who eats ten sandwiches a day can somehow get skinnier and taller by the hour. She says he weighs basically the same as he did when he was the world's fattest baby—except now he is five feet taller than he was then.

Dave lives with his mom and dad and one sister. His sister was the world's second-fattest baby, but now she is almost six years old, and she too is getting skinnier and taller by the hour, says their mom. It appears to be a family thing, says their mom, and eventually you kids will be ten feet tall and weigh ten pounds each, and we will have to live in a tall, thin tower.

It is funny to hear her talk about this, says Dave, because as my dad says she might be five feet tall on a hot summer day, and she is getting smaller by the year. She sure is getting shorter every year, though, and if this continues, soon she will be the size of my sister, and my sister will have grown to be Mom's former height, and everything will be all discombobulated.

Dave and his sister and mom and dad live in a cabin on Mount Hood in Oregon. Dave prefers to say that he lives on Wy'east, which is what the first people who lived on and around it called the mountain for thousands of years, rather than Hood, which is what some guy from another country called it one day, and *that* guy and his friends had guns, so *their* name for the mountain stuck, but it ought not to be the case, says Dave, that a guy with a gun gets to be the boss, especially of names, which are important. So Dave likes to say that he and his family live on Wy'east, so that is the name we will use for the rest of this story. Half of this story is Dave's story, after all, so he gets a serious vote on names in the story. That's only fair.

*

The cabin is near a small river called the Zigzag. It is called the Zigzag for reasons you can imagine. In the river there are all sorts of fish; Dave has counted nineteen species that he can identify and three that he cannot, yet. There are also a lot of other animals and insects, but Dave concentrates on the fish because they are interesting and good to eat. In the woods near the cabin and the river, there are all sorts of animals. Dave has counted more than seventy species and has drawn them on a chart in the cabin according to size. The chart hangs on the wall in his bedroom. His bedroom is the size of a black bear's den, says Dave, who actually crawled into a black bear's den once, after he and his dad made absolutely sure that no bear had been there for a long time. The biggest animal on Dave's chart, curiously, is not a bear, although there are some tremendous bears in these woods, but an elk called Louis, who is half again as big as the biggest elk anyone has ever seen. Louis may be the most hunted being in the long history of the mountain, says Dave's dad. You wouldn't believe how many people buy hunting permits every year for the express purpose of shooting Louis, and every year someone claims they did so, and every spring Louis emerges again from the snowy wilderness of the woods, not at all dead, and looking slightly bigger, as if he'd spent the winter lifting weights in a cave somewhere. That is one mountainous elk, so to speak, says Dave's dad, who says personally *he* will never shoot Louis, even if he had the chance, out of respect for Louis's remarkable persistence and intelligence in avoiding people who would like nothing better than to shoot him. And Dave's dad also refuses to even touch a gun anymore for various reasons. One of these days, if those hunters don't watch out, says Dave's dad, old *Louis* is going to learn how to use a rifle, and then it will be a donnybrook and brouhaha of rare proportions which we would be wise to avoid.

*

That is how Dave's dad talks, with words like *donnybrook* and *vainglorious* and *epistolary*, and he just expects you to know what he is talking about, says Dave, as if you too had read every book in the town library and every book in the bookstore's lending library and every book in the lost-and-found library at Timberline Lodge up the mountain, where Dave's mom works in laundry services. You would think that my dad had gone to college, says Dave, but this is not so, as yet. He *wanted* to go to college, but a war intervened, says my dad, and his personal compass got bruised and battered and set toward a new star. That's how he explains it when people ask him about his past. He never says much about being in the war except that not going to college allowed him the extraordinary gift and privilege of meeting and subsequently courting Mom. Dad says if he had never been in the war and afterwards come up the mountain to get some peace and quiet and recover his shaken equilibrium, he would never have met Mom reading a book in the sun in the woods near the lodge, and if he had not met Mom, he would not have the surpassing benediction of being allowed to be the dad not only of me but my sister also, a clean sweep of the possible genders of children, says Dad, so that really, rather than be all upset about missing college and having to be in a war, maybe he should be *delighted* at missing college and filled with gratitude for having had the honor to serve his remarkable country in a war, however foolish war in general is, and especially in this particular case, was. This is how my dad talks, says Dave, interesting but at angles other than most people do. You have to listen pretty close when Dad talks, partly because sometimes he doesn't talk at all for days, and then when he *does* talk, it sometimes seems like he is talking about something altogether other than what you thought you were talking about—but he's not.

★

Dave is a regular guy. He is not particularly strong or athletic or brilliant in school or handsome or talented in music. He is a terrible skier, even though he lives on a mountain covered in snow every day of the year and people come from around the country to ski there and most of his friends and schoolmates ski easily and well because they live there and everyone skis well except for Dave. He is not much for snowboarding, either, or cross-country skiing or snowshoeing, even though most of the kids he knows do those things well as well. He does like snow, and he likes sliding down the mountain on garbage can lids and old tire tubes, but he doesn't *love* snow, like his classmates. Most of his classmates either love snow or say they do, and they have ambitions to be ski racers and snowboard stars and travel around in cool vans and get free money from ski and snowboard companies for simply skiing and snowboarding with panache and brio.

Whereas in Dave's experience, skiing and snowboarding inevitably mean freezing and soaking and crashing into bushes and thickets and desperately avoiding trees and then slogging all the way back to the place where you started. In Dave's experience, cool snowy mountain adventures usually conclude with a bad head cold and something that you hope is only sprained rather than actually broken, which will cost the family money which we do not have.

However, Dave *does* love being in the woods, even in the snow, and he does love walking and running for miles and miles in dense and unpopulated forest and climbing above the tree line and gaping at the line of mountains running south in a straight line from Wy'east all the way to the California border on a good day. He loves that more than anything except his mom and dad and sister, and he loves that his mom and dad are cool enough to trust him to walk and run alone in the vast forests of the mountain, carrying only water and a compass and a poncho. They started letting him wander in the woods when he was ten years old. First he was allowed to wander anywhere within a mile, as long as he was home before dark and avoided the road and the river; as his dad said one million times, the highway was far more dangerous than anything he would ever encounter in the woods, even bears and cougars, and the river was where accidents went when they wanted to happen.

When Dave was twelve years old he was allowed to wander anywhere he wanted, as long as he brought a compass, a poncho, and a bottle of water. His dad went over topographic and weather maps of the mountain one million times with him until he was sure that Dave knew every river coming off the mountain, every road to avoid, and the most pressing concerns about weather; of all the places on this green earth where weather can hurt or kill you right quick, said his dad, this is the king of those places, more than a desert or an ocean. Snow comes fast, temperature drops fast, rain turns to ice fast, rivers burst their banks fast. Know where you are, and be wary of the weather; within those constraints, you are a free man with your time, if your domestic and academic responsibilities have been executed responsibly.

This was how Dave's dad talked, sort of scholarly but blunt. Dave's dad was a decent guy, although he was a real stickler for domestic and academic responsibilities. Dave's mom was not quite such a stickler that way, but she was a total stickler for kindness and tenderness toward Dave's baby sister and respect and reverence for everything else alive, as she said. We are omnivorous mammals, and so we are designed to have to kill and eat certain of our fellow beings of every shape and sort and size, but we will do so with re-spect and reverence for the inestimable value of that life we are taking in order to aid and abet our own lives, as she said. And we will make a concerted effort to not only defend life against those who would take it without respect and reverence but encourage and seed life where and when we can, which is why she planted flowers and vegetables all around the cabin and in any and all sunny spots nearby and volunteered one afternoon a week at the raptor recovery center on the other side of the mountain and stood up at town meetings and school board meetings to remind everyone that clean water was the paramount gift and virtue of their region and that their clear duty as residents was to defend clean water against any and all attempts to foul rivers and creeks and lakes. This was how Dave's mom talked, passionately but simply, and when she stood up to speak she sounded tall, thought Dave, even though she was hardly five feet tall and getting smaller by the year.

★

The last person in the cabin I want to tell you about is my sister, says Dave. She is five years old, but she is one advanced being, that's for sure. She rambles widely. Her name is Maria. She is al-most six years old. Her birthday is next week. She does not talk much, but she sees little things in the woods that no one else sees. She too is now allowed to roam on her own outside the house, but she has four markers past which she must not go, cross her heart. One is the big rock that looks like a hawk, which is as near to the highway as she can go. One is the huge red cedar tree that might be a thousand years old, which is as deep into the forest as she can go. One is the copper beech tree that someone planted many years ago, which is as close to the river as she can go. And the fourth point on her campus is Miss Moss's store, which is as far down our road as Maria can go. She signed a contract with Dad about all this, and she knows if you sign your name, then you are bound to keep your word. She has short red hair. She sleeps late in the morning but then stays up at night looking at books and drawing maps. She says her greatest ambition is to be me. I point out that she cannot be me inasmuch as I am me, and she says *we will see about that, Dave.* I say for one thing I am male and she is female and she says *maybe those are just labels, Dave.* This is how she talks when she talks at all, which she does not do so much. But she hears and sees everything, that kid. You wouldn't believe the things she sees when we walk in the woods. She found a bear claw one time stuck in a tree in a place where I had been leaning for ten minutes and never saw it. She has found deer antlers and animal bones and baby birds in nests and arrowheads and one time a hunting knife so rusted with what we thought was blood that our dad took it to the police station down the mountain in Gresham, just in case. One time she even found a pair of sneakers frozen solid inside a chunk of ice when we were up on the mountain past Timberline Lodge in winter, and how she saw those in the ice remains a mystery to this day, for they were new white sneakers inside a white block of ice among a pile and jumble of blocks of ice fallen off the Joel Palmer Glacier. Joel Palmer was one of the first white people on the mountain, and there's a story that his moccasins wore out as he climbed over the peak in winter, and he had to come down over the glacier barefoot. Maria says those sneakers must be Joel Palmer's sneakers, and he didn't want to get them wet, maybe, because they were so shining new. Our dad thawed them out and dried them carefully, and now they sit on the shelf over the fireplace with a card explaining how Maria found Joel Palmer's sneakers. See, a card explaining the exhibit for visitors, that is the sort of life we lead in our cabin. In our family, we leave room for the possibility that someone will come in and wonder about the new white sneakers above the fireplace, and if that happens, why, then, we are prepared for that.

2

ONE NIGHT, years before, late in the autumn, about a mile south in the deep woods from where Dave and Maria and their mom and dad live, a terrific windstorm on the mountain snapped off the top half of a vaulting Douglas fir tree. This fir tree was at that time more than four hundred years old and had grown in such an inaccessible ravine that it had never been logged before the national forest was established in 1893, so that even when it lost a hundred feet of height and its entire bushy canopy, even though it was now a ragged snag that looked sort of naked and forlorn, it still soared a hundred feet into the crisp air of the ravine, way up where only the ravens and falcons flew.

Year by year, as the tree slowly died, it was hammered and hollowed by all sorts of animals, from the smallest borers and beetles to the largest woodpeckers, and three times it was hit hard by lightning, which shivered and rattled it something fierce. Finally, about halfway up the trunk, what had been a small cavity became a fairly roomy hole, really a small wooden cave, about two feet deep by two feet wide. For a few years the hole was a nest for various birds; then it was taken over by a family of flying squirrels for several years; then it was the home of the owl who ate the squirrels; and then, after quite a long stretch of that owl's family and descendants, it had been commandeered by a lean brown animal called a marten.

This particular marten was a mother who knew that she would soon deliver her kits, and she had been looking for weeks for the exact right den for this momentous event; she had examined burrows and caves of all kinds, from stone caves at the timberline to the abandoned burrows of foxes to the hollow logs in

which skunks love to live, but none offered the defensible safety, sturdy walls, scope of grim maternal vision, and essentially weatherproof environment that she sought until she found the fir snag one moist spring morning. She evicted the badly frightened young owl who thought he had a perfect right to the hole inasmuch as it had been in his family for several generations, and she spent the next three days lining it properly with moss and fern and grouse feathers. When she was done, her only regret was that she did not have owl feathers, the previous occupant having left the hole too quickly to have contributed significantly to decor.

And in that wooden cave this April evening there is a birth; and then another, and then two more; until finally there is an exhausted mother, delighted but weary, and four tiny squirming nearly naked marten kits, none of them bigger than your thumb. The first three born are males, and the last, the tiniest, female. For a moment, after the last kit is born, she struggles with her larger brothers to find room to suckle; but then the brother born right before her shoves their older brothers aside to make room for the baby, and she too savors the first rich milky meal of her life. On and off for days and days the kits suckle and sleep, sleep and suckle, their mother dozing and occasionally rising to stretch and poke a wary nose out the front door.

Down below their tree, the snow melted, even in the shadowed parts of the ravine, and bushes sprouted new green fingers, and trees awoke from their long slumber, and all sorts of mammals and birds and insects found the doors by which their new generations entered this wild world; and there came a momentous day in late May when the mother marten led her four glossy kits, now the size of fists, headfirst down the fir to the redolent and seething wilderness below. She went first, showing her progeny how to grip lightly with their razor claws and walk confidently on the dense bark; the third brother, the one who had been kind to his sister, brought up the rear. Though he was the youngest of the brothers, he was noticeably the largest, and he seemed nearly twice as large as his sister. Tiny though she was, she learned quickest and was the only one of the four who did not tumble into the ferns at the base of the tree; instead, she leapt as lightly and deftly from the tree as her mother, while Martin, the youngest of the brothers, rounded up the other two and cuffed them back into line behind their mother. And so it was the five marten made their way to the river through an astonishing new world of trees and rocks, songs and whistles, bushes and scents, mud and flowers, all bathed in the high thin light of a mountain afternoon in spring. You could write a thousand books about this first walk alone, but of this opening adventure, Martin would remember only this one event: a honeybee rumbled by, and the oldest of his brothers leapt and snapped at it, and the bee stung the kit exactly between his teeth and his nose so that his upper lip swelled to epic proportions, and the kit could not suckle his mother for two days, so there was that much more milk for the other three, who enjoyed the largesse with a deep and humming pleasure as their brother moaned and bubbled and bemoaned the flying dagger it had been his misfortune to investigate.

3

DAVE'S DAD WAS A SORT OF LOGGER, as he said. He worked with two other men in a little three-man company that did selective logging on the mountain on contracts from the State of Oregon and Clackamas County. They also did a whole slew of other jobs, like hauling timber after forest fires, and maintaining and replacing signage in the national forest, and hauling drivers out of ditches after blizzards on the mountain, and helping repair bridges and washouts after storms and floods, and so many more things that if we listed them all, this page would go on for a week. Dave's dad also volunteered at the library in Zigzag once a week and occasionally did a little yard and carpentry work for people who needed it done but did not have any money, like Miss Moss. Dave's dad pretty much worked all the time, even on Sunday around the cabin doing this and that and the other thing, but he never made a fuss about it or seemed to sweat or move fast, and he always had time to sit and answer questions or stare at woodpeckers for a while if that's what needed to be done. What with Dave's dad's several jobs and Dave's mom's job in laundry services at the lodge, we seemed to have just enough money to get by, says Dave, if nobody got sick or broke anything and the car kept working.

Then my dad lost his job, says Dave.

Dad says that he didn't lose it, exactly, says Dave. He says that he declined to further participate in suspicious activity which he believed to be not only unjust but illegal. This is how my dad talks, even in a moment like this, when he is explaining to my mom at the table why he lost his job. It turned out that the two men he worked with had signed contracts to do work that Dad says is clearly against the law, not to mention poor business for the citizens of the mountain of every shape and stripe, and when he made his feelings known, the other men said grimly, *in or out, Jack,* and Dad said grimly, *out,* so he is out. Mom says she is proud of his decision and supports him without reservation, but her face is haggard, and she is asking to add Saturdays and probably Sundays to her job at laundry services at the lodge. Maria and I have talked about what we can do for money, and she says she will have to think about this more before she can come up with a plan, because she is not yet six years old, and perhaps turning six will afford her some new ideas. I myself, said Dave, have decided to snare birds and rabbits to eat, and then when the snow comes, run a fur-trapping line. I have read a lot about fur trapping, and I think a young man with some experience in the woods should be able to make a small profit, if he approaches the task with caution and diligence and persistence. If I prepare thoroughly this summer and scope out the right places for traps and familiarize myself with the lives and habits of the animals in question, I think I can be of material assistance to the family, which certainly, despite the fact that no one is talking about it, needs help.

★

There is a store in Zigzag that sells every single possible small important thing you could ever imagine you could ever need, if you lived on a mountain far from the flurry and huddle of stores in the city. In this store in Zigzag, you can buy string of every conceivable strength and fiber. You can buy traps. You can buy arrows. You can buy milk and cookies. You can buy tire irons and shoehorns. You can buy false teeth and denture glue. You can buy comic books and kindling. You can buy apples and pork tenderloin. You can buy kale and rock salt. You can buy explosive caps for removing rubble from a precarious situation. You can buy saws and drill bits. You can buy nightgowns and shotgun shells. You can buy old cassette tapes, and you can order iPads and iPods, which Miss Moss will have for you next week at the earliest, a phrase she much enjoys using for all sorts of things, only some of them having to do with the store; Dave remembers when he was little and asked Miss Moss when the sun would come up the next day and she said distractedly, *next week at the earliest*. Miss Moss also claims that she can order iGlasses and iWash, although no customer has as yet ordered those things. She once with a totally straight face told a small boy that, yes, she could order an iPanther, the most interactive mountain lion app imaginable, but it would not arrive until next week at the earliest.

You can also buy parts of old cars at Miss Moss's store, but the way that works is that you have to go out back behind the store in the clearing where there are old cars, tractors, trucks, snowmobiles, wooden carts and wagons, bicycles, snowboards, skis, ski poles, ski-lift cables, airplane seats, propellers, refrigerators, washers, dryers, pipes, card tables, shelving, planks, barrels, a toboggan, and many other things, and you find what you want and haul it to the back door of the store, where Miss Moss comes and stares at it with a cold appraising eye and offers a price, which you accept immediately, because, as Dave's dad says, Miss Moss knows exactly what things *ought* to cost, but sets her prices slightly *lower* for reasons that are murky. In this way, Dave found and bought a small longspring trap, only a little rusted, and enough strong wire to use for snares or trap anchors; and he walked back home through the woods, along the river, excited and afraid. Could he catch grouse and rabbits for the pot? Could he catch fox and marten? Could or should he kill animals just for their skins? Wasn't that just savage and brutal? But they did kill some animals for food, he thought, chickens and fish, mostly, and they did use the skins of other animals for coats and blankets.

The trap clanked against his shoulder as he walked along the river. By now, almost June, the snow was gone, this far down the mountain, but the river was still crammed with melt, and it raced and thrummed and braided in endlessly riveting ways. You could, as Dave many times had, just sit there in the sun with your back against a tree and watch and listen to the river sprint and thurble and trip and thumble; you had to invent words for the ways it raced and boiled and dashed and crashed, and indeed Dave had once spent an afternoon trying to write one long word that would catch something of the river's song and story when it was full of itself like this, not yet the shy trickle it would be in summer and fall, before the Rains came on All Souls' Day, and then the dim chamber of winter, when snow fell slowly all day every day for weeks at a time, and the woods were filled with soft slumps and sighs as trees shed their loads. Somewhere in the cabin, he had that piece of paper, he knew, for Maria had tried to read the word recently and only got halfway through; it was something like trilltrickleslipwhirltumlullrill, he thought; and he remembered that his mom had read it and said it sounded, by heavens, Welsh, didn't it?

He sat down, smiling. The trap was heavier than he had thought, and a brilliant warm sunny spring day like this was a rare enough meal on the mountain that it ought to be eaten slowly, savoring every bite; and dinner wouldn't be for a long while. He leaned back and sat as still as he possibly could and waited for the world to present itself, and soon enough he heard the rattle of a flicker, the hammer of a gray jay (the whisky jack, as his dad called it), and the shirring of a squirrel somewhere above him, nervous and curious. The river thwirled and bubbulated. He heard a raven's deep squark and a chipmunk's chitter and skitter. The squirrel above him crept closer and dropped pine seeds on his head and shoulders to test if he was alive or stone. He tried to be smiling stone. Take even breaths and fall into the moment and the light. The first few times he'd tried this, tried to get so absorbed in the sights and sounds and smells of the moment, he'd fallen asleep, but now he'd had enough practice at it to savor and relish the treeness of the trees, for example. Trees moved gently, if you paid close attention, and they brushed against each other, and you could only imagine their sensory apparatuses, their particularly sylvan and dendritic take on the world; perhaps, he had sometimes thought, they are staring at me and trying to dig the Daveness of Dave. That could be.

Damselflies whirred close, and four of them, one brilliantly red, landed on his knee and camped for a while; a small fish leapt from the river; a young male blacktail deer browsed a huckleberry bush for a few moments, its first spike antlers all of four inches high; and then Dave saw, one after another in a line like hikers on a narrow trail, five small lustrous golden brown animals slip out of the woods on the other side of the river. Four were smaller than the leader, who was clearly in charge, probably a parent, and the last one in line looked for all the world like he or she was the trusted deputy, bringing up the rear as a precaution against stragglers and mischief. Even as Dave watched, one of the smaller animals lurched to one side after a damselfly, and the last animal in line shoved the explorer back into place with an easy authority that made Dave grin. What *were* these animals? Not cat or fox, not squirrel or marmot, not mink or otter. Too small for bears, too big for weasels, too lithe for skunk. They looked rather like lean un-masked raccoons, though the coloring was all wrong, and they had none of the bearish big-butt waddle of the raccoon clan. More than anything, they looked like pocket-sized wolverines, but that wasn't possible, was it? Wolverines were bigger than dogs, and be-sides, no one had seen wolverines on Wy'east in a hundred years. But wolverines have cousins, don't they? Fisher and badger and . . .

Marten!

And just as Dave realized what sort of animals they were and blurted it aloud, they vanished back into the woods, graceful and silent as wraiths; but the last one heard Dave say the word and turned and looked at Dave, and he and Dave stared for a long instant at each other before Martin slipped under a fern frond, following his family, and Dave stood up, thrilled and stiff, and walked home to tell *his* family what he had seen.

4

MARTIN'S MOST ADVENTUROUS BROTHER, the one who had been stung by the honeybee and who was inquisitive about dam-selflies, the firstborn of the four, was so curious and headlong and headstrong and inquiracious about everything that you could write four books about his adventures alone without undue strain. He poked into everything—and by everything, I mean *every-thing*. Any hole, den, shadowed place, rockfall, deadfall of leaves and branches, nook, cranny, pool, rivulet, blind corner; in he went, curious and careless, and half the time he came out sprinting in terror, escaping in some cases literally by the hairs on his tail. He jammed his head into one den and discovered a very angry bobcat. He was driven from burrows by minks and weasels. He was stabbed above the right eye by the same owl who had been displaced from her hole in the fir tree and never forgot the indignity and was more than willing to punish the next stranger who appeared to be looking for a home. He was again and again stung by bees and wasps and hornets; he never seemed to learn that, small as they were, they defended their homes with alacrity and tiny awls. He was kicked in the jaw by a rabbit. He was chased headlong through a meadow by a fox. He was chased by a young dog and an old coyote. He was chased through another meadow by a grim doe. He drew the attention of a cougar near timberline, who marked his passage and filed away his pattern of movement and routes of escape when harried by a hawk. He drew the attention of a golden eagle above timberline, who watched him amble through the rock-fields, sniffing after pika and chipmunks; the eagle considered a sudden attack but calculated that her chances were better with a troop of golden-mantled ground squirrels slightly too far from their warren to prevent sudden death for one.

Martin, hidden in the lee of a rock nearby, watched with awe as the eagle arrived, huge and silent, and snared a sun-sleepy squirrel and was away in a flurry and rush of immense dark wings. Martin emerged carefully and watched the eagle flap away and somewhere in his brain stored the ponderous sound of an eagle on the wing. It would be useful to know that sound but more useful to remember that an eagle on the attack was silent and used wind as a cover for a sudden strike. He would remember these things, Martin would. More than his siblings, certainly more than his oldest brother, more perhaps even than his mother and his unknown father, he remembered what he saw and heard and smelled, and paid close attention to cause and effect, and drew his own mysterious conclusions.

*

Most of their first lessons from their mother were about what to eat and how to procure what they ate; inasmuch as marten eat pretty much everything, their culinary curriculum was extensive and demanding. How to catch voles and mice; how to chase squirrels through the trees at lightning speed; how to snatch insects from the air and slurp them from their lairs in rotten logs and under rocks; how to rob birds of their eggs and later kill the parents asleep in their empty nests; how to anticipate the circular path of tree-creepers and nuthatches and snare them unawares; how to swipe frogs from ponds and mudholes; how to pin a garter snake from behind and eat it like a wriggling stick of meat; how to tell a caterpillar chrysalis from a dead leaf and harvest the delicious interior of the former; how to strip berries from their prickly armor and which berries were best among the many available; how to dash in, steal a chunk of honeycomb, and dash out without undue damage except to the oldest brother, who, as usual, suffered the stings and lances of the infuriated bees at ten times the rate his brothers and sister did; how to stun beetles with a blow and eat them slowly as afternoon snacks; how to crack snails against rocks like nuts and savor the unshelled result; and even, in Martin's case, how to catch small fish in creeks and rivers by waiting patiently at the edge of a pool for a fish to hold against the current and then pinning it against the bank for an instant with a paw so that he could get his teeth into play. He taught this technique to his family and was interested to see that his mother and sister were deft at it before his brothers; and true to form, his oldest brother was so curious about the deeper pools in the Zigzag that he finally fell in and was bundled along for a hundred feet before he managed to crawl out, sodden and mewling for his mother.

*

The most and best meat, however, was what had died in the woods, and while all five of the marten were delighted to eat from dead deer and once, late in the summer, an elk, only Martin and his mother sensed the danger of carrion. In general, carrion close to the highway, deer and raccoons and skunks killed by cars and trucks, were safe from the possessive and powerful, but carrion deeper in the woods were usually claimed by their killers, and these shadowy and fearsome animals, as Martin's mother made clear, would be only too happy to kill and eat marten. Bear, cougar, lynx, bobcat, coyote, fisher, and fox: these were the creatures to beware, to flee without question; for all the astounding liquid speed of the marten on the fly, all but the bears were just as fast, in bursts; and several could and would rocket right up into the trees after their prey. There was no question of fighting or outwitting these creatures, and Martin's mother reviewed the lessons again and again, forcing her kits to know and fear those scents, to avoid carrion with too-fresh scent, to approach carrion knowing emergency escape routes, to avoid areas too open for instant flight into the canopy. In her own experience, the most terrifying of all these enemies was the fisher; as a juvenile herself, six years earlier, she had very nearly been caught and eaten by a fisher and had never forgotten that stunning speed and slicing teeth—all the more terrifying because the fisher had looked like nothing so much as a large marten. For an instant that was nearly her last on earth, she had stared at the fisher, interested and perhaps even inclined to be amorous, if it were indeed a large and lustrous marten, until it spun and attacked so quickly that she trembled to this day when she smelled even the faintest hint of its scent. According to all the biologists and hunters and trappers and attentive human residents of the mountain, there were no fishers on Wy'east, and there had been none for many years, just as there were supposedly no more wolves or wolverines; yet Martin's mother smelled the dark hint of fisher sometimes—just the faintest tendril, to be sure, but enough to make her move her kits into their sylvan den as quickly as possible.

★

Three of the kits stopped nursing when they were about five weeks old, although the second brother stayed by his mother's side and tried to nurse for another two weeks; something seemed slightly wrong with him, and he did not move as quickly or deftly as his siblings. His mother, even as she spent her days teaching the four kits how to survive on their own, tried to hunt for this one, as well, killing a mouse or a vole every other day and feeding it to him, the smallest of the brothers; but finally she stopped this effort, turning her energies to a new den in an enormous old cottonwood tree in a slight clearing by the river—a good place, she thought, with access to all sorts of food and good sight lines in case of attack. Here too she commandeered a large and roomy hole, killing the small squirrels in it and saving the bodies for her kits.

Her kits were three months old when she moved them into the new den. She led the way, leaping onto the cottonwood's trunk as light as a shadow and running up to the hole with something very much like pride in the achievement of new quarters. Martin, as usual, brought up the rear, nudging his siblings along, nearly carrying his second brother into the new den. This domicile was slightly smaller but wonderfully dry and thickly lined with moss and meadow grass, and their first night in the new den was a pleasurable feast of red squirrel, one for each member of the family.

But very little activity in the woods goes unseen, and more than one interested creature noted a new family of marten in the cottonwood. In the meadow, the rabbits knew that scent, and something of their wary fear was communicated to the voles and mice, the moles and shrews. In the trees and bushes, the jays, who see all things, shouted the unwelcome news to their cousins; a Cooper's hawk, big enough to snatch a marten kit given the chance, noted the den's whereabouts and calculated angles of attack if a wriggling line of marten meat should present itself apace; and even the deer for acres around were apprised of the news, though they had no reason to fear marten. One creature among them was most interested of all: a gray fox, hidden in an alder tree on the other side of the clearing. Thrice as big as a marten, hungry, smart, and experienced, she had subsisted on mice and voles and the first salmonberries of late spring, but a marten of any size would be a rare and delicious treat. Many animals in the woods would make a meal of the kits, but only a few creatures could catch and overwhelm an adult marten; and here was one of those very creatures, unbeknownst to the newest residents in the little meadow. As darkness fell, they slept, but the fox did not, her eyes sharp green stars in the dark alder thicket.

5

THE PROBLEM with trapping and snaring animals for profit and the pot, Dave discovered, was that it entailed what could only be honestly called murder. He even looked up the word *murder* in the battered dictionary over the fireplace to be sure that he was using the right word. *Killing with malice aforethought*, that was certainly what he was doing, and while the dictionary was careful to define murder as having to do with *unlawful* killing of *human* beings only, and he was lawfully killing beings that were not human, Dave did not feel much better about it. In a way he felt worse, because the dictionary was only emphasizing something he already felt was generally unfair, which was the way human beings assumed they were the best and coolest beings and had all final rights and say in the matter of life and death, without much or any consideration of what other beings thought or felt.

I mean, as Dave said to his dad one night by the fire, I know we eat other beings of all kinds, from animals to plants, and we live in houses built of the bodies of other creatures, and here we are in front of a fire built from the bodies of fir and cedar creatures, and this is all normal and ancient and the way we evolved, but sometimes it just sort of floods in on you that you survive by killing other creatures, and you get a little sad.

An excellent point, said his dad. But at least you are sensitive to it. That's a step in the right direction. At the moment, we do not have much of a choice about what to eat, our bodies having evolved in this way over millions of years, but at least you have a certain respect and honesty about the system. That's good. That's a step toward reverence. Better that than the arrogant assumption that you can kill anything you like any time you like. That's the wrong direction. That direction leads to more killing. Trust me on this one.

These kinds of conversations by the fire were probably Dave's favorite times with his dad. His dad was not much for sports and not much for hunting and fishing and not much for playing video games or watching television—although he did like watching movies with the family once in a while, the four of them curled up on the couch. Dave's mom and dad usually then fell asleep within minutes, and Dave and Maria would finish watching the movie and then gently wake up their parents, who would deny having fallen asleep and talk knowledgeably about the movie as if they had seen it, which they certainly inarguably had not.

★

The first animal who died at Dave's hands was a rabbit, for which he had meticulously set a wire snare. The rabbit, only slightly bigger than Dave's hand, had sprinted into it and strangled and was hanging limp and horrifying in the air like a small brown accusation when Dave checked his snares. It had only been dead for thirty minutes, perhaps—long enough to go cold, but not long enough to be wholly stiff, and after opening the snare that had choked it to death, Dave held it in his hands for a moment, wondering at how something so small could be so deft and vibrant in life and so infinitesimally small and weightless in death, almost as if its life had the weight and the loss of life shrank the creature to an empty skin.

He also found that he felt bad. He had not expected that; he had expected and rather looked forward to feeling triumph, that he had laid plans that worked, that he had procured food for the family in the ancient tradition of the hunter and provider. But instead, he felt small and mean, holding the shell of the rabbit in his gloves. He had planned to reset the snare along this path, clearly a rabbit run, but instead, he packed up his stuff and went home.

Skinning and cleaning the rabbit presented another whole set of logistical and emotional challenges, not to mention a rigorous examination in anatomy—is that a liver or a kidney? How could there be so little obvious meat? Should the internal organs, including a truly disgusting length of what seemed to be the colon, be buried or tossed in the river or securely bagged in plastic and placed in a garbage bin in town? Could it really be the case that he, Dave, the successful hunter, a man who had brought home meat from the wilderness for rabbit stew for his family, would have to ride his bike into town with a reeking bag of rabbit guts on his handlebars and then sneak it into the garbage bin behind Miss Moss's store?

He stared at the charts of rabbit anatomy he had downloaded from the Web and printed out for exactly this moment, when he had to separate the good parts from the foul parts, and after a moment, all the words swam together—the sacculus rotundus, the vermiform appendix, the squamous epithelium, the proximal duodenum, the convoluted jejunum, the ampulla coli. . . . Dave gave up. He carefully put all the disjunct parts of the former rabbit into a black plastic bag, tied it off with three tight knots, washed his hands four times in water slightly hotter than he could stand, and rode down to Miss Moss's store with the bag. Luckily no one was out behind the store, and he slipped the bag into the garbage bin and then went into the store to buy milk and coffee, feeling that he ought to pay for the loan of Miss Moss's facilities somehow. Also, he suspected that the rabbit would reek by the time the bin was ready to be emptied, and this made him feel even lower; so he bought a small bag of the fig cookies that Maria loved and everyone else hated. Miss Moss, handing him his change, stared at him over the edge of her spectacles for a moment but said nothing, and he rode home feeling small.

6

MARTEN ARE GENERALLY MORE ACTIVE by night than day, but summer, with its long days and lovely weather, was not only an attractive time to be out and about but provided a veritable grocery store of savory opportunities for eating, and Martin and his brothers and sister had the most delicious education during June and July. They tried to eat everything they could catch and anything stationary that smelled good. This led to some delicious adventures, like catching and eating moles, shrews, mice, voles, robins, jays, thrushes, towhees, warblers, woodpeckers of various sizes, snakes, and every sort of egg; but it also led to painful misadventures, like bees, wasps, hornets, skunk, porcupine, and what seemed like a house cat but which turned out to be a bobcat, which is a whole different order of cat than a house cat, and which slashed and tore at Martin and his oldest brother until their mother entered the fray in such a fury that even the bobcat, fully a match for an adult marten, quailed before such maternal rage. Martin was nicked and sliced in several places, the worst a cut on his shoulder so serious that his skin flapped open, but his brother, face-first into trouble as usual, was hurt so badly that Martin and his mother had to haul him back up to the den, where it took him days to recover.

*

As summer went along, the kits' education continued, and their various characters and personalities became more pronounced. The oldest brother, now nearly as big as Martin, continued to be either incredibly brave or astonishingly foolish, which are sometimes the same thing. The second brother, graced with preternatural patience, learned to hunt on his own, but only prey that did not flee and entail pursuit; he could catch mice and voles by waiting calmly along their avenues and byways, but he could not muster the energy to dash after squirrels, for example, like the others. This second kit was intelligent, certainly—not for him the constant stings his oldest brother endured, snapping after bees and wasps, the oldest brother never seeming to see the lurid stripes on wasps as flags of danger—but curiously weary, as if his reserves of energy, no matter how much he ate, were easily depleted by the briefest burst and flurry of activity.

Martin's sister, however, changed the most that summer, from the tiniest of the kits to the deftest; it was she alone who could decapitate an egg with the daintiest of blows, losing not a drop of the elixir within, and she who one day followed a young weasel into its burrow and killed and removed it so quickly that the furious mother weasel could do nothing but stare in a towering rage as her own kit was dismembered and eaten in a tree far above the burrow. Martin's sister also, like Martin, turned an interesting color that summer—if Martin was a dark golden bronze, she was such a deep glowing brown that she sometimes appeared to be black in certain lights. She did not grow large, but she grew muscled and sleek by the end of July; she and her second brother were by far the quietest of the four young marten—the brother seemingly from lassitude, but on her part almost a studied silence, as if sounds were dangerous and should be used only in the direst emergencies and situations.

★

And the kits learned about the most dangerous other beings on the mountain—bears, cougars, bobcats, foxes, dogs, coyotes, and most of all, people and their machines. Three times their mother brought them to within a hundred yards of the highway, huddled safely high in a towering fir, and made them watch the cars whizzing and the trucks roaring by: log trucks, construction vehicles, delivery trucks on their way to the lodge; hikers and campers, headed into the national forest; fishermen and hunters, scouting territory for when their seasons opened; tourists and vacationers in every sort of car and van and trailer; brightly clad bicyclists laboring slowly up the mountain or flying down at amazing speeds. And the plethora of smells along the highway! Oil and gasoline, burnt rubber and overheated steam—smells the kits caught nowhere else and which became instantly associated in their minds with whirring death. To them, the traffic was a species of monster, a sort of immense roaring steel snake big enough to eat the world, and they were afraid, and they cowered—even Martin and his too-bold brother, which is exactly the fear their mother had wanted them to learn and remember.

We have not spoken much of her, this remarkable and nameless female being, but in many ways, she was a walking wonder, as mother, as teacher, as leader, as defensive mastermind, as provider of food, as brave survivor of the trapline that had caught and killed her mate. They had been racing through the low canopy along the river, carefree and excited by what we would call a blooming romance in human terms, when her mate was snared by the thinnest wire snare either of them had ever seen, and it was his own liquid speed that killed him, for he hit the snare so hard that it tightened instantly, and he struggled for only a moment before he was strangled to death. His body hung in the air between two young alder trees, all his bristling energy gone, as if he had been instantly emptied of himself, leaving behind only a bag of dense gleaming fur. She walked around him, every fear and caution aflame to its uttermost pitch, sniffing his body, confused and angry and bereft, and then she slipped back into the high canopy and vanished. Inside her were the seeds he had planted for their kits, seeds that would become embryos in the winter and squirming, tiny kits in the spring—the kits he would never see. The trapper sold the skin for eighty dollars and considered that a good price, given that it was an early winter pelt; he might have gotten a hundred dollars or more if the male had been taken later in the winter, but you took what you were given by the woods, in his view, and were grateful. With the money, he bought sixty cans of fruit and vegetables, giving the canned peaches and pears and cherries to his daughter for her pantry and the tomatoes and beans and peas to the food bank at the church in Zigzag.

7

THE LAST DAY OF SCHOOL this year is three days earlier than usual, because of the state budget shortfall; teachers and students were officially on "furlough," a word some students looked up in dictionaries and most on the Web and about which they had to write a short final essay. Dave wrote his on how the American word *furlough* had come from the Dutch word *verlof*, or permission; and he grinned, sitting in the back of class, at the fact that as soon as he scribbled his final sentence, he had permission to run screaming out the door of the school and sail home on his bike along the river trail. Free! An early summer! No scholastic academic scholarly formal educational duties whatsoever absolutely until cross-country tryouts for high school in August! By which time he planned to be the most amazingly prepared freshman athlete in the history of Zigzag High, home of the Lightning Bolts! So fit and trail-tested would he be that the coaches would blink in amazement as he, Dave, smoothly caught up to and passed the experienced and cocky seniors, who would stare at him in amazement as he went by like mist whipped by winter wind! And the coaches would call him over, *Hey, kid!* And he would jog toward them, not even breathing hard, *Yes, Coach?* And they would say with real surprise and maybe even a hint of awe in their voices, *Hey, who . . . ?*

And just as he was about to say something cool like *my name is Dave, and that's a name you all will know soon enough,* he saw that young pine marten again, this time flying through the tree branches along the path just as fast as Dave was going on his bike. Not a squirrel, not a bird, certainly not any of the animals that couldn't get into the trees at all, let alone rocket along like lithe furry bullets. It was a marten, sure enough, and almost surely the same large young one he had seen in the clearing the other day; it was a curious deep golden brown color, not as dark as russet, not as bright as orange. He remembered this color particularly, for this one's companions, probably family, were all darker and, except for what must have been a parent, smaller. Dave skidded to a halt to get a better look at the animal, and to his surprise when he stopped, so did the marten, who crouched on a branch a dozen feet away and stared at him.

*

Now Dave had *heard* of marten, sure he had, from his dad and from hunters and loggers and skiers and even snowboarders and from his grade-school teacher Mr. Shapiro, who was a scholar of the mustelid family, as he said in his orotund sonorous baritone; and he had heard the most about them from a friend of his mother's in the laundry service at the lodge, who claimed that an entire family of marten lived in the drainpipes on the roof and used them as highways through the epic snowfall the lodge endured every winter, sometimes a hundred feet of snow from October through June. This was Emma Jackson Beaton, age thirty, who had a bright-blue Mohawk haircut and a steel ring in each eyebrow and a Maori tattoo that circled her neck like a scarf, all of which gave her an intimidating appearance, although she was the most gentle kindhearted soul imaginable and did double shifts without a murmur when Dave's mom was well and truly exhausted and needed a day off. Emma Jackson Beaton, young and dangerous as she appeared to be, was also supposedly a married woman— she always said *happily married*, although no one had ever actually met the mysterious Mr. Billy Beaton, who was supposedly a superstar surfer and spent months at a time on the professional circuit in Hawaii and Australia and Africa—although Emma Jackson Beaton *did* come back tanned and shining from her biannual vacations, about which she said little, though much speculation swirled through laundry services and even up into food services, some members of whom had private crushes on Emma Jackson Beaton, even though she was *happily married* as she always said, the two cheerful words as regular on her lips as *hello* and *pillowcases* and *snowplow*. The third chef had a crush on her, for example, but he was too awed by her Mohawk and marriage to say anything about his inchoate feelings; and one of the morning waitresses had a crush on her too but was too confused by the very fact of having a crush on a *girl* to say anything or even to admit it to herself except sometimes when she was almost asleep—that calm wild place which is the freest of all countries.

★

But Dave had not actually *seen* marten until the other day, and that was a glancing glimpse, really just a quick sense of heft and wriggle in lithe brown packages, whereas *this*—this was a *confirmed sighting*, as his teacher Mr. Shapiro would have said. Mr. Shapiro would then have pursued at least a cell-phone photograph or a snatch of iVideo or happily collected scat, but Dave didn't move a muscle, and just stared back at the marten. He realized somehow, in the deep part of his own ancient mammalian brain, that to move just now would be to break the moment and lose the connection, and he was fascinated not only by this most interesting creature but by the fact that it had stopped when he had and seemed just as fascinated by Dave as Dave was by Martin.

Rarely does a book switch viewpoints at a crucial juncture like this, but perhaps we should, just so we can get a good grip on the momentous nature of what's going on here. Dave, young as he is, has lived on this planet for fourteen years, almost fifteen—his birthday is October 4, same as the great explorer Joel Palmer, who walked over Wy'east barefoot. But Martin is, at this particular moment, only about seven weeks old; while he is no longer suckling milk from his patient and hardworking mother, he does still live at home with his mother and sister and brothers, and it has not yet entered his mind that in a few months he will be living alone and working for his living. In a sense, he is a new teenager too, like Dave, if you compare life cycles—an interesting and difficult project, that, as the fir tree in which Martin is sitting is itself rather a teenager as the life spans of fir trees go. So we have a teenager of one species sitting in a teenager of another species staring at a teenager of a third species. If only a young hawk would float over or an adolescent deer blunder by!

But their silent reverent contemplative moment, these three teenagers, is cracked not by a young sparrow hawk or elk but by the wildest most reckless bicyclist on the entire face of Wy'east, who can suddenly be heard rocketing down the mountain along the river path, getting ever closer and louder. Dave, who knows full well who this is and what it means for anyone in his path, smiles and immediately scoots his bike off the path and into the forest fringe. The instant Dave moves, Martin vanishes back into the forest, so fast and silent that Dave would use the word *evanesced* later at the dinner table when he told the story, and a man dressed head to toe in the most brilliant orange skin-tight jumpsuit shot past on a brilliant orange mountain bike, going faster than you have ever in your life seen a bicyclist go along a path featuring tree roots, rocks, whiplike branches across the path, stumps and jags of trees, and a shard of old highway drainage pipe just at the edge of town—which, if you did not know about the pipe and you hit it going fast on your bicycle, you would be thrown into the air and come down someplace near Japan, as Dave's dad says. That Cosmas, added Dave's dad, is the greatest most accomplished natural genius bike rider in the history of bicycles, but one of these days if he does not slow down he is going to break his neck, which would be a shame, because he's the nicest guy, and I'd hate to lose him. If ever there was a case where a town would be reduced by far more than one resident if we lost one resident, it's Cosmas. There's everything to like about that guy except that he is the wildest most reckless rider anyone ever saw. I wonder what the animals in the woods think of him when he comes rocketing down the mountain all dressed in orange and singing that song or whatever it is that noise he makes. What a nut. Sometimes I think that everyone in Zigzag must have taken a nut test to be able to live in this village. Your mother struggled to pass her nut test, but *I* passed immediately with flying colors. Isn't that so, darling?

8

YOU REMEMBER THE GRAY FOX in the tree, a few pages back? The fox that watched silently as the five marten made their way to their new den? The fox that noted that one of the kits seemed ill or indisposed or not quite growing normally and that another of the kits was slightly too adventurous? This fox noticed things like that. If you didn't learn to notice things like that in the woods, you wouldn't live very long. You needed to notice patterns and manners of behavior. If you paid attention, you could learn the ways that mice and voles and rabbits liked to travel on subtle paths and trails and roads through the brush. You could learn to smell their roads even through the snow and wait at key points and junctures and pounce at exactly the right time so that you wouldn't starve. You could learn that birds' nests were loaded with eggs in April but not in July, except for sparrows, who raised two sets of fledglings per year. You could learn that trying to steal eggs from hawks was in general a poor idea because they could and would and did fight back, and they had talons like razors. You could learn that young crows in June and July will crowd their parents for a while, moaning and gibbering and pleading for food, until they get a little cocky in early August and wander away from their parents far enough for an enterprising fox to pick them off without being battered by attacking parents. You could learn that carrion is delicious except when defended by the animal that caused it, and all of those animals were more than happy to kill and eat a fox if the opportunity presented itself. You could learn that human animals could and did set steel traps for foxes, and if a fox was caught in such a trap, the fox would be struck with a club until it was dead and then carried away to an unimaginable fate.

The gray fox had learned that lesson all too early and all too thoroughly. This was neither bad nor good, sad nor haunting, not for the fox; it was terrifying, yes, and she would never forget the scent of steel, the particular musky flavor of the scent the trapper used to mask his own scent, the scent of his leather boots and gloves in the snow, the scent of coffee that hung infinitesimally around his trails and traps; but all that information and all that terror was filed away inside her somewhere as useful material for survival. She did not wish to wreak vengeance on the trapper, although she had once watched from a snowy thicket as a fisher deliberately fouled and sprang several of the man's traps along a frozen creek. She wished simply to avoid the trapper and all of his works and things, which she did so thoroughly for so long that among the small cadre of trappers, male and female, on the mountain, there were stories of the fox they called the Rhody ghost, because she had twice been seen near the village of Rhododendron.

Those trappers who set for fox knew her mark, when she ran, she cantered her feet in an unusual style, but only two had ever seen her, one man twice. Oddly, the third sighting was completely on the other side of the mountain from the first two, but as the man who had seen her twice said, sitting by the fire at Miss Moss's store one afternoon, who knows the ways of foxes? Whatever you are sure of in the woods, don't be. You can study behavior and pattern all your life and read a thousand books and talk to a thousand biologists and spend a thousand days out there, and on the thousand and first, there'll be a fox that eats only ducks, or a beaver that's got his heart set on destroying a highway bridge that just doesn't meet his aesthetic standards, or a bobcat set on romancing a cougar, despite cultural differences and social bias and the excellent chance of getting eaten. All you can do is pay attention and hope you don't die. Farming fur is a hell of a way to make a living, and there's no real living in it, but those of us who do it, do it mostly for money but also for some sort of education, I guess. You learn things you never expected to learn in a million years—such as there is a fox out there who appears to be either a ghost or a genius at avoiding traps and trouble. I have a lot of respect for the fox population generally when it comes to intellect; it's pretty much a dead heat between people or foxes on the fox's native ground, but this one has surpassing gifts. You almost don't want to catch her except that her silver skin is worth a hundred bucks.

What if I gave you a hundred bucks *not* to catch her? said Miss Moss from behind the counter. She was kneeling down tinkering with something or other, and you couldn't see her face, but her voice was crisp.

Be tempting, said the trapper. But then you'd be on the hook for all the other animals I wouldn't catch, not to mention someone else might catch her, not to mention eventually that fox is going to die, and I might as well be the beneficiary of her pelt before it turns to dust in a cave somewhere.

It's interesting to me, said Miss Moss, emerging suddenly above the counter, how some animal beings on the mountain become famous among human beings, generally for their elusiveness. They are like football running backs no one can easily catch, and so their legends develop.

Also size, said the trapper equably. Bears, for example. Or Louis the elk.

Although I might argue, said Miss Moss, that Louis is famous not because he is big but because everyone wants to shoot him every year, and no one has yet in more years than any of us can easily remember. That animal might be a hundred years old. Though it *is* entertaining when hunters claim they shot him and they didn't.

Not so entertaining for the elk they *did* shoot thinking it was old Louis, said the trapper. But I am not picking on hunters who eat their meat. You have to eat, and you have to feed your kids; that's the agreement if you have kids—you have to actually take care of them. I have a problem with rack hunters, but who am I to talk, catching and skinning Rocky Raccoon? It's not like I eat him, after all. Which reminds me, I better get to work. I got a lot of work to do this summer before the season opens. You'd be surprised how little actual trapping a trapper does. Mostly it's walking and looking. They should call us wookers instead of trappers, or lawkers. You got to do a lot of walking homework in spring and summer before trapping exams in the fall. I thought I was all done with school when I graduated from Zigzag High, but no—still studying for tests all year long. Thanks for the fire, Ginny. My old cold bones feel better here than anywhere, and that's a fact.

Be safe, be well, drive careful, said Miss Moss, and she vanished again behind the counter, to tinker with something or other.

9

DAVE WALKED IN THE FRONT DOOR of the store, noticing that the bell that was supposed to jangle and clang when someone entered was broken. This was exactly the conversational opening he needed, for he was here to boldly ask Miss Moss for a job. His sister Maria said there was no way Miss Moss would be able to afford a helper, didn't Dave ever notice that Miss Moss was the only employee in Miss Moss's store? How could someone with no employees hire an employee suddenly? But Dave thought he would ask, and he had armed himself with information that only a sharp eye would gather about Miss Moss's store and environs: the broken bell; the vast incoherent disorganized welter of things out back that could be organized and categorized and offered for sale; and the fact that Miss Moss had no online presence whatsoever, even though surely the tourists and skiers and hikers and hunters and trappers who stopped at the store for one thing or another would be interested in being informed about products specifically aimed at their expressed interests and/or purchasing histories, to name the first three things that Dave had written down and had clutched in his hand.

But where was Miss Moss?

Right here, she said, once again emerging suddenly from behind the counter and smiling at Dave. What were you looking for this time, Dave? Traps for bears?

No, ma'am, said Dave. This time I am here to propose something.

You're here to propose to me? I am very honored.

No, ma'am, said Dave, blushing instantly and thoroughly. I am here to propose that you employ me in any capacity whatsoever, and I have several reasons and ideas about why employing me would be a good thing for the store.

I *have* been proposed to, you know, said Miss Moss. Twice. Well, one and a half times, to be accurate.

Ma'am? said Dave, a little rattled; he had been prepared to launch into his speech, which he had practiced for an hour with Maria, Maria acting as Miss Moss, complete with spectacles and sandals and wry amused tone of voice.

The first time was a little confusing, and I am not quite sure even now if the young man in question was actually proposing or sort of musing about what might *possibly* happen someday if the *stars* aligned, said Miss Moss. I think maybe he was talking about how a proposal *might* happen rather than actually proposing. It was very confusing. You'd have to count that as a half proposal at best.

Yes, ma'am, said Dave.

Whereas the second time was a legitimate and honest proposal, and made while he was kneeling too, which was impressive, said Miss Moss. An *excellent* proposal. The best I ever received, no question. A really memorable proposal. My favorite ever.

Did you say yes? asked Dave.

Well, now, Dave, what exactly were your reasons and ideas for employment here?

But her swift shift of gears caught Dave by surprise, and for a moment he was silent, trying to replace the thought of Miss Moss being proposed to with the coherent and persuasive speech he had memorized.

Dave?

Ma'am. Well, ma'am, there are several areas to discuss. One is what the store needs right now to get up to its best speed. The second is what the store could use to open new commercial vistas. The third is the character and responsibility of the candidate for employment.

Vistas?

Yes, ma'am.

Vistas.

Vistas, yes, ma'am. Areas of possible lucrative trade and income growth.

Dave, are you sure you are fourteen? Did you go to college already and not tell anyone?

Almost fifteen, ma'am. Heading to the Zag in September.

Hmm.

Let's look at each area in order. Right now, it seems to me that the store is efficiently run but not perhaps sufficiently staffed. It could be that the staff, because she has to do every aspect of running the store, is weary and cannot do more that needs to be done.

Good point, said Miss Moss. Such as?

Repair the bell over the door, said Dave. Computerize inventory and organize storage. Create and execute advertising and marketing plan. Establish social media presence. Research and execute online sales. Do something about the backyard. Research possibility of expanding hot food sales beyond soup and coffee. Other repairs and renovation as needed.

Persuasive, admirably detailed, and slightly embarrassing to hear, said Miss Moss. Excellent points. And the third area? The character of the applicant?

Honest and ready to work any hours possible, starting today, said Dave, mentally thanking Maria for that last touch. *Starting today,* that'll sound impressive, Maria had said, and she was right—it did sound impressive.

References?

Ma'am?

Character references. Anyone able to attest to your character?

Yes, ma'am. My parents. My teachers.

Maria?

Ma'am?

Your sister will attest that you are kind, honest, generous, diligent, steadfast, reverent, thoughtful, responsible, energetic, self-sufficient, creative, and good at heart?

I think so, Miss Moss, said Dave. I think she would. I'm sure she would.

Then you're hired, said Miss Moss. Anyone whose kid sister thinks the world of him can work here anytime. Welcome to the staff.

Yes, ma'am. Thank you, ma'am.

Eight bucks an hour to start, raised to ten in a month if you earn it?

Yes, ma'am. Very fair, ma'am.

Can you really start today?

Yes, ma'am.

Start with that damned bell, said Miss Moss, smiling. I have fixed that bell ten times, and obviously we need an expert on that project. Then go around and make a list of everything you see that needs repair, and we will prioritize. Give me four hours today, and then go home. Thank your sister for her character reference.

I'll do that, ma'am. And thanks, ma'am.

Good to have you on staff, Dave. I've never had a staff before. At the moment, you are the finest staffer I've ever had. Stay in that exalted state.

Yes, ma'am, said Dave, and he suddenly had a powerful urge to ask Miss Moss about the marriage proposal again, but somehow he knew this wasn't the moment. He went to fix the bell.

10

THE BEARS ON WY'EAST had many centuries ago quartered the mountain according to mysterious clan and tribal lines, and the rare battles between and among them were all occasioned by flouting of the lines; and every bear knew the ancient stories of arrogant young muscled bears who went deep into a forbidden territory and did not return, their bones scattered across the mountainside for all to see. And there were darker old stories too of wars between bears and cougars, for example, an enmity nearly as old as the mountain itself, or between bears and wolverines, despite the eerie similarity of their furious strengths, their capacities for a sort of grim rage few other animals knew or desired. Indeed, among the marten and the other members of the mustelid clan, there was at most a cold respect for the biggest of their tribe and no affection whatsoever. While the fisher, for example, could lose its temper when its kits were threatened or attacked, it did not and would not muster the savage, utter destruction of a bear or wolverine in full and uncontrolled rampage; the fisher preferred a sudden, swift violence and then a swifter disappearance so that there were hunting dogs, for example, who leapt after a hissing fisher and never knew the manner or incredible rapidity of the blow that caused their death, a terribly fast slicing of the jugular and instant retreat so that the dog found itself suddenly gushing out its life in the snow, a great weariness arriving like a tide.

But the marten, like the otter, fought rarely if at all, seeing no need for it except to assert territory or fend off danger to its kits, and the tools of battle rusted all the more because the marten was graced and given such astounding physical tools. It was the fastest and surest of all animals in trees and canopies, able and thrilled to rocket through the branches faster and more accurately than even the wood hawks who could arrow like small feathered jets through thickets, spinning and turning as necessary with an exquisite timing no human athlete could even imagine. And they were a muscular race, the marten—for all that they weighed less than ten pounds; they had steel chests and a boundless endurance that together spelled doom for all but the luckiest headlong squirrel or sprinting rabbit. Claws of razor wire, teeth like tiny daggers, the ability to hear a snapped twig from a thousand feet away, vision equally sharp day or night, and a coat of the thickest warmest glossiest waterproof fur, it was as if Time, who designs all beings and whittles them to their absolute essence, had decided to build the most perfect small mammalian hunting machine, mixing a bit of bear and lynx and hawk together into a small dose of cheerful, efficient predation, giving it the wildest wilderness for home and making its enemies few, relentless though they be—the hawk and eagle to pluck up wriggling kits, the coyote and lynx and fox to cull the old and slow adults, and most of all man, who did not even eat those he killed but stole their skins to make coats for himself, because he did not have his own fur or enough hair to keep him warm against the wind.

*

It was a brilliant summer. Day after day, the mist inherent on a mountain with glaciers and a permanent snowpack burned off by noon, the afternoons stretched as long and languid as napping cougars. The rivers and creeks burled along furiously right through the summer, when usually they slowed by August, as the last of the melt finished leaving the peak on its way to the ocean. The rains from the west that usually dropped their last loads on the mountain in June and July before petering out, exhausted, in the high sage desert beyond were scattered and confused this year and lost their way and ended up drenching British Columbia to the moist spluttering puzzlement of the British Columbians. The woods stayed wet enough from winter to fend off the late-summer fires that sometimes raged after lightning strikes, and the ferocious thunderstorms that sometimes roared along the mountain's shoulders were missing in action; no hikers or bicyclists or drivers tossed burning butts of cigarettes or cigars into the brush; no campers left their fires unattended or unbanked or forgotten; no boaters on the dozens of pristine tiny lakes accidentally sent sparks from fuel lines racing through the thickets. So the afternoons grew more crisp and clear and lovely and long by the day, and on the mountain that summer, every resident felt this, from the tiniest shrew to Louis himself, the elk bigger than any bear.

*

But Martin's youngest brother grew quieter and less active by the day. By early July, he no longer came down the tree from the den. He slept all day, as much of the family did much of the time, but he also slept, or seemed to sleep, at night, when their mother led the growing kits down the tree and into the woods to hunt. For a time, their mother and then Martin continued to bring mice and voles back for him, but finally he ceased even to eat and remained curled in a tight ball in the dim rear corner of the burrow, his eyes open. On the morning he died, Martin had just come back to the den, carrying a shrew just in case his brother was awake and hungry; his brother lifted his head a little but did not move otherwise or even blink.

As Martin watched, his brother's eyes dimmed, and his head sank back down onto his paws, and he died. He was three months and three days old when he died. Many other creatures died that day on the mountain, creatures of many species, death by many causes—predation, accidents, battle, age, illness, happenstance, perhaps a quiet suicide, who knows? And the larger the creature, the more noticeable the death, so that the aged electrician who had been a war veteran was widely mourned, and the old doe struck by a car on the highway drew a public works team to remove her body gently from the road, and the young eagle electrocuted by chance at a ski area was photographed by a dozen phones, her sudden death a viral sensation within moments; but Martin's brother was one of the thousands of small deaths, and no one knew but his brothers and his sister, who were saddened and confused, and his mother, who carried his body down from the den in her jaws, and the animals who found his body in the forest the next day, an unexpected and welcome provenance for many creatures, some too small to see.

So there were now three marten kits where there had been four, and from some ancient impulse, their mother again decided to move the den, from some old fear of death, from some sensible fear that there were larger animals in the woods who watched and waited with an ancient patience for one infinitesimal chance at such elusive meat; but before she could do so, the gray fox saw just such a rare chance, and seized it.

11

DAVE'S BEST FRIEND is a kid named Moon. Moon is real tall and skinny. He owns every mechanical technical engineered electric electronic computerized digitized shiny gleaming cool machine ever made, it seems. His house is so big that you could put Dave's entire cabin in the kitchen of Moon's house. Moon's *kitchen* is so big you could ride a bicycle in circles and never come close to touching the walls or stoves or sinks.

Moon has not one but three phones, all of which communicate with each other and probably hatch conspiracies when we sleep, says Moon. He has at least three computers and maybe four if you count the old one upstairs that no one uses anymore. He has so many routers and docks and plugs and wires and chargers that he keeps them all in a box so they don't wander off and electrify the cat by accident. His mom and dad work for technological companies that are so huge and vast and extensive and international and complex that neither Moon nor Dave knows what the actual products of the companies are. Moon says he thinks the companies actually just mint money on a contract from the government somehow, that they no longer have to manufacture anything but instead just hatch money, which they give in wheelbarrows and pallets to their shareholders and employees, who distribute it in turn to car dealers and housing agents and airplane companies. Mostly airplane companies, Moon thinks. Moon says the price for working for those companies is that you have to live on airplanes. Moon says his dad has reserved seat 3B on every flight offered by every airline in the United States for the rest of this year and half of next year, after which he has an option to renew. Moon says his mom does not go so far as to reserve the same seat on every flight on every airline, but she *is* partial to seat 2A. She is more of a landscape and wilderness person than my dad, says Moon, and she loves looking out the window, whereas Dad loves sleeping. My mom can look out any window of any airplane in any state and tell you within ten seconds where exactly you are and what mountain range that is and what agricultural products are being nurtured by irrigation thirty thousand feet below the window. She's amazing. I tested her last time we were all on a flight together, when we went to Costa Rica, and she was right every single time. I mapped out the trip beforehand and had it all downloaded to match the plane's flight plan. I would have tested Dad, but he was asleep.

Moon and Dave hang out. Those are the words they use for an answer when any one of their parents says, so what did you guys do today? *Hang out* can mean any of a number of things. Some-times it means eating or running or watching movies, but mostly it means lazing around in Moon's room playing video games or wondering what they are going to do next year when they are freshmen at the Zag. Moon's room is the whole second floor of Moon's house. Moon's parents' room with the fireplace and the hot tub and the exercise room and the sauna is downstairs, but they are rarely ever home at the same time, so when Moon's mom is gone and his dad is home, his dad sleeps in the den, and when Moon's dad is gone and his mom is home, she sleeps in the sunroom off the porch, so in general, Moon says, if you consider average occupancy and house volume, you could say that my room is the whole house, which is to say that I very probably have the biggest room of anybody on the mountain.

Not that Moon considers himself cool because his parents are rich. He is actually sort of quietly embarrassed that his parents are never home. He is politely awkward when other parents say courteously at school events, now, Moon, I do not think I have had the pleasure of meeting your folks, have I? He quietly wor-ries that if he and Dave make the cross-country team at the Zag and run in cross-country meets and Dave's parents come to watch, people will notice that Moon's parents did not come to watch because they are in Taipei and Brunei. Moon is not angry or an-noyed or hurt or resentful of his mom and dad; actually he really likes them and enjoys their company and even would say he loves them if he was being honest with someone he trusts, like Dave. And he likes their family house and the tremendous view of the rolling velvet foothills to the south and his phones and screens and cloud library in which last he looked there were more than five thousand movies and shows and six thousand songs on in-stant demand. But he is sort of quietly embarrassed that most of the time he is pretending that it's cool to be in a huge house alone, pretending to be happy that he can instantly obtain pretty much anything he wants, pretending to not mind at all that the mom and dad he really likes and even would admit that he loves work so hard for him that they don't actually see him much.

We do at birthdays and holidays, though, he says to Dave. You have to give them major credit points there. Not once that I can remember have both of them missed a birthday or a holiday, and holidays for us include the small ones that a lot of people blow off, like Saint Patrick's Day and April Fools' Day. You have to give them credit there. And my mom makes a point of being home for summer solstice every year. How many moms make a big deal out of summer solstice, huh? Not so many, Dave. Not so many.

12

IT WAS MARTIN'S HEADLONG older brother who was caught by the fox. Sure it was. You knew it would be, didn't you? He wasn't careful, Martin's brother. He didn't pay attention. He wasn't sensible. He ran out in the street after the ball without looking both ways. He rode his bike off the bluff without gauging the drop below. He saw something interesting and he sprinted after it without the slightest reflection or planning or caution. He had no reasonable doubt. He was brave and fearless and stupid and selfish. He was independent and carefree and careless and dead. He was afraid of nothing. Doesn't that sound cool? Isn't that what we all want, to be afraid of nothing? But he died. Maybe we *should* be afraid of some things. Maybe being afraid of a few things is a good way to not die. Maybe being afraid of some things is a survival tactic. Maybe being headlong and afraid at the same time is a good way to live. Maybe two contrary things can be true at once. Maybe a lot of things in life are like that. Martin's brother was caught by the fox just after dusk, just after he leapt headlong to the earth from the base of the tree, because the fox had watched the marten family leave the den again and again and had noted how the headlong older brother did not bother to stop and smell and listen to the waiting darkness, to use his amazing gifts of smell and hearing to sense what might be waiting, for good or ill; and so he died, because the fox set up for him and caught him in the split second he was available to be caught.

★

Martin's mother did move the den the next evening, this time to a small cave near the river; indeed, the new burrow was so close to the river that it had been the home of minks, until Martin's mother arrived. The new den was longer and thinner than either of their previous homes, but there were fewer of them now, and even Martin and his sister, by no means fully grown, sensed that this would be their last residence with their mother.

From this final home they ranged farther and farther afield, the kits; in much the same way Dave's parents let their children range within reason, so did Martin's mother let her son and daughter go. Day by day, Martin and his sister began to claim their own territories, drifting naturally toward landscapes they liked and found congenial. In general, Martin's sister liked remote meadows, where mousing was always rewarding, and fairly open woods, where birds were more likely found than in the dense woods and above timberline. Martin, however, liked the stimulation and bustle of country closer to human things; while he remained properly terrified of the road, he was not averse to exploring near the farthest-flung cabins, and it was Martin who discovered that the lodge where Dave's mother worked was a wonderful source of chipmunks and tiny golden ground squirrels. Something about human beings and their works interested him; dogs were annoying, yes, but the dog who could catch a marten in the woods had not yet been born, and the sheds and cabins and woodpiles and scraggly gardens and pastures of human beings were also a rich hunting ground for mice, voles, snakes, and moles. Woodpiles were especially trustworthy as meat lockers; Martin learned that if he tucked himself into a crevice and waited a few moments, the world would present him soon enough with a chipmunk, and there is nothing quite so delicious when you are sharp with hunger as a chipmunk. Not to mention that they are so wonderfully easy to dismantle, if you have the requisite tools, as Martin did. With total respect for mice and voles (also beautifully packaged and savory meat), and with a deep affection for the eggs of any bird whatsoever (eggs being the most easily opened meal of all), Martin loved nothing so much as a fresh steaming chipmunk when he was hungry. Entertaining to chase, just the right size for a substantive meal without having to drag remnants of it back to the burrow, and populous to the point of profligacy— the chipmunk was one of the great glories and beneficences of the mountain, and Martin was ever more curious about new places where even more herds and troops of them might be found. So he explored closer and closer to Zigzag High and Miss Moss's store and the lodge where Dave's mom worked and to the resort with nine holes of golf in the summer and to the laundromat that doubled as a used bookstore and chapel on Sunday afternoons for the Church of the Risen Lord, Wy'east Synod, and to the trailer where methamphetamine was made and to the vast cut in the woods through which telephone poles and wires marched for miles, a swath of open land scythed and mown regularly by a trail crew, a long, straight hole in the forest where trees used to be, some of them older than the telephone itself.

13

LIVING *ON* THE MOUNTAIN, you never get to actually *see* the mountain, said Dave's mom that night at dinner. Isn't that ironic? People come from all over the world to see this mountain, and here we are, and we never see it. If we never see it, does it really exist?

This made Maria laugh so hard she nearly shot milk out her nose.

How's the running going, Dave? asked his dad.

I was going to start morning and evening runs tomorrow, said Dave, but . . .

Everyone looked up from their plates.

. . . I got a job. At Miss Moss's.

Whoa, said his dad. That is *real* news. Holy moly. Congrats.

Doing what? asked Maria.

General service. "Dave-of-all-trades" is Miss Moss's term.

Dave, that's great, said his mom. That's just great. Hours?

Four a day to start. Six if things work out.

Wow, said his dad. That was a sudden decision. Admirable ambition, though. Prompt action. Admirable all round, I'd say, wouldn't you?

Absoluterlishly, said Maria without the hint of a smile, before her mom could get her affirmation out, and everyone cracked up.

Working more hours than his old man, Dave is, said his dad later in the kitchen. Maybe he should work more hours, and I will go to high school. We could do one of those switch things like in the movies.

I worry he thinks he has to take on more responsibility, said Dave's mom. He's fourteen. He's a kid.

Soon to be fifteen, and there's four players on this team, and you and I were working at that age. Personally, I think Maria needs to get a job. She's smart. She can run a homework service for kids or something. She's as useless wagewise as her dad at the moment.

It's unseemly of you to wallow, Jack.

Unseemly is a lovely word, said Dave's dad. Also *wallow*. I believe I'll check both of those words out of the library tomorrow and take them out for a ramble, put them through their paces. I bet if I harness them together properly, they would pull like hell.

You'll get work, Jack.

Sure.

You will, you know. Don't you just stand there and *agree* with me.

Okay, he said. Or *not* okay. I disagree, agreefully. Maybe I should have stayed in the service. Steady pay with the prospect of a pension if no one shoots you over twenty years. Did I ever tell you I had a friend in the service who loved calculating possibilities and percentages? He calculated we had a 40 percent chance of surviving our tour without substantive physical damage, which did not include illness, foot rot, psychological and emotional and spiritual trauma, sensory overload, and permanent gastrointestinal distress. He also figured out that anyone's chances of surviving twenty years in the service without substantive physical damage, given our cultural addiction to violence, was 8 percent. The only way to make it through a whole career undamaged was to get promoted as fast as possible, and the only way to get promoted that fast was to constantly and deliberately expose yourself to damage. You know what my friend did after the war?

Afraid to ask.

Accountant. I kept telling him that he should be a professional ironist or absurdist, but he said he liked to eat.

★

Dave and Maria slept upstairs in the cabin, Maria in the bear den, the half of the room with the roof slanting down sharply, and Dave in a sort of loft on his half of the room. Dave and his dad had discussed walling off the bear den with cedar planks or even building a wall of cedar down the middle of the room to give each child privacy, but Dave voted against both, as he liked puttering around with Maria, and Maria voted both down, on account of she liked talking to Dave and wandering into the bear den. Also, the den had the only upstairs window, which sometimes was obscured by snow so that the room had a gentle silvery cast to it. Dave and his dad did wall off the bottom of Maria's bunk bed with cedar, so she had a tiny wooden room for doing homework, which she loved, even though her homework to date had been mostly art projects and elementary alphabet stuff. Dave thought Maria actually liked the homeworkness of homework, so to speak, rather than the actual or ostensible learning *effect* of homework—she liked rulers and graph paper, pencils and pencil sharpeners, the old calculator she had purchased from their mom for ten dishwashing nights, the old compass she found at Miss Moss's for fifty cents, the Rapidograph pens she'd been given by an aunt or a godmother, the colored pens she wheedled whenever anyone went to the dentist or doctor or church or office of any kind whatsoever. She also loved maps and charts and had what their dad called a thoroueclectic collection of them pinned up all over her tiny wooden room: topographic maps of the mountain, of course, but also geologic charts, a map of the Zigzag River, a maritime map of Semiahmoo Bay in Washington that Miss Moss sold to Maria for three jokes about frogs, and a map of the interior of Dave's brain that she had drawn for a school project and which her mom wanted to frame, but Maria said, no, it was only an accurate map on the day I drew it, and maps that are not accurate are only curiosities, not utilities.

It was upstairs in the bear den that night that Dave told Maria about seeing the marten in the tree canopy near the river. She was fascinated, and they pored over everything Dave could find online and in his wildlife atlases.

You wouldn't *believe* how fast it whipped through the branches, said Dave. It was *shocking* fast. Faster than any squirrel, that's for sure. I was going pretty fast, as fast as I can go downhill, and it was flying through the branches, and it didn't even look like it was trying hard. And when I stopped, he stopped.

Or she.

Or she. Seemed like a guy, though.

Can I see it tomorrow?

If I see it again and you are nearby, I will signal to you, and you can come over without a sound.

Okay.

Okay.

Same signal as usual?

Yes.

The year Maria turned three years old, she and Dave had hatched a series of private signals, their own silent language, as Dave said. Left hand up meant *pay attention*; left hand balled meant *caution*; left hand flat meant *come over without a sound*. Signals with the right hand mostly meant *people*, and there were a whole array of these, mostly having to do with their parents: *tension in the kitchen; Give Dad a break—he's weary; Be careful—Mom is worried about something; Don't say anything about money*. There were two signals made with both hands: one meant *I love you*, although neither Dave nor Maria used that phrase and instead would say something like *You are slightly better to have around than a bad cold* if they had to put the message into words; and the other meant, essentially, *Let me be alone for a while.* The first signal was two open hands placed against your chest; the second was two closed hands huddled against your chest like two tiny locked rooms.

14

AS JULY LENGTHENED, Martin and his sister and their mother spent less time together; this was usual and natural and normal, the way of their species for millions of years, but Martin and his sister felt their mother's attention waning, one bright grain less per day, with some deep sense of . . . what? Sadness, regret, loss, nostalgia? We don't have good words yet for what animals feel; we hardly have more than wholly inadequate labels for our own tumultuous and complex emotions and senses. It's wrong to say that animals do not feel what we feel; indeed, they may feel far more than we do and in far different emotional shades. Given that their senses are often a hundred times more perceptive than ours, could not their emotional equipment be similarly vast?

Suffice it to say that Martin and his sister felt their mother drawing ever so gently away from them as the days lengthened toward solstice and shrank afterwards. They went their own ways from the new den, exploring different territories and coursing different landscapes, and they came together again only to sleep. Now that Martin and his sister were able enough hunters in their own right to survive and even to flourish, their mother ceased to bring them food and even ceased mostly to share it, although occasionally some deep chord of memory, perhaps, led her to bring home a vole to share and, once, a brush rabbit.

That was a day for the annals, if martens chronicled their doings. The last salmonberries and the first huckleberries filled the forest; grasshoppers and crickets leapt in the clearings like energetic appetizers; a new crow too young to fly had fallen near the burrow and made a lovely lunch; Martin had discovered and swallowed the contents of a swallow's nest artfully hidden under the eve of a woodshed near Miss Moss's store; and to cap it all off with fresh redolent rabbit, without the slightest effort expended in procuring it . . . well, of such repasts many a tale has been told among men and women and children—and perhaps among the other species, if we only could read their chronicles and annals. And to those who say animals have no chronicles and annals, no literature and sagas, no common memories and master storytellers, I say, are you sure? How would you know? Just because you have never seen them, they do not exist? Are you sure about that? Don't be. Whatever you are most inarguably sure about, as Miss Moss says, don't be.

*

Martin had his first fight in the opening days of July. This was with a male marten almost exactly his age and size. The battle was brief and savage. The cause of conflict was most of the left rear leg of a fawn that had been executed and dismantled by a cougar. The cougar had eaten most of the fawn but, in dragging the remains to a cache, lost some leg. The battle was short and intense and a great surprise to both combatants. The other marten had discovered the leg first, but there are no rules of possession and ownership and property and discovery that are inviolate except by adamant defense, and Martin was very hungry. He snatched a shred of the leg and was attacked, and he responded with a surge of swift violence so shocking to him—let alone his opponent—that when the battle was over, Martin found himself shaking with surprise and rage. You would have to call the battle a draw, if you were scoring the battle as regards injuries incurred and inflicted and rewards gained or retained. Both marten lugged shreds of meat away, and both were bruised and startled, and both sustained shoulder wounds that bled briefly and then were sore for days. Curiously, this was the first fight ever for the other marten, as well. We will not have time to delve into his life and story any longer than the end of this paragraph—and in a real sense, that's a shame, because this other marten has had a *most* interesting life to date, surviving somehow on his own after his mother was killed by a bobcat and his father was caught in a trap, and he will have a most interesting life over the next eleven years. He will, for example, be hit by lightning and assumed to be dead but then rise up spitting and utterly alive as if by magic. He will briefly find himself atop a running horse, which is a remarkable story all by itself. He will be a rare and perhaps unique case of a marten who learns to kill and eat porcupines after watching a fisher accomplish that potentially puncturous and eminently painful task. He will father more kits than we could easily count if they were somehow piled wriggling in front of us in a seething mewling pile. He will die finally in an act of stunning courage in defense of the object of his enduring love, a story which all by itself you could write three books about, and by heavens what a terrific movie it would make. And he is only one of a million, no, a *billion* stories you could tell about the living beings on *just this side of the mountain*. The fact is that there are more stories in the space of a single second, in a single square foot of dirt and air and water, than we could tell each other in a hundred years. The word *amazing* isn't much of a word for how amazing that is. The fact is that there are more stories in the world than there are fish in the sea or birds in the air or lies among politicians. You could be sad at how many stories go untold, but you could also be delighted at how many stories we catch and share in delight and wonder and astonishment and illumination and sometimes even epiphany. The fact is that the more stories we share about living beings, the more attentive we are to living beings, and perhaps the less willing we are to slaughter them and allow them to be slaughtered. That could be.

Yet some stories we must let go. Most. Almost all. We let them wander off into woods, dragging shreds of deer meat. We are sorry to see them go—how *does* a marten get atop a sprinting horse, anyway, and what *possible* combination of factors would lead to *that?*—but we cannot share them all, and we have to choose, and so here we choose to follow Martin, who watches the other marten go and then curls up high in a fir tree and licks his shoulder for a long while, pondering. He is so motionless in the crook of the tree that not even the swifts at twilight or the first owls of evening notice him there, and the owls see everything; or so they think.

15

DAVE PROVED INDISPENSABLE to Miss Moss within the first hour of his formal employment. The bell he had fixed over the door remained fixed, which Miss Moss called a blessed and inarguable miracle. Dave learned how to make milkshakes. He fixed the computer printer which for more than three months had been in the habit of eating every second sheet fed into it. He learned how to make grilled cheese sandwiches on the griddle, which is not at all the way you make them in a frying pan. He learned how to run the cash register and how to process credit cards and how to seed the tip jar with dollar bills to make the existence of the tip jar a subtle but alluring reality. By the end of his first hour, Miss Moss had crossed off six of the ten tasks she had in mind for Dave's first day, and she said, wander around outside and come back in ten minutes with some ideas about what needs to be done out there.

Yes, ma'am, said Dave.

We are going to have to find something other than *ma'am* for you to use, Dave, said Miss Moss. I don't think *ma'am* is going to cut it. Doesn't fit, quite. I am no madam.

I could stay with *Miss Moss*, Miss Moss, said Dave.

That's a lot of words, though, said Miss Moss. Not to mention the constant alliteration. Pretty soon, you would be calling me Missmash or Mossmush, and I couldn't bear that. For one thing, we would spend more time laughing than working, and we cannot afford that.

I could call you by your first name, if that's not too . . . forward.

You could, I suppose, said Miss Moss. I call you by yours, to be sure. But . . . I don't know. No one in town calls me by my first name.

The trapper did, said Dave. The man who was talking about the silver fox and Louis the elk and Rocky Raccoon, remember?

You heard that?

I was just coming through the door.

Were you? I don't remember that the bell rang.

No, ma'am. It was broken, remember?

Indeed I do, said Miss Moss, and you are the able youth who repaired it. Well, let's postpone nomenclature decisions for the moment. Right now I suggest you take a brief break from your labors and then scout around the perimeter and see what needs to be done out there and in what order. Prioritize loosely. The biggest job out there, of course, is inventory and organization of used goods—even I admit it's chaos out there—but that will take you all summer, so do me a favor and use your sharp young eyes to see what else needs to be painted, shored up, nailed over, resealed, cleared out, bagged up, cut down, stitched up, trimmed, snipped, shorn, pruned, burned, or cheerfully ignored. Fair enough?

Yes, ma'am, said Dave without thinking, and Miss Moss laughed.

See, now, Dave, we cannot afford more than a few minutes of

laughing per day, she said. We should probably set the limit at ten minutes or so on each of your shifts. That's healthy. Less than that, and we are dour, and more than that I'll go out of business. While I would go out of business *smiling*, still, I would go out of business, and then where would we be?

Yes, ma'am, said Dave, and he went out, smiling.

*

Miss Moss's store was built mostly of tremendous fir logs, although the whole structure rested on a solid foundation of stone, and Dave sincerely doubted that anything less than Wy'east destroying itself in a cataclysmic volcanic event would have the slightest effect on the building. It had been built more than a century earlier, and no one now remembered who had built it or why—titles and deeds and accurate county records were not common features in the early days. The brown people who had lived there for thousands of years laughed at the idea of people actually owning imaginary squares and rectangles and triangles of land and air, and the paler people who were intent on owning the squares and rectangles and triangles of land and air were often none too careful about who paid what to whom for what and why. Sometime after Joel Palmer walked on the glacier and before your mother arrived on the mountain, said Dave's father, that's when someone built Miss Moss's store, and what it was used for in its early days is a total and complete mystery. Probably a speakeasy or a church, which is finally the same thing—a place of rest and restoration.

Dave wandered around the building, looking at it carefully for the first time and thinking that it's amazing how we can see something a thousand times but never actually *see* it, you know? He'd been wandering around this particular collection of logs and cedar shingles and fir planks since before he could remember, mostly eating ice-cream cones and guzzling the very milkshakes he had just a few minutes ago learned to make, but he had never really looked closely at the tremendous heft and burl of the logs or the deft overlap of shingles or what sure seemed like cement patches here and there among the logs. For all the hours he had spent on the porch slobbering ice cream, he had never noticed that it was propped up on massive gray stone pillars that looked older than the world, and that the boards and planks that composed the porch seemed to have been cut from one unimaginably enormous tree. He had noticed, vaguely, all his life, that the porch creaked and croaked and moaned and groaned when you walked or sat on it, but he had never noticed the different chords and keys in which the porch sang, depending on where you walked. He had never noticed that the wooden railings, which he had assumed to be unadorned, were lined with faint forest motifs—ferns, huckleberry brambles, aster flowers. And the four sturdy railing posts, he now saw, had originally been carved as rough versions of four animals—bear, cougar, elk, and eagle— though the carvings, after the ministrations of a million hands, were gentled and softened as if by an invisible rain. You could tell, if you looked closely, that the two posts by the door, for example, were cougar and bear, but whatever blunt and violent dignity their anonymous sculptor had given them long ago was now much faded, and they seemed more like dreams of bear and cougar than powerful princes of the mountain.

16

MARTIN, BY THE END OF JULY, was ranging farther and farther afield from the third den, and more and more there were days when he did not come home at all but curled up in a tree bole, a windfall space, an abandoned burrow. As the days grew infinitesimally shorter and the nights longer, he began to spend more time hunting at night and sleeping during the day, although still, while summer offered such a bounty of foods and flavors, he made the most of the long light to explore new territory and familiarize himself with all sorts of landscape. He went down the mountain, all the way to where the highest apple and pear orchards grew; he went up the mountain along the river until the river vanished into nothing more than a trickle emerging from a stone; he went east around the mountain, discovering, among other amazements, a rhododendron jungle so thick that even he was briefly lost and confused; and he returned to the lodge where Dave's mother worked. Indeed, this time, he actually saw Dave's mother eating her lunch at a table outside the laundry with Emma Jackson Beaton, whose steel eye rings glinted alluringly in the sun, but the smell of people and their dogs and machines was powerful and frightening, and he withdrew silently when Emma and Dave's mother finished their sandwiches and went back to work. He marked the lodge firmly in his memory, though, as a good place to catch chipmunks and golden squirrels, some dozen of which he saw sprinting recklessly around the paths and porches. A deft hunter, it seemed to Martin, could make hay among such careless appetizers—at first light, perhaps, when the squirrels first emerged and before people were up and about, or at last light, when the squirrels were scouring the grounds for a last snack and the people were distracted by wine and sunset and alpenglow.

*

Even during high summer on the mountain there was enough morning mist and occasional gentle rain from the dense clouds wreathing Wy'east for animals to leave noticeable trails and prints, and by the end of summer, Martin was a serious student of the marks left both by residents and visitors. His first concern was the tracks of animals he could eat, and so he grew most familiar with the tiny prints of mice and voles, even unto the infinitesimal marks left by their trailing tails. He also learned to notice gnawed twigs and little piles of cut grass stems where a vole had fed; such piles, he learned, almost always meant a vole runway through the grass nearby, and a runway was an excellent place for a patient marten to procure a meal. Similarly the rabbits who established runways through grass and thickets and generally held to their highways for transport; the trick there was to choose a bend in the road and wait until eventually a rabbit slightly too comfortable with his or her usual commute turned the corner and commuted no more.

Higher up the mountain was the pika, the little rabbit of the rocks who lived in boulder fields and ravines filled with stone and rubble; their tracks, Martin learned, often did not proceed in a line but were spaced nine or ten inches apart as they leapt from place to place in their endless harvesting of grasses and plants and even flowers. When hunting pika, Martin learned to look for their harvest piles, deftly hidden under the rocks; when he found one with fresh-cut greenery on top of the pile, he would wait in a crevice for the enterprising farmer, whose winter forage would then become a pleasant surprise for others of his tribe.

The tracks and habits of shrews, marmots, wood rats, porcupine, gophers, birds, snakes, rabbits, even bats—these things Martin studied intently, daily, thoroughly, and the more he paid attention, the more he noticed. Among the snakes, for example, ones with spots were too big and dangerous for him to kill, but ones with stripes could be caught and were best killed by snapping their necks. Lizards were rare and delicious and best caught in the morning as they dozed on logs and rocks. Frogs were also rare and delicious and could be caught only at the edges of lakes and ponds, although tiny tree frogs could be found anywhere. Newts and salamanders were edible but should be approached with caution and eaten only in times of ravenous hunger; Martin had eaten a reddish one which made him sick for two entire days.

He was also a student not only of the animals that could and would eat *him*, given the opportunity—bear, cougar, fisher, coyote, fox, bobcat, wolverine—but of those who would neither eat him nor suffer him to eat them. Some, like elk and beaver and nutria and eagle, were significantly bigger than Martin and adamant about defense if affronted; others, like otter and mink and weasel, were muscular and violent enough to make an attack inadvisable, and Martin felt some vague cousinish feeling with those creatures in particular. And then there were skunks, which *seemed* edible but who not only put up a fight when attacked but emitted the most awful detestable foul funk imaginable. Martin himself had not been so foolish as to try to kill a skunk, but his sister had, and the memory of the stench she wore for days was unforgettable. Here and there, when Martin ventured near the terrifying highway, he caught that dense sharp loud smell again, and he vanished back into the woods as fast as he could.

17

THE TRAPPER'S NAME WAS RICHARD, although no one had ever once called him by that name—not his mother, not his father, not the teachers he briefly had in elementary school, not the drill instructor he had briefly had in the army, not even the Internal Revenue Service of the United States of America, which was not aware he existed and so did not call him anything at all. He had been called Dickie as a child, and to a few people he still was Dickie, Miss Moss among them; the few other people in the world who called him by name called him Dick. These latter folks were few and far between, however, for Dickie, while not quite a hermit, was awfully close to one—as close to a bona fide, no-kidding, old-style, old-school, quasi-biblical hermit in the woods as you are going to find in this digitous and electricacious day and age, said Dave's dad.

But those few people who did know him respected him, for he was a good guy, honest in his dealings, unfailingly courteous, and silently helpful when anyone needed help. Ten times every winter or more, he helped haul cars and trucks out of snowy ditches along the highway, materializing suddenly out of blowing snow with a large gray horse named Edwin. Twice every summer, he could be found battling brush fires that got a little out of hand and threatened cabins. Once every other year, he wrangled sandbags when the Zigzag River got a little bumptious and threatened cabins. Twice that Miss Moss remembered, he had quietly risen from a dark corner of the store when a visitor was being rude or vulgar or vaguely threatening, and something about his bulk and silence and clear sense of rooted residency made the rude visitor leave without further ado. Even the time he was bringing in his furs to Miss Moss's store and a bystander attacked him vehemently for indiscriminate slaughter of innocent animals, he lost neither his temper nor his courtesy, and Miss Moss says she will always remember his coherent and even eloquent remarks on that occasion, which were to the effect that he could not agree more that the animals who had given up their lives for his benefit were innocent of any crimes against *him*, not to mention any other human being of his acquaintance, but the cold fact of the matter is that their selective deaths provided his living, and his living provided a way for him to contribute to this community, and his labor and attentiveness to his neighbors of various species, he felt, was his way of paying taxes, and besides, if the bystander approached the matter from a slightly different perspective, perhaps she would comprehend that he was not so much a trapper as a rancher or even a sort of farmer; his work was to do his best to protect and conserve certain life-forms so that the health of their population in this place would provide him sufficient means to cull a minimal number of individuals in order to provide him with a living, by which living he could in turn protect and conserve certain life-forms.

In fact, added the trapper to the now-gaping bystander, he would, without undue self-indulgence or self-promotion, venture to guess that he, the trapper, did more on a steady basis to protect and conserve healthy populations of, for example, marten and fox and bobcats and mink on Wy'east than the bystander did; so that attacking him, the trapper, for the way he made his living was perhaps a misguided endeavor. And this was not even to inquire as to how the bystander made *her* living and what the *bystander* did to protect and conserve marten and fox and bobcats and mink on Wy'east.

There's absolutely no question that contributing *money* to various and sundry environmental protection agencies and entities is a useful and indeed crucial aspect of protection and conservation of healthy populations of small fur-bearing mammals in the forest here, said the trapper gently, but I think we can both acknowledge that there is also a useful and crucial role to be played by men and women like me who attend meetings of forest advisory councils, and speak at public fish and wildlife hearings, and walk in the woods enough to be aware of possible fire hazards and invasive species and unusual patterns of death or disease or degradation, and stay in touch with their elected representatives, and stay in constant contact with both the scientific and enforcement professionals, all of whom I know by name and nearly all of whom I have pulled out of some ditch or other when winter seizes the mountain by the throat. And finally, this is not even to begin to discuss the manner in which you also kill other living beings in the normal conduct of your day, from the mammals you eat, to the other sentient vegetative beings you eat, to the remnants of former sentient beings who now compose the oil and gas in your car, to the sentient beings who are destroyed by the dams that provide the electricity that *powers* your house and car. That *is* your car, sitting outside, is it not?

Miss Moss said that the bystander, to her credit, stood there silently for a long moment, and then stepped up and shook the trapper's hand and said something like *you are right and I am wrong* and then drove away, after which she and the trapper agreed on prices for his furs, and she made him a huckleberry milkshake to go, on the house, just because.

18

WIDE AS HE RANGED ON HIS OWN, however, and deft and able and experienced in the ways of the woods as he was fast becoming, Martin was still very young that summer, and many times his headlong curiosity and his innate caution were at war, and many times his survival was a near thing. Sometimes you could say that he was saved by his incredible senses and reflexes; very few animals in the woods are as liquid quick and preternaturally alert as the marten. As Dickie the trapper had observed more than once, the marten, like its cousin the mink, despite being a predator, was still small enough to be prey to a startling number of larger animals, including its own larger cousins the fishers and wolverines.

Not that I have ever *seen* fisher or wolverine on the mountain, said Dickie to Miss Moss from his chair by the fire, but I've *heard* stories of fishers eating marten, given the chance. Tough family, the mustelid family. Of course the wolverine would have no compunction eating the fisher neither. The wolverine, from what

I hear, has no compunction about eating *anything*. There's stories of wolverines eating tires and bicycles and llamas.

Llamas?

Llamas.

You just like saying the word *llamas*, said Miss Moss.

Also supposedly there was a wolverine that ate a double-wide trailer in Alaska, and there's a story of a wolverine that tried to eat a high school football team, but I am not sure about that one. I think that's apocryphal. Unless it was seven-man football.

★

But sometimes Martin was also saved from dangerous moments by a growing sense of . . . what word can we use? Something larger and deeper than caution—a sort of ever-growing awareness of subtle pattern, let's say. Without consciously filing information away, he constantly filed information away, and he never forgot anything he learned, from the way owls were more dangerous in the open than they were in the thick woods, to the way wood hawks could fly sideways through branches to pick off animals in the canopy, to the way fishermen along the Zigzag would occasionally leave their catch in easily opened wicker baskets while they went to answer the call of nature, to the way dogs were terribly dangerous in the open but not so dangerous in the forest, to the way the best huckleberries were higher on the bush closer to the sun, to the way that gray foxes could climb trees but red foxes could not, to the way that rabbit runs and the little clearings where grouse liked to take dust baths were good places to find the thin wire snares set by human beings for rabbits and grouse.

And much else, much else. More than we could account in a thousand books. Isn't that amazing that the lessons learned by one young marten on one side of one mountain would take us years to try to explain? But that's no exaggeration—the plethora and panoply of scents in his talented nose alone are beyond our mutual eloquence, and you and I would have to invent lots of languages just to get *close* to a few of the things Martin knew without having words for them; the rich, golden, sneezy smell of the grouse dust bath, for example. Within a few seconds, Martin knew how many grouse had been there and their genders and their approximate ages (four were chicks) and approximately when they had been there (five hours before), and he could hazard a guess at when they might return, for the bath was well worn, either by this one tribe or several; and he filed away this information somewhere deep in his brain. He did not *think* about evidence and implication as we do; he absorbed the evidence and drew conclusions and implications in another way that we do not yet understand and perhaps never will. We would be very foolish and arrogant to conclude that our way of thinking is necessarily better or deeper than his, especially as we don't actually understand his way; wouldn't that be like saying your language is better than another, though you do not speak the other? Does that make sense? No? Yet that is what our species has done for many long years. Perhaps the less we think we know, the wiser we are and the closer to actual understanding we get. Perhaps the more we learn, abashed and humble, about the ways other beings think, the closer we get to other ways of living.

*

Me personally, said Dickie from his corner by the fire, I don't think of myself as a trapper so much as a student of animal life and customs, specializing in the fur-bearing small mammals of this particular place. And while I know enough to make a small living on what I know, I know I don't know hardly a thing. Any one individual is enough to prove that whatever you think you know isn't very much. That silver fox is a good example. And there are many more. There's a bobcat over to Hood River who is a total loner, a hermit, as far as I can tell. I bet he's ten years old and I don't think he's ever been in love. He's got his territory, he defends it in season, and he must be a hell of a defender, because I have seen some worn and torn young male cats coming out of there *not* happy about having challenged the old guy who they probably thought they could knock off with one paw but they couldn't. But once he knocks off all the young pretenders, he fades back into the woods, and I don't see sign of him again until the next batch of cocky princes comes after him. So what's his story? I don't know, and if *I* don't know, you can be sure no one knows. Maybe he's got religion or he had a romantic setback that left a scar on his heart or he's got a political beef with his cousins or who knows what. And that's just one individual cat. Imagine what we don't know about *all* the bobcats on the mountain. Maybe they're working out some huge treaty with the cougars this summer, for all we know. Or there's a young genius bobcat on the rise who is going to persuade his companions to work together in teams like wolves so they can take down more deer or make a run at old Louis.

It would take a hundred bobcats to pull down Louis, said Miss Moss from the kitchen. Maybe a thousand. Louis is bigger than a bus.

You know I have never seen Louis? said Dickie. Me, who has seen a thousand amazing things in the woods, and I have never seen the one animal that everyone and his kid sister has seen? Bizarre.

I've seen him, said Miss Moss, emerging from the kitchen with two cups of coffee. I saw him from the lodge one day, at the edge of the woods. Emma was with me, and we just stood there staring at him. No question it was Louis. For one thing he was enormous and for another he knew it and was allowing us an audience, as Emma said. You know how people say the words *king of the mountain* in fables and stories? He's the king of the mountain. You should have seen his posture. I expected to see a court painter nearby.

Somebody will kill him eventually, said Dickie. That's what happens to kings.

Not this king, said Miss Moss. He'll live forever. He'll probably be elected governor someday. We elect actors all the time now, right? Plus I don't think he talks, which is a plus.

This is the best coffee I have ever tasted in my whole life, said Dickie.

Liar.

Except for the coffee you made yesterday.

Hmm.

Or the coffee you will make me tomorrow.

You hope.

I hope.

19

THE DAY that Maria turned six years old turned out to be a terrific day everywhere you looked. Dave went for not one but two runs and both times turned in personal bests. Dave's dad got a phone call and when he hung up the phone he turned and hugged Dave's mother so hard she said hey, you are going to crack my ribs! Emma Jackson Beaton did a complete no-kidding head-over-heels flip while snowboarding the glacier, a flip she had been trying to accomplish since last winter, and when she finally did it she lay down in the snow and made snow angels, laughing, and both the morning waitress and the third chef watched her from their respective windows in the lodge and sighed that she was so thrilling and lovely and inaccessible. Miss Moss was inundated by, in order, a group of Lutheran dawn hikers, a group of German skiers, a college summer botany class, a book club reading only books of alpine adventure in alpine settings, a Forest Service trail crew, a group of

Pacific Crest Trail hikers who had smelled bacon and broke their vegan vows, a group of snowboarding competition judges, a group of nudists who thankfully weren't yet, a group of Finnish fishermen, a wine club, and a flower club, and that was all before noon.

It was a Saturday, and Dave worked at Miss Moss's between runs, and then he had the afternoon off for Maria's birthday party. Maria had specified that she wanted a "real picnic," with baskets of food and running in a meadow and someone playing a guitar. She had seen her party in a dream and was quite particular about it. She invited six friends from kindergarten and she specified that each member of the family could invite up to three friends each. Her mother invited Emma Jackson Beaton and two friends from the library; her father invited his two former partners from the logging concern in an effort to mend bridges; and Dave invited Moon.

It was the most beautiful Saturday you could ever ask for at the Saturday store, as Maria said. The meadow was an easy walk along the river; it was the same meadow where Dave had seen Martin for the first time. Emma Jackson Beaton brought a ukulele, which she could almost play and which was, when you thought about it, a cousin of the guitar, was it not? And there were not one but three picnic baskets of sturdy burly wicker and many delicious and savory things to eat, and children ran headlong and laughing through the meadow, and Dave's dad's partners lit cigars under a tree and allowed as they were sorry for the misunderstanding, and Dave's dad said is that anywhere within an acre of an apology? and the brothers said, well, sort of, we guess, you might say so, and they all three smoked for a while, grinning.

Also in the meadow of course were many other guests either resident therein or visitors passing through on business, and Dave and Moon made a list of all the other beings who attended Maria's birthday party and presented her with the gift of themselves, as Moon said: crickets, grasshoppers, beetles, ants, worms, wasps, bees, hornets, damselflies, dragonflies, moths, butterflies, swallows, jays, crows, warblers, a tiny woodpecker, squirrels, chipmunks, and what sure seemed like a peregrine falcon, although it went by far too fast to get a good look. Also Moon was sure he saw a deer's long sad face in the shadows under the trees, and Dave pointed out that if you considered the meadow to be an endless vertical space as well as a finite horizontal space, you could include geese, cranes, ravens, and what probably was an eagle, although it was too high to see clearly.

Usually a bucolic scene like this one, in a mountain meadow, on a lovely summer afternoon, either turns dark for some reason—contrast is such an interesting literary device, isn't it?—or is arranged to house some character revelation; a meadow is a kind of open stage, when you think about it, a sort of theater in the round, with our cheerful subjects gathered in the center, and we readers, and perhaps a deer, watching from the edges. But this bucolic scene is just what it is, happy and warm and sunny and gentle and friendly and cheerful. Dave's dad, having received the phone call that gave him a maintenance job at Zigzag High, is happy to have made some peace with his former partners. Emma Jackson Beaton is secretly delighted to be around children, because she loves children and wants more than anything to have sons and daughters and has never told anyone, and she plays the ukulele all afternoon as deftly as she can, because she never wants this afternoon to end, because the meadow is as crammed with children as she someday hopes her house will be. Moon is happy to be shyly among lots of people, which is rare and intimidating and thrilling for him. Dave is happy for his family, and he finds himself watching his mother's pleasure in Maria's pleasure; being happy at someone else's happiness, he is beginning dimly to realize, is a form of love. The ladies from the library are happy to be out in the sun and wind, especially as one is "Unabled," as she says, and never hardly gets out into meadows without major logistical help.

Near the end of the afternoon Maria sits by this lady and they get to talking and the lady says now, Maria, I am *so* honored to have been invited to your celebration, and I thought long and hard about what to give you as a present. I am not in a position to buy things, but I have the sense that you are not the sort of young lady who measures things by their price as much as by their worth, am I right? So my present seems small, but I hope you will find her companionable, and she opened a small papery box in her lap, and out hopped a finch, who hopped right up her chest and onto her shoulder. The lady reached up gently and slipped her finger under the finch and put her on Maria's shoulder. The finch whistled suddenly and Maria laughed aloud in surprise and pleasure. The lady smiled and explained how the finch had come to her, but she thought Maria would be a much livelier and more mobile companion for a creature who really ought to see more of the world than an Unabled person could offer, so that if it was okay with Maria's family, perhaps the finch could live with Maria, and the two young beings could travel together, as it were, and keep an eye out for each other's welfare. So that is how Maria came to be walking home from her birthday party with a finch riding on her shoulder as Dave and Moon carried the picnic baskets, and Dave's mom and dad brought up the rear, holding hands.

20

WE HAVE THIS IDEA that there are *Domestic Animals* and *Wild Animals*, but it's not such a clean dichotomy, of course; there are lots of animals who live between those worlds, who are wild in nature but quite comfortable around people and their domiciles and habitats.

Some are readily seen, like raccoons and sparrows and deer and squirrels and coyotes, who are all flourishing, tribally, what with the vast and savory dining opportunities that people provide, consciously (bird feeders, tossing nuts to squirrels, salt licks for deer) or unconsciously (providing cats for coyote appetizers, garbage cans for deft raccoons, warm basements and bulging pantries for our friend the house mouse). But some are not so readily seen; the smallest, of course, like the myriad insect and arachnid clans, and the quietest, like the swifts living in the chimney and the swallows under the eaves of the toolshed. And then there are the many creatures who populate the edges of our settlements, the abandoned houses, the empty mills, the derelict cottages, the riddled boats, the slumping cabins heavy with moss, the logging-camp barracks where once a hundred men wrestled and roiled, now left for the forest to reclaim.

And this is especially true of Dave's village. There are deer living in three houses on the east side of town, where a developer's dream failed and not even the county saw a point in maintenance; those three houses, each exactly the same, were to be the vanguard for a resort community, for which the streets were platted and the rights of way cleared through the timber. But now many years have passed, and the only way you can tell what were to be streets are the lines of young alder trees between the ten-times-taller firs.

Deer in the dining rooms and kitchens, deer in the garages, deer in the downstairs bedrooms; all sorts of birds living upstairs and squirrels in the cramped attic; garter snakes in the laundry room, warmer than the rest by virtue of its soundproofing; the porches front and back colonized by bees and wasps, the chimney filled with swifts, ten generations of moles aerating the faint remnants of the lawns; shrews under the driveways, possums in the playhouse, carpenter ants slowly grinding the walls to the finest golden dust.

For a while one family lived in one of the houses, waiting the population of the others, to no avail, and finally they surrendered and returned to the city, leaving behind scraps and shards of their lives, now turned to use by other families. See, the small daughter's red wagon, filled with rainwater, the common pool and spring for sparrows and juncos and robins. The bag of compost fallen from the father's truck, now thrilling with earthworms. The latticework cupola in the garden, now a city of spiders and occasionally a rest stop for a haughty heron between ponds. The doghouse, so painstakingly and meticulously built by the son as a form of therapy and concentration and penance and prayer after a sea of troubles; for the last five years it has housed a pair of foxes whose kits annually explore the yard and garden and houses with awe at the wonders of the world. Were there ever fox kits like these, so well housed in carpentered wood? Who found, hidden and wrapped in a blanket in the garage, the very rifle once fired at their great-grandmother, to no avail? Who found, hidden beneath the floorboards in the third house, a small bag filled with a white powder that smelled so much like medicine that no creature would eat it, though the fox kits happily licked the vestiges of salt from the sweat of the boy's fingers on the bag and left the powder to sift away in the eddying winds of winter in the room.

*

Subtly, gently, without obvious sign or signal, it became clear to Martin that his mother and his sister would stay together in the third den, and he would leave and make his own way; so in his wanderings farther and farther afield, he began to look for a den of his own. He explored likely holes in old trees, he investigated windfalls, he poked cautiously into burrows that looked uninhabited and unattended—although this, he discovered, was a chancy business; twice he was challenged by furious residents with flashing teeth, and once he evaded being bitten on the nose by an angry marmot by a hint of an inch.

For some reason, he found himself drawn to possible dens right at the line where the biggest trees gave way to smaller juniper and alpine fir; for one thing, there seemed to be an endless supply of squirrels and chipmunks in the tiny meadows and rockslides there, and for another, he felt a curious security with the open face of the mountain looming behind him. Above timberline he was dangerously exposed to eagles and the bigger hawks, and even to the rare enterprising owl who ventured up this far after Rodentia, but there was an endless supply of good denning possibilities among the rocks, and he was close enough to the canopy to escape easily from any serious threat. Plus he found himself drawn somehow to the lodge; while he had no urge to den anywhere near it, he did find himself passing it regularly in his rambles, and often he would perch lazily far above it on a warm rock in the broad light of the alpine afternoon and watch with interest as people and dogs and cars milled about below him, the people in their jackets and sweaters as bright as birds, the dogs addled by the alluring scents of chipmunks and sandwiches, the cars climbing eagerly up and then wearily retreating back down toward the city. Occasionally Martin would turn his attention to the people who slid down the mountain on pieces of plastic, some of them screaming as they did so, but they were not as interesting as the activity around the lodge. It was the lodge that interested Martin most. He could not have explained, even in a common language, why all this interested him so; it just did. Some things fascinate us and some do not. Some things call alluringly and some do not. Some things sing and some are mute.

21

DAVE RAN AND RAN and ran and ran. He ran in the morning and he ran in the evening. He ran down along the river and back up along the highway. He ran the track at the high school. He ran along the corridors in the woods cut by telephone crews. He ran along game trails. He ran loops around and above and below the lodge. He ran up empty ski runs through grass as high as his waist. He ran around lakes and ponds. He ran mountain bike trails. He ran off-road vehicle trails. He ran around and through golf courses. He ran logging roads. He ran Forest Service roads. He ran up ravines above timberline that were arid and dry in summer and twenty feet under snow in winter and roaring with snowmelt in spring. Once a week he ran with Moon who started their runs gasping and barfing and then slowly got his wind. Once he ran with his dad, who quit after half a mile, laughing at how ancient and useless he was, like an old horse; I should probably be traded in for a new model down at the dad store, he said. Twice he ran with older guys from the high school track team, who did not speak to him and pointedly pulled away over the last mile. Once he was running along the river and a tall thin shirtless guy with long hair floating behind him like a cape pulled alongside, running as effortlessly as a breeze, and they ran together for three miles, and then the guy said thanks for the run and he vanished into the woods suddenly. Once he was running down the river trail when behind him he heard a cheerful voice shouting, *watch out Dave watch out!* and Cosmas shot past him going what sure seemed like eight thousand miles an hour. That time Dave had to stop running because he was laughing so hard his breathing got messed up. You would laugh too if you saw a huge guy dressed in an orange jumpsuit rocket past you on a bicycle while singing at the top of his voice.

The thing is, said Dave's dad later at dinner, you can never tell what *song* Cosmas is singing. Isn't that the great mystery of our time? What *is* that man's music? If you could find that out, you would have the key to everything. It's like the secret code to the universe, the Song of Cosmas. Or a new book in the Bible. But you never can tell because all you ever hear is a loud snatch of it as he goes by like a freight train. And why the orange jumpsuit? There are so many pressing questions in this life, don't you think? Pass the butter?

★

It was Dave's mom's habit when she worked the day shift in the laundry at the lodge to sit and eat lunch with Emma Jackson Beaton outside the lower laundry delivery door, where she and Emma sat like the queens of the nether reaches, as Emma said, and ate their sandwiches. Sometimes they sat silently all through their sandwiches and watched ravens float around the mountain chuckling in their dark amused voices, but often they had interesting conversations that took interesting leaps and turns, like today.

Tell me about the eminent Mr. Billy Beaton, superstar surfer, said Dave's mom. Is he in Hawaii today or Australia or Africa?

Mr. Billy Beaton, said Emma through her sandwich, is off the grid at the moment, you could say.

Due home anytime soon?

Not to my knowledge, said Emma. Have you ever noticed that ravens croak one way when they are aloft and another way when they are stationary? Do they have a flight vocabulary and a landed vocabulary?

I hadn't noticed, said Dave's mom. You have a sharp eye for the birds, Emma J. B.

I like the ravens, said Emma. They have a sense of humor. I

mean, they can tear a dead animal down to the bone in an hour, but they have a sense of play about the whole thing. I admire their panache, you could say. I used to think about being a biologist.

And then you met the eminent Mr. Billy Beaton?

Then I ran out of money and got this job where I get to be interviewed by my esteemed and gracious colleague Gracious McGracious.

Haw, said Dave's mom, and being actually a gracious and perceptive soul, she bent the conversation toward other matters, but she did wonder then and later about Mr. Billy Beaton. What was the story with Mr. Billy Beaton, and why, even if someone casually looked through sports sections of newspapers and past issues of surfing magazines at the library, was there no mention at all of Mr. Billy Beaton? Were there such things these days as superstars no one knew? Many things were changing these days, and perhaps there was now a new kind of superstar who quietly asked reporters and bloggers not to mention his feats, perhaps for spiritual reasons or for some incredibly deft and subtle marketing effort; could it be that the more mysterious you were, the more famous you became? If your face was never seen and your voice never heard and your actions legendary but undocumented, but there were rumors and intimations of your existence, did you exist? Can someone be mythic and real at once? It's awfully tempting to be merely logical here and begin to wonder if there even *is* a Mr. Billy Beaton, thought Dave's mom as she and Emma brought their chairs back inside the laundry, but then again, that which a lot of people call God operates on exactly this principle. It's a puzzle.

22

UP AND UP COMES a very old bear through the thinning juniper and alpine fir and into the tumbled rock fields, and Martin watches from a high stone pillar. This is an ancient bear; her fur is grizzled gray on her haunches and a brilliant white on her muzzle, and she picks her way slowly and painfully up the slope, paying no attention to the scurry and scuttle of marmots and pikas in the rubble around her. Her enduring idea is to go higher to die for reasons no one will ever know and no biologist could ever really explain; something deep inside her mind wishes to finish her story high above the dense moss and green light of the forest, and lie down for the last time amid sharp rocks, under a blue sky, near the ice, maybe even *in* the ice if she can get that far.

Martin watches cautiously; even an old bear has paws like huge hammers, paws big enough to break all the bones a marten has— bones Martin preferred uncrushed.

The bear enters a blind alley among the boulders. Martin watches to see if she will clamber over the stone wall. She rears up, slowly. Something is wrong inside her, some dark illness of the blood, some slow freezing of the bones, some gray exhaustion of the organs; Martin can hear her wheeze in pain. But she no longer has the energy to leap or climb, and she turns around and contemplates retracing her steps down out of the alley to find another path up the mountain. But something in her finally calls it quits, and she backs up to the vaulting wall and folds herself down, grunting with pain, and then she is still, watching the sprawl of slope below her, waiting for . . . something. Who knows what she is waiting for? A raven, endlessly curious, alights on the wall behind her, out of range from any sudden leap, and cocks its head in puzzlement; but the bear does not even turn her head. Martin wonders if the raven will jump down, hoping for a tremendous windfall of protein, but the raven also is old and experienced and knows that the bear is not yet dead. After a few minutes the raven floats off, perhaps to share the news of meals to come. But Martin stays atop his pillar and watches. Damselflies whir past, shadows lengthen, the ravens establish a loose perimeter. The sun declines over Martin's shoulder. The long cold shadow of the mountain reaches for the bear; and then it is night, and the curtain slides over all, and Martin slides silently off his pillar and back down into the woods, as noiseless as a shard of moonlight.

★

By late August, Martin sensed the impending winter, and he doubled his search for the right den; but he also had the oddest urge to range wider and wider before he settled on a home, and what had been daily jaunts of several miles now became journeys of many miles. He explored every lake he could find: Scout Lake, Wahtum Lake, Ottertail Lake, Lost Lake, Blue Lake, Rainy Lake, North Lake, Badger Lake, Clear Lake, and Frog Lake, which indeed featured frogs; something about lakes fascinated him, and he much enjoyed milling through cattails and marsh looking for small delicious meats. He went down the mountain far enough to cautiously skirt the towns of Brightwood and Rhododendron, on the west side, and to see the town of Parkdale in the distance, to the northwest; but towns of that size reeked of oil and gasoline and rubber and dogs and trouble, and he stayed high in the canopy and safely deep in the forest fringe even while examining them with interest for hours at a time.

He saw much that puzzled him in these voyages of curiosity, but he was already experienced enough to gauge which astonishments were fraught with danger and which were by some few degrees safer. In general, anything having to do with human beings should be watched with immense caution, let alone approached that way, while interesting things and places without the smell of human beings could be explored with a little more freedom, although by now he had developed an extra sense for escape routes and situations that, given the right enemy, could prove fatal. Seemingly empty dens and burrows, for example—tempting as it was to just stick his nose in on the good chance that they were either abandoned or rented by something good to eat, there was also a chance that they were occupied by something big and violent enough to eat him. The most memorable lesson he'd had along these lines was from a bobcat, which rocketed out of its burrow in a windfall with horrifying talons and a quicksilver fury Martin evaded by the thinnest of chances. He had fled instantly into the trees, but the cat flew up the trunk right behind him, and for the next few seconds, Martin's early death was a distinct possibility; death was less than an inch behind his golden tail until the cat abruptly abandoned the chase and leapt back snarling to the forest floor. Martin sprinted on for another few minutes, changing directions faster than any football player could ever emulate, until he was sure the cat was gone. But again, he filed away some crucial information in some deep file folder in his brain: the bobcat's incredible sprinting speed, a match for his own in a brief burst; the fact that it could and did rocket up into the trees after him; and the fact that it apparently was not a long-distance pursuer through the canopy, although this last was not a data bit he could bank on, given the small sample size.

Had he known it, the only animal capable of surpassing his liquid speed through the canopy and killing him far above the ground, other than raptors, was a fisher, his larger cousin among the mustelids; but no fisher had been seen by people on the mountain for many years. Thus no young marten had filed away knowledge of that particular manner of death and communicated it to his or her kits—just as no mountain marten knew that the largest of their cousins, the fearsome wolverine, could and would eat marten, given the chance, as no wolverine had been seen on Wy'east for a century. Not even Mr. Douglas the trapper had heard of wolverine in this forest, and he alone among all the men and women on the mountain had sought out the oldest residents and walkers in the woods and asked their tales and solicited their stories and welcomed the memories of the stories they had been told by the oldest before them. So it was that Mr. Douglas knew stories from before even Joel Palmer walked over the glacier barefoot, stories of the occasional wolverine—or carcajou, as the oldest First People called them—stealing kills from bears and cougars and killing snow-floundered elk and confronting human beings with a grim violent confidence that no other animal showed. But the animals in those stories had not been seen by human beings on the mountain since before the trees were felled to make Miss Moss's store.

23

ONE DAY AT THE END OF AUGUST when Dave reported to work at Miss Moss's, she was waiting for him on the porch with the trapper. Your assignment today, Dave, she said, is to accompany Mr. Douglas on his expedition through the woods and keep your eyes peeled for entrepreneurial opportunities for the store. You are a sales agent for things I do not know we are going to sell yet. I think we need more entrepreneurial innovation and product variety, but I am not in a position to explore those opportunities as much as you are, and I would like you to spend your shift today studying the possibilities with Mr. Douglas. Mr. Douglas will be responsible for safety and edibles. I have implicit trust in Mr. Douglas and you can be sure he is a trustworthy and personable companion. Report back on your progress tomorrow. No need to return to the store. I'll credit you with up to eight hours, depending on your progress and the nature of the country. Feel free to pepper Mr. Douglas with questions. His reputation as a taciturn man is undeserved in my experience. Questions?

No, ma'am.

Away with you, then. Safe passage, gentlemen.

And off they went on one of the most interesting days that Dave ever had in his life. Indeed he would remember this day for many years to come, and often accounted it a sort of beginning for the life he led. To be completely honest with you here, Dave had a slightly higher opinion of his woodcraft than perhaps was totally accurate, but to give him credit, he also was not fulsome or cocky about it, and he was quick to acknowledge his betters— and in Mr. Douglas, within the first few hundred yards of their journey, he discovered his better.

Let's start by learning to be silent, said the trapper, and for the next hour they were, as they picked their way along the river through a series of old clear-cuts and windfalls. For a few minutes, Dave noticed, being silent was no effort, especially as Mr. Douglas set a fairly rapid pace, but then he found the lack of conversation a little unnerving; but after another twenty moments or so of wanting to ask questions and make observations, he noticed that he did seem to notice more when he wasn't able to speak, an observation he made to the trapper when they paused finally and Mr. Douglas asked what he'd been thinking.

For the next hour, then, said Mr. Douglas, let's concentrate on walking silently while not speaking. Let's slow down and walk carefully. Look down and see where your feet are headed. Pause when necessary to negotiate your next step. See what's down there, rather than just walking through it. We spend a lot of time not seeing, it seems to me. Report on what you noticed.

At the end of this second hour, Dave was able to say that he had seen salamanders, two kinds of frog, what might have been a lizard but it was way too fast for even rough identification, and the vanishing tail of a dark snake that might well have been after what might have been a lizard.

That all?

No, sir, said Dave. Lots of crickets, grasshoppers, beetles, snails, spiders, caterpillars, moths, butterflies, quick small brown birds with tiny tails that I believe were wrens, more than a few sparrows, two towhees, a thrush, and a large bird that I believe was a blue grouse. Also various feathers—this one I am almost sure is an owl, and this is surely a jay feather. Also several beer bottle caps, a plastic knife, and a pencil.

Sharp eye, Dave. That pencil still work?

Yes, sir.

Keep it—another lost treasure of the vast and mysterious forest.

Yes, sir.

You don't have to call me *sir*, Dave.

Yes, sir.

Want me to call you *sir*?

No, sir.

Want me to call you Elmore, or Mohammad?

No, sir. Dave is good.

Alright, then, Dave. What say we go for a couple of hours now as quietly as we can and keep our eyes peeled, this time for animals and their habits and customs and trails and territories. Animals live in certain ways, and when you pay close attention to their ways, what they like, what they are most comfortable with, that's when you go down a few layers deeper, sort of. Know what I mean? My job is to catch some of them, but the larger pleasure isn't the money, it's the literature of their lives, so to speak. And it's very humbling, which is refreshing. You never get to the end of knowing about them. There's always something new that the books and Web sites and grizzled old veterans of the woods don't know. That's a good thing to remember. Whatever you know beyond the shadow of a doubt out here, you don't. On the other hand, a working knowledge of habit and probability is a good thing. If you are looking for mink, for example, you're probably not going to find a whole lot of them above timberline. That narrows down your search engine, so to speak. Ready?

Yes, sir.

So we'll just walk and talk quietly. You ask anything you want and tell me anything you see, and I'll do the same. We'll be quietly companionable. Two students in the biggest school there is. Both of us working for Miss Moss.

Can I ask you about Miss Moss, sir?

No, sir, said the trapper, smiling. She's not on the agenda. For one thing we are both on task here, and for another I don't know anything for sure about the estimable Miss Moss. She's a mystery from head to foot and tip to toe. No, sir.

And off they went for two hours and then a lunch break and then two more hours, looping back downhill another way and eventually back to the store. And indeed they walked and talked quietly, and Dave never forgot, all the rest of his life, the gentle murmur of the trapper's voice in the shadows as he talked about how most predators of any size like to establish territories, which he called yards, and how they would patrol their yards every day, rain or shine, and how any encroachment on their yards was a flagrant offense, and how not only would they defend their yards against enterprising members of their own species seeking to snatch some new yard but also sometimes against members of other species even if they were larger and dangerous, and how some animals seemed to have a détente or treaty going for reasons you couldn't really tell. And on top of that, some individuals of some species established their own treaties for their own reasons—for example, a cougar he knew that just would not eat deer no matter what, even when apparently presented with the world's easiest chance at venison for dinner. Who knew what was up with *that*, said the trapper. You could speculate that maybe she, the cougar, tasted poisoned meat or associates deer with pain or trouble or something, but you don't *know*, and it's all the more mysterious because every other cougar on the mountain would take a train and a *bus* to get deer for dinner. But there you go.

They talked about marten and what they ate and where they lived and when the kits left their dens to establish their own yards, and they talked about foxes and how usually on the mountain there were few red foxes and lots of gray foxes, but lately in the last few years there were montane foxes, which are red foxes particularly adapted to mountain life, with thicker coats and more muscle in the chest, seems to me, said the trapper. And they talked about deer and elk, and mink and otter, and bears and bobcats, and how in the old days there were lynx up here and fisher and wolverine but probably never much badger; your badger is not much for mountain life, all things considered, said the trapper. And they talked about chickarees and chipmunks and bats and birds and snakes and skinks and every other sort of animal the trapper knew and Dave was curious about. And they stopped, here and there, and stood silently when a resident presented himself or herself—an owl half-asleep in a tree bole, two rabbits in a clearing, a king-fisher rattling down a creek on a blue trail in the air. At one point, Dave turned and could have sworn he saw a golden brown flash of fur in the canopy, but it vanished so quickly and thoroughly that he didn't mention it to the trapper; and later that night, in his bed-room, he realized that to have mentioned the young marten would be to have instantly endangered it, for the trapper would have marked the spot and returned to look for sign. He fell asleep, ex-hausted and pleased. When he awoke in the morning there was a bright yellow warbler feather on his chest, a gift from Maria in gratitude for the owl feather he had left for her the night before.

24

INDEED IT WAS MARTIN in the trees above Dave and the trap-per, watching curiously. By now he recognized the smaller hu-man being as the one who ran without being chased, and something about this particular being drew Martin like a lure.

He could not have explained it, even given a language we could understand; it was a feeling composed of interest and even affection. He *liked* this being, felt a certain empathy for it, much like he had felt for his lost brothers and felt still for his quiet sister, despite not seeing her much anymore as summer waned. He was intrigued by Dave; he felt some inarticulate assurance that Dave was not dangerous, and he liked both proximity to him and sprinting through the trees overhead as Dave flew along the forest trails. Granted the eloquence in our tongue he already had in his own, he might have said simply that he liked Dave and felt somehow that Dave liked him too.

Which increasingly was the case. Now when Dave went for his morning and evening runs, he looked automatically into the trees to see if the marten was there, and almost every day there Martin was, the distinctive golden brown burnish of his fur evident to an eye looking for just that characteristic color; and Dave would smile, and say *ready?* and take off, upriver or down depending on the bounce in his legs, and above him to one side or another the marten would float along effortlessly, flying along branches so fast and gracefully that Dave would have sworn on a Bible that there were times the marten's feet touched nothing but the crisp clean air.

This is probably a good time to stop and talk for a moment about the really amazing athletic machine for which we use the word *marten*; and let's use Martin as an example, as he is right there above us, in midleap between fir branches. Let's freeze time for a moment and zoom in on Martin and take a close look. He's four months old today, still growing, but already you can see the size and build of the mature creature he will be in a few months. He's almost two feet long already, if you count his tail; his thick furry tail is about six inches long and a little darker in color than his body, as are his feet and legs. On his chest there's a patch of lighter fur than his generally golden brown body; it looks like he's wearing a permanent bib. Rather large triangulish ears, black nose and eyes, black burst of whiskers. Serious claws, when he unsheathes them. Small teeth, but sharper than any knife. Alert and attentive at all times, capable of long periods of absolute stillness and then instant violent action so fast that he would be a blur to your eye if he was moving at top speed. Weight, about two pounds now; in a few months he will grow to be close to three pounds. In essence he is a furry muscle in the woods, quite comfortable on the ground and in the trees. He can climb anything lightning fast and is the king of the forest insofar as using the canopy as a highway. While his favorite food is voles, caught on the floors of forest and meadow, he much enjoys squirrels of all kinds and is the only hunter of squirrels who can follow them to the highest, thinnest branches; not even the fisher, being heavier, can achieve that dangerous elevation. He eats everything else he can find, of course, but given his druthers, like today's late-summer bounty, he would have a vole for breakfast and then some thimbleberries and a cricket as a midmorning snack and then another vole for late lunch, followed by huckleberries in the afternoon, most of a dead white-crowned sparrow, some early white-oak acorns—which were not quite as toothsome as he had hoped—and then, delightfully, a young flying squirrel, which was just waking up in a cottonwood tree for its own evening hunt. All in all, an excellent day food-wise; had Martin known it, this would be one of his best dining days of the year, for heavy snow will come all too soon on the mountain to cover much of the larder. Savor these last days of summer, for autumn on Wy'east will be short, and soon cometh winter; and winter on a mountain eleven thousand feet high is thorough and inarguable.

★

The hole in the cottonwood tree where Martin had found and eaten the flying squirrel was roomy, angled out of the prevailing wind, relatively inaccessible from other predators, high above a creek filled with fish and crawfish and snails, relatively close to two meadows with good hunting prospects, and equipped with the remnant of a branch that served as something like a porch or deck by the front door. After cleaning out all evidence of previous occupancy, Martin moved in, driven by some feeling that he must have secure housing before the seasons changed. He could feel the change, somehow—the chill now, after dark, and the beginning of leaf loss among the deciduous trees; the reddening of vine maples and yellowing of birch and aspen trees; the ripening of first acorns on the burly white oak trees in meadows; the first salmon and steelhead returning to their native streams; the male deer and elk growing restless and testy with each other. From his perch in the afternoon sun, he could hear the clash of their antlers like faraway swords.

Driven by another inchoate feeling, he sought out his mother and sister, and for two days, all was as it had been in the beginning—his mother bringing food to their den, Martin and his sister chasing each other comically, the three of them curling up for naps. More than once, Martin caught a faint and final wisp of the smell of his brothers and remembered them curled in the dark of their natal burrow. But early one evening, as he and his sister and their mother filed out of the burrow for an early evening hunt, they went one way and Martin another; and they would not see each other again for a very long time.

25

THE FIRST DAY OF SCHOOL at Zigzag High is always officially three days after Labor Day, but freshmen with athletic aspirations were required to register early for physicals and interviews with coaches and team captains, so at ten in the morning on the first day of September, Dave was waiting nervously by the back door of the gym amid a remarkable gaggle of boys and girls, only a few of whom he even vaguely knew. More evidence, says Moon quietly to Dave, that there are a lot of people living out in the woods about whom we do not know a thing.

Not that you would know them anyways if they lived in town, says Dave.

Town? says Moon. What town? Is the Zag a town? A wide place in the road with a store and a gas station is a town now? Did I miss the meeting at which the Zag was christened a town? I'll tell my folks next time they're home.

Moon has been persuaded to register for a sports physical, but he has yet to choose a sport. He says he will feel it out as the day goes along. He says he will listen to each coach and each team captain and see if there's a place where their agendas meet his. He says you can tell a lot about coaches and captains by the way they explain what it is they want. He says that there are all sorts of ways they talk about what they want, and you have to listen carefully as if they are speaking in code, which basically they are. The coaches and captains who dwell on glorious victories over bitter rivals are interested in war. The coaches and captains who talk about each member of the team rising to his or her best self are interested in weight lifting. The coaches and captains who talk about the team as a family are the sort of people who will cut you from the team without the slightest hesitation or compunction if you get hurt. You have to listen carefully before committing yourself to things, Dave, says Moon. You have to tread very cautiously in water this deep.

Isn't that a mixed metaphor? asks Dave.

I think you are committing to running without knowing anything about the people you will be running with or who will be telling you where and when to run and in what direction, says Moon. Is that wise? Is that the approach of a sensible man?

Are we men? asks Dave. At fourteen?

I'm serious, Dave.

Moon, says Dave, smiling, I am going to try out for the cross-country team, and I hope I make it, and that's that. If I make it, great. If not, I'll run on my own. I like running, and I am no good at any other sport. Like you.

It turned out that the cross-country team had three captains—two seniors and a sophomore who was so clearly the best on the team that there was no way not to make him a captain. To Dave's relief, all three of the runners and the coach seemed relaxed and honest and direct folks; secretly, he had been worried that Moon was right and that the captains and coach would be grim martinets or screamers. The seniors talked about summer training, academic expectations, and how the team mixed and matched for travel slots during the actual season, depending on performance and attendance and health. The coach talked about how the team was really a collection of individuals who ideally supported each other but were in the end responsible for their own training; his role was only to help runners train, choose the best for meets, and make sure everyone got the same chances and opportunities. It's a loose team, and you are on your own together, is the best way I can explain it, he said. We are not much like the other teams here, with organized practices and such. We just stretch and run and then stretch. Sometimes we have meals together. I drive the bus. If your grades sink below a B, you're off the team. If you miss school for disciplinary reasons, you're off the team. If you fight or curse at anyone, you're off the team. Otherwise you're on the team. You freshmen might not make the traveling squad, but you're on the team. You get your uniforms at the end of the first

week of running, if you make it that far. Once you get your uniform, only you can take it away from you. Questions?

The sophomore spoke last. He was a tall thin boy with a pony-
tail that hung to his waist, and he was barefoot and shirtless.
Dave could see each detail of each rib on his chest. He looked
like he might have about an eighth of an ounce of fat on him, or
less. He spoke quietly. He said that running was an ancient human craft, and we ought to honor and celebrate such a gift. He
said he would be at the back door of the gym every afternoon at
three o'clock, starting today, and that anyone who wanted to run
with him was welcome to do so, for as long or short as they
wanted. He said it would be an honor to run with anyone who
wanted to run with him, because running was memory and
meditation and fitness and witness, and those were good things
to achieve collectively.

Even the kids who usually sniggered at talk like this did not
snigger, partly because the sophomore was one of the best three
runners in the state already and partly because of the sheer calm
dignity with which he said his piece. You'd feel like a heel
laughing at a guy like that, as Dave said later to his dad. He was
speaking right from his heart without any fuss and bother. He
wasn't selling anything or showing you how cool he was or anything like that. You got the sense that this is exactly who he is, no
more and no less.

Alluring, isn't it? said his dad. That's the final frontier for all of
us. To take off as many masks as you can pry off and just be you.
Was that the end of the tryouts?

Yep, said Dave. I passed my physical, and I'll show up for the
run at three o'clock and see if I am really in shape or not.

What sport did Moon choose?

Basketball.

Isn't basketball in the winter?

That's why Moon chose it. He says he gets to say he's trying out for basketball, but he doesn't actually have to do anything. He says he picked basketball because it's a metaphysical idea for the next three months.

Unusual boy, your boy Moon.

I'll say.

Do his parents know he chose basketball?

He says he will inform them by all modern means of electronic contact tomorrow. His mom's in Russia and his dad's in Kuwait.

Unusual boy, your boy Moon.

I'll say.

Kuwait?

Kuwait.

I've been in Kuwait.

Your turn for the dishes, Jack, said Dave's mom, and Dave's dad said, your wish is my command, madam, and he extended his hand to Maria and said won't you join me, young lady? And she said I accept your invitation, frog king, and everyone cracked up, and that was that, but later Dave looked up Kuwait in his atlas and wondered.

26

THE THING ABOUT ANIMALS, says the trapper, sitting by the fire and ostensibly talking to Dave but pitching his voice loud enough so Miss Moss could hear him in the kitchen, is that we totally take them for granted, and we arbitrarily divide them into categories that don't actually apply, like domestic and wild. The animals we think are tame would mostly happily escape their prisons given the chance, and the ones who are not fenced in are, in my experience, cautiously interested in human beings. And *we* are wild animals too, of course. We forget that. We're just mammals with attitude. In a lot of ways our skills pale before their skills, and in a lot of ways we are terrible at fitting into our environmental niche. Why we achieved this dominance is sometimes a mystery to me, and a dangerous dominance it is too. The whole point of *our* evolution, it seems to me, is for us to find a way to fit back into the world as it is, rather than try to remake the world to fit us, but not everybody thinks like me.

And a good thing too, or we would all be philosophizing by the fire and keeping Dave from doing his work, said Miss Moss's voice, wandering out of the kitchen by itself.

Mr. Douglas grinned and got up and left money for his milk shake on the counter and said good-bye to Dave and Miss Moss.

I'm off to the woods for a while now, Miss Moss, he added, but I will be by in October to outfit for the season.

It will be a pleasure to see you when you are back, said Miss Moss, coming out of the kitchen to shake hands. It seemed to Dave that they shook hands very slightly longer than people usually shake hands, but there's only so much you can read into how long people shake hands, and Miss Moss's hand was a little moist from doing the dishes, anyway, so maybe that's why their hands stuck together that extra couple of seconds. Probably that was it.

*

Martin sees the trapper leave Miss Moss's store. Martin is high in a beech tree behind the store, staring down at the jumbled welter of stuff where Dave found his trap. Martin watches Dave wander among the stuff; today, Miss Moss has asked Dave to begin *the Count,* as she says.

Long past time for someone to know what's out there and what's useful and what's not so we can sell the former and recycle or scrap the latter, she says. You would think the proprietor of the store would know what's out there, but you would be wrong. The proprietor, in her defense, bought the store with the clearing already almost full of Stuff, and she has not had time or, to be honest, inclination to conduct proper inventory, whereas she was trying to keep body and soul together and the business extant and the wolf from the door.

When did you buy the store? asks Dave.

Many moons ago.

Your folks owned the store?

No, no, says Miss Moss, recovering herself from some sort of reverie. I bought it from the sweetest couple, Mr. and Mrs. Robinson—Alton and Alicia Robinson—just the nicest friendliest gentlest people in the history of the universe. They had owned it for fifty years and they were getting kind of worn and weary, as Mr. R. said. You know them, don't you? They're the old couple with that little old black Ford Falcon car. They go everywhere in that car and they never go anywhere without each other. They only travel as two. They live out of town a ways in the woods. I keep telling them they ought to move down into the city away from the ice and snow, but they'll never leave the mountain. Now *those* two people are mountain people from the old days of mountain people. I doubt they have been down to the city more than three times in their whole lives. Both of them were born up here and schooled here and worked here all those years and never wanted to live anywhere else. You see them here and there in that little old car. I bet that car is fifty years old too. You wouldn't believe a little old regular car like that could survive this long on the mountain, but you would be wrong there. I bet that car has half a million miles on it. I kid you not. They sold me the store for a price slightly below what it was worth, I thought. And then they worked for me for thirty days, the two of them together, so I would understand all the little quirks and corners of the business, who could be trusted and who couldn't and who drank a little and who would deliver supplies when he said he would, that sort of thing. The sweetest gentlest people ever, the Robinsons. They must be ninety years old or more. No one knows how old they are. I don't think they know how old they are. They might be two hundred years old for all anyone knows. Mr. Robinson in particular likes to play with people's heads that way and sometimes he says he knew Joel Palmer before he walked over the mountain. *That Joel Palmer,* says Mr. Robinson, *he was a wild kid, wore through a pair of shoes every week, his poor mother was in here buying shoes regular as rain.* Old Mr. Robinson, what a lovely man, and Mrs. R. is twice as so. You'll see them go by in that Falcon sometimes, going about eight miles an hour. You can identify their car by the sound—it sounds like a bicycle with baseball cards in the spokes, pupupupupupupupup. *We are in no particular hurry,* says Mr. Robinson, *and this way we don't use hardly a drop of gasoline. We only use the gasoline going up the mountain, and we just coast down.*

Do they still come in the store? asks Dave.

Not so much, says Miss Moss, and she falls silent a moment. Not at all recently, come to think of it. Maybe I should pop out there one of these days and see if they are okay. The nicest sweetest gentlest people you could ever imagine. Much like the woman to whom they sold the store, who seems to be keeping her sole and valued employee from the execution of his duties, isn't that so, Dave?

★

And back out in the clearing, Dave set to work, first counting how many of each thing there was and then hauling and dragging things into cousinish piles—car parts with car parts, tools with tools, various and sundry scraps of wood thrown together into a corner so at least when someone needed wood you would know where to go.

Martin watched from the beech, curious. It is a capital mistake to think that animals spend all their time chasing after food, pursuing romance, engaged in conflict, or at rest—just as it is a capital mistake to try to define human life by such broad and limited categories alone. Much else happens of a subtle and unassuming nature, a good deal of it having to do with curiosity and playfulness and a sort of . . . what words shall we use? Contemplation, meditation, pondering, a general quiet open absorption in the swirl and seethe of the world? We sit on park benches and beaches and couches and hilltops, listening and dreaming seemingly to no particular purpose. But isn't it often the case that when we cease to move and think, we see and hear and understand a great deal?

So Martin was still as a stone on his branch and watched the boy and for once did not seek for pattern or calculate how matters below might result in small and delicious meats for him;

and the boy worked steadily through the afternoon until finally enough of the chaos had been roughly ordered that he could sit a moment and rest.

It was hot amid the piles of metal and wood and plastic in the clearing, and Dave knew his mountain summers well enough to suspect a breeze in the trees, so he leapt up the pile of wood and into the beech, walked right up a slanting branch like a fence line, and sat down. Indeed there was a lovely breeze right in his face, and he closed his eyes and shivered with the subtle pleasure of being at rest after substantive work, and his sweat dried just enough to be comfortable but not chilled, and then he opened his eyes again, and saw, not five feet away, curled on the branch above him like a furry golden hat, a marten!

27

ABOUT EIGHTEEN THOUGHTS ran through Dave's head at once—wonder, fear, amazement, hesitation (was this really a marten or a cat with serious muscles or some new species of tree badger or a mink that had totally lost its way or a pygmy fisher or small otter wearing someone else's jacket or . . . ?), awe, fascination, curiosity, trepidation, astonishment, respect, reverence, something like pride (no one he knew, other than Mr. Douglas, had ever been so close to such an elusive and legendary animal), and finally startled recognition—this was the same marten that ran through the canopy when he ran the river trail! Its color was unmistakable—a sort of deep bronze, a bright russet, a dark burnished golden color utterly not the color brown, although now that Dave was close enough to see detail, he saw the darker legs and feet and the lighter patch of fur on the marten's chest, looking exactly like the bib he and Maria wore as babies.

They stared at each other. The wind casually commented on the shapes of leaves. A beech tree in September still has a lot of leaves and there was a lot to say. Two crows opportunistically hopped around in the new arrangement in the clearing below, on the general principle that Dave's labor might well have un-covered or unsheltered small and delicious meats. Very faintly, Dave heard the bell on the front door of the store jangle and the warm tone of Miss Moss's voice greeting a customer. A truck lumbered uphill outside the store and a small old black Falcon puttered downhill. Martin's left ear twitched. Dave knew beyond the shadow of a doubt that if he moved even an eyelash, the mar-ten would vanish in an instant.

Martin was fascinated. He had never been so close to such an elusive and legendary animal, and he examined Dave with care, from the worn red sneakers on his feet to the bright red ban-danna on his head. A large animal, but perhaps not a predator, was Martin's initial feeling; he couldn't see any talons or teeth, though the animal's scent smacked of danger—this was the scent of highways and dogs and cars and wire snares, all things to be avoided at all costs. Yet this animal was somehow riveting, and Martin noted how its breathing slowed after a couple of minutes, how the muscles in its naked face lifted the ends of its lips toward its eyes, and how it finally made a quiet sound almost like a small creek murmuring.

If I *say* something, it'll vanish, Dave thought. But if I make some gentle sound . . . Can you make a sound that indicates non-violence? A friendly sound? A sound that is meant and received as hey, we are all good here, how's it going, lovely day, isn't it? A sort of noncommittal, nonconfrontational sound? But I don't know his language and he doesn't know mine. Or her. It is male or female? How do you tell with martens? On the other hand, he or she doesn't know if I am male or female, either. What am I thinking about this for? This is not the time to get into questions of gender.

I thought about just humming or singing or something, but what came out of my mouth were words, Dave told Maria later. I didn't even think about what I was saying. I was just trying to get some quiet things into the air before he vanished. I think I said something like *hey, I have a younger sister; what about you?* I think that's what I said but I am not sure. I said it as quiet and gentle and calm and murmury as I could. I was just trying to extend a hand and say hi without moving my hand, you know? And there was a minute there when I was saying something like *so my sister just turned six years old, she's the best sister ever, we don't have any brothers yet, although who knows in the future,* and right then Miss Moss came around the corner saying Dave? And the marten vanished so suddenly that you would swear it just evanesced on the spot, like it de-atomized itself. I swear I never took my eyes off it, and one second it was right there, staring at me, all golden brown with darker legs and that white bib on its chest, and the next second it was just absolutely inarguably incontrovertibly gone.

What did you do? asked Maria.

Climbed down and went back to work.

Did you tell Miss Moss?

I didn't, no, said Dave. I wanted to but then I just didn't for some reason, and then the moment to tell her passed. You know how that happens, that the moment you should say something just slides by, and then what you had to say doesn't fit the next moment?

Yep.

Then later I thought, well, if I tell her, she might tell Mr. Douglas, and he might set traps for the marten.

That's true.

But I felt bad that I didn't tell Miss Moss.

Are you going to tell her tomorrow?

I should, said Dave. I really should. I like Miss Moss. Plus, all this happened on her property, so technically she should know, right?

But he didn't tell her the next day or the days after that. Every time he thought this would be a good time to say, Miss Moss . . . ? the bell would ring, or a truck would rumble past, or she would step into the kitchen just out of range of his voice, and he would go back to work, thinking, alright, I'll tell her next time I get a chance, this time for sure.

But he didn't.

★

Martin slid away into the canopy as the woman came around the corner and barked, and some instinct in him knew this was not a time to linger. Plus he was hungry. He explored a few interesting cavities in trees, finding nothing to eat, and finally he descended into a clearing, where he explored rotten logs until he found what he was looking for—a vole's burrow with a vole in it. In Martin's experience, you could almost always find voles, if you looked assiduously, especially in clearings left over from logging; many small animals flocked to these sudden meadows, where sunlight and piles of brush the loggers called slash provided lots of succulent new plants and cover. The mountain was thoroughly dotted with these cuts, and Martin thought of them as something like pantries, where he could almost always find something good to eat, from voles to mice to shrews to birds to insects to berries.

Late in the afternoon he made his way back to his new den in the cottonwood tree and curled up to sleep just before sunset. He was sleeping more in the day now and abroad more at night as the summer waned, and even in his warm burrow, he could feel the deepening cold in the evenings. He lay half-awake for a few minutes, listening to the world outside and fitting the sounds into the quilt of his experience; the whir and flitter of swifts leaving an old fir snag nearby, the first quiet calls of an owl. The owl got his attention for a moment until he recognized that it was a screech owl, too small to cause him problems, and he closed his eyes again. The last sounds he heard clearly and identified in some deep recess of his brain were that of elk making their way past the base of his tree; one of these animals, at least, must have been very large, for it forced its way easily through a huckleberry thicket so old and dense that Martin had thought it impenetrable to any creature bigger than himself. In the morning, remembering the sounds of the immense elk in the bushes, he found a wealth of scattered berries on the ground and breakfasted with pleasure. Of all the berries to be found on the mountain, from the blackberries near people places to the fat orange salmonberries near creeks, from the blueberries in clearings and meadows to the thimbleberries that tried to hide themselves with leaves the size of birds, huckleberries were the most savory and delicious, and Martin ate so many that he went back up the cottonwood for a nap.

28

TO MOON'S INTENSE SURPRISE, basketball did not begin on December 1, which was listed as the date of the first game of the season, but a mere two days after he signed his name to the tryout sheet. The coach was the mathematics teacher, and he called Moon the next day and told him to be in the gym at noon the day after.

For what, sir?

Conditioning. Officially we cannot practice until October, but we sure can get in shape in September.

Yes, sir.

Wear sneakers and shorts and a white shirt if you have one.

Yes, sir.

No earrings, nose rings, eyebrow rings, nose studs, tongue studs, necklaces, earbuds, rings, bracelets, or hardware or software of any kind.

Yes, sir.

Ever play before, Moon?

No, sir.

Signed up as a joke?

No, sir. My parents want me to play a sport during my high school years, and I thought I would begin this year and perhaps get better than awful at something over the next four years. I am not much of an athlete.

Refreshing ego you have there, Moon.

Sir?

Admirably small. Refreshing.

Yes, sir.

Why basketball, Moon? Other than you thought we didn't start for a while.

Indoors, sir. I am not much for the cold.

You live on the tallest mountain in the state, and you are not much for the cold.

No, sir.

Ever pick up a basketball before, Moon?

No, sir.

Any idea of the game at all?

Yes, sir. I have watched thousands of games. Sometimes two or three a day. I like watching the flow and spacing of the game.

You do.

Yes, sir.

The flow and spacing.

Yes, sir.

Moon, how old are you?

Fifteen last month, sir.

Fifteen.

Yes, sir.

Moon, no basketball player who ever played for me ever used the words *flow and spacing of the game* to me, that I remember, and I have been coaching ball for thirty years, and I remember every kid who ever played for me.

Yes, sir.

Moon, you come to the gym an hour early, and find me. See you at eleven.

Yes, sir.

No earrings or nose studs.

No, sir.

The flow and spacing of the game.

Yes, sir.

★

Moon was at the gym earlier than eleven. He was excited. He was terrified. He hoped he had on the right kind of sneakers. What did he know of the right kind of sneakers for sports? He hoped buying the ones he saw on the players in television was a good idea. He was nervous. But he found that he was confident, a little. He wasn't stupid. He could figure anything out. Dave had often said so. Moon could repair anything with wires and batteries. You just think it through patiently, he said to Dave, and wasn't basketball a thing with wires and batteries, if you thought about it? Patterns and geometries, ways of passage, angles and energies? So if you could understand the pattern and flow, the way people and the ball moved and why, you would get it, right? He had tried to explain this to his dad last night on Skype. He loved his dad but couldn't find easy ways to say that, so he explained his theories about basketball at length. His dad, to his credit, listened patiently. He was in Kyoto now. Moon's mom was in New York, but she was actually on her way home to Oregon for four whole days before she flew to Hong Kong. They hoped to meet in Singapore for a date.

Moon?

Sir?

Good to see you're punctual.

Yes, sir.

Three laps around the gym. Let me see you run. Run easy, like you are running on the beach. Speed is not the object.

Yes, sir.

The coach watched as Moon loped around the gym, carefully not cutting the corners of the court. Hmm. He's got height. He runs easily. He's not breathing hard. Doesn't know what to do with his arms. Doesn't know what to do with his body yet. Still.

Now do me a favor and run sideways for a while.

Sir?

Just sort of slide sideways as fast as you can for a while, back and forth.

Around the gym?

Right here.

Yes, sir.

Hmm. Good feet, thought the coach.

Halt.

Yes, sir.

Moon, do you know anyone on the team?

No, sir. I don't really know anyone at school yet. I know a few of the kids coming in as freshmen. Not many. Well, a couple. Well, Dave. You know Dave?

The runner? His dad works here?

Yes, sir.

Not yet.

He'll be a great runner, sir.

If you say so, Moon. Now pick up a ball and just sort of putter around with it, you know—dribble a little, shoot a little, just fiddle around. Pretend I am not here and you're a little kid in the playground just fooling around.

Moon tried this, but he discovered that what looked so easy and graceful on television was not at all the case with a real ball. For one thing, the ball felt huge and clammy, and for another, it didn't seem to be bouncing quite as truly and accurately as it should ideally bounce. On television the ball seemed to be almost attached to the hand of the dribbler, generally, but this was not at all the case here. Also shooting was harder than it looked; you had to guess at the parabola and force of a shot, depending on all sorts of factors. On television, generally, the ball fell through the hoop as if the hoop was magnetized, but here he kept missing shots and then having to sprint after the rebound, which disdainfully flung itself into the far corners of the gym.

Time, said the coach. Moon, come sit down for a moment.

Sir.

You really want to try out for basketball.

Yes, sir.

You want to make the freshman team?

Yes, sir. I can't make the junior varsity.

We don't have a junior varsity, Moon. We have two teams, basically older and younger, although there's some interchange. We don't have enough students for three teams. I think you can make the freshman team if you channel your energies. You run well, and I have the feeling that once you actually play games you will get a feel for the sport. My only advice is don't try to get good at the game yet. Just play it—does that make sense?

No, sir.

All this next week, we will mostly be running and drilling to get your body used to what the game asks. The week after that we start practice games. After that we will do both drilling *and* games. My advice to you is kill in the drills but not the games. The other guys will be way better in games. Don't worry about that. You try to be good at the drills first. Then the next step, okay?

Yes, sir.

They'll tease you, Moon. They will. Don't let it get to you. Just smile and accept it. You can't ignore it, because they're right—you're terrible at basketball. But you won't always be terrible, if you go slow and learn the game right. Okay?

Yes, sir.

The only way to make them stop teasing you is to kill the drills, okay? You win the sprints, they'll stop. You drop out last in the sweat drills, they'll stop. Okay?

Yes, sir.

I admire the fact that you're here, Moon. Takes courage to try to do something you never did before. That's sort of what school's for, in the end.

Yes, sir.

Sure you're doing this for yourself and not for your folks?

Mostly for me, sir. But some for them too. I want them to be happy.

The coach stared at Moon for a minute. Yet another kid with all sorts of stories and pain and grace swimming inside him, and I might see a tenth of it, he thought. Yet another one. I wish to god I could do more for these kids. But at least he's trying. Heaven help him this week.

Alright, Moon. Shoot around until the other guys come. Today's mostly drills. You'll be fine. They'll razz you because they don't know you, and they want to see who you are. They're not really as cruel as they'll seem this week. Kill the drills, and that will quiet them down.

Yes, sir.

I'm proud of you that you're here, Moon. Takes guts.

Yes, sir.

I'll be prouder at the end of the week if you don't quit, though.

Yes, sir.

You can if you want, but I hope you don't.

Yes, sir.

You can call me Coach if you want.

No, sir.

Alright, then.

Yes, sir.

29

YES, IT WAS LOUIS who burled his way through the huckleberry bushes at the foot of Martin's cottonwood tree. Sure it was. With a sort of panache or sense of ownership or blunt curt amused disrespect for huckleberrybushness. What thicket was this, to think that it could fend off the elk of elks? But Louis was not arrogant. Confident, yes. Sure of himself and his place in the world, yes. Aware of his elevated status among his tribe, yes—but not overweening or brash or brazen in his approach to or understanding of the other tribes. He fit his place with grace and assurance; that is the best way to say it. He did not seek to be king of the mountain except among the elk, and there he wished not for power or control or domination but only to be left alone by challengers, whom he defeated and dispatched as quickly as possible, to conserve his energy, to reduce damage, and perhaps, in some subtle way, out of respect for the brave young males who challenged him for what he considered his family. He had done the same, of course, when young, and somewhere in his bones, he knew his time would come, and he would limp away from some powerful attacker and spend his last years wandering alone and desolate. But not today, not this season, not this year.

Autumn was the intense season for Louis, the season of challenges and of hunters, and when the challengers of October were vanquished and the last hunters of November evaded and bollixed and led deftly into sucking mud and trackless marsh and the snow began to fall densely in December, there was a last dangerous period when cougars and bears and even bobcats and coyotes scoured the hills for prey slowed by snow or too old or ill to, bound away with an athleticism nearly as stunning as their high-desert cousins the antelope. This last flare of danger was especially so for Louis and his fellows, because they were often wounded and sore after battle and much thinner after their exertions in love and war. But until he dropped his antlers in January, he was armed with enormous razor-tipped knives on his head, and even after he shed his antlers, he had his huge rock-hard hooves, powerful enough to smash a skull as easily as an egg. It was very rare, now that he had attained his full growth, that he himself would be attacked, but it was not so rare that his tribe of female elk would be stalked by a hungry cougar or rushed by a bear from ambush. But Louis, at twelve years of age, weighed more than a thousand pounds and was a terrifying eight feet tall when he reared and slashed with those awful hooves. More than once he had landed a blow that instantly killed the attacker, who was then in his or her turn eaten by the many smaller animals and insects to whom a bear carcass was a mountain of meat, a promontory of protein, a feast beyond imagination. Who knows if among the ravens and the marten, the vultures and the jays, the weasels and the bobcats, stories were not still told of an alp of fresh food found splayed on a brilliant hillside, with no evidence of its provenance but the prints of many elk, one among them immense?

*

While much of Martin's time was spent pursuing and digesting the many savory delights available to the predatory tribes generally, he was also attentive and curious about the many things he found on the mountain that he could not eat, and could not understand their use or role or provenance. Beer cans and bottles, for example. As a rule, bottles were found near creeks and streams and rivers, and cans along the roads and trails. He once found an unopened bottle actually in a stream, and he fished it out and played with it for a while until it slipped out of his paws and smashed, releasing a frightening fizz and a foul smell like something had died and fermented in the brown glass.

But he also found bullet shells, condoms, spoons, fishing lures, cigarettes and cigars and tobacco chaws in every conceivable form of redolent dissolution, rum and whiskey bottles, pornographic magazines, bicycle wrenches, candy bars, compact discs, earbuds, arrows, lug nuts, hubcaps, apple cores, eyeglasses, sunglasses, hats and caps, gloves, old tires, and once a set of upper dentures, which fascinated him because he recognized them as teeth but could not imagine why they were out here on the forest floor, unattached to any jaw or cranium that he could see.

Most of these objects he approached with immense caution, for they smelled of human beings, and human being smell was dangerous. Sometimes he would watch for a while and let other animals explore them first to see if there was a snare or trap involved; jays and crows and ravens and nutcracker birds were especially useful here, as they were curious beyond belief and would cheerfully zoom in and poke around anything new and especially shiny they noticed without seeming to care about possible dangers; but they never seemed to get caught in traps that Martin noticed, so either they were deft escape artists or perhaps too light in weight to set off a snap trap or be snagged by a snare. Or, as Martin began to think, perhaps they knew human beings best and understood their habits and patterns and knew which things were deadly and which were lost toys or careless garbage— although not even the ravens, generally the subtlest of birds, were beyond mistakes. Martin had once seen one starved to death by a plastic six-pack holder, into which the bird had inserted his head from curiosity or to entertain his companions; but then he could not get it off, and eventually it had snagged irretrievably, and the raven eventually died. His companions brought him snatches of food for a while and begged him to eat and made what were perhaps encouraging remarks and admonishments to persevere; but he died. By the time death came, he was so withered and reduced that none of the bigger scavengers bothered with his corpse, and he was left to the insects and the weather. You can still see his bones if you climb up the mountain a ways and look for a spire of rocks like the mainsail of a clipper ship; in among the spiny juniper there is the plastic six-pack holder, hardly weathered at all, and from it hangs the amazing skeleton of a raven, one of the kings of the mountain for years beyond counting.

30

I LIKE IT a lot more than I ever thought I would, said Moon, answering Dave's question about basketball practice. You bet they ragged me, those guys. But they ragged all the freshmen, so I didn't feel too bad, and it turned out the coach was right—the more you killed the drills, the less the older guys ragged you. I told the other freshmen that, and they told me Coach told them the same thing. He's an interesting guy, Coach. Usually coaches are supposed to like the older guys who they know and trust and be hard on the new guys they don't know. Weed out the weak ones or something. But he treats everyone the same. He doesn't yell or anything, either. Coaches on television are always yelling. He says why should he yell when you know what you are supposed to be doing and you are trying to do it? He says we don't yell at him when he makes a mistake, so why should he yell at us? Plus he says yelling is counterproductive, and those who get yelled at learn to tune it out, so what does a guy who yells do then? Whisper? This is the kind of thing he says before practice. He gives a little speech about something, and it's never about basketball, it seems. It's always about how to *approach* it or something. Interesting guy. Of course then he runs us so hard in drills and scrimmages that guys puked the first week.

You puke? asks Dave.

Just once. You?

Not yet, says Dave. Although I have been so tired that I knew if I tried to eat something, it wouldn't stay down in the basement.

How's running?

It's a good thing I ran a lot before practice, that's all I can say.

Getting ragged?

Actually, no. I think the seniors would like to, but the sophomore guy sets the tone somehow, and no one rags anyone. Plus, we are running so hard we don't have time to talk.

You going to make the team?

I don't know, Moon. The first cuts are next week. They keep twelve guys, and there are a lot of older guys. There's six of us freshmen, and I am thinking they might keep two. How about you?

I think I might make the second team just because there's not a lot of guys and they need me to practice, said Moon, but I don't mind either way. I promised my mom and dad I'd try out, which I did. Making the team would be gravy.

How was it having your mom home?

Man, it was a ball after the first couple days. When she or Dad get home, they are way too parental for a while, and we have to find the balance, you know? Like there's too much cooking and sitting together talking about Things That Matter. The best way to be with your family is just to be with them without an agenda, right? Like your family does. You say yourself, sometimes the best times are when no one says anything, like watching a movie or just hanging around reading and napping and goofing and stuff.

I guess.

You okay?

Yeah. I worry about my mom. She's awful tired.

Didn't she cut back at the lodge? When your dad got work?

Said she did, but she didn't. You know how they are. It's like if they say they are *going* to, that counts, even if they don't actually *do* it. There's always some good reason, like someone switched hours or she's covering Emma's shift or there's overtime or something. But she's awful tired. You can tell.

You tell your dad?

He knows. He *says* things to her, but he can't make her change.

Maria?

Maria could. We are sort of keeping her in reserve for when we really need her, my dad says. She's like a secret flashlight you pull out when everything looks dark.

How's she doing?

Loves school. What a shock. Although her thing now is that first grade is for little kids and she wants to apply to fourth grade. She says school should be like colleges where you apply wherever you want and they say yes or no, rather than have to march up the grades like a ladder. Dad says she has a point, but he says the school district is antediluvian and dinosophomoric. You know how he talks. When's your dad coming home?

He says he will be home for the first game of the year, no matter what, even if I don't make the team. He says he's so proud that I gave it my all that he will be there either watching me or sitting with me.

That true?

You want another sandwich?

Moon? That true?

Because *I* am having another sandwich. I could eat ten sandwiches right about now. I'm starving. You want another one?

*

I'll *prove* I deserve to be in fourth grade, thought Maria. I'll prove it beyond the shadow of a cloud. I'll walk home from school by *myself*. Like the big kids do. *I* don't have to take the baby bus. I am not a baby. The baby bus is for little kids who are afraid to walk home by themselves. I know how to cut through the woods like Dave does. I am demure for my age.

And, her plans laid, she quietly collected what she would need for a jaunt through the woods and did her level best to forget the ironclad rules about frontiers and limitations on her urge for ramblage, as her dad said, although she found that every time she set her mind to forget the rules, they came back clear as if they were written in the air before her eyes—the four boundary points of her compass, the corners of her world, the edges of the allowable universe other than school . . . the big rock that looks like a hawk near the highway, the huge red cedar tree in the forest, the beech tree near the river, and Miss Moss's cabin below the store. I promised, she thought. I signed a contract. I gave my word. But that was all before first grade. Things have changed. Circumstances are different. Therefore promises are different. Plus those rules are for little kids in kindergarten. But I should be in fourth grade and not even first grade. I'll prove that the rules shouldn't apply. Once I show Mom and Dad that there's no reason anymore for the rule, then there doesn't have to be the rule, and I can walk home every day by myself and not have to take the baby bus.

Still, she felt uncomfortable. She put a compass and an orange and a spoon and a thin jacket and a cap and two candy bars in her backpack. At the last second before she zipped it up tight and went to bed, she put in the owl feather that Dave had given her, just because. You never know when an owl feather will come in handy, she thought. What if she met an owl who was one feather short? Wouldn't that be good, to hand an owl an owl feather? And what if the owl was very grateful then, and decided to be her friend? Wouldn't that be good? And maybe that owl talked to the other owls, and all the owls on the mountain would keep an eye out for Maria's family. That would be a good thing, to have all the owls keeping an eye out for you, because they see everything. Probably no animal in the woods sees as much as an owl. That would be a good thing, she thought, and she fell asleep.

31

USUALLY WINTER ON WY'EAST begins slowly, with plenty of small practice snowstorms dusting the meadows and clearings and frosting the forest and replenishing the brilliant gleam of the glaciers and snowpack on the peak. Usually there is no snow to speak of in September and about five inches falls in October and thirty in November and fifty in December and sixty in January, and then the snows taper back down through the forties in February and March down finally to zero inches by July, although you never know; plenty of climbers and skiers have seen sudden snow in the highest reaches of the mountain in summer, usually late in the afternoon, when the wind shifts course and fogs roll in and climbers lose their bearings. On average, September's snow was a tenth of an inch, according to all the charts. But averages skew.

It started on a Friday morning. Dave's dad was fixing a bus at the school. Dave was in geometry class. Maria's first-grade class was discussing how arithmetic was a language as well as a tool. Dave's mom was at the lodge working with Emma Jackson Beaton, who had a *terrible* cold and should *not* have been working but was stacking up vacation days so she could, she said, surf with Mr. Billy Beaton on the west coast of Africa. Miss Moss was in the store, feeding an entire busload of Swiss Presbyterians. Mr. Douglas the trapper was in his cabin reviewing his finances, filling out his Oregon Furtaker License Application (*fifty* dollars this year!), reviewing season opening dates and special regulations (no beaver trapping on the mountain at all now, for example, and no bobcat trapping west and north of the peak), and pondering whether to even bother with trapping weasel and coyote this year at all; while there was open season on both all year long, the pelts sold for relatively little, and it would be better resource management, he decided, to focus on bobcat, marten, mink, and fox. He was tempted to try for otters, but of all the animals he knew, otters were the most entertaining and interesting, and not even penury could persuade him to set for them. He rationalized this by explaining to himself that he would spend enough time in and around creeks after mink that the extra wet time for otter would just inevitably lead to pneumonia, which he could absolutely not afford, given the state of his rickety and wheezing finances.

But he laid his plans for red fox (opening day October 15), marten (November 1), gray fox and mink (November 15), and bobcat (December 1), and he checked his traps and gear and winter clothing for the fiftieth time and then decided to split more wood; it looked awfully foreboding outside, and it was always an excellent idea to lay down more wood to dry. You just could not have too much dry wood for the fire, in his experience, and more than once, he had built stacks as tall as his cabin—although, to give him credit, he then often gave a lot of it away, sometimes as barter for food or gasoline but often as friendly gestures or as the sort of thing people do when they bring casseroles or pies to those who have been hammered by illness or death. Easily a dozen people around Zigzag had found half a cord of good dry cedar in their sheds or porches or under tarp and immediately knew whence it came and thanked him for it when next they met. Mr. Robinson, in fact, claimed that he could tell just from the look of the cut who had split the wood; that man wields an *amused* axe, he said, a remark which Mrs. Robinson found entertaining every time she heard it, which was often.

★

Dave's dad knew that it was going to snow. He could tell. The clouds were pregnant, it was too cold for rain, and there was a sort of *glower* in the air; that is the best way to say it. A sort of chilled expectation or premonition—like the air was grimacing, and soon it would begin to cough relentlessly.

He checked in the school's shed for sand, salt, shovels, and the snowplow attachment for the tractor. He checked to see that there were not only tire chains but backup tire chains. He dug out the spare generator and tested it. He dug out the sump pumps on general principle. He contemplated the layout of the school and prevailing wind directions and access points and road grades and laid his plans for bus egress and parent ingress. He wandered by the cafeteria and asked about food supplies on general principle. He found snowshoes and cross-country skis and ski poles in the shed and cleaned and oiled them just in case. He filled the gas tanks of the school's two trucks and one all-purpose tractor.

But the morning passed without snow, although the chill deepened; and the lunch hour passed without snow, although the air grew grayer and denser; and not until the first buses were driving off and the sports teams started practice did the first hesitant pellets and then flakes fall. For more than an hour the snow was merely flurries swirled this way and that by eddies in the wind, and Dave's dad began to think that it was a brief fluke in the seasonal cycle. He stood by the shed for a moment to watch the cross-country team return from its daily run and start interval training on the track. Dave was fifth in the straggled line of returnees, running easily, neither trying for a dramatic finish nor easing up, but finishing just behind the lead pack of three seniors and the tall thin sophomore. Dave's dad watched with a complex mix of feelings—unutterable pride in his son (that kid was two years old two minutes ago, and look at him now those scything legs!), a sigh that he was so damned skinny (how can he possibly compete against those kids—they are twice as thick as he is . . . he looks like a heron running with deer), worry about him not being dressed properly (aw, a sleeveless shirt and shorts in *snow* for heavens' sake), and deepest of all, beyond any words he could have summoned to drape on the feeling, a sense of impending loss and the cruelty of time and the yaw of mortality. Very soon, all too soon, Dave would go away—college, work, the navy, traveling, who knew? And while his dad, from layers one through fifteen of his soul, was delighted and thrilled and proud and happy that this would happen, pleased that things looked good for Dave to grow into a cool and responsible young man over the next four years, enough that he could launch into a stimulating life of his own, which every good dad wants for his kid, he also felt, silently, at level sixteen, in the innermost chamber of his heart, a terrible sadness that there would come a day when, look for him as he might, there would be no Dave in the cabin, in the school, on the mountain, and good and right and healthy as that would be, it would also be a hole that could never be filled by anything or anyone else. He loved Maria with a deep and powerful love, but he had two children, and one is not two.

These were his thoughts as the last of the runners staggered through the fence around the track just as the snow picked up its pace. The wind had died, and the snow fell thicker and thicker; even the cross-country coach, who usually ignored the weather, noticed the shift from scatter to storm and finally called everyone in and sent them home. The runners, gleeful at their early escape, sprinted toward the gym and hot showers, laughing. Dave didn't notice his dad by the shed, and his dad didn't say anything as the boys ran past; he just watched his son float up the hill to the gym, snow in his hair, laughing.

32

JUST AS DAVE reached the gym door and his dad turned to lock the shed and Dave's mom settled into Emma Jackson Beaton's car, calculating that she would be home a full twenty minutes before Maria's bus dropped her and the other three kids from their neighborhood at the bus stop, from which they walked twenty yards (Alicia), forty yards (Aidan), seventy (Honora), and ninety (Maria) to their cabins, Maria stepped into the woods behind the grade school, fishing for the compass in her backpack. She noticed the quiet increase in the snow but didn't worry about it; most of the trees along the trail home were firs and cedars with arms as wide as the world, practiced at catching snowfall and shucking the weight as necessary. Plus this was September, and it never snows in September.

She's mapped out the trail in her head and on her lunch bag: through the woods for two hundred yards to Snag Creek, then up the creek four hundred yards until it met the river, then up the river four hundred yards to home, quick and easy as pie. On the last leg she would go right past Alicia's and Aidan's and Honora's cabins, and maybe she would wave at them if they were in their windows, and they would be amazed and jealous that she had walked home *All by Herself*. Honora, she knew for a fact, was not allowed to walk even to or from the *bus stop* by herself, and that was only seventy yards, or two hundred and ten feet. Poor Honora.

Through waist-deep ferns and arches of vine maple, around massive firs and bigger cedars, through a secret little ravine filled with dwarf yew trees with their bright red berries; past rotting stumps with their ladders of fungi and immense slugs, around boulders with bright-green and bronze blankets of lichen and moss, past a stump exactly as tall as Maria with a new tree exactly as tall as Maria growing out of it; past skittering thrushes and towhees and wrens underfoot, past a tree with a massive rusted wire cable locked to its base so tightly that the bark had shrunk above and below from the pain, around two little sudden tiny black pools of muddy water in the path as dark as ermine eyes; and there was the creek trilling gently in its bed of rocks and pebbles. Part one of the journey successfully accomplished!

Here and there, alders overhung the creek as it descended gently in a series of small pools, but for the most part it was open to the sky, and now Maria noticed uneasily that actually it was snowing heavily; any relatively flat surface already had several inches of new snow, and the path along the creek could be discerned only as a white line between the edge of the woods and the creek. She had worn her high-top sneakers today, thinking that they would be better in the woods than her other shoes, but she had not even conceived the possibility of snow. Snow in *September*? No way. But it sure was snowing. It couldn't possibly stick. Yesterday was sixty degrees, and tomorrow would probably be seventy—that's how September had been her whole life. It was always the last lovely month of summer, and then rain in October, and snow in November, and this was most certainly *not* November.

But it was inarguably snowing. You can *object* to reality, her dad liked to say, but you cannot successfully *argue* with it, so she formally registered a protest but reached into her backpack for her blue cap and red jacket and set forth up the trail along the creek. Within minutes her feet were wet and cold, and she began to hurry.

★

This being Martin's first experience of serious new snow, he was enjoying himself immensely. He flew through the canopy after squirrels, the chase sending sheets and plummets of snow to the forest floor. He studied the wonderfully evident tracks of rabbits, their origins and destinations written on the ground nearly as clearly as their scent in the air.

Chasing a grouse through the trees, he drew near to the high school and froze silently as a sudden line of runners passed below him on a trail; but then he saw that one of the runners near the front of the line was the human animal from the beech tree, and from some deep impulse he left off grouse hunting and followed the boy for a while—not as fast and freely as he did when the boy ran alone, but discreetly and from a farther distance, so none of the boys saw hide nor hair of him but only vaguely noticed a flurry of falling snow here and there off to the side.

When the runners turned to head back to the school, though, he faded back into the woods, and here again we have to thrash after words for what was going through his mind—or really through his entire electric muscle of a body—for the marten often thinks and feels and acts all at once. He was interested in the boy for reasons he did not know. He felt some subtle connection, some inchoate wish to know that animal and its ways. He did not wish to befriend it, eat it, or defy it, which were generally his range of possibilities; he felt some *curiosity*, some mysterious urge to know that particular story is the closest we can get to it. Yet he was already immensely cautious, young as he was; this wariness had stood him in good stead, and would do so many times again in his life, and was a crucial and constant part of his consciousness. So it was that he instinctively knew that being seen too much or too clearly was dangerous, and so he faded back into the forest, drifting generally toward the river. He was not hungry enough to work for squirrels or to pick up the grouse's trail, but the Zigzag was always a rich vein of possibilities, and it may be that he was idly pondering crawfish or how to catch a water ouzel when he noticed a small red jacket below him, slowly slogging through the deepening snow along a creek.

33

SURE, MARIA WAS LOST. Sure she was. Wouldn't you be? By her calculations she had gone up Snag Creek four hundred giant steps, which should be four hundred yards, but there was no Zigzag River where it was supposed to be, and now the snow was slurring from the sky like people were dumping it off the sides of immense trucks with enormous shovels. Twice she had slipped and fallen, once almost into the creek, and her sneakers were wet through and growing colder by the minute. She had stopped twice to check her map and to eat a candy bar. Now she stopped again to calm down and to think slowly, like her dad said you should do when you are rattled. When you are rattled, make the rattle stop, and then you can think clearly again, he said.

Okay, Dad, she said aloud.

Go slow, she said in his voice. Prioritize.

Dad, there's no river, and there should be, right here.

Can you hear it?

No. I hear water, but that's the creek.

Can you get a better view? Higher?

Good idea.

She climbed up on a huge fir trunk fallen across the creek.

I don't see it, Dad.

Can you keep going up the creek?

My feet are awfully cold.

You scared?

Yes. I am really scared. My feet are awfully cold.

But when she tried to say something wry and warm and fatherly in his voice, nothing came out of her mouth, and she started to cry.

*

Mr. Douglas and Miss Moss were in Miss Moss's store playing chess by the fireplace. The snow was so heavy that traffic up the mountain had ceased for the moment, and the store was quiet, and the snow fell so thickly outside the windows that there was a silvery light everywhere except by the fire. Mr. Douglas had carved the chess set. The queens looked rather like Miss Moss, but all the other pieces were animals: the pawns were chipmunks, the rooks were ravens, the knights were owls, the bishops were falcons, and the king was some sort of new animal equidistant between wolverine and bear.

A bearverine, Mr. Douglas had explained when he first presented the set to Miss Moss as a birthday present. There may be such creatures in the woods. Who's to say? Not me. Who knows what's out there? Not me. I know a little but not a lot. Your move.

Miss Moss dearly loved to play chess, but what with the press of duties at the store and her weariness after duty at the store, she did not play as much as she would like. Mr. Douglas dearly loved to play chess and he played anyone anywhere anytime. His favorite games were against Mrs. Robinson, who was a deft and masterful player and who as a girl had been county champion.

Where was that? Mr. Douglas had asked when that little tidbit slipped out one day.

O, long ago and far away, she said, smiling, and Mr. Robinson laughed aloud in the kitchen, and Mr. Douglas had thought—not for the first time, either—that someday, if he was very lucky, he too would be able to speak in complex secret affectionate amused code with someone in such a way that people who heard you would not know what you meant but would understand full well that you were speaking a dual language of your own made of sweat and laughter and tears and work and time and arguments and lust and labor and respect and annoyance and witness and some sort of reverence that has nothing whatsoever to do with religion and everything to do with love.

Check, said Miss Moss. Her owl was threatening his bearverine, and the only way out was to lose his falcon. He reached for it but then paused; more than once while playing Miss Moss he had moved too quickly to address one problem and then been snagged by the second and subtler trap.

Outside, very faintly, they heard a car mumbling uphill

against the snow, going very slowly; so slowly that Mr. Douglas realized how deep the snow was.

I'd better get out there with old Edwin, he said to Miss Moss. There'll be people in the ditches for sure. Can't believe it's snowing like this in September.

Your move, said Miss Moss.

Want to call a halt? Pause it where it is?

Your move.

I am registering a protest against undue and overweening pressure.

Move.

I feel cornered and harassed.

Move.

He looked up from the board to see if he could see her eye, but she was intent on the board. He stared down for a moment and moved his falcon. She immediately moved a chipmunk.

Mate.

A fascinating word, that, said Mr. Douglas, staring for a moment and then reaching down and gently placing his bearverine on its side. Do you know where it comes from, in this usage? Ultimately from the Persian, in which the meaning is something like *ambushed* or *surprised*, as in war, where you are suddenly invaded or overcome by a force beyond your ken. How apt and suitable, how very accurate. For me, anyway. I acknowledge being invaded or overcome. I admit it with humility. You win. I'd better go. If I know Edwin, he will be annoyed that we are not out there already. He knows when more than six inches of snow fall, we are on ditch duty. You'd be surprised how accurately horses can measure snowfall. I don't know how he does it.

Be safe, said Miss Moss, not looking up from the board. Be careful. Please? Come by for coffee later. I'll keep the store open until you come back. Be careful. Please?

★

Martin followed the red jacket, curious. This was no animal he recognized, and his angle of vision and the density of snow were such that he didn't realize it was a human animal until it sat down suddenly and made high plaintive noises. Was this some sort of territorial statement, or was it calling its companions? He couldn't tell—you never really were sure about anything with human animals, other than the fact that you could never be sure about what they were doing or would do—but he found that he had the same subtle interest in this one as he did with the one who ran through the woods every day. Had he been versed in a dozen languages, he still would struggle to define the feeling he had for the running one in particular—some hint of deeper interest, some kind of subtle assurance that it was not overly dangerous and would not cause him harm; and to a lesser degree he felt this same odd inexplicable feeling of relative safety and interest about the one in the red jacket by the creek. So when she finally stood up again from her huddle in the snow and continued to shuffle up the creek, he followed at a safe distance, high in the canopy, as the snow grew thicker and the daylight thinner.

34

DAVE AND HIS DAD are home in the cabin, worried about Maria. She should be home. Mr. Douglas is riding Edwin slowly through the snow along the edge of the highway, wondering if the car he and Miss Moss heard slowly laboring up the mountain could possibly against all sense and reason in such a storm have been Mr. and Mrs. Robinson's old Falcon. Dave's mom is still in Emma Jackson Beaton's car about half a mile from the milepost where Emma will drop her off so she can slog through the snow to the cabin and begin to worry about Maria. She should be home. Miss Moss has battened down the hatches and shoveled the front steps of the porch and hauled in more firewood and hauled four cots from the attic and stacked them by the fireplace just in case. Moon is in the vast kitchen of his house staring out at the vast snowfields that used to be the vast lawns around the house. Louis the elk, having had much experience of sudden storms, has led his extended family to a thick grove of cedars where the interleaved and interwoven branches above catch most of the snow, leaving a relatively protected, relatively open area beneath where the elk huddle together, their collective steam sighing up into the canopy. And there are so many other beings we should go visit here to see if they are okay, to see what they are doing, to hear what they are thinking—what they worry about, the shape of their hearts and dreams. Mr. Shapiro the elementary school teacher, for example—there he is shoveling a path to his cabin from the highway turnoff. As he flips a load of snow over his shoulder he gets a searing stab of pain in his back, a flame so sudden and terrifying that a fearful sweat breaks out on his brow, steaming his spectacles. And there's the tall thin sophomore runner with the long hair making ramen noodles for his two little brothers in their mossy trailer deep in the woods. And there's the Unabled Lady at her piano trying to write the exact music that snow makes when it falls on cedar duff. And there's Moon's basketball coach on the phone, canceling the loose scrimmage he and the coach from Joel Palmer High were planning as a surprise for their boys tomorrow. And there is the gray fox who ate Martin's older brother, snapping the neck of a grouse who had been hiding in a rhododendron thicket. And there is the old tough loner hermit bobcat who lives over to Hood River; for some reason known only to him, he has climbed to the top of a stone outcrop in his kingdom and is gazing out upon his lands and possessions, the snow gathering on his fur. And there is Cosmas, wearing not one but two bright-orange jumpsuits in deference to the cold, standing with his bicycle at the top of a hill where the power line cut through the trees has left a steep corridor down which he is about to ride his bike for reasons known only to him. And there are Mr. and Mrs. Robinson in their car, the engine silent, the snow falling more thickly by the moment. Mr. Robinson appears to be asleep. Mrs. Robinson appears to be awake, but she is not moving at all one bit. She is leaning on Mr. Robinson's shoulder. His jacket covers all of her and the right half of himself. Her eyes are open but they appear to be fixed on what would be the horizon if you could see anything like a horizon through the snow that has blanketed the windshield and the windows and the rear window too. The passenger window on her side is open about five inches, and the snow has sifted in and covered her right shoulder and neck and face and eyelash and the right shoulder of Mr. Robinson's jacket and Mr. Robinson's right hand, which is the most gentle shade of blue imaginable—something like white having an idea about blue. The car is gently tipped to one side, but not so much that either passenger has sagged noticeably, although a jar of creamy peanut butter has escaped the grocery bag in the back seat and fallen to the floor behind Mr. Robinson.

*

Emma Jackson Beaton left her car running at the milepost and hiked into view of the cabin with Dave's mom, although Dave's mom kept saying the whole way, *you don't have to do this* and *I will be fine* and *what if a plow comes along and crushes your car*, this last remark making Emma laugh out loud.

When was the last time the county ever plowed up here? she said. What would be the point? As soon as you plow, another two feet of snow falls, and you are right back where you started. Plus it snows in *summer*. Technically today is summer, you know. I could see snow falling tomorrow, on the first day of fall; that would be apt. But summer? There are times when I wonder why anyone actually lives up here. Are we nuts or what? Just half an hour down the mountain, four inches of snow is a *catastrophe,* and all the way down in the city, if six *snowflakes* fall, the governor declares an emergency for a week, and everyone goes to church. I can see *visiting* up here if you are a snow freak or you worship alpine flowers or whatever, but actually *living* here all year round, are we nuts or what? Hey, there's Dave.

Dave?

Mom, Maria's not home.

What?

She wasn't on the bus. Dad checked. She was at school all day, but she didn't get on the bus. Two of the kids in her class said she decided to walk home. They said her pack looked bigger. Like it was stuffed with stuff. Dad and I were waiting for you. Dad will go down the river, and I will go along the road. She's real smart, Mom. Don't worry. She's smart. She won't panic. Don't worry.

But before he even finished speaking, his mom was running through the snow to the cabin.

Why don't I drive you, Dave? said Emma Jackson Beaton. I have to drive that way anyway, and if we don't see her on the road, you can cut back up this way along Snag Creek.

Dave was about to say no thanks, but actually this made sense, and he said okay. He slogged back to the cabin to get the pack he and his dad had prepared. He could hear his mother sobbing and his dad trying to be calm and almost getting there. He tapped on the kitchen window and caught his dad's eye and made a gesture like hands on a steering wheel, and his dad nodded, realizing this

meant Emma Jackson Beaton. Dave slogged back up to the milepost, and he and Emma started slowly downhill along the road
you couldn't hardly even see anymore unless you lived there and
knew where it used to be before the world went white.

35

I SHOULD HAVE brought Joel Palmer's sneakers with me,
thought Maria. She is standing under a cedar tree where the
snow is thinner. Those are *magic* sneakers. I could have walked
on top of the snow and been home by now. The cedar suddenly
dropped a load of snow in front of her and she startled and cracked
her elbow against the tree trunk. She reached in her pack and
got the orange and ate half. Her feet were *freezing*. She was awfully tempted to eat the other candy bar, but she didn't. I can't
stay here, she thought. I'll freeze if I stay still.

Dad? she said. Dad?

But she couldn't hear his voice.

Dad, should I stay here or keep going up the creek?

Far away, she heard a sharp crack; it was the sound of a
branch snapping under a load of snow, but she took it as sage advice, and she stepped out from under the aegis of the cedar and
set forth up the creek again. By now the snow was so deep she
couldn't see the trail at all, but luckily it wasn't cold enough to
freeze the creek, and she made her way slowly along its edge, slip-
ping here and there but not crying even when she cracked her
knees and elbows. Little kids cried when they fell down, and she
was not a little kid, and that was that. She had a candy bar and
half an orange and Dave's owl feather, and the owls were watching, and soon the creek would say, hey! see, *there's* the river! and
then she would know exactly where she was, and she would be

home with her feet perilously close to a roaring fire, and her mom would drape the biggest red wool blanket ever around her, and there would be soup and hot chocolate, and this would be a funny story. The whole family would tell this story, laughing harder each time. Remember that time when Maria walked home and she was barely six years old, and it snowed like crazy, but she made it? Can you believe that kid? You want to see the sneakers she wore? They're right there on the mantelpiece next to Joel Palmer's sneakers. Dad said they were *heroic* sneakers. He said they had carried a being of just as great courage and perseverance as old Joel Palmer, and he cleaned and shined her sneakers and put them right up there with old Joel's sneakers, see?

★

But Martin noticed how the red jacket was slower and the light fainter. It was alright for *him* to be abroad in a snowstorm in the dark—he rather liked the snow, the darkness was his natural winter habitat, and it would have taken a snowstorm ten times worse than this to keep him in his den—but the red jacket was probably one of those animals, like rabbits, that ought to hunker down in a storm and take cover and retreat to den or burrow or hole and doze and muse until the snow stopped and day broke. The only animals out in a snowstorm at night were hungry ones big enough to capture smaller weaker ones trapped or hampered by the weather. With great respect for human animals, whom Martin knew for a fact were quite capable of killing any and all animals in the woods, this particular one in the red jacket looked relatively small and weak.

What prompted Martin to do what he now did? Again, we have no words for something—an impulse, a decision, a feeling, a sudden act—and by now we should be getting comfortable with the idea that there are more things we cannot explain with words than those we can; there are more things beyond the reach of our thousands of languages than there are those for which we have even inaccurate and reductive labels or ostensible theories. Perhaps this is why we keep inventing and reinventing languages, to try to explain ever more of the endless things that defy explanation. Perhaps this is the greatness and the foolishness of the human animal in a nutshell.

So it was that Martin sped along the canopy web above Maria and leapt off a bowing branch into the snowy twilight. And so it was that Maria stopped, startled and frightened, when a small golden brown animal landed with a plop and a puff of snow ten feet away from her. And so it was that Maria met Martin and Martin met Maria. Neither would ever know the sound that others used to indicate them, the particular sound we call a name, but neither would ever forget the moment they met, either. A moment of stunned witness, of caution, of amazement— imagine, on Maria's part, if an animal you had never seen alive before in your whole life suddenly dropped out of the sky and stood staring at you from ten feet away. And imagine, on Martin's part, being so dangerously close to exactly the kind of animal that had sawed the skin off his father, sold the skin for fur trimming on a coat, and chopped his father into stew-sized pieces for a dog. Shouldn't there be fear and trepidation in the air? But there wasn't. Each was cautious, each absorbed, each startled by such an incredible moment but immediately fascinated by what would happen next. It's such a wild and amazing moment, actually, that we ought to just leave it for a bit and let them savor such an unbelievable thing by themselves. So there they are, staring at each other, the snow falling silently, the last light ending just as this sentence does.

*

Maria's mom knew that she should stay in the cabin in case Maria suddenly staggered out of the snow onto the porch, but she could not help making little forays out into the storm—first to the tiny meadow on a tiny bluff fifty feet up the river where Maria had taken her first steps in this world, and then to the huge red cedar tree that might be a thousand years old, which was one of Maria's favorite living creatures. She thought about slogging back out toward the highway to the big rock that looks like a hawk, but she knew Dave would look there. Dave would also look in at Miss Moss's store. He and Emma Jackson Beaton would have four eyes along the highway. Traffic would be slow to nil because of the storm, so that was one less worry. But Maria would not have come along the highway. She would have come through the woods. She should have come up along the creek and then along the river. That was the best way from school to the cabin, and Maria would know. But her husband would search that way thoroughly. And now other people would help. Other people would be out looking as soon as they heard. People were like that. You wouldn't stay inside if you knew there was a child lost outside. Even people who couldn't go outside would camp out at their windows and keep their eyes peeled. She called three friends and told them, and they called three more each. She called Miss Moss, and Miss Moss said there was hot fish chowder on, and in about eight minutes Maria would walk in the door, and Miss Moss would bundle her up by the fire and spoon so much hot fish chowder down her throat that she would have gills and scales for weeks. Miss Moss said she would tell Mr. Douglas the trapper, and he knew the woods better than anyone, and if she didn't walk in the door in eight minutes, Mr. Douglas would find her in nine. Maria's mom made a fire, and then she made soup, and then she made Maria's bed, and then she stepped out on the porch and cried so hard she hurt her back.

36

YOU WATCH THAT SIDE, and I'll watch this side, said Emma Jackson Beaton. What color was her jacket?

Probably red, said Dave. Probably.

They'll find her, Dave.

Okay.

She's smart. She'll know what to do.

Okay.

Can't believe it's snowing like this in September.

Yes.

How's school?

Good.

You're running? You made the team?

Yes.

You want me to stop asking questions?

No.

Okay.

And they inched along silently. It was eerily quiet—no other cars, no trucks, no birds, no faraway sounds of saws or engines, no wind filtering through the trees. Emma was thinking of Dave's mom and the morning waitress and the fuel filter and her useless ratty shredded awful stupid hateful windshield wipers and her oldest brother, who just discovered he had a savage cancer. Dave is thinking of Maria's face when she is absorbed and thrilled by her homework. Emma is thinking that if *you* were a kid and it started snowing like crazy, wouldn't you head for the highway where you knew there would somehow be people rather than try to hurry home through the woods? Dave is thinking that Maria of course would have mapped out her adventure and almost certainly would have made a copy for her personal private archive, which was their old toy chest upstairs. Emma thinks she sees a red jacket in the forest fringe, but it is a scrap of orange traffic cone. Dave sees Mr. Douglas looming out of the storm atop old Edwin, and he says could you let me out here, Emma? She slides the car to a halt, and Dave gets out, and she says, Dave, they'll find her for sure. I absolutely know that for an absolute fact, and he says thanks, Emma, thanks for looking, and she slides away slowly, only one windshield wiper even making a token effort at clearing away the snow.

★

Martin turned and bounded a few feet away through the snow and stopped to look back. Maria stood transfixed. Was this a marten? Was this the marten Dave saw in the beech tree? What did it want? Was it dangerous? Martin bounded back once to Maria and then back away again. She took a step forward. He bounded away again. She took a step forward. He leapt onto a tree trunk and turned to look at her. She took one step back. He leapt down again, this time vanishing into a snowdrift for an instant. She took a step forward to see where he had gone, and he leapt onto the tree trunk again. She stepped back. He leapt down on the other side of the tree and turned to look at her. She walked around the tree. There was a space of about eight feet between them that they both felt comfortable with, and for the next minute Martin bounded ahead through the snow and Maria followed. She noticed that his tail left a print but his feet sinking beneath the surface of the dry snow did not. She noticed that he was leading her slightly away from the creek, which worried her, but then he leapt onto the lowest branch of an enormous cedar tree and stared at her. For a moment she stood silently and stared back, and then her feet hurt so suddenly that she wanted to cry but didn't. Martin skittered down to the base of the trunk and then back up again to the low branch, all in two seconds, and she noticed a long crack in the trunk. When she walked around the base, she saw that the whole bottom of the trunk was hollow and dry; some combination of the massive overhanging branches, a ridge or brow of bark just above the doorway, and the angle of the entrance had protected the hollow not only from snow but apparently from rain and dew, for the space was dry as bone, though ribbed by spiderwebs and musty with wood rot and what looked like red sawdust. It was also remarkably roomy, easily five feet by six, with space enough for Maria to almost stand up comfortably, and she began to wonder if she had been led here on purpose. But when she backed out of the hollow to look for the marten, it had vanished. The snow was still falling heavily. Maria stood for a moment and watched the fat flakes descend silently. The creek was perhaps twenty yards away; she could hear it faintly, perhaps a tiny bit louder than usual. She undid her backpack and found the owl feather and poked it into the trunk in such a way that someone who walked past would notice it, and then she crawled inside the hollow and took off her socks and sneakers and rubbed her feet for a long time. For a while her feet were stinging and icy, but after a while they warmed up and she made a mound of sawdust over them and propped her socks and sneakers up to dry. She ate the other half of the orange and one bite of the candy bar and talked to her mom and dad and Dave for a while and then wrapped herself tightly in her jacket and heaped more sawdust on any exposed Marianess, and then she fell asleep.

Along about midnight, a bobcat emerged from the white whirl and was about to poke into the hollow to see if there were mice or bats to eat, but a sudden furious attack by some animal in the low branches sent him retreating hurriedly back into the storm. At about four in the morning the snow stopped and when dawn finally inched around the mountain from the east side at about seven in the morning, you never saw such clear placid innocent blue skies in your whole life. You wouldn't believe that a crisp clean beaming summer sky like that had just delivered such a whopper of a storm, but it had.

★

Maria's mom finally sat down in front of the fireplace and tried to pray. She wasn't much for prayers and religions and churches and all that theater and ritual and pomp and that sort of thing, but she was bone dry and at the bottom of her hope and at the top of her fear, and finally in complete and total desperation, she tried to pray. First she tried to remember the shapes of the prayers she had heard as a child, but as soon as they came back to her memory she knew them to be empty and lifeless, mere shells and jackets. Then she tried to aim her thoughts at some sort of divine being, but the very idea of the force that sparked the universe to life looking anything like a human being at all let alone a shaggy grandfatherly guy was so silly as to be cruel. Then she remembered her grandmother telling her once that the urge to pray *was* the prayer, so she spoke aloud to the firelight and the sifting snow and the uncountable beings on this the ancient holy mountain and asked that they bend their beneficent dreams toward her daughter, that she be safe and warm, that she be huddled and protected, that she soon be found and carried home, that she be unbroken and unafraid, that she be wrapped sooner than soon in the arms of her mother from whom she had come, smiling even at birth, mere moments ago in the larger scheme of things. In this way did Maria's mother pray all night long by the fire until dawn.

37

THEY SEARCHED ALL NIGHT. Sure they did. Wouldn't you? Everyone did. Miss Moss later counted more than fifty people all told who searched the woods and the road and the river and the ravines and every shed and garage and drainpipe and cut bank and bus shelter and outhouse on the chance that Maria had taken shelter from the storm. Nearly every person mentioned so far in the previous pages of this book was either out in the snow in the dark that night or ready in some way to assist in matters of information or transportation. Some took up sentinel positions along the route that it was thought Maria had taken, from the school into the woods and up to the cabin. Moon was one of these, and he kept himself warm by practicing rebounding off a fir tree, one hundred rebounds with the right hand leading, one hundred with the left hand leading, one hundred with both hands firmly on the ball, repeat. Cosmas in his bright-orange jumpsuits for once abandoned his bicycle and hiked every power line cut he knew for miles around on the chance that Maria would seek an opening in the woods so as to be more easily seen. Maria's friends Alicia, Aidan, and Honora huddled together in Honora's bedroom all night making WELCOME HOME MARVELUS MARIA! posters and cards to be pinned up everywhere at school, because she *would* be found, and after a day to sleep and recover, she *would* be back at school, and she *would* be fine, and that was *that*, as Alicia said over and over.

★

Emma Jackson Beaton almost found her; she and the morning waitress came down Snag Creek from where it met the Zigzag river and found the cedar tree where Maria had dropped half

an orange peel; but this was farther down from the tree where Maria slept, and Emma and the morning waitress, even after ranging in ever-increasing circles from the orange peel, found nothing more. Maria's dad almost found her; he hiked all the way down the river and Snag Creek trails, shouldering desperately through snowdrifts and then all the way back up again, his heart black; but he found neither hint nor hair, print nor sign nor her owl feather signpost, though he stared at every square foot of snow and bark and branch and rock and thicket for a message, a note, a missive however slight or coded . . . twigs arranged in an *M,* a frozen mitten pointing out where he should go to gather his baby girl into his arms and press her face into his chest and wrap her inside his jacket and smell the apricot shampoo she loved the best.

★

It was Mr. Douglas who found her, a few minutes after dawn. Dave was aboard Edwin, slowly making their way up the creek, Dave thinking the slightly higher vantage point would help.

Mr. Douglas was ranging through the forest away from the creek, thinking that Maria may have holed up in a deadfall, when he saw the long crack in the cedar bole and went to investigate. To his surprise his heart flopped when he saw her red jacket. She woke only when he touched her neck to feel her pulse. For a second she was frightened, and then she recognized him, and he smiled, and she smiled, and neither said a word, and she stood up and reached for her socks and sneakers, but they were frozen, and Mr. Douglas took off his big gloves and put them on her feet, and she stepped out of the tree, blinking in the light, and he scooped her up as if she weighed six ounces and ducked out from the overhanging branches and called for Dave.

My backpack? said Maria. My sneakers?

We'll get them later, Maria.

Thank you.

Any time.

Thank you for finding me.

My pleasure.

Did Miss Moss send you?

Yes, said Mr. Douglas. Yes, she certainly did.

★

Martin watched them go, the red jacket on the horse with the human animal who ran through the woods and a larger human animal following on foot. Then he came down the trunk and smelled Maria's backpack and sneakers. There was something good to eat in the backpack, but tearing it open was too much trouble, and he was weary after a long night. By now the sun was actually hot, and the melt was starting in full force; indeed it would get up to seventy degrees today, and by the end of the third day after the storm almost all the snow was gone, and the creeks and rivers and ditches on the mountain full to bursting, so much so that the highway bridge two miles down the mountain would have to be examined by county road crews, what with the river slamming away at the center stanchion and throwing sheets of spray over the road. Martin made his way home, not even stopping to explore a little clearing where he was sure he could smell vole tunnels under the snow, and once in his burrow, he curled up and slept the rest of the day, dreaming for some reason of rabbits twice as big as any he had ever eaten, yet.

PART II

PART II

38

WE HAVE NOT SPENT as much time as we should have discussing the rest of the . . . what should we call Zigzag, a village? Not
quite big enough. Certainly not a town, or god help us all a city.
Settlement? That sounds prehistoric. A gaggle of cabins relieved
by the occasional larger structure, none taller than two stories
except for Moon's house? An osmosis of small dwellings with a
few communal in purpose, that is, a library, school, gas station,
and store? A populated crossroads? What *do* we call a very small
community? A hamlet? Is *community* even an accurate word if
many of the people there have no particular interest in their
neighbors and indeed moved there largely because of the pau-
city of neighbors and privacy thereof? There is more than one
hermit here. There are people who do not ever answer a knock
on their doors. There are people with bristling signs nailed to
large trees around their cabins stating in no uncertain terms that
solicitors are not welcome and trespassers will be shot. There is a
man who wanders alone in the woods in summer stark naked
playing an oboe, not very well. There is a woman who has built a
vast city of her own device from small slivers and splits of wood in
a trailer next to the trailer in which she lives alone. She takes
photographs of the tiny city and pins them up on the inside walls
of the trailers. There is a man who wears a Cub Scout uniform
he has tailored and sewn himself whenever he is at home in his
cabin, complete with the woggle that gathers his neckerchief.
There are two men who started their own religion and are at-
tempting to recruit lucrative disciplage. There are men who were

in wars and never escaped. There is a woman who eats only plants she gathers herself from the forest. There is a man who escaped from prison more than thirty years ago and changed his name and burned off his fingerprints on a stove and makes his living as a technical writer for manuals for household utilities. What is a hamlet? You could draw any number of circles trying to contain all the people who live within a mile or two of the Zigzag River, and you would end up leaving people out, not to mention all the other beings of all the other kinds who live in those areas and were not counted, either. Is a community a verb more than a noun? Doesn't it change every day, really? So the entity we call a hamlet is reduced, or added to, hour by hour? Is a hamlet more accurately measured as a story than a number? Especially if we are focusing in particular on human beings—we would be foolish to say of Miss Moss, for example, that the words *female* and *storeowner* and *tall* and *thirtyish* and *kindly* and *unmarried* describe much of real substance about her, isn't that so? A great deal of who she really is are stories we do not know, stories she may or may not share, stories perhaps even she does not know the meaning and shape of quite yet. People are stories, aren't they? And their stories keep changing and opening and closing and braiding and weaving and stitching and slamming to a halt and finding new doors and windows through which to tell themselves, isn't that so? Isn't that what happens to you all the time? It used to be when you were little that other people told you stories about yourself and where you came from, but then you began to tell your own story, and you find that your story keeps changing in thrilling and painful ways, and it's never in one place. Maybe each of us is a sort of village, with lots of different beings living together under one head of hair, around the river of your pulse, the crossroads of who you were and who you wish to be.

★

Spring arrived on the mountain in layers or bands; up high, at six thousand feet and above, spring might finally arrive inarguably in June, whereas down low, below a thousand feet, it starts as early as February, with crocuses and forsythia and daphne flowers and tree frogs and snowdrops and daffodils. Mid-mountain, where the Zigzag River flows, it probably starts the day that harlequin ducks arrive in the creeks, or the day you hear flycatcher birds singing, or the first time you see a bright shocking tanager all red and loud and orange and defiant against the snow. Ground squirrels and chipmunks emerge from their dozing dormancy. Bears emerge and stagger downhill for grass and insects; they start their annual eating binge with salad and appetizers, as Mr. Douglas says. Some warblers pause and eat and then move along, and some like the hermit warbler arrive and stay. Lots more frogs start singing, as does every sort of owl. Deer and elk antlers start growing. Newts start crossing the roads and trails in such numbers that you have to watch where you are walking or suddenly you are oppressing the four-fingered populace with your cruel and unconscious heel.

Me, personally, says Maria's dad to Maria, it's the first time you hear a thrush in the woods. *That's* when spring begins. Now that might be along about late May, in a late winter, but after that, winter's done. It just doesn't have any gas left after that. It might lose its temper and drop a last tantrum of a snowstorm, but it can't keep up its bad temper. You hear a thrush, you know that we'll have a summer day eventually. Maybe just the *one* summer day, same as usual up here, but by god, we will have *one*. I hope. You need help up there?

No, sir, says Maria from the roof, where she is scraping moss.

Make sure of your footing, remember.

These are my magic sneakers, Dad.

Ah yes, says her dad. Indeed, they are. In about an hour, you'll grow out of those sneakers, you know, and then they go up on the mantelpiece with old Joel Palmer's shoes. I think we ought to build a shoe museum for the greatest shoes ever. Imagine the shoes we could get for the museum. There's Jesus's sandals and Gandhi's sandals and Meher Baba's sandals. What is it with spiritual visionaries and sandals? Mohammed wore sandals, too. Although Mandela wore sneakers, didn't he? And old Dorothy Day too. Although she lived on the beach and probably wore boat slippers. Probably a lot of the great visionaries wore sneakers but their hagiographers thought sandals were cooler for the hagiographic paintings. I bet Jesus wore high-tops.

What's hagiography?

It's when someone cool is reduced to only being a saint. It's like a polite insult. You need help up there?

No, sir, says Maria. I think I am done. Can we go get a milk shake now?

Sure. Listen, can I ask you a question?

Sure.

Is something bothering Dave? He seems grumpy lately, and when I ask him, I get a lot of no answers.

He seems a little . . . remote.

You guys still talking at night before bed?

Not as much. I miss that. I miss Dave. Can we get a milk shake now?

You can get one for each mom you have, how about that?

★

Martin's first birthday was the first wide-open wild-blue un-clouded balmy gentle warm everything-melting-at-once day of April, and he celebrated by dozing most of the day, a habit he had developed during the long winter; there had been many cold days when he had been out hunting and eating for all of four hours and sound asleep for the other twenty. But day by day now, he felt something stirring in him—not just more energy, and a hunter's utilitarian pleasure at lovely newborn things to eat, but some gnawing curiosity he had never felt before. He found himself ranging farther and farther afield again, much as he had in the fall when searching for the right den, but he did not know what it was that he wanted.

His travels this time took him all the way around the mountain, far up into the ice fields, and far enough down the mountain that he explored orchards and tree farms for the first time, marveling at their unnatural geometry. He met and sometimes bristled at, and three times fought with, other male martens; he met and was interested in but did not further pursue the first female martens he had seen other than his mother and sister. He briefly saw and certainly clearly scented an animal that looked very much like a very large marten and might have been a fisher; he saw scrawny tousled bears tearing up rotten logs for grubs and gorging on anything green they could find in bulk. Twice he saw the enormous elk who had shoved casually through the huckleberry jungle under his den, although both times he and the elk were more than twenty miles from Martin's home in the cottonwood tree.

There is much else to report about Martin's first winter, but it *is* his birthday, so let's celebrate the manner in which he has not only survived, as many marten kits do not, but flourished. Before he was a year old, he struck out on his own, established a territory, found and furbished a suitable dwelling, became a skilled and enterprising harvester of meat and fruit, explored a great deal of a tremendous wilderness, survived a number of attacks and battles, discovered the first rudiments of a fishing technique unique among his species, and later familiarized himself with the doings and dwellings of human animals sufficiently to satisfy his curiosity without endangering his life, became an accomplished and soon-to-be-legendary robber of nests in his endless search for the golden glory of fresh eggs, learned how to catch and eat snakes without being lashed by their whipping tails, and discovered what amounted to a secret village of easily accessible squirrels and chipmunks around the lodge, a food source he wisely tapped only when he was very hungry on the general theory that the less he was seen, the safer he was. He had also discovered that the chipmunks in particular had relatively short memories—if he took one every other day, they became cautious and skittish and increasingly hard to kill, but if he only visited once a month, sliding out of the canopy at dusk and along the wall of the outdoor swimming pool and into the drainpipes, he was assured of a fat careless chipmunk scrabbling for the last scraps of food spilled on the trails around the lodge. Indeed, for his birthday present, let us give him just such a gift, which he snares with a sudden lightning dash from the drainpipe and carries back up into the canopy to eat in peace.

39

DID I EVER TELL YOU ABOUT KUSHTAKA, the Otter Man, who saves kids from freezing to death in the woods? says Mr. Douglas to the counter where Miss Moss would be if she was not in the kitchen making soup.

Yes, you did, says her voice, winding around the doorway where people have written their phone numbers for many years; if you squint a little, you can see Mr. Robinson's first phone number, written in 1939.

Did I?

Several times. A number of times. Perhaps twelve. Or twenty.

A consistent peccadillo of mine, he says, smiling. Among many others. An incalculable calculus, Ginny. Your move.

You move for me, says her voice. I am amidships the soup.

I wouldn't think of moving for you, he says, coming around the doorway with the phone numbers; he notices Mr. Robinson's number with a pang. No one can do anything for you. That's sort of the problem.

I have a problem? she says dangerously.

That's not what I meant, he says. I mean that you don't let me do anything for you, and I would very much like to do things with you. For you.

Garlic, she says.

He crushes a head of garlic in his fist and hands it to her. What's the soup?

Miscellaneous general kitchen whatever vegetable. Deliveries are tomorrow.

Would you like to come for a ride on Edwin? He's restless.

He is or you are?

It's a yes-or-no question, Ginny. No need to get terse.

I'm awfully busy.

I see.

And Dave's not due in for an hour.

Noted.

But yes.

Yes?

Yes.

Yes, yes?

Yes to going for a ride on Edwin.

He and I are honored. Back in a bit.

No no—I'll come with you now. The soup can wait. God forbid you ride up on a horse and sweep me away.

Would that be so bad?

Yes.

Yes, yes?

Yes, no.

★

It had been a long winter for everyone and everything. Moon's father had politely asked Moon's mother to vacate the premises after something somewhere somewhen had happened that neither Moon's dad nor his mother would explain to Moon. I think it has something to do with wandering affections, said Moon to Dave. My dad explained it without explaining it. He's good at that. I think that's why he gets paid a lot of money by his company. He explained *around* it, you know what I mean? My mom wasn't coming home anyway for another three weeks, so it's sort of a moot point, their separation. Can you be separated if you are already separated? Isn't that a double negative, which inherently negates the proposition?

The bobcat population had taken a serious hit from Mr. Douglas's traps, as had the foxes, although the marten and mink populace had only lost a few members; numberswise it was a whopping bobcat year for Mr. Douglas, and among the pelts he brought in to the store for registration was the old hermit bobcat who lived over to Hood River and had long defended his territory with adamant guile. He had stepped into the simplest of traps, in the most obvious of settings for a trap, and Mr. Douglas was so startled to find him there one morning, asphyxiated but not yet frozen, that he spent an hour tracing the cat's movements prior to arrival at the scene. If it didn't sound so damned weird, he said quietly to Miss Moss, I would say that he did it on purpose. I tracked him from his cave up in the rocks right to the trap, a straight line, no hesitation. It wasn't an accident that he got caught. He knew right where the set was, and he walked right into it like he decided to call it a day and get it over with quick. From his prints I think he might have stood by the trap for a while thinking god knows what before he just stepped right into it like you would step through a door. Which is what he did, I guess. Average bobcat this year is about a hundred dollars, but I will get three hundred for him. I feel weird about it, though.

On the other hand, Dave's dad had been promoted to maintenance chief at school, and Dave's mom had finally gone to the doctor and been diagnosed with vitamin deficiency, which she had addressed with dietary change and the construction of a rudimentary sunroom in the southwest corner of the cabin. Maria had designed a lesson plan in mapping, geography, and satellite-based navigation systems for grades one through four, which she led so successfully at those grade levels that Mr. Shapiro had asked her to consider offering it for grades five through eight. The Unabled Lady had completed a song cycle based on the music of falling snow, which she played through twice at the adult center in Gresham, though her head now nodded forward over the piano lower by the day as her neck and shoulder muscles grew infinitesimally weaker. Moon has actually made the second team in basketball, against all expectations and predictions, although he never played a single minute in games and only got to wear an official practice jersey in practice when one of the other players was sick or missing, which is why sometimes he wore jerseys that hung almost to his knees and other times jerseys so short and tight that as the other players said it sure looked like Moon was wearing a sports bra or a tube top rather than a basketball jersey; but he laughed too.

Also Dave had finished the cross-country season third on the top team, behind only the sophomore who ran like an antelope and one of the senior captains. He learned to draft behind other runners for the first mile; he learned not to try to stay with the sophomore no matter how tempting it was to match pace with him; he learned to ignore remarks and comments and elbows and hips from other runners; he learned that rhythm was his best friend and adrenaline his worst enemy except in the last few hundred yards; he learned how to attack hills and how not to cruise downhill but maintain speed; he learned what it was like to be spiked by runners both ahead and behind him; he learned how to run in mud and how to look for the driest line of firm ground across moist meadows and fields of muck; he learned that the brightest sunniest days were harder on runners than cold cloudy days; he learned to hold his spot in a knot of runners and keep his balance and pace when jostled; he learned that the thing he loved best when running alone was available to him still in a race—a sort of mindless, almost musical pleasure, if he could manage the vagaries, as the coach said—the prime vagaries being adrenaline and opposition. You cannot ignore the other runners or the course, said his coach, nor can you disregard your own excitement and nerves and insecurities. The trick is balance. I can't teach you that. *You* have to teach you that. It comes from experience. Get your rhythm down, know where everyone else is, set your goal based on your pace, and then fly. If you can see the leaders in the last half mile, try to catch them. I don't care if you win a race. I care if you did better than you did last time. My goal is that everyone sets personal bests every race. Will that happen? No. Might it happen? Yes. Has it ever happened? No. Could it happen? Yes. Will I be annoyed if you don't get better? No. Should *you* be annoyed? Yes. Listen, I want you to have fun, but I want you to push too. I want you to enjoy this but see what else you have inside you. It'll hurt to find that out sometimes. Deal with it.

*

It was Cosmas who found Mr. and Mrs. Robinson the morning after the storm. He had been walking up the road when he saw a broken vine maple bush. Something had sheared away half the bush and crashed into the woods. The snow was infinitesimally shallower where that something had passed. He followed the trail of shallow for a few yards into the silent forest and found their car. It was so covered with snow that the only sign of automobility was the radio antenna, itself capped with a tiny fingertip of snow. He knew whose car it was. He knew what the silence and undisturbed snow meant. He felt some great twist or throb in his chest like a sudden wave crashing. He walked around the car and saw Mrs. Robinson's open window, and he bent and peered in and bowed his head. Mr. Robinson's hand on her shoulder was the most gentle blue color imaginable. Mrs. Robinson's door was locked, but Mr. Robinson's door was not. Cosmas opened Mr. Robinson's door gently. At such an angle you would expect the driver to fall out or slump out, but Mr. Robinson was unmoved. There was frost on his eyebrows and on the tip of his nose and on the rims of his spectacles. Cosmas closed the door again gently. He noticed that liquids of two colors had wriggled downhill from under the car in tiny creeks, probably from the smashing the underbelly of the car had endured as the car plowed through the forest. By now the melt had begun, and Cosmas could hear dripping in every meter and rhythm imaginable. As he stood by Mr. Robinson's door, the tiny fingertip of snow slid off the top of the radio antenna, and the loss of weight made the antenna sway ever so gently for longer than you would think. You wouldn't think such a tiny thing would make such a big guy as Cosmas weep, but you would be wrong about that. He wept silently and helplessly into his beard for a few minutes, and then he went around to Mrs. Robinson's side of the car and opened her door and rolled her window up gently just in case ravens started getting ideas, and then he walked as fast as he could back to the road and down to Miss Moss's store where there was a phone and the phone numbers of the police and fire station and Forest Service and doctors and nurses. Those phone numbers were at eye level on the doorway to the kitchen, about halfway between Mr. Robinson's phone number in 1939 and the phone number of the kid from Rhododendron who was about eight feet tall and ended up playing college ball and one time wrote his phone number so high up that you couldn't read it unless you stood on a chair.

40

IT HAD BEEN A LONG WINTER for Emma Jackson Beaton also. In December she had finally accepted the ninth invitation of the third chef for dinner, as long as no one uttered the loaded and freighted word *date*, inasmuch as she was a married woman, and they had dinner and really enjoyed each other's company, although Emma insisted on driving herself to the restaurant so that she could drive home alone and not get into the whole chess match of who drives whom and who paid for what and who expects or hopes for what because of who is driving or paying. But that was that, undatewise, with the third chef, although he several times afterwards suggested with honest genuine interest and no agenda that they have coffee or go for a walk or catch a movie or snowboard together or drive east up onto the high sage desert where there was occasionally sunlight just to see what sunlight might feel like in winter. Probably we will get burnt a shade of red not invented yet, he said with a smile. But she declined politely each time, and after a while he got the message and went back to watching her from the window sometimes, dreaming.

Emma Jackson Beaton had also accepted the invitation of the morning waitress to go snowboarding together, and the shimmering implications of this event were a lot of the reason why she had had such a long winter, as she explained to Dave's mother one afternoon outside the doors of the laundry service. It was actually a sunny day, almost balmy, but so much snow had fallen at the lodge and been shepherded into towering walls to clear paths and trails for guests and visitors and employees that they sat between walls of snow fully twelve feet high, each woman wrapped in a thick coat, although the light was so bright off the vast fields of snow on the mountain that they both wore sunglasses.

Was it fun?

It was a ball, which is sort of the problem, said Emma.

Which means?

I'd like to do it again.

Snowboarding?

Having such easy relaxed fun with . . . her.

Isn't that easy? You just go snowboarding or have tea or whatever. What's the problem?

I have the feeling she wants us to be more than friends, said Emma.

★

Hardly ever does a story just stop, right in the middle of the crucial moment like this one, but we had better do so now, because this is a huge moment, and Dave's mother knows it, and she also knows she has about eight seconds to craft a gentle remark, the exact right thing to say to get Emma Jackson Beaton talking. She can't be blunt here, not yet, because Emma will just clam up and erect heat shields and draw her curtains shut. Nor can Dave's mom leap to conclusions or say anything wise or give cogent advice; she has to say something that will draw Emma out, let her walk into what she clearly wants to talk about but is very afraid of talking about. It turns out that having a conversation with someone you like and respect is harder as you go deeper, isn't that so? Conversations are easy on the surface, where there's just chaffing and chatter and burble and comment and opinion and observation and mere witticism or power play, but the more you talk about real things, the harder it gets, for any number of reasons. For one thing, we are not such good listeners as we think we are, and for another, everyone in the end is more than a little afraid of saying bluntly and clearly what they really think and feel—partly because we are nervous about how it will be received and partly because once you say something true and deep and real, it's been *said*; it's out of your heart and out of your mouth and loose in the world, and you cannot take it back and lock it up secret again, which is, to be honest, terrifying.

★

Do *you* want to be more than friends? says Dave's mom.

★

You know, we spend all this time these days freezing video on our various electric devices and running it back and skipping forward, but we can't do that with real events in real time, and we miss an awful lot of nutritious and fascinating context with real events. Like here, for example. There are two ravens overhead going south-southwest at such a clip that you have to wonder where they are going in such a hurry. There is a chipmunk behind the two women, exactly one inch from the laundry service door, which is ajar exactly one inch, which is just enough to admit a curious chipmunk. In the two seconds that it takes Dave's mom to ask Emma her question, the earth spins approximately a thousand feet to what we call east. A tourist on the lodge portico above and to the right of the laundry service door feels a baby twitch inside her womb for the first time ever. A sharp-shinned hawk just inside the trees that the two women can see from their table slices open the breast of a downy woodpecker, whose last sight in this world is a lovely dense lattice of fir branches overhead shaped just like a nest.

*

Yes, says Emma. Yes, I do.

*

Again, Dave's mom knows this is a freighted instant; the wrong words in reply will make Emma huddle back inside herself; nor is silence an option, for silence will itself be a comment reeking of shock or disapproval. And again the reply must be crafted in such a manner that Emma continues to think aloud; in so many ways, this is what friends are for—to allow you to speak freely, to speak yourself toward some clarity of heart, to think aloud and thrash toward being able to say what it is you feel, for the chasm between what you feel and what you can articulate is vast and wide. And this is not even to mention how very often what we say has nothing whatsoever to do with what we truly feel.

*

Then I am delighted for you, Emma. That's wonderful, to feel that ripple of fascination with someone, isn't it? It's always such a *surprise*—like a window opened suddenly, or a light clicks on where you didn't even suspect there was a lamp. Of course, it's always fraught with confusions and complications, but it's such a lovely thing, the surprise, isn't it?

★

And now the shoe is on the other foot; Emma is silent as she tries to bring the right words to her own lips. She feels six things at once: a surge of warmth for Dave's mother, who understands how sweet and painful this is; a shiver of fright that she has actually just said the thing she felt but absolutely could not say; the urge to laugh that Dave's mom has just perfectly encapsulated the shock and muddle of suddenly feeling something for someone you had no idea you felt something for; a thrill that the thing is spoken and out in the open; a mammalian pleasure, subtle but real, that someone has actually listened with care and attention to something you said; and the dawning realization that sometime soon now, the question will arise that she has long dodged in town and at the lodge, even while knowing somewhere deep inside that it would eventually come up somehow somewhere somewhen and could only be avoided by leaving altogether and reinventing herself once again somewhere else, as she had so many times done before. *What about Mr. Billy Beaton?*

41

MANY SILLY AND HILARIOUS and peculiar things had happened that winter also, it must be said, and for every sad and freighted moment, there was one loaded with nuttiness and laughter. A nine-year-old girl had won the lodge's annual open snowboard competition, defeating a former Olympian and a professional who had once been ranked fourth in the world, and at the awards ceremony, the former Olympian bent down and said something rude and dismissive to her, upon which she punched him right in the gonads, a moment which instantly went viral and registered more than ten million virtual hits around the world. A young cougar claimed an exit ramp of the highway and refused to be dislodged by firecrackers and police dogs, and finally the Department of Fish and Wildlife had to come and shoot it with a drug dart—but the first shot went awry and hit a young deputy, who was unconscious for two hours, and when resuscitated, he said that he had dreamed he was a baseball bat. A young skier trying to do flips was caught in a fir tree upside down, and it took hours to bring him down safely, during which his friends stood under him and threw peanut-butter sandwiches up to keep him *fortificated*, as one of the brothers said to a television news reporter. Six men proposed to six women on the portico of the lodge during the winter, two proposals occurring during howling snowstorms, and five of the women said yes. A brand-new refrigerator wrapped in an enormous green bow was found more than a mile deep in the woods from the highway, with no discernible evidence of how it got there. A man deep in the woods built an entire small hut out of bicycle parts, with a pedal for a door handle. At a Forest Service hearing about clear-cutting a huge new swatch of old forest, Cosmas got up to speak, and opened his mouth, and a winter wren flew out, causing a ruckus. An older man down the mountain about a mile became convinced that he was a traffic light and stood in the middle of the highway making signals with his arms until his daughter came to retrieve him. Maria and Dave got a cell phone to share, which Maria immediately commandeered and programmed to chirp like a finch rather than ring, which Dave found mortifying. Miss Moss, on a trip into the city, got two tiny tattoos on the palms of her hands, one reading *no* and the other *yes*. Moon scored his first basket of the season in the last game of the season, but at the wrong basket; the other team laughed, and Moon's teammates started a fight that led to a flurry of technical fouls. Mr. Douglas, following his most remote trapline one morning, found evidence of more than thirty bobcats having gathered together in a clearing. By the depth of their footprints and the prevalence of scat, they must have all been there together for hours, he told Dave the next day. What could they possibly have been doing? Was it a meeting of some sort? An election? A spiritual thing? Was it some sort of conspiracy being hatched to get the guy who had a great bobcat pelt year? You never know what's going on in the woods, I think. Whatever you are sure cannot possibly happen probably just did. Me, I am going to walk nervously for a while. You never know with bobcats. They don't say much, but I think they are a deep tribe. They might be plotting to catch and skin me. If I vanish suddenly without a trace, you'll know why. If that happens, I leave my estate such as it is to you. Maybe they have their own courts and prison system. Hope I get a defense attorney, you know? Maybe I should learn to speak bobcat just in case. You'd hate to not be able to converse clearly with your attorney, isn't that so? Especially if your attorney has claws like steak knives.

★

Martin had seen many odd and interesting things in his travels that winter, but nothing as odd and haunted as the empty timber camp he found one afternoon, so deep in the woods that even he was not quite sure where he was in relation to his den. He was, that day, more than thirty miles from home and filled with some strange energy that forced him through the woods like a headlong verb in a forest of crowded nouns.

Even Martin, sharp as his senses were, didn't realize at first what the strangely shaped clearing used to be before the forest

took it back from the human animals; it was only when he noticed a peculiarly hollow sound underfoot, as he trotted along
what had seemed to be a hillock, that he knew. It turned out this
was the old camp barracks, now completely overgrown with
wild vines, moss, and grass; time and weather and the woods had
slowly turned what was probably once a neat wooden structure
into a large green swell or ripple. Martin, curious, explored inside, and found a few shards of old axes and saws, probably left
behind as useless when the men cleared out, and long ago rusted
almost to anonymity. He also found a cooking pan so thoroughly
worn in the middle that it was nearly translucent, and one logging boot (providentially filled with nesting mice, which provided lunch), and several frail dry sheets of paper still nailed to
the walls. These he smelled carefully, hoping for salt, a feature of
many old human animal things, especially paper and cloth; he
could smell nothing after so many years of dust. Many a man's
eyes had been upon those calendar pages and pinup posters, but
not so many fingers, and those fingers now long dead.

Martin explored the rest of the abandoned camp, finding an
outhouse and a cook shed but no more evidence of the presence of
thousands of men than a knife handle and, curiously, a stack of
thimbles nested in each other many years ago and now rusted
together permanently. It was interesting to think that this place
for many years had been a hive and a hotbed for men, men singing and brawling and eating and snoring and marching in and
out of the woods six days a week and often quietly on Sundays
too—men arguing and patching up arguments, men fighting
with fists and shovels and sometimes with knives, men burying
some companions and sticking up for others, men counting their
money and men weeping for loneliness, men eventually packing
up the camp equipment and cleaning out the barracks and the
cook shed, men leading laden horses and mules away down the

trails and never coming back, so that the camp that for years thrummed and bustled woke up the next morning after the closure silent as a chapel. Animals must have crept slowly back into what was once dense woods and then was a clearing in the ancient timber and then a humming camp of men, with the whine of saws and thunk of axes and rattle of plates and swirls of cigar and pipe and cigarette smoke and clink of forbidden surreptitious bottles. First the spiders, delighted at being left alone to build their cities, and then other insects and then chipmunks and squirrels and mice and birds, claiming territory for themselves, and then the animals who preyed upon those animals, but never again a human animal, never again for eighty years, not a scavenger nor a hiker nor a hermit nor a trapper nor kids looking for secret places to lose their consciousness or virginity. Though men in the city had maps with the old timber camp marked, though men in office buildings had records of the ownership of the site, though men in government recorded taxes paid for the right to ignore the site, no man ever again set foot in that clearing, and year by year, it grew less human and more sylvan, less a clearing and more a green pause in the thick forest. The alders and bushes and grasses loved it for the sunlight, and they leapt from the soil as if called to attention by the sun and rain; and no man would set foot in that place again for another twenty years, which is long past the end of this book, so that we have nothing to say of that young man when he does arrive, or the small green-eyed child he carries humming on his back.

42

MARIA AND HER PET FINCH had taken a while to get to know
each other, but as spring stretched and yawned and warmed, a
certain affection and respect finally cohered, and by May they
were the best of friends, attentive and interested in each other's
adventures, each wishing genuine joy and substantive work for
the other. The finch listened carefully as Maria explained her
homework and various projects for school (among them video-
taped interviews with her family, a series of paintings of crawdads, and a sculpture of a falcon made from toothbrush bristles),
and Maria listened carefully as the finch tried to teach her the
three basic bars of music on which finch languages are based; no
matter what kind of finch you are, you can piece out what another
kind of finch is singing if you know the basic building blocks. It is
interesting to note, as Maria discovered many years later, that the
finches, which populate most of the world and have been developing in many different environments for many thousands of
years, can, if placed together in the same environment, communicate in rough but understandable terms. How this could be so,
and how finch languages might have a common root or even a
single masterful original singer, is a mystery that the finches as a
genus have not seen fit to share with human animals, yet.

Maria's finch was, according to the bird books, a Cassin's finch,
a mountain bird, but he, the finch, was startled and not especially pleased to be called Cassin's finch, as he, the finch, had no
knowledge of Mr. Cassin, and no particular interest in Mr. Cassin,
either, all due respect. Maria explained to him, the finch, that
Mr. Cassin was a man in Pennsylvania who was interested in
Western birds and drew and painted them in books, for which

service to the study of birds his name was attached to all sorts of birds and even an insect that spent seventeen years underground before emerging to sing for one summer. But the finch remained unconvinced that even such admirable service to basic familiarity with other animals quite deserved your name being placed on other animals in a possessive sense. Because Maria paid close attention to and had come to great respect for the finch, for example, should he, the finch, then be called Maria's finch? Conversely, if he, the finch, had come to similar respect and attentive reverence for Maria, should she, Maria, be called the finch's Maria? The whole question of where identification, which is generally a harmless and beneficial step toward understanding, slides infinitesimally into possessiveness, which is a harmful and damaging step toward prison, is a pressing question, they decided, and not one to be easily or immediately solved. It's more of a question to be asked one Cassin at a time, as Maria said to Dave drowsily one night in the bear's den.

★

That same night, the night that Dave told Maria he was sorry for being so grumpy lately but he just was, for reasons he couldn't figure out, it was like he had the flu in his soul or something, Martin came as close to death as he would come in his first few years. It happened in this way. The night was moonish and bright. The snow was nearly gone even in the deepest shadowed places in the woods and wholly gone in meadows and clearings. Martin was exploring an opening in the woods where a timber company had clear-cut in a hurry, leaving slash piles in which lots of small meat lived. The piles, some of them twenty feet tall, were filled with mice and wood rats and chipmunks and ground squirrels, and Martin patrolled the cut as a rancher managed his herds, culling here and there.

Something about the weather, perhaps, made Martin just a tad careless, a touch off his usual meticulous awareness of danger; it was a warm evening after a bright sunny redolent day, and he'd slept deeply until the afternoon and then spent an hour trying to catch fish in a creek, to no avail, although he remained convinced that he could and would learn to do this well. He had watched raccoons in the water, and mink and otters, and while he could not and would never swim, he could and would, he thought, learn how to trap fish in pools and either snatch them with his teeth or snag them with his claws or even bat them up onto the bank, out of their fitted element. Perhaps he was musing about just such matters as he walked across the moonlit clearing toward the first of the slash piles, because he did not hear or sense the owl who swept in behind him, low and silent, and sank its tremendous talons into his back on either side of his spine.

*

What saved Martin's life? If anything, it was his instant reflexes; as the owl's razor-sharp talons touched him, he instinctively leapt to the side, and it was perhaps this infinitesimal shift that kept the owl from getting her usual firm and fatal grip. A great horned owl attacks silently, from above or behind, and sinks its enormous talons into its prey, four talons on each foot, closing two on two like dual locks. With a small animal, like a vole, the impact and shock of the attack is often enough to cause death; with a larger animal, like a rabbit, the owl's talons will sometimes sever the spinal cord on impact, or the owl will do so with her blade of a beak as soon as she has flown up to a safe perch with her catch. But Martin was not small; he was himself a ferocious predator, and his next instinct, after trying to dash aside, was to fight back furiously.

The owl had not expected this. She was six years old, in the fullness of her physical prime, experienced, hungry, and a mother with two chicks gibbering in her nest; taking a young marten was fully in the realm of the possible, and Martin was not at all the first marten she had killed and shredded. He was, however, the first to contort himself in such a way that his back claws raked at her tail, which staggered her flight. This was again an infinitesimal thing, a little hitch in the beat of her wings, but it was enough to bring the owl back down toward the ground; her grip on Martin was already not as firm as she would like, and the interruption in her wing beat caused her to sink back to earth.

But earth was Martin's domain, and the instant he felt his feet touch ground, he twisted savagely, and he and the owl crashed in a heap. The owl's talons were planted in Martin's back, but her grip was not sure, and Martin, enraged by the terrible pain in his shoulders, now had the footing he needed to counterattack. While the owl was much bigger, with a wingspan of almost five feet, she and Martin both weighed about two pounds, and Martin was fighting for his life, whereas the owl was both out of her element and rattled. Martin twisted again, faster than the eye could see, and one set of the owl's talons were dragged out of his back. The owl tried to leap up and away from the chaos, but she was still hooked into Martin with the other set of talons, and his weight caused her to crash again; but in the instant of open space that her flight had created, Martin slashed at her chest and tore a hole in it. The owl, furious and desperate, hammered him with her wings, but as she did so her other talons lost their remaining grip, and an instant later Martin's teeth were grinding inexorably through the dense mat of feathers at her neck. She raked his belly with her talons, she battered him terribly with her wings, but seconds later she was dead.

Martin bled from his back. He bled from his belly. He bled from a slash on his head where her beak had cut him to the bone of his skull. He was enraged and exhausted and shocked and shaking and furious. The moon was brighter than ever. The clearing was absolutely silent; every single denizen of the slash piles and the freighted air and the burrows below knew of the battle and huddled waiting for the coast to clear. Martin knew dimly that he needed shelter, needed to clean his wounds, needed to go to ground for a while, for he also knew he was now sentenced to a week of great pain and total inactivity, a week when he would be weak and utterly vulnerable; but the tide of rage rose in him again as he stared at the owl. Grunting with pain, he tore open her chest and ate his fill. When he could eat no more, he limped inside the nearest slash pile and curled up to sleep. He was as weary as he had ever been, but before he closed his eyes he licked clean every wound he could reach, tasting the owl's blood as well as his own; and then he slept.

43

IT TURNED OUT that the day Mr. Shapiro the teacher hurt his back shoveling snow was the last day he was an elementary school teacher, for something in his back had broken and didn't heal, and he had to take leave from teaching, and then he had a small surgery, which didn't work, and then he had a whopping surgery, which worked some but not much, and by then he had used up all the vacation and disability days he could possibly take from the school district, and he had to accept a severance package that would extend his medical insurance while allowing the district to hire another able-bodied and energetic teacher. By the first days of spring, however, he had adjusted enough to what he called his new friend Tom Pain to sign up as a substitute teacher at the high school level, which is how, in late March, Mr. Shapiro and Dave and Moon found themselves back in a classroom together.

Mr. Shapiro was pleased to see the boys; Dave had been one of his favorite students ever, and Moon had always seemed like a boy who would blossom later in life, probably not in high school but some years later. Moon seemed to be the sort of student who would muddle through high school, work a year or two, tiptoe into community college, wake up amazingly both intellectually and ambitiously, and then soar through a university, and then who knows? Moon would probably end up being governor or god help us all a teacher who would face kids just like himself, if the universe had a sense of humor.

And the Moon that Mr. Shapiro met again in freshman history was the same Moon as before, although a startling four inches taller and, astonishingly, a basketball player; he was a friendly boy with a quick wit and an admirable kindness to others, if not a particularly diligent or intellectually curious student. Whereas High School Dave was a different Dave altogether than Grade School Dave, it seemed to Mr. Shapiro. The younger Dave was just the sort of student you always envisioned having as a teacher—eager, curious, creative, willing to take suggestions and directions seriously and then run with them. However, the New Dave, as Mr. Shapiro thought of him, was a surly boy who grunted his answers to questions, pointedly refused to participate in class, did only the minimum amount of work required to earn a B, and was consistently last to arrive as class started and first out the door when it ended.

Mr. Shapiro asked the other teachers about the New Dave and was met with a general accounting of a boy who had been by all accounts friendly, curious, hardworking, personable, and engaging from the minute he walked into the school in September until approximately the last day of winter, after which—as the Spanish teacher Ms. Ishimira expressed it—an evil vernal demon occupied the boy formerly known as Dave, creating a lazy, sneering, untrustworthy, rude, vulgar, grumpy, disgruntled, sarcastic, supercilious, crude, offensive, snide young man whom no student wanted to be with, no teacher wanted to teach, and no one except perhaps Jesus or Nelson Mandela could reach, which was a shame, because the Old Dave was a fascinating boy whose thirsty curiosity was often the best part of my day, she said, and then she burst into tears.

I have a cold, she explained, which makes my eyes water profusely, and Mr. Shapiro said he understood perfectly, as he was subject to the same phenomenon, and he found that blueberry tea was an excellent panacea.

*

One thing you learn as a teacher is never to call out a student in front of the other students; a direct attack sends students diving for cover behind their masks and walls and shields, and those defenses are already so formidable that students sometimes trap themselves behind their walls and cannot easily scale them, and so imprison themselves for years at a time. Nor does a private conversation always pay dividends; to be asked to stay after class, or to be invited to a formal discussion after school, usually prompts a furious period of wall construction, which not even the most brilliant or empathetic teacher can breach. So it was that Mr. Shapiro bided his time and waited for the right moment. He had the time—his substitute assignment, filling in for a maternity leave, was for the rest of the academic year, which did not end until June—and he had been a teacher long enough to learn a preternatural patience, a skill he sometimes thought the most important of all in his beloved profession. In a lot of ways, as he and Mr. Douglas had once discussed, teaching was like hunting: both were disciplines in which preparation and patience were most of the work, and moments of intense action were actually quite rare, and often all your preparation and patience went for naught, anyway, and the quarry slipped away untouched.

But Mr. Shapiro's moment with Dave did come, finally—a last-period class on a day of incredible rain, epic rain, pelting rain, ferocious rain, inarguable rain, silvery sheets and swells of rain, a day so thoroughly and decidedly and roaringly wet that all after-school practices were canceled, even for the track team, which was inured to bad weather. The official announcement had just come over the sputtering ancient public-address system, and as his class filtered out, Mr. Shapiro asked Dave to stay behind a moment.

Dave sat down, annoyed.

What?

Dave, we need to talk.

I haven't done anything wrong.

And no one said you did. I just wanted to talk.

What about?

Dave, is something wrong at home?

No.

Health problems in the family? Too many hours working at Miss Moss's?

No.

You don't . . . seem like yourself lately.

I'm fine.

Are you?

I just said I was.

Pause.

Well, Dave, said Mr. Shapiro, this is sort of exactly what I wanted to talk about. Forgive me for being blunt, but you are a lot ruder than you used to be, and it's no fun. You do your work, your grades are not a problem, but you're incredibly rude. Why?

No reason, said Dave.

That's not an answer.

Mr. Shapiro, if I am doing my work and my grades are fine, what business is it of yours?

Pause. Another thing Mr. Shapiro had learned in his years as a teacher was to at least try to stay calm and count to ten, although he noticed he never actually got all the way to ten; eight was his personal record.

Look, Dave, he said, I am not stupid, and I know things have changed since you were in my class in sixth grade. I get it that you are now a teenager and close to being a man. But the guy everyone liked for his friendly kindness then seems to have abandoned ship. I am here if you need help. Being a teacher is more than grading. And you must know that I am not the only teacher or student to wonder why you are so curt and rude these last few months. I just got here, as you know, but your other teachers here have mentioned it to me.

Dave opened his mouth and closed it and opened it again and closed it and sat there simmering. What could he say? He had nothing to say. He was angry and ashamed and annoyed and angry. He just wanted to be who he wanted to be. He didn't want to be what anyone else wanted him to be. Everyone had an idea of him and he was none of those Daves. He just wanted to be left alone and people were always after him to be something or do something. Couldn't people just leave him alone? What was so hard about leaving a guy alone when he wanted to be left alone? Was that so hard?

Dave?

I have to get home, Mr. Shapiro. If we don't have practice, I have to get going.

There being nothing more to say, Mr. Shapiro said nothing, and Dave grabbed his stuff and left, yanking the door shut just hard enough to say something without saying anything, and

Mr. Shapiro stood by the window and stretched for a while like the therapist said he should every day but he didn't.

But all the way home, Dave felt a shiver of shame for the way he had spoken to Mr. Shapiro, and when he and Maria were in bed that night and she said *what's the matter*, he told her, and she got out of her bed and padded over to his and hung her face an inch over his face and said *be tender*, and then she padded back to her bed. You know how when you are going one way in a river,

and you stick your paddle in and hold it in the right spot for a second, and the whole boat turns? It was like that for Dave after that. Years later he would tell his own kids about those two words from their aunt Maria at that exact moment and how those two words woke him up and cracked something, and this is one of the thousand reasons why your aunt Maria is so cool, although all three of you already know *that*, don't you?

44

RIDING AN *OLD* HORSE through a forest is a lot easier than riding a *young* horse in the woods, said Mr. Douglas to Miss Moss, raising his voice a little so she could hear him clearly, although he was talking frontward and she was sitting behind him on Edwin. Because your older horse, for example Edwin, knows not to be rushing along headlong but rather to meander and pick and plod his way along and not be knocking his companions off his back with untoward branches and things like that.

Meander is a lovely word, said Miss Moss. That's a dollar word.

Thank you.

As is *untoward*. You hardly ever hear that word.

Thank you.

Are we allowed to be riding a horse in the national forest?

Yup. Nor does Edwin leave, ah, evidence. He saves that for home.

A meticulous being.

It's more that he doesn't like conducting his toilet outdoors, I think.

Ah.

Like most of us.

Ah.

Although he is meticulous about many things.

Such as?

He likes his hair brushed a certain way.

Ah.

God help us if you brush it any other way. He gets sulky.

Ah.

And he likes his food served a certain way.

Such as?

Mash cooked just so, with honey. You forget his honey, he lets you know about it right quick, and in no uncertain terms, neither. And it has to be a *quart* of oats—no more, no less. *Two* carrots, not one or three. And he's not much for walking in the rain. Snow he doesn't mind, but good luck getting him out in the rain. He just doesn't see the point of moist. There have been times when I needed him to drag someone out of a ditch in a thunderstorm, and he just takes refuge in metaphysics. He's an obfusticator. He gives you that look, you know, and then you know you are in for an *hour* of debate. It's like living with a theologian.

How did you and Edwin meet?

Blind date.

Pardon me?

Edwin was a police horse in the city, you see, and they were just about to retire him, and my date and I went down to meet her brother, who was the policeman who had ridden Edwin, to pick him up, the brother, to give him a ride to dinner where we would meet *his* date, and that's how I met Edwin. He was just standing there, and we became friends, and I worked out a deal with the policeman. He was happy that Edwin would be up on the mountain. He said Edwin had always liked the mountain but that he, the brother, had never had occasion to get up there with him.

Did you see your date again?

No.

Why?

To be honest, Ginny, I didn't like the way she used her beauty as a tool. I didn't like that at all. It seemed selfish and sort of cruel.

What did Edwin think?

Of what?

Of your date.

I don't think he liked her much, either, but unless you are dealing with food or hair or rain, it's hard to get a clear opinion from him. He keeps a poker face. I mean, I have known him for years, and I have no idea what he's thinking right now.

*

This is what Edwin is thinking: When are you going to ask her again? It's past time. Are you going to sit up there babbling about hair and rain or are you going to get down on your knees and ask the poor girl to marry you or what? If it was me, I would be down on my knees already instead of rattling on and on about oats and policemen, you silly oaf. You asked her the once, and she declined, but she didn't decline permanently. Do you not remember the way she declined? She declined as gently and mildly and sweetly and affectionately as you could ever possibly decline an invitation to marry. That no was about as close to yes as you can get with a no. Me personally I thought she was gently closing the front door and flinging the back door open. Me personally I would be down on my knees as soon as we came across a dry place to kneel down. Do you think a being like her comes along more than once in a lifetime? I could tell you stories of the beings I know who never met the being they should have spent their lives with or spent their lives with the wrong being or mated with the wrong being and had to pay for that mistake the rest of their lives. Do you think you get many chances to ask this sort of question of this sort of being? In fact, if you do not kneel down, I will damn well kneel down and get the whole thing started myself as soon as I find a dry place. As if there's a dry place on this mountain in May. The only dry places are probably caves or sun-soaked meadows or the hollows of old trees like the one Maria slept in. Fine—the first cave I come across or the first hollow tree or the first high dry sunny meadow I see, I am going to kneel down and make it clear that this is the time and this is the place and this is the person. Fine.

★

Maria's final assignment in first grade, the big spring project due at the end of May, was to portray her domicile, in a medium to be chosen by you, the student. You can, said the teacher, write, paint, draw, sculpt, video, build a model, or portray, in any other form or manner you like, the place where you live. This is a Creative Project, so I am not going to tell you what to do. But I do want you to think about it first, and then work hard at it, okay? Don't leave it for the night before and make your mom do it or just copy what your older siblings did in this class. Part of this project is to get you ready for next year, when you will be asked to do more work on your own, and part of it should be just fun, a way to see your home in a different light. The one thing I will ask is that you think of your home as a verb, not a noun—think of it as a thing in motion, not just a place. Do you see what I mean? I am more interested in what *happens* inside your home than in the actual building. Think about that for a while before you do your project.

And Maria did think about it for a long while. She climbed and clambered all over the cabin, on the roof, along the eaves, and in the dark dry crawl space below reachable only through the trap door in the woodshed. She took notes in a notebook and photographs with her cell phone, and she interviewed her mom and dad and Dave, and conducted a population survey of the beings in the house—animal and vegetable—from insects (Arthropoda) to mosses (Bryophyta) to Dad (Paternosotra, said her father), and finally she set to work. First she drew a map to the scale of one foot of house equaling one inch of map, in which she recorded every being's movement in or on or through the house for one hour on a Saturday morning. Then she drew a second map, noting every being's lowest and highest physical presence for the same hour; Dave, for example, went from sprawled on the floor by the fireplace to standing on the roof staring at the sky in which he was sure for a moment that he had heard sandhill cranes. Then she drew a third map, noting the places in the house where the most paths crossed the most times during that hour; she labeled these Crossroads and colored them in green. Then she drew a fourth map, noting the places where not a single being had been during the course of the hour; she labeled these The Arid Lands and colored them in red. Then she drew a fifth map, in which she redesigned the cabin so that all the Crossroads were in the same room and all The Arid Lands were in a closet. Then she added a sonic map, showing, in different color inks, the musical tones of all utterances and voicings in the house over the course of the same hour. To this she added a recording of each tone, captured on a thumb drive. Finally, she wrote a two-page essay called "A Poem Without Any Words" about all the places in the house that she loved because beings she loved were somehow connected in the most subtle and gentle ways to those places—the place on the wall next to the thermostat where her dad leaned his right hand as he used his left to turn the heat down at night, so that after years of turning down the heat there was a gentle vertical poem on the wall written by thousands of nights of turning down the heat; and the tiny poem on the headboard of her bed in the bear's den where the finch rubbed its beak every evening before going to sleep; and the infinitesimal penciled poem on the frame of the porch door where Dave had written his rising elevation over the years; and the gentle sag in the couch like a cupped leather palm where her mother had fallen asleep curled like a cat every third night or so for years; and the tiny nick in the kitchen wall that was the poem of the frying pan kissing the wall when you hung it up after cleaning it and it swung and tinked the wall once before coming to rest; and many other things, too many to list here, for eventually paragraphs have to end, even the most warm and lovely and riveting ones, like this.

45

THE UNABLED LADY LIVED ALONE, for complicated reasons having to do with money and love and loss, but another woman came every morning to help. This was Mrs. Simmons, who was about the same age but had a body that moved more freely than the Unabled Lady's body did, so Mrs. Simmons did the laundry and cooked a bit and cleaned the bathroom and windows and did things around the house that needed to be done. She was not a nurse, quite, although she was a competent and gentle assistant in moments of medical and physical stress. She was not a caretaker, either, quite, as her service to the Unabled Lady was recompensed partly with money but also with vegetables from the garden and a share of the gifts that occasionally came the Unabled Lady's way through the largesse of the community, such as elk tenderloins and deer burger and the occasional huckleberry milk shake, and rides to the city and homemade ale and pears and cherries from the vast orchards to the north and east of the mountain, and books from the library's overflow sale, and one time an American flag with only forty-eight stars, which the Unabled Lady and Mrs. Simmons traded back and forth every few months just for fun, taking turns hanging it proudly in awed celebration of and gratitude for—as the Unabled Lady liked to say—Mr. Thomas Jefferson's skills with the first draft and Mr. Benjamin Franklin's skills as an editor thereafter.

Mrs. Simmons came every day but usually only for a couple of hours, as she had three other housecleaning jobs per week, and it should be said here, before we go any further in this sentence, that she did superb work. She never rested at all but filled her two hours thoroughly; as she often said, there were always more things to be done than you could possibly do, and sitting even for a moment allowed old weary in. You best keep in motion, as she said, so as old weary cannot get a toehold. Old weary is a slippery thing. It is the most amazingly patient of things. It will get you in the end, anyways, but if you keep in motion, old weary cannot get footing. One thing I have learned in life is just that. Old weary will take you in his arms eventually, but you got to dance and fence with old weary until then. O yes. Old weary is so polite and gentle. He is so warm and friendly that you want to just lie down and say alright, old weary, you have your way with me; I am ready for you. But when you do that you will be dead, and when you are dead you just can*not* get your work done, and that is a fact.

Mrs. Simmons had a number of unusual convictions about life, one of them being that no person of sense would drink water from a faucet or hose or tap, because who knows what is inside those pipes and what mutant germs are living in there having sex, and besides, *snakes* can get in there, you know, that has *happened*. So Mrs. Simmons, when thirsty, drank from the clear cold water that the Lord Himself Bless Jesus provided us poor creatures of the soil, which is to say creeks and springs and rivulets and even sometimes the river when it was not gray with snowmelt in the late spring. So it was that at the end of her two hours today, Mrs. Simmons does kneel by the little friendly creek that marks the edge of the Unabled Lady's yard, and she leans down to slake her thirst, having earned refreshment ten times over by the sweat of her brow and the honesty of her labors and the kindness of her heart, and something breaks inside her chest, and all the parts that have for the last sixty years worked relatively fine with only the occasional soreness and pain do now stutter and altogether halt, and Mrs. Simmons leans ever so slowly down and down into the creek, and her nose touches the water, and then her lips, still pursed to accept the clear cold water that the Lord Himself Bless Jesus provides, and then ever so slowly the rest of her face, and then her head, and then her neck and the first few inches of her chest and shoulders, but then old gravity calls a halt to the pro-ceedings, and there, with her face and head beneath the surface of the creek and her eyes open and amazed at what they saw last in this life, rests what used to be Mrs. Simmons. Old weary has come at last.

*

The Unabled Lady did not notice Mrs. Simmons in the creek for quite a while, being absorbed in a piece of music at the piano that might under the proper circumstances grow into something like an oratorio; also she and Mrs. Simmons were quite comfortable with the idea that each could quietly do her work in another room without having to be constantly bantering and nattering about nothing and its second cousin, as Mrs. Simmons said. So it was twenty or thirty minutes before the Unabled Lady looked up and checked the time and did not see Mrs. Simmons in the kitchen or hear her in the bathroom or hear the squeak of windows being cleaned or hear her humming in the laundry room. Odd, she thought, and she wheeled away from the piano to the window to see if Mrs. S. was puttering in the garden, though it seemed early for that yet, this high on the mountain. And then she saw Mrs. S. kneeling by the creek, and she knew.

She was so *still*, as she told the policeman later. She was *never* still.

The Unabled Lady had a cell phone; sure she did. Who would be without a cell phone these days, especially in her situation? Of course she had a cell phone. But, she slowly realized, the phone was in Mrs. Simmons's right-hand apron pocket. Mrs. Simmons was in the habit of calling her oldest daughter when she was finishing a shift, just to rest that blessed child's mind about her ancient tooth-less thoughtless mother, and often she would make this call outdoors, partly for the ostensibly better cell reception and partly so as not to disturb the Unabled Lady at the piano.

So, then.

Listen, we have all read epic adventure stories. We have read them all our lives and had them read to us, and we have or will read them to our children and very probably will have them read to us again when we are near the end and old weary is reaching for us also. But consider how climbing a mountain, or grappling with a bucking boat or bronco, or wielding a sword or wand or gamma gun, is a lot easier when you have legs and feet under you for general balance, and then consider that the Unabled Lady does not have any legs and feet anymore for reasons having to do with cocktails and cocaine and cars and then a slow dying of nerves in the body, and now she needs to get from the house all the way up a steep uneven rocky trail not six inches wide, lined with dense fern and bramble and currant and snowberry, with not one but two fallen fir trees across the trail, each one fully three feet in diameter, before she can reach Mrs. Simmons's right-hand apron pocket and call for help. Consider the next hour and four minutes— for it will take the Unabled Lady an hour and four minutes to traverse the hundred yards between the moment she sits in the window, steeling herself, to the moment when ever so gently she wraps her arms around Mrs. Simmons and pulls her from the creek and folds Mrs. Simmons onto a little bed of moss on the bank and then calls the police and then collapses exhausted and sobbing next to Mrs. Simmons in such a way that their faces are both looking up at the sweet wild blue of the sky—as one of the greatest epic and courageous adventures of all time. Consider what it might feel like to lower yourself out of your protective chair and down onto the moist earth, so recently covered with snow and remembering the cold wet of it yet, and scrabble and roll and haul yourself up a wet rocky tiny trail, your hips and stumps being rubbed raw by stones and thorns, your shoulders burning, your breasts scratched mercilessly by the bark of the fallen trees, your jacket caught and held by branches, your shirt torn and stained. Consider what it might be like to stop, exhausted and sobbing, after making it over the first fallen fir and having to pee so badly from shock and fear and despair that you just do, right there, into the fir duff, and then you crawl on up the trail, dreading the next fallen tree. Consider what it might be like to slip and lose your balance as you haul yourself over the second moist tree and fall heavily on your right side in such a way that your right hand, your strong hand on the piano, is caught under you in your fall and is twisted in such a way that you scream in pain. Consider the desperate strength with which you grasp the body of your friend around the middle and yank with all your might and nothing much happens, for Mrs. Simmons was a substantial woman and you are not, until you scream with rage and loss and haul her bodily out of the creek and fall backwards with her onto the mossy bank. Consider how you weep from the bottom of your soul as you brush her hair away from her sweet lined stern face and fold her long thin arms over her flat chest and reach into her pocket for the cell phone and make the call and talk to the dispatcher and give him directions and then lie down next to Mrs. Simmons, so close that your shoulders touch, and stare at the sweet wild blue of the sky and the way that all the fingers of all the branches are webbed and woven, all reaching for each other all the time. Consider that.

46

MARTIN SAW ALL THIS. He saw Mrs. Simmons bend to drink from the creek and never stop. He saw the Unabled Lady crawl sobbing from the house to Mrs. Simmons and then lie there also in the moss staring at the sky, the two women dripping and silent. He saw the police car arriving and the policemen running and the radio blaring and the emergency vehicles later. By then it was dusk and when everyone was gone he slipped back into the woods to hunt, for he was very hungry, and in May there were new young things and many eggs to eat for a marten who knew where to look.

In the morning he was again possessed by the urge to ramble widely; it was almost as if some force was steering him through the woods in search of something he did not know. He was restless and annoyed and uncharacteristically testy, and twice he attacked tiny birds he would ordinarily have ignored. All day he slipped through the woods, a shadow in the canopy, a dark rumor among the squirrels, who feared a marten even more than owls and hawks, for raptors could miss a strike and then veer away disgruntled, but martens rarely abandoned a chase. Had the squirrels known it, this relentless pursuit was a mark of the whole mustelid family, who, once launched on a project, rarely gave it up, be it battle or burrow. From the smallest weasel at one end of the clan to the bearlike wolverine at the top, the mustelids were generally musky, intent, ferocious at times, much hunted for their dense fur, and famed in lore and legend for their intelligence, their long memories, and their skill as hunters. Even the anomalous members of the family, like skunks, were noted for their combative temper (as many a whimpering and stinking dog could attest), and those of a more playful mien, like otters, were ferocious underwater when chasing their favorite food and had no particular enemies among the larger predators, except for human animals. Martin had only once in his life seen an otter even attacked by another animal, and that had not gone well for the bobcat, which leapt away in pain and shock after being raked across the face by the otter's claws. Martin had drawn two lessons from that fight: be even more cautious of otters, who were bigger than he was, and an otter away from water is out of his or her element and thus subject to attack.

In the afternoon he found himself up near timberline, and he ranged through the thin forest with a fidgety unease, although his senses were sharp. This high and dry on the mountain, it was a sea of different scents than down in the thicker woods of firs and cedars, and he could smell juniper and hemlock, woodrushes and violets, windflowers and rock cress, and even currants and serviceberry. Currants were a favorite fruit of his, and he stopped for a moment to nose through the currant bushes to see how far they were from fruit—and that is when he saw her.

*

At exactly the same elevation at exactly the same moment at exactly the other side of the mountain, Mr. Douglas reaches up and helps Miss Moss descend from Edwin's back—which is, as Mr.

Douglas has often said, more like the deck of a tall ship than it is the spinal segment of a member of the equine family. Miss Moss then helped unpack the duffel bag that Mr. Douglas had slung over Edwin's capacious rear parts. From the bag, she drew, as if from an inexhaustible vault of treasures, a bottle of cold wine, two sandwiches, two enormous carrots roughly the size of small baseball bats, and a candy bar so old that the brand name of the bar and the company that made it were utterly obscured.

How old exactly, said Miss Moss, is this candy bar?

My grandmother gave it to me when I graduated from high school, said Mr. Douglas. I have been saving it for a special occasion.

Right about now would be a good time to ask her, thought Edwin, glaring at Mr. Douglas.

Edwin, my friend, I am going to borrow this blanket from you, if you don't mind, said Mr. Douglas, sliding the blanket off and snapping it twice before draping it over a fallen log. Don't glare at me like that. It's not that cold, and you have plenty of fur.

It's not the blanket, thought Edwin. Look at the poor girl. She's rattled. Either give her some wine or ask the question, for heavens' sake. The one complaint I have about you after all these years is that sometimes you hesitate a beat too long to do things. Sometimes you have to just jump into the moment and logic be damned. This is one of those moments, my friend. If you don't do something in the next minute, I will kick you from here to Mount Jefferson.

Ginny, listen, said Mr. Douglas. I don't know how to dance around this anymore. I think of you all day and night. I love your honesty and humor and hard work. I love talking to you and listening to you. I trust you. I'd like to be your partner in everything we do. I think I could be the best trustiest lovingest partner you could ever have.

In the store?

Ginny, really, listen. I am trying to say that, I, you, could, we could, I think, that we, I don't know how to say this.

I am going to kick you *past* Mount Jefferson, thought Edwin. I am going to kick you all the way to California.

Let me try to say it, then, said Miss Moss. The woman is always supposed to wait patiently and sweetly, but I am neither patient nor sweet. I love you too, Richard David Douglas. I love your company, and I trust your heart. But I don't want to get married. Every marriage I have ever seen was a sort of gentle or awful jail bound by expectations and assumptions. It seems silly at best and cruel at worst. The wedding is performance art, the honeymoon is a pretense of dewy intimacy, and the only real benefit is a tax break. I don't want a tax break. I want you. Why can't we be married without being married?

Maybe I will kick *her* to California, thought Edwin.

Even the birds in the clearing paused to hear what was coming next.

Well, said Mr. Douglas slowly, because I don't want to be married without being married. I want to be married to you and only you the rest of my life, if at all possible. It matters a great deal to me to be married. There's something about saying yes to each other boldly and publicly that seems wild and brave to me. I would invite the whole world to our wedding if I could— animal, vegetable, and mineral.

Mineral? thought Edwin. There'll be rocks at the wedding? Where would they sit?

Would you like a sandwich? asked Miss Moss.

I would not like a sandwich, said Mr. Douglas, and both Edwin and Miss Moss saw something in his face they had never seen before, some complex wrangle of pain and humor and anger and affection and respect and sadness that washed over his face like wind shivers a lake. I would *not* like a sandwich, he said again, and he held out his hand to help Miss Moss up off the log, and she took his hand and stepped toward him, perhaps to kiss him, but he bent and picked up the blanket and put it back on Edwin. She stepped back, her face a mask, and they packed up the duffel bag again and rode home.

47

FOR NEARLY THE ENTIRE academic year now, Dave had tried and tried and tried to talk easily and naturally and comfortably and unconcernedly to girls, to no avail. He tried to be casual. He tried to be flippant. He tried to just engage them in normal conversation as if they were actual human beings. He tried to pretend they were guys and therefore not alluring and causing him to mumble and stammer. He tried being dismissive. He tried being mysterious. He tried being attentive and solicitous. He tried ignoring them altogether. But none of this worked, and every single day, every single class, every single minute in the tidal surge in the hallways as he was carried upstream and down by the crowd, he was entranced and awkward and bumbling and a complete idiot with girls—and not just the girls he found attractive, either, but with girls he was not attracted to *at all*. He was a total stammering idiot with them too, which was just *dispiriting*, as he said to Moon.

Plus this whole thing with girls made you a grump, said Moon helpfully.

You're not helping, said Dave.

Just because you can't talk to girls didn't mean you had to be a total butthead all the time. Even your sister says so.

Moon . . .

And *she's* a girl. You can talk to her—what's the problem with other girls? Just pretend they are Maria plus ten years.

I wish I could, said Dave. But I can't. I just want to be normal. Why can't I be normal? You're normal, almost.

I don't want to go out with any of them, which means I don't get nervous, said Moon. They are just people, you know. They're just like us.

No, they're not. They're beautiful, and we're, well, look at you.

I am a god, said Moon. *I* am a member of the B team. Sure, I don't get to play much in games, but I didn't get cut from the team, and I am not failing any courses yet. The secret is to reduce your expectations. My only goal this year was to not flunk out. My only goal was to not give my parents a chance to send me to an expensive prestigious famous boarding school where everyone wears polo pants. The whole basketball thing was a bonus, and my attitude is that the coach could come to his senses tomorrow and cut me like he was supposed to in the fall. He's clearly deluded, but I am not going to bring that to his attention.

You are so weird, said Dave. Were you this weird when we met? When did we meet?

Kindergarten, remember? We were both four years old when kindergarten started, and everyone else was older than us. We held hands at nap time, remember?

I didn't mean to be surly, you know. I just felt so . . . discombobulated. You hate to use the word hormone, but I guess sometimes it's real. I just want to be normal. I used to be normal, and now normal is like a foreign country.

I know, said Moon. Let's eat.

Eating is not the answer to all problems, you know.

It is when you have stuff for *great* sandwiches, said Moon. Come on, let's eat, and then I'll go for a run with you. Running always cools you out. I think running is insane, myself, but I'll start out with you, and then you can keep going, and I will quit like an intelligent guy and come home. I have to clean the house later. My folks are coming home.

At the same time?

Yeah, weird, huh? I'll make name tags for us to wear around the house.

They home for a while?

A week. Amazing, huh?

Are they . . . together?

Dad says an illness is now on its way to healing, with sufficient attention and light.

What does that mean?

I haven't the faintest idea. I think she did something, and he was hurt, but they like each other enough to try to reboot the system. He talks like that when he wants to tell me something he can't figure out how to say. He says this is why God invented metaphors.

When was the last time they were both home for a whole week?

I can't remember. Probably when they hatched me.

Maybe it'll actually be fun, Moon. You know? To be together.

I guess. Maybe. It could be. I guess.

★

There was a church in the Zag, sure there was; what self-respecting hamlet does not feature a church of some flavor? Churches being such an ancient habit among all beings, of course. Did you think that human animals were the only animals with sacred places and haunts? There are many chapels and prayer rooms and shivering places where beings go to meditate or be shriven or observe the timeless rituals or to try to crack open doors in their hearts. Mountaintops and benches along rivers, huts and hermit cells, groves and copses, altars of stone and wind, old airplane hangars, moist wooden cabins, clearings in the woods where many feet have flattened the eager grass and many voices are raised in prayer and supplication . . .

But the Zag, populated by only a few human animals, has had to toss all its religions together into one former state highway repair building, long used for the storage of sand and gravel and plows and cement mixers and shovels and a small, relentless tractor named Frank. After more than fifty years of steady use by the state, the building and Frank were sold to the village for a nominal fee (one dollar for the building, eighty for Frank, who was a very fine tractor), and now the building, and sometimes Frank, were used by men and women and children of every conceivable faith tradition, from Christian to Jewish to Hindu to Buddhist to Pantheist to Wiccan to Druid to Muslim to Zoroastrian. Even Lutherans were welcome, though hardly any came; occasionally one would wander by and poke his head in and see, say, Cosmas in his orange jumpsuit singing Van Morrison songs, and he, the Lutheran, would withdraw quietly and return to his car and drive away slightly too fast.

For a while after the state sold the building to the village, the faith traditions took turns holding court, as it were—Hindus one week, Zoroastrians the next—but soon it became evident that all the traditions wished to have some sort of weekly service, just to stay in rhythm ("to stay in *practice*, get it?" said Dave's dad. "Religious *practice*, get it? Does anyone get it? Anyone?"), so they slowly learned to share a weekly event. The first few weeks were awkward, as people sang and knelt at different times, but slowly they got the hang of it and lost their prickliness about identity and heritage and individual charism and ownership of the Truth and what words to use for the things they all had in common but called by different names. After a year or so, to be honest, if you polled or questioned the congregation anonymously after church service, you would find that in general they quietly enjoyed the new color and jazz of the event and found it sweeter and deeper than their own home ritual in which most of them had swum half-conscious for many years, perhaps more for nostalgic than spiritual reasons. Indeed, the new service, as Cosmas would have said had he been asked, was not unlike an estuary into which all manners of water pour—fresh and salt, muddy and clear, sun warmed and storm whipped—and do estuaries not produce more life and nutrition than any other aspect of landscape we know? Well, then.

48

AND JUST BEFORE THAT DAY WAS DONE, Louis led his herd, his clan, his tribe, his companions, his cabal, his extended family of wives and aunts and children male and female, uphill another few hundred yards to a high meadow he knew, where there was excellent browse, fairly open forest fringe in case of the need for sudden escape, and a tireless little creek of water, so recently ice from the glaciers above that even the elk, a hardy race, were careful to sip rather than gulp.

Here they pitched camp for the night, Louis standing first watch—cougars were fond of attacking in the first dim moments of dusk, before moon and stars emerged and allowed shadows. He watched as his companions chose their sleeping places and settled down. He noted the yearlings in particular, for he knew, as they did not, that these were their last days with their mothers. Soon the mothers would give birth to new calves, and there would be a sea change in affections, and the yearlings would be banished and exiled, the spike bucks to try to survive on their own another year until they were strong enough to challenge such chieftains as Louis, and the young female calves to survive and grow until they too could mate and mother at age two.

Louis's group was the only one of its kind on Wy'east; the custom of elk on the mountain from time immemorial was for the males to range alone all year until the battles for primacy among them in the fall, and then the joy of sex for the winners, and then ranging alone again until the next battles began. But Louis had changed this pattern for his tribe, and while none of the other bulls of his class and heft had done so, several had noticed; and who knew when a second chieftain would also decide to keep a family of wives and aunts and progeny together through the hard winter and the melting spring and through a bright summer before having to defend against the brash young challengers of autumn? Who knew? And perhaps that is how all things change; one decides to try this, and another notices and decides to try also, and then there is a new idea loose in the world, from which even newer ideas might someday hatch. And there is time and time enough for such ideas to flower, over the course of millions of years and ideas, and while some beings do not change—having found the idea in which they wish to stay forever, like the ancient ideas in which crabs and crocodiles and dragonflies live—other beings *do* change, some constantly, like the human beings, who were once animals who snarled and hooted and hunted and were hunted, animals little different from their omnivore mammalian cousins. But ideas bred easily among the human beings, and their snarls and hoots became songs and poems, and their solitary pursuits became plans and plots, and their slabs of split stone became swords and rifles, and so they commandeered the world, or tried to. But once they were dominant, their ideas began to wither, their success being poison to their dreams, and there were those among them who wondered if some subtle wildness had been the food of their greatest creativity, and if their salvation as a species, and their dwindling chance to clean and balance the world they had fouled and rattled, depended on something in them that yearned for trees and ice, waters and animals, mountains and caves, mystery and attentiveness, the humility before wonder that once they had thought merely their lot and fate, but was instead perhaps their greatest gift and grace.

*

Louis was often called the king of the mountain by human beings on the mountain and by hunters who came from below to try to kill him for his annually gargantuan antlers, a few inches longer every year than the year before. But while he certainly was chieftain of his own tribe and conqueror of the grim brawny challengers who fought him every fall, he was not at all chieftain of any other beings than his family. Indeed, there were many chiefs among the elk, and not all male, either, which would confound the human scientists, if only they knew. Down by Badger Lake, for example, there was a tribe of elk who chose a female elk among them for wisdom and direction and tolerated the series of males who assumed their ostensible leadership; the Badger Lake clan understood that a powerful male was not only a reproductive necessity but a good defense against predation, and in general they humored him—although one year the winner of the autumnal battles was a cruel male, whom they endured for only a month before driving him away one night in a roaring thunderstorm.

And there were chiefs and visionaries and prophets and mayors and teachers and singers and hermits and sages and thieves and liars and healers among all the beings on the mountain, of course—among the owls, the newts, the worms, the grouse, the beetles, the toads, the crawdads, the wasps, the moths, the bears, the gyrfalcons, the hawthorn maggots, among every clan and tribe that flew and ran and leapt and slid and swam, and among the stationary beings also. Did you think that among the trees and sedges there are not more distinctions and differences and nuances than we know? Did you think they were not each one its own self, individual and inimitable, like but unlike every other of its kind? There are famous cedars among the cedars, for example, famous not just for age and girth and height and weight and sprawl but for many other reasons beyond our ken. Did you think that the other beings were not like us, each one alike as a species and each one utterly unalike as an individual? Yet this is so. And just as among us there are threads of light and dark in each one of us, and in every group and in every place and in every time since we first stood uncertainly and began to walk, there are similar threads among all the other beings. Did we think we knew the world so well that we knew this could not be so? Yet it is so. And among the weasels there have been some who would not draw blood, and among the deer there have been killers, and among the quiet kestrels there have been exuberant singers, and among the grasshoppers there have been some who remembered much and shared their memories and imparted their tales to beings of other shapes (including, famously, a grasshopper who told a dragonfly such a riveting story that the dragonfly returned the grasshopper to earth alive), and among the salamanders there was one who could heal with a touch of her tail—though that was many years ago now, and only the oldest cedars and pines and sturgeon and turtles remember hearing about that one, the turtles remembering best, as they are moist cousins and neighbors of the salamanders, and several among them had been released from illness in that way at that time. Illness is a form of prison, and being freed suddenly from prison is an unforgettable story not just for one but for everyone.

49

ON THE OTHER HAND, says Mr. Douglas to Dave as they are chopping firewood for Miss Moss, let's not get carried away with the whole noble animal thing. There's an incredible amount of murder and mayhem among the animals of the world of every species. No being can avoid eating other beings for sustenance. That's just how it is. It could be that we all eventually evolve into eating air and water and light and so progress past the eating each other segment of the history of the world, but I am not sure that it is coming anytime soon. Animals eat animals eat insects eat vegetative beings or prospective vegetative beings or seeds. That's just the way it is. Now there *are* some biologists and such who will say, well, there's no murder in the animal world other than with human beings, but that's silly talk if you ever met a weasel with blood rage in his eyes. And there are plenty of animals who will plan and carry out assassination. There's a lot more going on out there than we are aware of. I wouldn't be surprised if there are gangs of chickadees or whatever running huckleberry extortion rackets. You never know. Whatever you are sure of, don't be. That's probably the best way to approach natural history in general.

Yes, sir.

Don't call me sir, Dave. That's unnerving. I am not yet forty. When I am forty, we can go with the honorific. It'll fit better.

Yes, sir.

Dave . . .

Yes, Mr. Douglas.

You *could* call me by my first name, Dave. Guys who chop

wood together don't use titles. Plus I am calling you by your first name, right?

Miss Moss says no one calls you by your first name except people who don't know who you really are.

Miss Moss is a woman of remarkable perspicuity, but even she is not always right. Trust me.

Yes, sir.

Dave . . .

Mr. Douglas. Sir.

*

Two days before school ended in June, Dave was on his way from his last class to track practice when someone says Dave? And he turns, and there is a girl named Cadence who sits second row second seat in geometry. She is a big girl, and some kids call her fat, but Dave doesn't (a) see where size matters, particularly with girls; you either like them or you don't, you either find them attractive or you don't, you either want somehow to know more about them or you don't, it was all impossible to explain, and in his view it has a lot less to do with how tall or round or slight or busty or how their hair looks, or what clothes they wear, than with something about the way they carry themselves, their electric self, their relaxed lack of disguise, something like that; and (b) he had more than once stared at her in class thinking she was actually lovely but she was the sort of lovely that guys like Dave didn't think of asking out because (a) asking *any* girl out is terrifying, and you are safer not to ask anyone out—that way, you will never hear a girl say *let's be friends*, which is code for *I don't ever want to kiss you*, and (b) lovely high school girls are always already going out with college guys, which is why no one at school ever sees lovely girls with guys from school, and (c) even speaking in a friendly fashion to a lovely girl is to essentially ask to be beat up by the grim college boyfriend, who is probably a wrestler or a martial arts instructor, and of course he has a car and money, which, as Moon says, are the two first necessary tools in the girlfriend operation manual, not that *he* had ever read the manual.

But here is Cadence, who is lovely, actually talking to Dave, who is only Dave, her face eighteen inches from his face, her green eyes right in front of him like headlights, her voice direct and unadorned with no fake music in it, and there is no looming college boyfriend in sight that he can see, either, although he surreptitiously looks around, just in case.

She is saying that maybe they could go for a run together sometimes. She is saying that she tried out for the lacrosse team this past spring and didn't make it because she wasn't in good enough shape, although she has decent stick-handling skills. She is saying that she is going to really get after it this summer in the area of getting into great shape, and she knows she needs to run a lot, so maybe they could run together and he could teach her about pace and rhythm and the proper technique and things like that. She is saying she has already made some changes in her diet and that side of the getting-in-shape equation is taken care of, but she really wants to do the running part right, and she knows he is third on the team already as a freshman, and that's just so impressive, and she has always thought he was a stand-up guy from what she can tell in class, and she knows this is a little forward, but what does he think? About the running-together idea? Maybe just once to see how it goes?

Dave?

I would, I would like that, he says, and he can feel a flush rising right up his neck and colonizing his face from the bottom up so by the time he says the word *that,* the heat is rising up his forehead like someone is pouring a gallon of embarrassment into his brainpan.

That's great, she says. That's just *great*. You tell me where to be when, and I will be ready. Remember you're a real runner and I am not, so have mercy on me, okay?

You bet, says Dave. This'll be fun.

Tomorrow?

You bet. Tomorrow's great.

You'll text me? Where to be when?

You bet.

Okay, Coach.

You bet, says Dave, thinking, *you bet?* You bet *is the best you can say? Idiot.*

This is so generous of you, says Cadence. I was afraid to even ask.

You bet, says Dave, and Cadence says thanks and sort of vanishes from his vision scope, and he feels like a robot, and if he could actually kick himself, he would do so—right in the posterior parts, as his mother says—except just then he hears the coach's three sharp whistles, which means time for stretching, and he returns to planet earth and runs to practice, thinking, *you bet? you bet? what an idiot. But hey, a run with Cadence, with* Cadence! And then he realizes, of course, *duh, stupid,* he didn't get her number! *Idiot, fool, bonehead! But* Cadence! *Cadence asked* me *for a run!*

50

BUT A *RUN* IS NOT A DATE, says Moon in his kitchen. It's important to remember that. You want another sandwich? A date is something with food. If you are not eating together, it's not a date. Food is sexy. If there's no food, it's not really a date. It's an encounter, or a getting acquainted. You can go to the movies or walk through the woods or ride in horse sleighs or whatever they used to do in the old days with chaperones or whatever, but if your mouths don't have food in them, it's just a business meeting. Trust me. Turkey or ham?

And you would be an expert on dating . . . why, exactly?

I pay attention, says Moon. I know the code. I watch carefully. I am getting prepared.

For what? You're asking someone out?

Well, not right now. But eventually, sure.

When?

I was thinking in about two years. Spring semester, junior year. May.

Two *years*?

That gives me time to get everything in order, vet the candidates, get the campaign organization up and running. Grassroots organization is the key, I think.

Are you insane?

No, no. Sensible.

You're beyond insane.

Dave, why leave it all to chance? Why not approach the whole thing in a sensible fashion rather than just careen from girl to girl like a pinball?

You're . . . I don't know the word that means insane cubed.

Look, Dave, I have watched my parents. They met in a bar. Total accident. In fact, Dad was with a date, and Mom was with *her* date, and you can imagine how messed up their opening moves with each other were after *that* kind of beginning. They never thought about what kind of person they wanted to be with or anything. No preparation at *all*, and now they each live different lives and have troubles, although lately I have to say they sure seem to like each other more.

But every couple starts by accident, says Dave. You can't plan it unless you have an arranged marriage or whatever.

Mostly this whole romance thing is a bust, or a way to sell chocolate and clothes and dinners in restaurants, says Moon. I wouldn't be surprised if it was invented by corporations. All I am saying is that all the trouble could be reduced by a little coherent management of the initial process. It could all be a bit more sensibly organized. You could break the problem down into component parts and approach them one by one. For example, why wait until I develop a crush on someone in school? Why not choose candidates now and consider pros and cons carefully? Why does the whole process have to be like a car crash?

Dave wants to fall down laughing at the sheer inane Moonness of this speech, but something inside him is intrigued and he says, because it *is* a car crash, and you can't pretend it isn't. It's not a math problem. You like people a certain way or you don't. It's not like a software program, Moon.

There *are* arranged marriages, though, says Moon, and supposedly mostly they work. Here's your sandwich.

I bet they work, says Dave, munching away, because their cultures expects them to, and also I bet there are a lot of those that don't work, but the people in them don't tell anyone, including themselves, and also I bet a lot of the ones that work do so because the people in them are startled to discover that the spouse they were assigned is actually a gentle cool person. Maybe surprise is the reason arranged marriages work. Maybe being surprised continually is the key to the whole thing.

In which case I am right, says Moon. If we got *assigned* a partner, that would be a better system than the car-crash system. You'd *have* to be surprised if you got assigned a partner, and you had to figure them out without the whole car-crash part. Maybe there should be a national database and a Department of Assigned Spousal Units. Talk about your Homeland Security, man.

You are nuts to the ninth power, says Dave. Another sandwich? One more. Then let's go shoot hoop.

★

Martin approached her cautiously. He had seen and scented female marten other than his mother and his sister, of course, many times, but he had never been this close, and something about her was wholly different—alluring, frightening, tense.

He circled her carefully; she snarled and bared her teeth when he came too close, but she did not attack him or flee; she seemed cautiously interested, as well. A sparrow hawk hovered over them for an instant and then vanished; two small blue butterflies wandered past, twining their flight patterns; and a cricket chose that inopportune moment to launch right past Martin's nose—his final leap, for Martin snapped his jaws faster than the eye could register, and the cricket was a thing of the past.

Martin stepped closer, and again the female snarled, but Martin's fascination for once overrode his caution, and he came even closer. But this time, she attacked in a rush, and he leapt back, almost losing his balance for an instant in the currant bushes. For an instant he lost his temper and was about to attack in turn, but again that strange combination of interest and allure and tension arose in him, and he began to pace and circle her again. At one point she turned to leave and he cut her off so fast she was stunned, and she a marten, one of the fastest animals on earth. For a few moments, there in the currant bushes, high on the mountain among juniper and hemlock, not far from a ravine where icy slate-gray glacier melt thrashed and roiled among sand and boulders, the two animals stared at each other, absolutely absorbed in attentiveness in and with and through every sense—their noses questing for every hint and suggestion, their eyes registering every flick of fur and flow of muscle, their ears catching every tone and subtone, even their tongues forever registering the taste of those first few moments with each other. All the rest of her life, she would associate him with currants and juniper, and he would think of her whenever he crunched a cricket or tasted the sharp high tang of timberline.

51

EMMA JACKSON BEATON STANDS by the laundry services door and says I have something to tell you. Two things, actually. I know this sounds weird, but just stay with it. The first thing is that there is no Billy Beaton. I am not Mrs. Billy Beaton. I am not Mrs. Anybody. I am just Emma Jackson. I made him up and I bought myself a wedding ring because I didn't want anyone to ask me out anymore. All I had ever been was someone's girlfriend and I could never get clear of boyfriends long enough to figure out why I wasn't happy with any of them for very long. So many of them were really nice guys but I wasn't excited much and soon they would be unhappy also, because they could feel that, and we would break up, and another guy would ask me out immediately, and I could never come up for air, and I felt terrible about all these unhappy boyfriends. I felt awful about making everyone unhappy all the time. I got the tattoo on my neck for that reason too, to sort of scare people off, but it didn't work, and people kept asking me out. I didn't feel attractive, and I could never believe that they thought I was, so I always suspected they just wanted to get me in bed, and that made me feel worse, so I finally got a ring and invented Billy Beaton, and the ring was like a magic wand I could wave to create some space. That's when I came here to work in the lodge too. I wanted to get as far away from everything as I could. I wanted to be a new person. Being Emma Jackson was never much fun, but being Emma Jackson *Beaton* was always fun. People stopped asking me out because they saw my ring. All I had to do to stop making boyfriends unhappy was wave my ring and say the name Billy Beaton. All I had to do was go away once in a while to be with Mr. Billy Beaton. All I had to do was go somewhere sunny. Even *I* believed in Billy Beaton after a while. He was fun to tell stories about and the more stories I told about him the more he was a real guy. He protected me. I really came to like him. He was never mean or unkind, and he was never disappointed by me, not once. I never made him sad or didn't like him as much as he liked me, and he was always there to protect me when I needed him. All I had to do was say his name and there he was, sort of. But not anymore, not now. Telling you about Billy Beaton means I just killed him. I feel terrible about that. Poor Billy Beaton. But I *had* to tell you. I couldn't not tell you. You have been so kind and gentle, and I am so glad Maria is okay, and I love your family, and *you're* the reason why your family is so gentle and funny. I want to be like you somehow. I don't know how to do that, because the other thing I have to say now that I have told you about Billy Beaton is that I really, *really* want to be more than friends with the morning waitress. I want that more than anything I ever wanted with any boyfriend, even Billy Beaton, the best boyfriend I ever had. This is really scary for me, to feel that and to talk about it, but I can say it to you because you are kind and gentle. So those are the two things I had to say. I suppose you could say that I have been telling one lie for a long time about Billy, and I have been telling another lie to myself about how I feel about her, and I am sorry for telling lies. I didn't know what else to do. I'm sorry. I'm so sorry. I'm . . .

But Dave's mom has risen and opened her coat and wrapped each side of her big coat around Emma Jackson too so that she and Emma are both standing inside the coat, and Emma Jackson leans her face down on Dave's mom's shoulder into the thick soft wool that smells like woodsmoke and coffee and burnt toast and laundry soap, and Dave's mom brings up her left hand and very gently puts her hand on the bottom of Emma Jackson's neck, and they stand there for a really long time not saying anything at all. It might be that Emma Jackson is crying or weeping or sobbing into the coat, but the coat is so amazingly thick that it absorbs any and all sound like the sound had never been born. Whatever kind of wool that coat is made from is the kind of wool where sound goes to die, and that's a fact.

★

There was a boar raccoon over toward Dollar Lake who liked to tear one leg off frogs and toads and then leave the frogs and toads to live or die. He would catch them and tear one leg off and then poke at them to watch them wriggle in pain and then leave them there in the mud, not even eating them. Sometimes he would catch a frog and tear off one leg and impale the frog on one thorn like a shrike does but then impale the torn-off leg on the next thorn, so that the frog would be wriggling on one thorn while staring at his or her leg on the next thorn. Sometimes he would catch several toads and tear their legs off and leave the legs all in a row on a rock while the rest of the toads lived or died. He never ate any of the frogs or toads he caught and dismembered, and he did this for two years until one night when he came down to the lake looking for frogs and toads and something happened. He waded into the shallows to wash his hands. There was a full moon. The raccoon noted the brilliant path the moon cut across the water. The lake was as still and quiet as he could ever remember. He walked another step into the lake, feeling for crawdads, when dozens of frogs erupted from the lake and fell upon him like small, wet, green sticks. He snarled and flung them off and grabbed one and tore it in half, but dozens more erupted from the lake and covered him completely and then dozens and dozens more, too many to count. He fought savagely, but dozens and now hundreds of frogs leapt from the lake and fell upon him and crammed themselves into his mouth between his gnashing teeth—so many that he could not get purchase with his teeth, and he began to gag. Now dozens of toads leapt from the banks of the lake and fell upon the raccoon also, and if you were standing on the shore of the lake you couldn't see even a hair of the raccoon, because he was so covered with dense frogs and toads. More and more toads and frogs leapt from the lake and the bank, and their soggy weight forced the raccoon out farther and down into the lake. He fought desperately, ripping and shredding at the brown and green blanket of frogs and toads with his paws, but their weight was too much, and he could not breathe with the frogs cramming themselves down his throat. Their weight forced his head under the lake, and more dozens and hundreds of frogs now came up from below and hauled him down. The surviving toads struggled back to the surface and back to the shore, but the hundreds and hundreds of frogs, so many that if you were underwater and were watching this, you would see nothing but an amazing seething knot of frogs, stayed with the raccoon as he sank. There was a last struggle and writhing and then he died. For another few seconds, the ball of frogs fell slowly and silently and then it gently hit the lake bed just at the edge of a deeper pool. At the impact on the lake bed most of the frogs released and rose toward the surface. A few escaped the raccoon's open mouth as his body began to roll slowly into the deeper pool. As the last surviving frog of the ones who had crammed themselves headlong into the raccoon's mouth launched up and away from the body, an immense pike emerged endlessly from the dark and took the raccoon and turned with it back into the depths of the pool.

52

AN ABSOLUTELY BRILLIANT JUNE DAY, crisp and redolent, just enough breeze to charge the air but not so much to demand a jacket; and something about the light, the sheer delight and pleasure of it high above the valley and the city, high above highways and huge slow rivers, electrified somehow with the glint of glaciers and the ripple of snowmelt, aware of bears and elk and cougars and eagles, brought lips and fingers and noses and beaks and paws closer together; so that as Dave's mom and dad sat on the porch ostensibly having a family budget meeting at which Dave's dad was going to propose jocularly that they put Dave up for sale and pour the proceeds into Maria's education, they instead kissed gently, each surprised by the other, each startled and moved by the sudden quiet charge of the moment. And Dave and Cadence, running uphill along the river, more than occasionally jostled shoulders ostensibly at narrow points in the path but not always. And Martin and his companion were also sprinting through the canopy above Dave and Cadence for reasons they could not have articulated and occasionally they too jostled seemingly by accident but not. And there is Dickie Douglas the trapper reaching gently for Miss Moss to assist her down the steps of the store after they had tiptoed back toward warm after that cold moment on the mountain. And there is Louis nuzzling his newborn twin sons, the two of them with enormous noses and feet and otherwise seemingly built of thin brown sticks, so far. And there is the Unabled Lady with her hands cupped like a bowl in her lap and Maria's hands cupped inside her hands and the finch burbling while standing in the double bowl of their twenty fingers. And there is Emma Jackson and the morning waitress holding hands as they pick their way along a creek looking for first thimbleberries but also scouting for, as Emma says, secret huckleberry havens and refuges. And there is a bobcat mother cuffing her sons and a kestrel father ever so gently handing the large intestine of a vole to his daughters, and there is Mr. Shapiro scratching the dog who appeared last night on his porch and knocked on the door for admittance and curled up in Mr. Shapiro's favorite reading chair as if he had been doing so for years. And there is Cosmas on his knees smoothing out the soil over the graves of Mr. and Mrs. Robinson as he plants tomatoes and beans and garlic because he knows they would have wanted to be working and productive even after their expiration dates. And there are Moon's parents dancing very slowly in the kitchen as the milk for their coffee boils over quietly but they don't care, and Moon comes in and sees them and steps back abashed and embarrassed but then for some reason he could never explain he steps forward and wraps his arms as long as a story around both his parents, and there is a delicious, brief moment before Moon's mother says oh my god the milk!

★

Listen, this dog on Mr. Shapiro's reading chair—let's take a minute and listen to his story, because it's an amazing story, and you hardly ever hear a story like his. This dog was born in a breeding shed on a farm that didn't farm anything anymore except puppies. The biggest cutest ones were sold and the runty awkward ones were thrown out of a speeding pickup truck in the deep woods where they would live for a few days and then become meat. The dog on Mr. Shapiro's chair had been a runty awkward one who also annoyed the breeder by having the wrong father by accident. When the dog was two months old he was thrown out of a pickup truck as it sped through the deep woods. This was near a mountain the old people called Loowitlatkla, the fire mountain. In the old days, the mountain called Wy'east, where Dave and his family lived, was in love with the mountain called Loowitlatkla, where the puppy landed in a mat of ferns and lay unconscious for a few minutes, but their love affair didn't work out, although the two mountains still gaze at each other across a huge river and dream of what still might happen. The dog awoke after a while and limped to a creek and drank and took stock of the situation. Luckily this happened in late spring so there were lots of small newly born creatures to find and eat, and as his first summer wore on he learned how to lie in wait for rabbits along their runs and how to wait patiently for squirrels to venture to earth. Here and there, he found dead things that were good to eat—like once a buck deer gut-shot by a hunter and abandoned in a thicket—and then in the fall he discovered a small river with a healthy salmon run. By winter he was twice as large as he had been when he was thrown out the window of the truck.

The winter, though—that almost killed him. Several times he was so desperately hungry that he ate bark, and he lost a fang in a brief savage fight with a cougar over a deer carcass, and once when he fought a coyote for a rabbit he was slashed so badly across the chest that he nearly bled to death—although he killed and ate the coyote who slashed him, which may have been just the meat that saved his life.

By his next spring, he was gaunt but alive, and he enjoyed another three seasons of hunting, the only terrifying moment being an encounter with a bear. When the snow melted in May, he began to travel. At first he followed the remote logging road from which he had been thrown as a puppy, then he followed a county road that descended the mountain slowly, and then he found himself in a wide valley of farms and ranches and orchards and vineyards. Had he known he was less than a mile from the puppy mill where he was born, and had he the slightest urge for vengeance, he might have paused there and wreaked silent havoc, for the man who threw him from the truck kept chickens and ducks and geese. But his nature was peaceful, and on he went.

He did not know his destination, but he knew his direction, straight south. He traveled by night to avoid human beings and their cars; he ate as he went, catching squirrels and birds who had never encountered a dog so fast and deadly. He grazed here and there in fields and orchards, developing a lifelong taste for wine grapes and carrots. The one time he felt flummoxed, by a tremendous river far too wide to swim, he soon found a highway bridge and crossed so early in the morning, in such a dim mist, that the only driver who saw him assumed that he was a whopping large coyote, which he reported to his fellow workers at the airport, who didn't believe him, as usual. That crazy Henry Hutto, always making stuff up, they said, but for once they were wrong, and Henry Hutto was essentially right.

Still south, but now slowly up the gentle slopes of another mountain; through industrial wasteland and suburban villas, through schoolyards and playgrounds, across the campus of a community college, always up toward the glacial air he could smell like a new home; always avoiding trucks of any kind, always avoiding human beings, always moving at night and napping during the day, being seen only once, when he caught and ate an arrogant cat in a yard right in front of a four-year-old boy, who watched with interest; and finally to Mr. Shapiro's door at night and wearily into the reading chair. There are so many ways we could close this chapter of this dog's story for a moment before coming back to him later, but let's stop right here with Mr. Shapiro on the couch, staring at the dog, and the dog in Mr. Shapiro's reading chair, staring at Mr. Shapiro, the two of them puzzled and delighted at having met each other at last.

53

SILLY AND INEXPLICABLE THINGS HAPPENED on the mountain every day, every moment. How could they not? Such as a
garter snake unaccountably attacking a rabbit and not being able
to get more than a snatch of the rabbit's tail in her mouth and the
terrified rabbit taking off a high speed with the snake bouncing
along grim and addled behind the rabbit for a while until the
snake finally was dislodged and was cocky and sore for a week.
Or the day Cosmas was riding his bicycle headlong down a trail
faster than fast and he, no kidding, no exaggeration, *ran over a
wolverine dozing in the sun* even though biologists say with absolute conviction that there are no wolverines on the mountain,
but by gawd there is at least *one*, as Cosmas will tell you with
absolute assurance. Or the time a guy was fishing in the Salmon
River and snagged a trout by the dorsal fin and yanked up to
dislodge the fish but the fish stayed hooked and went flying past
the fisherman's face and landed in a jay's nest, and was *that* jay
ever surprised! Or the young osprey on the Zigzag who dove on
a glittering fish and ended up with an Elvis Presley action figure
complete with rhinestone Las Vegas cape. Or the bear who
smashed open a nest of honeybees who specialized in huckleberry nectar, and the bees conspired to retaliate not with indiscriminate attacks on the general corpus of the bear but with
ferocious concentrated attention in consecutive waves of twenty
on the bear's testicles, which led to a bear with nuts the size of
pumpkins. Or the time a troop of Girl Scouts were boating on
Lost Lake as part of a weekend retreat, and just at dusk an enormous white sturgeon leapt out of the lake and crashed back
with a crash so loud that the troop leader thought an air force

jet must have broken the sonic barrier overhead or somehow a whale had been planted in the lake unbeknownst to any and all. Or the Presbyterian clown convention that showed up one day at the lodge, every one of the clowns dressed head to toe in comic performance gear. Or the bow hunter who pursued a buck deer for hours and hours one day and finally got close enough to get a shot off, and suddenly a set of antlers came flying at him at such high speed that they impaled an inch deep in the tree he had providentially hidden behind. Or the time Miss Moss, walking along the river at dusk, found a tiny smoldering campfire, no bigger than a half dollar, with a tiny frying pan the size of a dime next to it. Or the day that Maria found the perfect bed of moist clay in the woods, just the right consistency for molding birds, and she sat down and made four sparrows, and then she went to wash her hands in the creek, and when she looked back, four sparrows were taking flight from exactly the spot where she had left the four clay sparrows, and there was no clay to be seen where a moment ago there had been four clay sparrows.

★

And deep mysteries too, things that no one could ever explain and in most cases no one ever knew or apprehended or discovered—a new species of snow flea mutating in a dark crevasse on Joel Palmer's glacier; a blue bear born to two black ones but alive only for a day; a place where trees and bushes and ferns decided to intertwine and make a small green cottage complete with walls and a roof and a door; a cave with the bones of a creature eight feet tall inside; a pencil lost by Joel Palmer at nine thousand feet of elevation on the south side of the mountain, long ago encased in ice and now some twenty feet beneath the surface, waiting to be found in the year 2109 by a young woman named Yvon, who would be amazed that the pencil never wore out no matter how much she used it, as if it had patiently stored up words for two centuries; and much else, more than we could account even if this book never ended and its pages and pulses went on forever, and it was the longest book in the history of the world. Even then, it couldn't catch more than scraps and shards of the uncountable stories on the mountain, of bird and beast, tree and thicket, fish and flea, biome and zygote. And this is not even to consider the ancient slow stories of the rocks and their long argument with the lava inside the mountain and the seething and roiling miles beneath the mountain, all the way to the innermost core of the sphere, which might be a story of metallic heat so intense that to perceive it would be your final act in this form; another mystery.

And of course there are many mountains on and *in* the mountain, says Mr. Douglas, sitting by the fire. It's not like there's *one* mountain. Wy'east is a vast amalgam of ideas of mountains, and stories of mountains, and lies about mountains, and misperceptions and illusions about mountains. People always want the mountain to *mean* something, to be some kind of holy destination or refuge for revelation, but it's just a temporary upthrust, and soon enough it will be mud in the valley, and what was the valley will be twelve thousand feet high, probably with shopping carts on the peak, frozen into the glaciers, if there still are glaciers then. That's the way of the world. What's up will be down and et cetera. Think of the mountain as a wave that will soon enough crash to earth and be subsumed; it's just a real *slow* wave, by our lights, being made of stone. Like the hearts of certain people I know who are making soup in the kitchen as we speak.

He said this with a smile, but Dave saw that the smile had a jolt of pain in it; but before he could say anything, Miss Moss swept out of the kitchen and around the counter, and before Mr. Douglas's smile got all the way to startle, she was extending her hand to him and saying, Richard, come with me, and he was up in a flash, and they were out the door hand in hand so quickly that her voice saying, *Dave, you are in charge for a couple hours, thanks*, had to wander back through the doorway to find Dave's ear. A moment later he stepped out on the porch to see if they were arguing or what, and there was neither sign nor hint of their presence, and just then, a cavalcade of white vans filled with students pulled up, ravenous and singing, and he ran back to the kitchen.

★

For a few moments, Miss Moss and Mr. Douglas walked hand in hand through the woods where the path was wide enough, but then when it narrowed, Miss Moss led the way calmly sure of the way, and Mr. Douglas followed closely, curious as to destination. As far as he could tell they were walking toward the river but he forbore to ask and she declined to tell. No words were offered or exchanged whatsoever on either part, and the only discussion extant was between a kingfisher, aggrieved, and a heron, dismissive. There was a hint of a suggestion of fertilization by one tree to another, but Miss Moss and Mr. Douglas passed by too quickly to catch gentle inquiry or ready reply. At the river Miss Moss did not pause but stepped into the tumbling thigh-deep icy water without removing her shoes or socks or pausing in any way to acknowledge or ameliorate the frigidity of the water, which not so long before had been snow. Upon reaching the middle of the river, she turned and gestured firmly and inarguably to Mr. Douglas, and he too strode forward into the river without the slightest hesitation, although he was wearing his best woods boots—the ones he worked on relentlessly and almost daily with mink oil to achieve not only complete and inviolate waterproofing but also a rare and astonishing suppleness for which he had often suggested to Miss Moss there ought to damn well be a word invented like *supplicity* or *pliabliss*.

As he arrived in the middle of the river, praying quietly that he would not unaware unbeknownst step into a deeper hole, thus allowing the river to reach his reproductive parts and cause him to quail and utter high-pitched noises of dismay, she took him by the hand and led him to a massive boulder, upon which they climbed together and on achievement of pinnacle stood facing each other, and she stepped forward and cupped her hands around his face and kissed him long and soft and tender and said, I love you, Richard David Douglas. I want to wake up in the morning and find you in the bed again like a large hairy miracle. I want to talk to you every night over dinner. I want to make love to you and argue with you and maybe have children. I want to be with you as long as we can before something or anything or death bears us away. I trust you, and I love you, and I don't want to lose you, because we don't have good words for how to be together. I am, here and now, on this rock in this river, asking you to be with me as deeply and truly and honestly and gently as you can possibly be, if you want to do that. I hate the word *marry*, but I love the idea hiding behind it. I hate the words *marriage* and *wedding* and *commitment* and *joint tax return*, but I want the thing under those words, and I want that thing with you, Richard David Douglas, and with no one else. So I won't say *marry*, but I ask you here and now if you want that thing too. With me.

Yes, he said, as clearly and crisply as if no one had ever said that word before, and it emerged fresh and amazed from his mouth like a new child being born. Yup. Yep. Sí. Oui. Hai.

Richard?

Haan. Ndiyo. Baleh. Naam.

Dickie, are you okay?

Ayo. Da. Evet. I am trying to say yes in every language there is to cover all possible bases and eventualities. I am going to say yes so many times and in so many ways there will never be a question henceforth about it. Bai. Kyllä. Avunu.

Avunu?

That's from India, I think. Or Japan? No, Japanese is hai!

Richard, how do you know all this?

I have been studying to say yes for two years. In case the chance ever came up I wanted to be ready.

You are the strangest person I ever met.

Merci. Danke. Grazie. Arigatō.

I love you more than I can say. More than I understand.

Yes.

We'll have to work out a lot of things.

Yes.

I am a puzzle and a conundrum and a thunderstorm.

Avunu. Hai! That is *so* true. That is so . . .

But you are no picnic, either. You are a wilderness. You have a head like a rock.

Ginny, he says, dropping all his masks so suddenly so thoroughly it's a wonder they didn't bounce off the boulder and plop into the river, Ginny, I want to see and hear you deeper than anyone else ever does, ever. I want to watch you grow and ache and deal with stuff and laugh and cry and nurse your sons and get old and lose your temper and laugh so hard you pee. Avunu, yes, I do. I say yes. Hai! Let's go for it. Let's just promise to try like hell and work out the details and problems as we go. You want to try like hell, too, Virginia Mary Moss?

Yes, she says, and she starts to cry. Hai!

Hai! says Mr. Douglas. My feet are freezing. Let's go sit by the fire and kiss for the rest of the day. Dave can take care of the store. Nice kid. Hai!

54

ON ANY ONE DAY ON WY'EAST, one million living beings
lose their lives. They die, are killed, are shredded, fade out, are
gulped, expire, decease, pass from this plane, cease to function,
demise, commence decomposition, transition to the next stage,
initiate cellular breakdown. This is the way it is. Some live a
day, and some live a thousand years. Some are smaller than this
comma, and some are taller than you can measure with your eye.
Some are serene and eat sunlight and rain and do not slay their
neighbors and do not battle for supremacy and sex and speak a
patient green language. Others are vigorous and furious and
muscular and speak the languages of blood and bone. This is the
way it is. They are all brothers and sisters in time and light and
water and weather. They change, they morph, they evolve, they
go extinct, they sink back into the earth from which we all came
and shall return. This is the way it is. It may be that every death is
mourned, though most go unremarked, and every day's million
deaths causes a million other hearts to sag. Who is to say that is not
the way it is?

And here is one death today: the fox who ate Martin's
brother, the fox who waited in the darkness with only her eyes
flickering, the fox with the canter recognizable by trappers, the
so-called Rhododendron Fox, the fox called ghost and dream
and fiction by men who heard the stories but never saw her
once—that fox is hunting at dusk and picks up the scent of marten. A marten is a meal, and the trail smells like two marten,
which would be a meal sufficient and then some for her new kits
also. She follows the two marten. As far as she can tell from the
scent trails, one marten is a female in estrus, and the other a male

with prospects. She suspects that the female in estrus is scouting for dens and burrows in which to eventually give birth. She ponders the implications of this for a moment; marten kits are delicious bits of meat and much easier to catch than adult marten, who tend to fight savagely when attacked. Yet marten kits are not born until late winter or early spring, and the fox is hungry right now, and her new kits are hungry right now, so she follows the two adult marten into the deepening dusk.

★

A gray fox can climb trees and run along branches and leap from branch to branch, much as a marten does. The gray fox occasionally dens in trees, as marten do. A gray fox is lightning fast in bursts, as a marten is. The gray fox hunts night and day, altering patterns depending on season and available crops, much as marten do. But a gray fox is longer and taller and heavier than a marten—a large marten might weigh three pounds, where a large gray fox might weigh twenty pounds—and thus the gray fox, given the chance, catches and eats the marten, despite the marten's liquid speed and incredibly quick reflexes. The percentages are not with the marten, you might say. The marten may elude the chase; the fox may miss his or her strike; the marten may lead the pursuing fox into a situation more dangerous to the fox, like a hunter or a hound or a highway; but in general, a fox intent on catching and eating a marten or two has an excellent chance of doing so and history on its side.

But not this time.

★

As dusk gave way infinitesimally to dark, the two marten made their way first through a vast clear-cut and then briefly along a logging road and then down a sharp slope and through what a human observer might call a small foul city of incredible garbage—the detritus of an entire civilization, splayed and dumped and tossed and moldering in a little dell into which everything thrown down the slope from the road ended up smashed together in a pile fully twenty feet high adamant with stench and stink. There were hundreds of old tires in every size from child's wagon to bulldozer. There were hundreds of smashed jars and bottles that had once contained beer, whiskey, mayonnaise, rum, jelly, jam, oil, petroleum jelly, cream, gin, soda, and pretty much any other substance you can imagine. There was an entire mobile home in pieces. There were bits and parts of cars and trucks and bicycles. There were televisions dating back more than seventy years. There were parts of cows and pigs and dogs and cats and birds and goats and llamas. There were guns and knives and half an assault rifle. There were diapers and records and compact discs and cassette tapes and false fingernails and two bathtubs. There were computers and computer printers and cords and coils and hammers and spatulas and bullet casings and mattresses and do we need to go on? Why would beings throw garbage into the homes of other beings so that the animals who lived there must leave, and the plants who live there are choked to death by weight and darkness and chemicals, and the whole foul mess will be there for a thousand years like a lurid sin until the blessed day when a shiver in the earth from Wy'east grinding its teeth drops the whole awful mound into a sudden crevice, never to be seen again?

★

The female marten had seemed intent on a certain target or idea as she and Martin came down through the clear-cut and through the garbage pit, and soon it was evident to Martin what it was she sought—a tremendous fir tree standing nearly in the middle of a creek, approachable only by deft footwork along a ridge of boulders leading to it like a road of rocky teeth. Halfway up the ancient tree was a spacious hollow in which Martin thought he could smell the faintest scent of bees. But whatever residents the hole had housed were long gone, and Martin understood that his companion was choosing this as her home—the den in which she would give birth to their kits. For a while, she allowed him to explore the space and investigate the infinitesimal scents of other former tenants; he thought he could smell red squirrels and perhaps also an owl, although that scent was so very faint that it might be only the record of a one-time visit, perhaps to eat the squirrels.

Suddenly, according to some mysterious decision in her part, she drove him out, and he backed hurriedly out of the hollow and down the tree to the boulders. A minute later, she joined him, and they leapt back toward the forest. Both were hungry, and Martin was sure he had seen not one but two birds' nests near the garbage pit. They had also passed near a huckleberry thicket, and no marten in summer passes up huckleberries, given the chance.

One nest was empty, though, and the other contained nothing but broken eggshells, so Martin led his companion toward the berry bushes; but just as they crossed a small clearing crowded with ferns, the fox struck.

★

The ambush is an ancient and effective technique, because it entails surprise, which means unpreparedness, which usually means death or injury leading unto death. In almost all cases of violent combat, across all species, he or she who sustains the initial injury loses the battle, being drained of energy and force, not to mention essential liquids. Yet evolution or time or a fitfully merciful creator or some unimaginable referee interested in competitive balance and the persistence of infinitesimal chance also arms all beings with a quiver of intuition or extrasensory perception or awareness beyond the range of understanding—we do not have good words for this, but it is indeed true, as you well know, because you have experienced it, and have been startled and intrigued by it too: a premonition of impending trouble, the sure knowledge that someone is looking at you though you cannot see the stare, the certainty that there is someone behind you though no sign or signal was given.

And Martin had this gift in spades, partly because he had made his way alone in the world from a very young age and had survived in part by cultivating and trusting this mysterious gift—more times than he could count, he had leapt away from disaster at the exact right moment or struck a killing blow in the dark without clearly seeing his prey. He had also been given something like a gift of geometric calculation and was already, not even two years old, a master at gauging a chipmunk's desperate direction, a squirrel's final leap, the dart of a fish in a pool. And as we already know, he was also given gifts of unusual size and . . . what word should we use here? Courage, bravery, fearlessness, defiance—don't they seem a little too *human* as labels to describe Martin's unusual attitude? If we spoke marten, as it were, perhaps we would know the word for what drove Martin in the next few minutes, but without that word, we will have to just account what happened.

★

The fox, knowing that she would have but an instant's advantage, struck at the leading marten, thinking that a killing blow there would allow her to spin and attack the second before the second could flee; it was none of her concern which was first on the trail, the male or female—although given a choice, she would kill the male, who offered more meat.

But the first on the path was Martin, and even before the fox launched herself from her crouch in the ferns, he felt . . . something. Did he hear the infinitesimal quiver of her muscles as she tensed?

Did he smell an iota of her slaver in the dark? Had he somehow screwed his senses to an extraordinary pitch, given the darkness and the dense vegetation crowding the trail?

So Martin was ready to dodge, before the dodge that saved his life and that of his companion; but the fox, slashing savagely as it shot past, sliced a long deep wound in Martin's hip. The fox spun and came for Martin again, but to her shock, this first marten, the large one, was leaping directly at *her*, and before she could recover, she had been bitten deeply on her snout and slashed so deeply in her right eye that she could not see. She staggered for an instant, and then, incredibly, was attacked again, this time from two directions—the large marten almost under her, clamping its jaws in her throat, and the smaller one tearing and shredding at her right leg, on her blind side.

For the first time in her life the fox was terrified. She had been fearful before, she had been in fights before, she had been attacked before, but never by two animals at once, and *never* by marten. In her experience, marten fled instantly into the canopy when pursued. Instead her attack had missed, she had lost an eye, she was in screaming pain, and she was now being throttled by one marten and bitten by another. She clawed desperately at the one at her throat and kicked furiously at the one behind, but she could not get her killing jaws into play. Suddenly, her rage gave way to a despairing urge to get away, to shake off these savage little creatures and sprint away and huddle in her den and lick her wounds; but for all she clawed at them, they kept their jaws locked in her, and now her breathing staggered and slowed; Martin ground his jaws deeper and deeper into her throat with a grim fury that only his own death would have quelled; she choked and gagged, and a moment later she died. The marten at her throat, sensing her death, drove deeper and tore her trachea in half before releasing his grip.

For a moment now, the little clearing was silent. The two marten lay exhausted and bleeding; some of the bruised and crushed ferns slowly tried to stand again. Nighthawks flew past, wondering at the three spent bodies below. A beetle detoured around the massive thicket of the fox's tail. For a moment, not a sound, as if the world held its breath; and then Martin staggered upright and began to lick his companion's wounds. She did the same for him a moment later, and then, wearily, hungrily, they tore the fox open and ate their fill.

55

WHEN DAVE ARRIVED at the store for work he found a note on the door that made him smile. The last time Miss Moss set foot outside the boundaries of the store during hours of operation was known only to the owls, who knew everything, as Dave's mom said.

Just as he turned the soup pot back on to simmer, as instructed, Emma Jackson Beaton came in and sat at the counter and asked for soup, and as soon as it was simmering, Dave served her a bowl.

What is this exactly? This is terrific.

I think it's Miss Moss's Everything Soup.

This happens every Wednesday? I'll be back for this. There are things in here I never saw before. I think there's okra, and I am pretty sure I saw a persimmon. Plus if I am not mistaken there's antelope in there. This is incredible. Also there's a chess piece. And a turtle.

Really?

No. Great soup, though.

I'll tell Miss Moss.

Dave, have I ever told you how much I admire your mom?

No, but I see how you get along. You're always laughing. Not everyone gets along like that with people they work with.

Your mom is a very wise being.

I know.

Do you? Many teenagers don't see their parents for who they really are at all. I sure didn't. I was a jerk to my parents.

Really?

Really really. I left home at seventeen mostly because I knew I was being a jerk but couldn't figure out how to stop. Are you a jerk to your parents?

Pardon?

Are you?

No. Yes. Well, I don't think so. Well, I was for a while these past few months. I mean, I really respect them and how hard they work, but they treat me like a kid, and I am a man. Almost. Partly.

At fifteen?

Fifteen and a half.

Is there more of this soup? I think I tasted rutabaga or maybe bear.

Dave gets her another bowl, and she closes her eyes and inhales redolent tendrils of steam.

What do you want to do when you graduate high school, Dave?

I don't know.

College?

My folks want that.

Job?

Maria wants me to be a mapmaker so we can start a map company. She loves maps.

What do *you* want?

I don't really know. I like to run. I like living here. Maybe coach and teach, I guess. Although I wouldn't be much of a teacher. I was a jerk to my teachers this spring, I think. I feel bad about it now. I was rude to Mr. Shapiro.

Why?

Not sure. I just felt . . . weird.

Weird like?

Like everybody wanted me to be something I didn't know *I* wanted to be. You know what I mean?

Yup. Although for me, it was the other way around—I didn't know I wanted to be something I didn't know I already was.

Pause.

What? says Dave.

Emma laughs.

Dave, listen, she says. There is no Billy Beaton. There never was. I invented Billy Beaton so I could act married because I was tired of guys asking me out. I like guys, but I think I love a person who happens not to be a guy. It took me a long time to get to there. It takes a long time for people to figure out how to make joy soup, you know what I mean?

I think so.

Ah, what do I know? I just think you are luckier than you know, maybe. Your mom is a very wise woman, and your dad is a kind man, the best kind. You already know your sister is the coolest person ever.

She's decided to be governor, you know. Dad wants her to try for president, but she says she doesn't want to leave the mountain, that she can be governor from here.

I don't think I was ever so scared as when she was lost.

Me too, says Dave. Me too.

For a moment they are both caught in the blizzard again, terrified, and then Dave says she still won't talk about that night.

She says she knew she would be found and that she knew Edwin would know where to look. She says we should remember that while Mr. Douglas gets credit for the save, it was Edwin who carried him to the right place. She says Edwin is sort of a genius, and he just doesn't say anything about it, because he's not a boaster. She says Edwin has a minor ego and doesn't need the strokes. She says Mr. Douglas is right about Edwin not liking to be wet and there's an amazing story why that's so. She says Edwin loves honey because he long ago did something for the honeybees in the city, and now they look out for him and deliver honey if necessary. She says there are about a thousand more stories like that about Edwin, and someday she will write them down if he will allow it.

I'd read *that* book, says Emma, and just as she pronounces the *k* in *book*, the doorbell jangles, and Moon comes in, and Emma buys him a bowl of soup just because.

★

Dave's mom had a name. Sure she did. She had lots of them. She'd been given one at birth by her mother, overruling the one her father wanted to give her (Dandelion!, complete with the exclamation point), and she'd been given her dad's surname, as was customary in the culture into which she had been born. And then she was given the middle name of an aunt to whom her parents owed a thousand dollars for their mortgage deposit; the name paid the debt. Then she got another name when she was thirteen, as was customary in the religion into which she had been born, and then she took another name when she was nineteen, as the result of an experience with drugs, and then she took a name made up of numerals for a while, as an act of protest against the dehumanizing economic system into which she had been born. Then she was briefly married to a man whose surname she took as her own, as was customary in the culture to which she had been born, but when that man turned out to be a liar and a thief and a stain and a blot on the world, she handed him back his name on the day she concluded their six months of marriage— actually handing it back to him one morning on a piece of paper between two slices of buttered toast, a divorce sandwich—and then again assumed her father's surname as her own, partly for the peace and safety of being again huddled beneath the long name she had as a child. But when she met Dave's dad and married him, she did not then accept his surname as her own, as was customary in the society into which she had been born, but adopted her mother's first name as her new surname, reasoning that she had long worn her father's name and had once worn another man's name, and now she would wear her mother's name as a form of reverence and respect—a decision to which Dave's dad, as he said to Dave with a smile, could only assent, debate not being part of the program, and your mom's decision about her names being her own decision, of course, names being personal things and really only labels and bits of sound when you think about it. And besides, I adore *her* mother, your grandmother, a woman of remarkable grace, so much so that I think *I* will adopt her name too as a surname, one of these days, if she will let me. I think you have to fill out a form or something and then get it stamped by a butterfly and submit it to your grandmother for review. Something like that.

★

Here's a question for you: why do we use the word *mate* when we talk about nonhuman animals achieving a physical confluence of bodies and spirits? Why do we not use the word *mate* with human animals? We use all sorts of *other* words for human animals when we describe moments and relationships like this, but none of them have the flat ostensibly neutral rudeness of *mate*. It's inherently inaccurate simply by the limit of its nuance. It's not a big enough word. It doesn't look into the corners and levels and languages and confusions and epiphanies and subtleties not just of the physical moment of confluence but the layered dance that ideally leads to and enhances the moments of shiver and serenity. So why do we force such a poor word on animals? Did you think that human animals were the only animals who seethed and boiled and sagged and sang with feelings as complex and staggering as the thousand kinds of wind? Did you think we were the only animals whose bodies sometimes wrapped and coiled and curled and slid and slipped and wrestled and grappled as the brains and hearts inside those bodies swirled in eight directions at once, and then after it all, they both subsided, came to rest, achieved equilibrium, tired and thrilled, and everything afterwards was different? For that is the case for all animals, including, early one morning in late July, Martin and his companion; and inside her, the seeds for two kits are now set in place, side by side, to wait patiently through the winter and be born in spring, long after the last page of this story.

56

SPEAKING OF COMING TO REST, speaking of subsiding and equilibrium, nowhere in this book have we come to a point of utter stillness, when all beings are at rest. It's been action action action all the way, go go go, walking and running and sprinting and riding bicycles and cars and a large horse, fights and arguments, a woman with no legs hauling herself sobbing through the mud to help a friend, a small girl huddled inside a tree listening to a howling snowstorm. But let us here pause and rest. Let us see beings at rest. Let us choose a moment when the labors of the night are done and the labors of the day not yet launched. Let us range about the hamlet and the woods and the river and the west side of the mountain and visit each being with reverence and affection. We have been with them a long time in this book, and we have come to know and appreciate them a little, at least, and let us go together and look at them sleeping and wish them well and savor their slow, regular breathing and pray for them by our silent witness.

So here is Dave, sleeping on his right side, facing the slim moon, snoring gently. Here is Maria, asleep in the bear den, maps pinned on every surface, even her blanket a map of The Journey of Joel Palmer on the Glacier, woven by her mother. Here is the finch, sleeping in a nest of old shoestrings Maria made for her in the corner of the windowsill so the finch could see her natural element. Here is Martin, asleep in his den in the cottonwood tree, and there is his companion, asleep in her tremendous fir tree in the middle of a creek, her den smelling ever so faintly of honey. Here is Mr. Shapiro asleep on his couch, sitting up, the only position in which he can sleep because of his back, and there is the dog asleep on the reading chair, and neither of them remembered to turn out the reading light. Here is Dave's mother asleep curled against Dave's father like a vine against a fence, both of them dreaming of Maria. Here is Louis asleep in a bed of ferns while near him sleep his wives and children, one of his sons sleeping on his back with his legs folded against his chest like the biggest hairy praying mantis ever. Here is Emma Jackson asleep on her left side, facing the slim moon, and the morning waitress on her right side, facing the huge poster of a surfer that she and everyone else always assumed was Mr. Billy Beaton, though it is not. Here is Martin's mother, asleep in her new maternal den in a cave in a ravine with her three new kits; and here is her daughter, Martin's sister, asleep in her own first den, a former red squirrel nest high in a fir tree that Joel Palmer himself had once leaned against for a moment to smoke a meditative pipe and eat gobbets of dried salmon. And here are Mr. and Mrs. Robinson together in their grave, garlic and tomato and bean plants rising from the soil above them. And here is Mr. Douglas asleep in his cabin in the last days he is an unmarried man sleeping alone, wearing nothing but his threadbare wool socks under a blanket made from all the old beach towels his mother had ever given him as a child in their shack by the sea. And bobcats and coyotes and trout and herons and snakes and beetles and turtles and toads asleep, and the pike that ate the raccoon asleep, and the armies of the frogs asleep. Here is Cosmas asleep outdoors on a burlap sack on the very pillar of stone high on the mountain from which Martin saw the bear slowly climb to her ending in the approaching shadow. Here is Miss Moss asleep in her bed with her spectacles placed carefully on a table exactly eleven inches away so that in the morning her right hand can reach for them without her mind being involved quite yet. Here is Edwin asleep standing up in his shed, and in his dream he is speaking the language of bees, and they are laughing in their strange electric way, because he is telling jokes about human beings and their odd and confusing adventures bumbling through the delicate and impatient world. Here are Moon's parents asleep in their bed, so big it has an area code, as Moon says; but their feet are touching. Here is Moon asleep at his desk, the right side of his face pressed against a page about Bill Walton in a book about the greatest basketball players ever, pressed so firmly against the page that in the morning, ever so faintly, if you looked very carefully, you would see Bill Walton's headband on Moon's cheekbone. Here is Dave's running coach, asleep, and Moon's basketball coach, asleep, and falcons and snails and swans asleep, and everyone in the lodge asleep, and trees and bushes and sedges and asters and ferns asleep, and fleas and midges and mosquitoes asleep, and even all the little lakes around the mountain for an instant are still as glass, unrippled, shining, frozen without ice. For an instant, all over the west slope of the mountain, for a sliver in the river of time, every single thing animate and inanimate is utterly still . . . except the Zig-zag River, which never sleeps and is always a story that wants to be heard by the sea.

★

At the end of July, Moon went down to the city for two weeks to a basketball camp at a college, and although Dave ran every morning with Cadence, worked at Miss Moss's store every afternoon, and hung out with Maria almost every evening, he found to his surprise that he really missed Moon. This was a startling state of affairs. They had been friends for years, but in the way of guys had never put it in words; they just were friends, arguing and laughing and banging shoulders on the basketball court and diving into lakes and eating.

Mostly it seems to me we eat, if you have to say what it is that we do when we do stuff, said Moon when he came back from camp in August. I mean, we eat, and then we do something or think about going to do something, and then we eat, and then we think about maybe getting something to eat. Are girls like this? What does Cadence do?

Not eat, says Dave. She says she's fat, and all she eats is avocados. Me personally I think her skin is a little green lately, but I am not going to tell her that.

You guys make out yet?

What?

You know what I mean. Did you go further?

Moon.

Well?

No.

No, what? No, you didn't go further, or no, you didn't even make out yet?

Well, no, that I don't want to talk about this, and no to the other questions also.

You didn't even make out?

No.

Why not?

She's not my girlfriend.

Yet.

We just go for runs, and we talk, and she eats avocados, Moon. That's all.

Don't you want to go further?

Yes.

Well?

Well, yes, I want to go further, but I am not sure with Cadence.

Who cares with who?

What?

You heard me.

Actually, I think that should be *whom* there. Who cares with *whom*?

You heard me, Dave.

But that's crazy, Moon. You are actually saying to me you don't care who you do stuff with—you just want to do stuff? Who it is doesn't matter? You're actually saying this to me?

Well . . . yes.

That's crazy.

Why is that crazy? Are you going to marry the first person you do stuff with? Or wait to do stuff until you are sure enough about someone to marry? That could be forever.

I don't know. I haven't worked it all out. I want to do stuff, you bet I do, but I like Cadence, and just doing stuff with her unless I really like her and she really likes me . . . that just seems cold. It's more complicated than just doing stuff.

Is it?

To me it is, I guess, says Dave. I figure I'll just wait and it'll figure itself out. Meanwhile I just like running with Cadence and talking, although I am not much for avocados. Also let me point out that the guy lecturing me about being cool with just doing stuff with people who you don't even care about who they are has never done stuff or even had a date.

Yet, says Moon. Actually I am going to have dates starting the second week of school. I am going to ask girls out starting in September. I'm moving the program up a year from the original plan. I feel that I am ready. One date a week. If no one says yes in September, I'll go through October. That will be six total asks, and I am figuring I'll hear yes twice, so I will have a choice. I'll test drive them in November, and the winner will be Miss December, and right around Christmas, we will do stuff. Girls get gooey at Christmas. Things change after you do stuff, so if she doesn't like me anymore after that, I'll take winter break to regroup and then start again second week of school in January. You have to have a plan. It's time to launch the plan.

You're crazy.

Am I? I'll be doing stuff by Christmas, while you will be running through the snow with a green person. Who's crazy, you or me?

You, says Dave, and for the first time ever he is angry with Moon, really angry, so angry that he has a sour taste in his mouth. Because, he says, after you do stuff with someone you don't even like, if you get that far, and she gets it that you don't even like her and all you wanted was to do stuff, she'll be so hurt even *you* will feel like shit. Mark my words. I know you, man. This is not you. This is some weird cocky you, and it stinks. Did you go to basketball camp or idiot camp?

Don't be such a geek, Dave. This isn't like when our parents were kids and had to get permission slips to make out. Things have changed.

Have they? Girls don't feel bad anymore when guys are jerks? Is that so?

Man, what's with you? You spend too much time with Cadence while I was gone? You look a little green too, come to think of it.

I'm out. See you.

Dave, come on. No need to get mad. Let's go eat.

Maybe this is a goof, says Dave. In which case I am a prize idiot and you got me. But even if it's a goof, it's slimy. There's guys who do think like this, right? Guys who are going to ask my sister out on a date just so they can do stuff? Guys who don't care what kind of person she is at all? Nine years from now Maria is the girl who gets asked out in September so she can be Miss December? I'm out. Call me when you want to play ball.

Dave . . .

But indeed, Dave is out, and Moon watches him run smoothly across the vast lawn of the vast house, and he feels like an ass. He makes a sandwich and then for no reason does the laundry and even folds the sheets and towels, for no reason.

57

IT IS SAID AND WRITTEN and reported that marten in North America are generally solitary except for the mating season in spring and that they prefer to hunt alone and that sometimes fights and battles will erupt when marten encounter each other at the edges of their vast territories (as big as six square miles, often bounded by rivers or mountain ranges or other topographic features, like clear-cuts and lakes and scarps and marshes) and that

they will range much farther afield than you might think an animal weighing three pounds would like to go, but all these remarks, of course, are data, bits of news, akin to a few branches ostensibly representing a forest. They are true facts, as far as they go; yes, many marten are solitary except when impelled by dreams of congress, and yes, many marten establish and defend startlingly large territories against competitors for the food and congress therein, and yes, many marten will range ten miles in a night and thirty miles in a week when young and seeking a territory of their own. But the very men and women who say and write and report these facts are the first to admit that there is so very much more we do not know about the lives and habits and personalities and characters and lore and idiosyncrasies and cultures of marten. So Martin's continued interest in and affection for his companion, long after the seeds of their kits were planted and Martin—according to our science—should be ranging afield alone, was unusual by our dim lights and not at all unusual by his or hers. His habit of bringing her voles and mice and squirrels, without even kits yet to explain his paternal urge, was just what he did, two or three times a week. Their napping together, without an explanatory urge to congress, was their mutual occasional pleasure, as was his now nearly daily habit of racing through the canopy above Dave as the boy lengthened his daily workouts to prepare for cross-country practice and the opening of the school year. Why a marten, untamed and untamable, in his second year of life, at nearly his full growth and grace and musculature, should choose early in the morning to rise from his den and make his way through the forest to a certain tree by a river and there wait quietly until below him a young man, noticeably taller since spring if not an ounce heavier, should arrive and stretch and tighten the laces of his running shoes and look up to find the marten and nod in acknowledgment of their—friendship? companionship? arrangement? respect?—is a mystery not even a book devoted to the intricate mysteries of some creatures on a particular mountain can explain. And yet the marten does this every morning, and the young man does this every morning, and their two or three seconds of absorbed acknowledgment is something gentle and wild and mysterious and beyond any words we can find in our dictionaries and translation software. They attend, they see, they witness. The young man nods, he inclines his head, an ancient human-animal gesture of respect and peace and even reverence. The marten stares, he twitches an ear, he shifts his grip on the branch. The young man sets his watch, and then away they go, not sprinting but cruising easily to start, although more than occasionally they will both sprint the last quarter of a mile, the marten winning each and every time. On days beginning with the letters *T* or *S,* they run upriver first and finish downhill; on the other days, they run with the river and then run toward the ice to finish. They run every day. The young man thinks he should also now be running every afternoon, but his sister has persuaded him, using charts and graphs, that he is better served athletically by spending the afternoons with her, usually swimming in a lake, although here and there they have ridden bicycles along the intricate trails Cosmas has made in the power line cuts—and even once, for a hilarious and frightening moment, raced Cosmas along the trail by the river, but Cosmas went so incredibly fast that Dave pulled up breathless at a little clearing—coincidentally the very one where he had first seen marten after he bought his traps at Miss Moss's store. Maria would long remember the afternoon they raced Cosmas, for they saw a tremendous salmon holding in a pool in the river, a fish bigger than any she had seen in her life, and never was there a fish so gleaming and brilliant and green and red and speckled and massive and akin to a long intent muscle in the water. It hung there in the pool effortlessly, facing into the current with only the occasional twitch of its tail to indicate that it was alive, and for the longest time, Maria and her brother hung over the lip of the pool, staring. They did not think of trying to catch the fish or of doing anything but staring in awe, and finally, for no reason they could tell, it moved gently forward a few inches, and then, as smooth and fast as the river itself, vanished upriver. Though the water upriver from the pool was no more than two feet deep, neither Dave nor Maria saw the slightest ripple or roil, not the slightest swirl or boil. They rode home silently, smiling.

★

Miss Moss and Mr. Douglas, after consulting with Maria, set the date for the Unwedding Ceremony as October 4, Joel Palmer's birthday, and Maria's dad said yes, she could take her magic amazing lifesaver sneakers off the mantel and wear them to the Ceremony if she chose, as she would be in the key position of Lordess of the Rings.

Yes, there would be rings exchanged, even though this was not a Wedding, a Marriage, or a Religious or Civic Event in any way shape or form, said Miss Moss. No civic or religious entity or organization has the slightest role or authority in this matter, which is a private matter.

More like a public private matter, said Mr. Douglas, grinning. A communal personal matter, you might say. With pie. And beer.

After a good deal of discussion, Miss Moss and Mr. Douglas decided not to have the ceremony in the store—despite how cool it would be to have a fireplace and a kitchen available—or in the former state highway repair building, because even a free-form church shared by every faith tradition conceivable was too much of a Church for Miss Moss, although Mr. Douglas voted for the church for a while on the theory that it would provide easy access for Edwin and they could even invite Frank the tractor, which would be fun; imagine a tractor ever so slightly in his cups!

Emma Jackson and the morning waitress and most of the rest of the staff from the lodge offered to provide food and drink and setup and teardown wherever the Ceremony was held; the master of the lodge, a lean old cheerful man with a glass eye, offered the lodge's capacious back deck for the Ceremony with its glorious view of the snowy hunched shoulder of the mountain, but Miss Moss declined, politely, and Mr. Douglas explained about the public private nature of the Ceremony—to which, of course, the lodge master was invited, as he and Mr. Douglas had fished together many times, mostly for steelhead.

Dave's dad and the cross-country and basketball coaches offered to erect tents or temporary wooden platforms or stages as directed by the happy couple if necessary. Mr. Shapiro offered to provide cases of the very best wines and beers. Moon's parents offered to pay any and all costs for the Ceremony, including a honeymoon, if planned; Mr. Douglas again explained about the nature of the Ceremony, which had no proviso for a honeymoon, as it was not a Wedding, a Marriage, or a Religious or Civic Event in any way shape or form.

It's a not-wedding, I guess you could say, said Mr. Douglas. An unwedding. It's a plighting of troth without the usual frippery and drapery, as Ginny says. The county and the state are not involved, the federal government of these United States is not involved, no ostensible religious authority is involved, there are no tax breaks, there are no forms or permits or licenses, there will be no banns announced or notes in the newspaper, there will be no tweets or posts or alerts or photographs or recordings, there will be no hired band or caterer or event manager, and all beings of every shape and form are invited. Last I looked, there was a horse and a finch coming, and Mr. Shapiro's dog, which looks like a coyote on steroids. I am very grateful for the generosity of your offer, but what we would prefer is just you all there as our guests.

Where is there? asked Moon's father. And when? I am off to Swaziland, and I believe my wife is headed to Tasmania.

The when is October 4, and the where is To Be Determined, said Mr. Douglas. Miss Moss is in charge of where, and some observers think that she may well announce the where on the morning of October 4. *Some* observers think this is nuts, but *some* observers are not in charge of the Ceremony. *Some* observers think the Ceremony ought to be held on the rock in the river where the reason for the Ceremony was hatched, but this idea did not get past initial supervisory review and has not been accepted for appeal as yet.

58

FOR LOUIS, the long hot days of September were a series of terrific battles, one after another, with a series of challengers, each of whom was large, furious, covetous of the possibilities of congress with Louis's female companions, and majorly muscled. Some days he was involved in two battles lasting an hour or more each, and there was a three-battle day which, for a while, late in the last afternoon, he did not think he would survive. But he won that battle, and he won the others. By now, after years of battles, he was a master at judging his opponent and using his experience to unsettle the opposition's intent. Young challengers, for example, who were newly grown into their muscle and power and proud of their heft and size, could be worn down by their own energy, so to speak; the trick was to let them charge you in all their glorious fury, accept the charge, but decline to hold your ground. Louis would allow them to push him halfway across the battlefield in clouds of dust before shaking them off and resetting the stage for another furious charge from the young prince. After an hour of shoving Louis from place to place, even the strongest young buck was exhausted, at which point Louis would suddenly blaze up and charge, irresistibly. In the first years of his chieftaincy, he would lose his temper and sometimes gore an opponent or trample a fallen foe, but experience had taught him not only patience but a sort of serenity. It was enough to win the battle, and the winner did not, in Louis's view, have to actually vanquish a foe—just defeat and dishearten him.

But this year he was nearly as exhausted as the young bucks he defeated, and when an older and more experienced challenger fought him, he won now by wile and no longer by strength. Twice he defeated a veteran challenger by topographical maneuver— once driving a foe into toppling off a small ledge, once trapping a challenger in a muddy dingle with poor footing. Once he was so desperate and weary that he calculated his final charge in such a manner as to drive his opponent into a copse of trees, where the challenger damaged a hoof. And the battle he had survived this third afternoon, the one that left him so exhausted that he could not stand, was the first in his whole life in which he had con-sciously, deliberately, calculatedly done his best to blind his oppo-nent, done his best to jam the razor edge of his antler into another elk's eye, to gore a fellow animal in such a way as to cripple it, and he had tried to do this not once but twice, succeeding the second time and causing his opponent to retreat with his shredded eye dribbling down the side of his face.

We are so sure that we know what animals do not feel. We measure their brains and record their behaviors and analyze their communication and map their sensory apparatus, and we con-clude they do not feel regret, shame, the grit of mortality on the tongue. Perhaps we are right to be sure; perhaps they are not re-flective and meditative in the ways we are; perhaps they cannot think and feel as we do; but then again perhaps *we* cannot think and feel as *they* do, and perhaps they are meditative and reflective in ways we cannot understand. Perhaps Louis, wearier than he had ever been in a long and tumultuous career, feels sad and proud at once that he was what he was, and this is now ending. Perhaps he feels a rush of affection and loss and pain for his par-amours and their children grown and new, with whom he must soon part and see them gathered under another chieftain; perhaps, as he finally lifts his head to stare out at the brilliant meadow where so many of his battles were fought, he feels some sort of dark joy that the end of his story is nigh and weariness at an end.

*

As he wanted to cover a good deal of the mountain, Mr. Douglas had boarded Edwin that morning; trapping season for marten opened in five weeks, and he wanted to scout the possibilities as thoroughly as he could. The season for marten was again the first day of November through the last day of January, and if he got off to a good start in the first two weeks of November, he could then focus on gray fox, mink, and raccoon, all of which were trappable beginning in mid-November and closing in March; bobcat, on which he also wanted to concentrate this winter, were December through February. The three-month red fox season opened in October, but Mr. Douglas calculated that (a) he would be occupied learning how to be Miss Moss's . . . unhusband?, and (b) he had never seen a red fox on the mountain, although there were now vague reports of montane fox, a red fox particularly suited to alpine reaches. This was something to explore next year, he thought, as he and Edwin trotted upriver, both of them wary of Cosmas and his headlong bicycle. Once again he had concluded to leave the otters alone, even though otter pelts were worth more than a hundred dollars each; his sensible self had remonstrated with the rest of him on this matter, especially as he would now be welcoming Miss Moss into the financial chaos of Richard Douglas Incorporated, but he felt somehow that he and the otters had an understanding, and he could not bring himself to trap animals who spent glorious sunny days like this playing merrily on mudslides and careening hilariously into the river, not even bothering to hide as he and Edwin strolled by.

Marten and bobcat, though, would bring good money—the current price was over a hundred dollars per skin for both animals—and if he had a good year with them and filled in where he could with fox (twenty-five dollars each) mink (twenty dollars), and raccoon (ten dollars), plus the occasional coyote, if possible (thirty dollars, and the season was always open on the poor creatures—what did that say about human beings that no authority saw fit to give them a safe season?), he could post a very good year indeed—which, added to the miraculous situation with Miss Moss, would make for what Mr. Shapiro liked to call an *annus mirabilis*, a year of wonders.

He was just pondering where he would set for red fox next year when Edwin stopped suddenly, snorting uneasily.

What? said Mr. Douglas. This is a meadow. You and I know that we are looking for good marten runs, none of which entails a meadow.

Don't you see the elk in the thicket? thought Edwin. Maybe I have been wrong to admire your sharp eye over the years.

Although . . . what's that? said Mr. Douglas quietly. In the thicket. That's not a lion. It's big, though. Bigger than deer. Not a bear. Is that an elk? Why is it down? Let's go see.

I think that's the biggest elk I have ever seen, thought Edwin, and I am not happy about approaching an elk bigger than me. An elk that big will have serious antlers, and I do not have antlers, and you don't carry a rifle, and we are screwed if there's a misunderstanding. What if he thinks I am a very ugly elk and am challenging him? What then? It's the rut, you know. Can't you smell that? Smells dangerous to me. I think we should retreat forthwith, myself.

But Mr. Douglas gently urged him on, and they walked very slowly forward. Soon enough Mr. Douglas could see that the animal in the thicket was indeed a tremendous elk, but something was wrong with it. Was it sick? It should have exploded out of the thicket to flee or charge at this close range, but it lay there sick or exhausted or even wounded. His temper flared—had some idiot tried a potshot out of season? Archery season was finished, and rifle season didn't open until October.

Maybe it was this spurt of anger that made him dismount and approach the elk—a dangerous idea under any circumstances, and more so with an animal of what appeared to be epic size. But Mr. Douglas was no fool; he was the sort of man whose experience soaks into his very being so that now when he was in the woods he made decisions calibrated by many thousands of hours of attentiveness and caution and respect and even reverence. And here, without consciously thinking about it, he knew that he and Edwin were safe and that the elk, incredibly powerful though it appeared to be, was not going to come roaring out of the thicket, hooves and antlers flashing like axes and knives.

On the other hand, he was not foolish enough to approach too closely or too abruptly, so he and Edwin stood together a few feet away, gaping at the animal's war wounds. Welts, slices, cuts, one serious hole in the left shoulder; trickles of blood on chest and haunch; dusty from head to hoof; a powerful scent of sweat and musk and blood and thrashed vegetation; and a patent obvious bone weariness you could very nearly feel.

This one is close to death, thought Edwin, and Mr. Douglas nodded soberly. Of course Edwin was right and this was the rut, the season of epic battles among elk on the mountain. Mr. Douglas had forgotten about the rut, being so concentrated on planning his traplines. And here was inarguable proof of the awful price of the rut, the wounding and killing of those who went to war.

And something in him was moved, suddenly, by the utter exhaustion of the being in front of him. Such a king he must be or have been—and not only able in battle but an intelligent chieftain of his companions to have survived and flourished so. But here he was, helpless, curled in a thicket, a tremendous life very nearly at the end of its energies. Perhaps this was merely a lull, after which it would rise again and slowly be restored, but perhaps these were its last moments, and none of its own to witness, but only a quiet horse and a silent man.

Then Edwin walked forward and pushed through the scrim of the thicket and knelt down slowly alongside the elk and leaned in and rested his head upon the head of the elk, and for long minutes, all was still, and no being stirred, not the elk nor the horse nor the man nor insects and birds nor creatures in the dust and soil below. Mr. Douglas stood amazed, staring at the two massive beings before him; and then, as if by some subtle signal, the birds sang again, and insects whirred, and Edwin stood up, and the elk lifted his head and regarded them. As Edwin stepped gingerly out of the thicket, he looked at Mr. Douglas, and Mr. Douglas understood, and they turned and walked downhill together, Mr. Douglas not climbing aboard until they were back among the jungled firs. As they stepped beneath the trees, Mr. Douglas thought he heard a slight thrash and rustle behind them, as if a very large elk had arisen, but neither he nor Edwin turned around to look, and they went on, silent and thoughtful.

59

SCHOOL BEGAN ON THE NINTH DAY of the ninth month of the calendar invented by a man for whom a crater was named on the moon. The first serious homework assignment in second grade was a one-page report on What You Did This Summer. Maria turned in a seven-page report with a cover made of cedar bark about mapping not only the topographical and zoological features of her "area of residence" but also a brief essay about the interesting possibilities of mapping emotional landscapes and finding ways to add story to maps—so that the truly useful map, as she wrote, would exhibit not only the readily evident physical aspects of a place, such as promontories and water features, but also local lore, notes on beings past and present, and something of the songs and story of that place as distinct from other places, even ones thought to be similar by the usual categorical measures, which are, of course, shallow and insufficient to the mapmaker who wishes to account a place in any kind of seriously layered way, rather than simply the topographical—or even worse, merely the concrete and macadam and cement ribbons we call roads and streets.

In fact, as Maria wrote, warming to the task, we miss a wonderful chance in cartography and mapmaking to discover, in the layered accounting of a place, more of it than we could in any other single endeavor; to "map" a place is essentially to try to tell its stories, and the creative mapmaker sees this as a remarkable opportunity to plumb and explore, to study not only spatial but verbal, oral, musical, spiritual, literary, tactile, climatological, geologic, dendritic, atmospheric, electric, criminal, political, theatrical, and other narratives. For narrative *preserved* is the bailiwick of the dedicated mapmaker, and her task and pleasure in that responsibility is today made all the more attractive and interesting by the advent of new technologies for showing and sharing the wealth of narratives that are to be found in all places, be they famous or ostensibly obscure—the latter being, of course, a silly and unfair label, better phrased as *not well mapped as yet*.

Maria's teacher asked her to stay after school on Friday for a few moments so they could discuss her report. Maria, delighted to speak freely about all this—Dave pretended to be asleep whenever she spoke of narrative mapping—walked her teacher through the more complex three-dimensional aspects on her iPad, like flow function (showing river level and volume by season, correlated to snowpack depth on the mountain), selected animal population ebb and flow (the otters were particularly interesting when correlated with highway traffic patterns), and even a selection of recorded stories filterable by the teller's gender and age. Female storytellers, Maria contended, were twice as likely to tell stories of a spiritual nature, defined broadly, than males, who were almost twice as likely to tell stories of adventure and misadventure than females—although, Maria had to admit, the control group here was small, and she had not been able to recruit stories from beings other than human beings.

The first time you see a person actually gape—open his or her mouth in astonishment, and (entranced or amazed or astounded or stunned or awed, whatever word you like) forget to close it again for a few lovely seconds—is a truly remarkable moment. It doesn't get enough credit as an Incredible Life Moment. We are all over the Incredible Life Moments of birth and death, and kneeling down to ask for marriage, and the cold moment the word *divorce* first enters the kitchen, and sporting moments and moments of sudden violence and sexual moments, and moments of mass hysteria like elections and concerts, but the little extraordinary moments that are not little, those should be in the hall of fame too, yes? Like the moment you realize you just did work that was play to you. Or the moment you realize you aced a test because it was fun and you love the subject and it didn't feel like a test at *all*. Or the moment when you wanted to reach for the bottle with every iota of your being, and you kept your hand still, clutching so tightly to the newspaper that you couldn't get the ink off your fingers for two days. Or the moment someone you so wanted to say yes said, gently, *yes*.

This was that sort of life moment for Maria, who looked up, smiling, after saying she would have *loved* to try a thorough insect population map but just didn't have the time and saw her teacher's lower lip, thick and lovely and gently lipsticked still, even at the end of the school day, hanging loose and astonished before its owner hauled it back up toward its partner. That was maybe the moment, Maria said to Dave many years later, when I started to realize that not everyone was like you and Mom and Dad, letting me chase whatever I wanted to, but also that I was *right* to chase after stuff I wanted to, even if a lot of people would think I was nuts.

Did she think you were nuts? asked Dave.

No, said Maria grinning. But she said I would be doing a lot of independent study the rest of the year.

Studying what? asked Dave.

Otters, of course! said Maria. If you had eight months to study whatever you wanted, wouldn't you study otters? Sure you would. Otters rule!

*

I'd study marten, if I had the chance to study one animal for a lifetime, Dave is saying to Mr. Douglas. They are in the kitchen of Miss Moss's store, and Dave is making Everything Soup, and Mr. Douglas is poring over cookbooks on the off-chance that *someone* he knows will ask him what foods she ought to have at the Unwedding.

Why marten?

I think because no one knows anything about them, says Dave. No one even knows they exist except trappers and forest biologists and game wardens and people like that. I bet if you asked the next hundred people who walked into the store about marten, maybe one would know who you are talking about. Everyone else would think you meant Martin Somebody or Somebody

Martin. But trappers know. And I know. I've seen them. They are the most amazing animals. You know how most animals look like some other animal? Like a fox looks like a coyote or an osprey looks like a hawk? Marten don't look like anything else except fishers, and fishers are three times bigger. I'd like to study them partly because they fascinate me and partly because no one knows anything about them, and if we knew more about them, maybe we wouldn't wipe them out.

We're not wiping them out here, says Mr. Douglas. They're pretty healthy on the mountain. Lots of deep forest and squirrels here, and it's protected land, you know, so they ought to do well forever here.

Except for trappers, says Dave, and he says this half politely and half challengingly—the former a Dave tone Mr. Douglas knows and admires and the latter a Dave tone he had not heard until now.

Trappers do more to preserve populations than anyone else, says Mr. Douglas carefully, looking at Dave; but Dave is staring into the soup pot.

Trappers respect animals more than anyone else, continues Mr. Douglas. Trappers know how animals live and if their populations are healthy. Trappers never take more fur than the population can bear. We did in the old days, sure, but not anymore. Who do you think tells the state scientists how to set limits and seasons? Where do you think the data comes from? From trappers. We know if a population is declining, and we are the ones who provide the numbers to the foresters. It's not like the old days when people would just take everything and move on. For one thing, there's no more On to move on to, and for another, we're a lot smarter about balance. Trappers are more environmentally alert and astute than any of your next hundred people walking in the door, Dave.

It's killing, says Dave very quietly into the soup.

Dave, what's in the soup?

What?

What's in the soup?

Well, says Dave, well—everything.

Name the ingredients.

Carrots, garlic, potatoes, onions, peppers, peas, leeks . . .

All killed for your soup.

Pardon?

Did you think the carrots weren't alive before they got pulled from the garden? The garlic, the leeks? Sentient beings, every one of them. They're born, they grow up, they sense light better than we do, they know how to eat minerals from the soil better than we do, they have enemies and communities and relationships beyond our understanding. Yet we yank them up and cut them up and eat them and don't think twice about it. And in the refrigerator there are pieces of chickens and pigs and cows and deer and ducks and salmon. It's all killing, Dave. Why is my profession crueler than any other way we kill beings for food and clothes? Why is that? At least in my profession it's me and the animal, one on one, a battle of wits, and believe me, I lose the battle most of the time. There's factory farms in my profession, but trappers scorn them. You want to earn the price of a mink pelt, go catch a mink. I don't have truck with fur farms. But even at that, why is a mink farm any different from a piggery or a cattle ranch or a cornfield or a vineyard? Riddle me that.

All killing, says Dave, even more quietly than before and again speaking into the bubbling soup.

Mr. Douglas pauses a long moment. He can feel his ire rising—he's been attacked before for killing sentient beings and scalping them and selling their skins, and his articulate defense is there on his tongue, ready for tart delivery. Yet he likes Dave, he understands something of Dave's anger and confusion, and he too was once fifteen, furious at the brilliant half lies and eloquent excuses of adults, their shoddy bargains and easy rationalizations, their willingness to ignore and forget the inconvenient and unremunerative.

Yes, says Mr. Douglas, all killing. There's no way around it, yet. I tease the vegetarians and the *veeeeegans* for their prim arrogance, but you have to secretly admire the effort when it's not about being cooler than the next person. We do kill and eat and wear and use other beings all the time, from food to clothes to cabins and firewood. We do. Maybe someday we will evolve to just eating carrots and leeks, although that's still killing sentient beings, you know. But meanwhile you can at least kill with respect. You can at least acknowledge the fact that the chicken and the carrot gave their lives for your nutrition. I don't suppose that the chicken and the carrot care much about your respect after the fact, but it's at least something. Religious people would say something about reverence right here, but I don't speak their language.

I wish you wouldn't trap for marten this year, said Dave suddenly. I wish you would take a year off. Focus on bobcat, like you were saying. Raccoon, mink, fox. Maybe leave the marten alone, give them a break. Like farmers let a field go fallow to recover. You said yourself there's not all that many marten, not as many as there used to be. You said so yourself. You said they used to be all over the country from sea to sea anywhere there was serious forest, and now they're not. Now they are only in the north and west where there are still serious forests, and there will be ever more people and ever less serious forest and so ever less marten, right? You said so yourself. So why go for marten this year? Give them a last year off. No one else traps for marten on this side of the mountain. You're the only one; you said so yourself. If the world keeps going like it's going, there will be just little islands of serious forest, and the marten can't stand that; they like to amble and roam. You said so yourself. You talk about respect—take a year off out of respect; give them a last year where they can ramble and roam and no one sets traps for them. Close the season the day before it opens. You could do that. You're in charge of marten trapping on this side of the mountain. Give them one last year when no one knows anything about them except you and me. I won't tell anyone. I won't even tell Miss Moss. I'll make up the lost money for you, working extra in the store. We don't even need to tell Miss Moss. I'll just say I am stashing extra money for college. If you don't give the marten a break, who will? And you don't lose a dollar on the deal. They win and you win. My mom says that the birthday present system is all flawed and that on your birthday *you* should give everyone *else* presents. Isn't a wedding like that? So you are giving the marten a present in honor of your wedding. You're giving Miss Moss a present so cool she won't even know about it. Isn't that sort of the coolest present of all? A present that's not a thing? You say yourself we have too many things in our lives. Remember how angry you were at all the stuff dumped in the woods? Here's a chance to give a present that has nothing to do with things and everything to do with respect, isn't that right? Mr. Douglas?

60

FOR NO REASON HE KNEW, Martin went more and more to his pillar rock above timberline and crouched there contemplating the sprawling vast wilderness below his feet. Sometimes he watched the sky and marked the patterns of the ravens and noted the way eagles used flyways above ravines. Did ravines channel thermal lift, perhaps? Other times he focused on the border between the dense fir forest and the last band of trees and bushes before all green surrendered; that border, he knew from experience, was a good hunting ground, as denizens of both thick and thin forest crossed borders looking for food. Still other times he paid attention only to the rock jungle below him, a wilderness itself of nooks and crannies and tiny caves; this was the kingdom of pika and chipmunk, ground squirrel and marmot, and here too Martin had made many a meal, especially in this season, late summer and early fall, before the snow returned and covered it all ten feet thick.

But he had already eaten this morning, a fat golden squirrel near the lodge, and now he perched atop his pillar, pondering, watching, attending. He did not doze, not here in the open. More than once, ravens had swooped on him, taking a chance on causing a fall that might lead to meat, and once an owl had attacked him here at dusk—to the owl's regret, for Martin had slashed it deep enough that the bird staggered off dripping blood. So today he gazed, he meditated, he paid attention. By now, almost two years old, almost fully grown, experienced and seasoned, survivor of much conflict, he was a serious student of pattern, for apprehending and understanding the ways and habits of creatures was the best road to safety and supper. But there was also something in him that *enjoyed* seeing and learning for more than simply utilitarian purposes.

And he *remembered*; perhaps this is his greatest gift, more than his liquid speed and quickness, more than his astonishing sensory machinery, more than the way he was the most cautiously curious and adventurous of all his species on the mountain, the only one who silently drew close enough to schools and stores, lodges and ski runs, boat docks and orchards to apprehend human animals and their symbiotic companions among other species.

He remembered, and not just facts and patterns necessary for survival. He remembered certain angles of light pouring in the door of their burrow when he was a mewling kit with his sister and brothers, and he remembered the first time he saw Dave in the clearing by the river, and hearing the clank of metal traps. He remembered carrying a shrew to his sickly second brother and nuzzling him with it and seeing his brother raise his head for an instant and then sink back and soon after die. He well remembered being chased to within a whisker of death by a bobcat; he remembered every instant of the savage fight with the fox; he remembered the scent of the huckleberry bushes in which he had seen his female companion for the first time. He remembered the wild sound of Cosmas singing as he whizzed down trails and clear-cuts on his bicycle, the lovely savory tang of the first chipmunk he'd ever eaten, the dark safe warm joy of his mother's milk before dawn. And so much more—the ice cave in which he found the skeleton of a bear twice as large as any living bear he'd ever seen; the remote meadow where three times he had seen people on their knees weeping and beating their chests with their fists; the glacier pit, far from any trail, where he had found a tiny frozen new human being, covered with snow.

★

The Unabled Lady is now so hunched over from her slow illness when she sits at her piano that she thinks pretty soon she is going to be playing the piano with her nose, which would actually be interesting, like having an eleventh finger. But that day is not yet come, and she thinks she'd better use the time before she is permanently bent to write one last glorious piece of music for ten fingers and not eleven. She thinks maybe she will write it for the Unwedding, because she very much admires Miss Moss, who sometimes brings her stacks of chicken sandwiches, and she very much likes Mr. Douglas, who stops by to fix things occasionally, after which they watch football games and drink beer. She thinks maybe a song will be the right and only thing she could present the young people as a gift for the unceremonious unoccasion. She thinks maybe someone else will have to play it by then, which means she'd better get in touch with Emma Jackson, who plays a terrific piano—something no one knows except the Unabled Lady, who has been teaching Emma quietly for more than a year. She thinks she will try to write a piece of music that has everything on the mountain in it. She thinks this is crazy; therefore she will do it. She sits down and starts noodling at the keys and scribbling notes and dreaming and humming, and the morning slides into afternoon and melts into evening, and all that time she tries to write down Mrs. Simmons's amused smoker's cough and the way the finch used to cock an eyebrow at her if she started a piece in the wrong key and the way buzzards flitter the silver lining of their wings to each other, probably signaling secrets, and the way the little creek in her yard burbled and thrilled and trilled and murmured and how she still dreamed sometimes of her legs as they were before the accident and her husband's smell like sweat and mint when he was naked when they were young and the way the baby she never had would have suckled desperately at her breast and belched like a barge and the faint groan of logging trucks early in the morning away on the highway and the chime of ice in the fir trees and the reek of cougar urine on the porch one morning and the sound of dirt falling on her husband's coffin made of juniper and jack pine and the screech of Cosmas's bicycle as he braked to a halt when he came by occasionally to sit and listen and hardly ever speak. Maybe listening is a kind of music also, she thought. Maybe I should write a piece of music that has listening in it, places where the piano stops talking. Yes. I want to write a piece of music that has everything in it, including room for the parts of everything that don't make a sound. Yes. The music of breathing and waiting and smelling and listening and savoring. The music of being afraid but going on anyway. The music that you write last and best for someone else to play.

61

OFFICIALLY, BASKETBALL WORKOUTS did not begin until October 1, but Moon and everyone else who wanted to play ball for the Zag was in the gym or the weight room or both every afternoon, partly to be sure the coach saw you at work and partly from the sure knowledge that when tryouts started, if you were not in tiptop shape and on your game, you had no chance, for it was clear from the first open gym period that there were a *lot* more ballplayers this year, somehow, and something was different about the ones who had been merely good last year—Moon among them.

It had been evident from the first few minutes. Usually ten or fifteen guys might show up for open gym, some serious about scrimmaging but most just horsing around or killing time before a later theater or choir practice or a ride home. But this time nearly thirty guys were there when the door opened, with more straggling in later. For a few minutes, guys milled around, shooting freely at either end and on the lower baskets on the sides, and then the varsity captains, brothers whose dad worked at the lodge, set up teams for brief scrimmages, knockout fashion— winner stays on court, loser to the end of the waiting teams. To their credit they did not pack teams with last year's players, although they did anoint their respective teams to open play. Moon's team was first challenger, and they won, mostly because he got nearly every rebound at either end of the floor. They won a second game, a third, a fourth, and in each game, Moon hammered the boards as hard as he could, although by now the other players were diligently trying to keep him out of the lane. By the fifth game, the coach was standing outside the gym doors, watching. By the seventh game, Dave and a few cross-country guys were watching too, as word had spread. Moon's team finally lost to a team that the brothers did pack with last year's starters, but when the game ended, guys shook hands and meant it. Moon had scored only two baskets in eight games, both on the simplest of shots from as close as you could possibly get to the basket, but even the coach, who had tried to keep track of rebounds and blocked shots, had lost count.

Man, that was amazing, says Dave on the way home. People stopped what they were doing to watch *you* play ball. *That* never happened before.

Moon laughs. I tell you, Dave, he says, I know what to do now. I know where to be without thinking about it. And I know what not to do and where not to be. It's like I finally speak the language. You know how when you are trying to learn something and you have to think about each part of it, and then finally you realize you are just *doing* it without thinking about it? That's what it feels like. That's the first time it ever happened like that. I felt totally comfortable, like I knew what I was doing for a change. I don't think I ever felt like that before, except while making sandwiches.

You going to tell your folks?

Well, says Moon, Dad is in Borneo, and Mom is in Iceland, I think. Although today she might still be in Denmark. Not sure of the schedule. I would Skype them, but what would I say? That I didn't totally geek up for a change?

You know, says Dave, what if you actually turned out to be a good ballplayer and I turned out to be a good runner? What if we turned out to be good students? What if we were actually good at the things we wanted to be good at?

Unthinkable, said Moon. Apocalypse. Armageddon. That would mean we would have futures. Nah. I just had a good game, and you had a good run. Let's not get crazy.

Hey, come for dinner, says Dave. Maria will be thrilled.

What's for dinner?

Trout. Somebody at the lodge caught a mess and gave them to us.

What a coincidence, says Moon. Trout is the only thing I eat now, for religious reasons. I am in a new religion where I have to eat huge amounts of trout. In butter. With mustard. A little salt. Dill, if you have any.

You can explain your religion to my mom yourself, you goof.

I might have to move in if there's trout every day at your house. We might have to switch places. I always wanted a kid sister anyway and Maria is the Cadillac of kid sisters. I think she is going to be governor someday. I bet she is governor before she graduates from high school. If I become her brother now I will be in good before she is elected, and she will give me a cushy post. Is that Maria on the roof? Why is she on the roof?

Moon! says Maria's voice. Are you staying for dinner? Say yes. I need your help with a project. Do you have your iPad? Say yes.

Where are you, Madam Governor?

Up on the roof, says Maria. I am making a galactic map, and *you* are going to help me. Right after dinner. Dinner is trout. Mom says she knew you were coming for dinner as soon as she put the first fillet in the pan. She says she could hear you smelling it from a mile away. Help me down? Let's eat. Then you can help me. Hi, Dave.

Hello, Governor, says Dave with a smile. Good day?

Great day. Did I tell you I love you today?

You did this morning when I left.

Did you tell me you love me?

Once this morning and twice last night. Let's eat.

★

I think I love you, says Emma Jackson to the morning waitress, but I don't think it's working out, and I don't think I want to be together anymore, because I don't feel like we fit, although I think I love you. I'm so sorry. I feel awful. But I love you, and I want to be honest and straight. So to speak. I'm so sorry.

They are sitting on the edge of Emma Jackson's bed. Her bed is narrow. There is a faded blue blanket on it. The blanket was woven by her grandmother. There is a small desk by her bed. On the desk are photographs of her parents and her grandparents and her brother who was a sailor before he. Emma and her family never finish that sentence anymore. On the walls there are three paintings by the morning waitress. The morning waitress loves to play with shape and color and considers most works of art to be too nervously representational and not willing to simply play with shape and color in ways that perhaps make the viewer reconsider the shape and color of the things we think we know, like desks and beds and morning waitresses.

I love you too, says the morning waitress. I think we do fit. I think we fit great. I'd like to see how we could fit even better. I'd like to try to fit with a house and children and work. I'd like to try to fit in other places like Wales or Nicaragua. Somewhere by the sea. I think you came to the mountain because you should be by the sea and yet you are running away from it because of your brother. I think you and I fit, but you don't fit here. That's what I think.

They sit silently for a few minutes. Emma Jackson reaches for the morning waitress's hand to hold hands, but the morning waitress smiles and lifts her hand and cups Emma Jackson's face and says, listen, I would wait years for you if I thought we had a chance, but I think you have a long road before *you* fit with you. That's what I think. I love you, and I'll always want to know if you are happy. You stay in touch, okay? Just send me a card here and there with one sentence. Write a poem in one sentence, and I will translate the poem to see if you are getting close to fitting you to you. Will you do that?

Yes, whispers Emma Jackson.

Maybe what will happen is that you will actually meet Billy Beaton. Or Miss Billie Beaton.

Maybe.

But it's not someone else, you know.

I know.

You'll get there.

I don't know.

I think you will.

I'm so sorry.

I love you too, Emma.

Will you be my date at the wedding?

Unwedding. Yes. Of course. A not-date at a not-wedding. How apt.

I'm so sorry.

Me too.

And they sit there for another four or five moments, inside love and pain and love. If you were a painter, you could paint the lean slump of their bodies, the stilled birds of their hands, the bright shapeless paintings behind them, the drift of dust motes, the faraway thrum of cars leaving, the thrill of thrushes, the seethe of the wind. If you were a painter, you could try to paint the way people who love each other can be untogether. You could try to paint that. It would be hard to paint, but you could try if you just used shape and color. You could have two shapes of two different colors almost touching but not quite, not anymore.

★

Cosmas is not on his bicycle for a change. He is in his orange jumpsuit kneeling on Mrs. Robinson's grave. Hers is on the right. He has already worked Mr. Robinson's grave this morning. Mr. Robinson is on the left. That is how the Robinsons moved through the world together when they were alive, and that is how they sleep together now that they are in another form. Cosmas is wearing an orange bandanna. He is thinking that Mr. and Mrs. Robinson have produced a *stunning* crop of tomatoes. It's hard to get good tomatoes this high on the mountain, what with the dusty ashy soil and the cool nights and the way the sun sears through the thin air sometimes on wild hot days, but the Robinsons, by god, have done it with verve and panache. You could do better with the basil next year, says Cosmas very gently, but your garlic production is superb, and the tomatoes are just crazy good. I am going to eat two tomatoes for dinner tonight in your honor and save the rest for the wedding. Yes, wedding. That's what I came to tell you this morning. Yes, Miss Moss and Dickie Douglas. Finally. *She* asked *him* finally *in* the river. He says she only asked him finally because she was weary of him asking her twice a day. He says he would have asked her twice a day for the rest of his life if necessary. He says you can hear no any given number of times as long as there's a chance someday of having yes in your startled ear. She says it's *not* a wedding and *not* a marriage, and there's no marriage license and no joint tax filing and no joint checking account. Yes, she has a bee in her bonnet about all that, but they *are* actually plighting troth on Friday. Dickie says the day was chosen because it's Joel Palmer's birthday and Maria gets to wear the sneakers found in the glacier, but Ginny says Friday is the one day of the week named for a woman, and that's the day for her. She says Friday is named for a woman who lived on a snowcapped mountain and could see through time. Yes, they asked me to be the celebrant. No, I am not to use the words *preside* or *wed* or *join* or *marry* or *pronounce* or anything like that. Ginny says she and Dickie are coming to an agreement with their friends and neighbors, and we are all there to celebrate together, and no one is in charge of the moment, not even she and Dickie, but because I am the tallest of all of us, I can stand with them and be master of ceremonies, sort of. She says their only request of me is to wear my jumpsuit and not some flowing billowing robe or gown or cloak or whatever. She says orange is the color of October and that will be apt and suitable. She says Dickie wanted Edwin to be master of ceremonies but Edwin declined, which is a good thing, because where would we find an orange jumpsuit big enough for a horse? She says she wishes more than anything in the world that you two were there and that she will certainly weep bitterly that you are not standing there next to her beaming as she too takes the leap you took toward each other, because that's why she is leaping toward Dickie, because you leapt toward each other every hour of every day, and she saw that and admired that and watched your gentle patience and affection and respect and reverence for each other in every little aspect of your lives, which were of course not little at all, which she says is the greatest lesson she ever learned and what she wants to try to reach with Dickie. She says if she and Dickie can be anything like you two, then she will account their lives a roaring success even if the generator in the store keeps wheezing and dying and the milk keeps going bad a day too early and Dickie brings in one too many raccoon pelts, a woman can only take so many raccoon pelts hanging in the shed to dry before she goes stark-raving mad and starts wearing orange jumpsuits and growing vegetables in cemeteries and talking to the graves of friends. I'll come tomorrow to collect the garlic, okay? And then Friday morning for the tomatoes. You keep working on the tomatoes until then. I'm thinking we could try turnips and parsnips after that. I think we can get one more crop in before snowfall. You want to try kale? Think about it. I'll be back tomorrow for the garlic. I miss you awfully too. I miss you terribly. I wish I could hear your voices. I wish I could hear you laugh. I bet you are laughing right now, right through the tomatoes. These are unbelievable tomatoes. I miss you. Sleep well. I'll be here in the morning.

62

THE DOG WHO HAD DECIDED to live with Mr. Shapiro, the one who had survived his first year in the deepest wildest forests in North America, generally arose with Mr. Shapiro in the morning and companionably ate breakfast with him, and then, when Mr. Shapiro went off to work, the dog explored generally, soaking up information and scent, studying the style and story of his new place. For the first few days his explorations were of the cabin and yard and neighborhood, trying to make sense of ostensible boundaries. The other dogs nearby, after some initial disagreements and debates, agreed to allow him free passage through their territories. The human beings nearby, as a rule, did not care overmuch about a trotting dog, although the golf course manager was rude and intemperate in his language and twice tried to hit him with low flat drives with a five iron. The two adult coyotes who lived not far from the right-field fence at the high school were afraid of him and went to ground at his approach; and it was only one testy raven who ever harassed him on a regular basis. The dog thought more than once that he might catch and eat that damned raven, more on principle than from hunger, but the conflict was resolved one morning when the dog actually did catch the raven, who had come an inch too close, and pinned it to the ground with both of his front paws and communicated in clear and relatively patient fashion that he had no particular problem with ravens individually or collectively or as a species, and any raven that had a problem with *him* was mistaken in that belief and imprisoned in a misguided concept, and that further harassment was a poor idea from every conceivable angle and that henceforth he would expect, as the raven could expect, not quite friendship as much as something like a truce or a polite neutrality or an agreement not to disagree. The raven understood and expressed something like an apology. As the dog thought later, the raven's apology could not be said to have been delivered with anything like what you would call grace, but it *had* been genuine, insofar as he could tell, and certainly the raven did not afterwards dive upon or otherwise harass or badger the dog or fly off to recruit his or her companions for a confrontation in numbers.

So it was that the dog began to fit into his new community, and by subsequently avoiding the greens on the golf course, he found himself for the first time in his life not subject to attack; a refreshing state of affairs. As Mr. Shapiro said later, the first condition for substantive and nutritious relationships is the safety and security of all parties concerned, after which denser webs may be woven—and the denser the webs among beings, said Mr. Shapiro to the dog, the less likely a breach of the peace, could that be the case? The thicker the threads, the less likely their sundering? The dog, curled on his chair, considered all the cases he knew of sudden violence between and among mates and partners and tribes and packs, but he refrained from comment, aware that his experience was not comprehensive of all possibilities. He very much liked hearing Mr. Shapiro propose and speculate, ponder and wonder, consider and offer conjecture; a warm and affectionate voice being the one thing the dog had never heard in his whole life and to him something very much like fresh water when you are desperately thirsty.

*

Cadence weighed herself one morning, and she had lost eight pounds. The vice president of the senior class asked her out that afternoon after seeing her at the store. She said yes. Dave said no when she told him. She said she would make her own decisions about whom to date or not date thank you very much. Dave said that he was under the impression that they had a special relationship. Cadence said that yes they did but that did not mean that she could not date whomever she liked. Dave said that the only reason the vice president had asked her out was that she was skinnier. Cadence said that might well be the case, but she would find out his motivations and character for herself, and was he calling her fat? Dave said well, that pretty much meant the end of their running together, didn't it, and he was *not* calling her fat. Cadence said that would be a mean thing to do to quit running with her because he was jealous. Dave said he wasn't trying to be jealous or possessive, but he didn't think it would be much fun for *him,* at least, if they went running together while she was dating another guy. Cadence said she understood how he felt, but she could not behave according to someone else's dictates or rules. Dave said he understood, but part of the problem maybe was that he had been about to ask her out but had not done so because he was not sure what she would say and because they had a special relationship that he really liked and because he didn't want to ruin that, but now he is kicking himself because he should have asked her out. Cadence said she understood but that even if he *had* asked her out, she would have accepted the invitation from the vice president, because she was not ready to be dating only

one person at the present time. Dave said actually he *was* ready to
be dating only one person at the present time, and he had rather
hoped it would be her. Cadence did not say anything, but Dave
could hear what he thought was crying on the telephone, and
then Cadence said I have to go now, and maybe we should take
a few days off before we talk again, okay? Dave said he understood, and he turned off his phone and felt a stagger in his
stomach. His mom and dad and Maria were out, and he packed
two sandwiches and two bottles of water and left a note on the
table that he was in the woods and would be back for dinner, and
he stepped outside and walked upriver and vanished into the
woods.

⋆

Martin spent the morning hunting and the afternoon ranging
restlessly again. He could feel the imminent change in seasons, he
could smell it, he saw it everywhere he looked: vine maple past
its brilliant autumnal color, the last berries shriveled on brown-
ing bushes, geese and cranes croaking overhead, the elk finishing
the rut and settling into their winter clans and companies; school
buses on the highway, the ebbing of summer tourists; soon the
weasels and hares would turn white, and the bears would lumber
into their winter bunks and barracks, and the snow would fall—a
flurry or two at first and then the first steady snows and then the
deluge.

Up and up he went, drawn by some inchoate urge to be
above the forest in the last brilliant bit of summer. He skirted the
lodge cautiously—even with fewer tourists, there were always
human animals in the woods and trails near it, pressing their
faces or bodies together, holding bottles and cans to their mouths,
sleeping, reading, chanting aloud, clanking and clambering along
the trails, raising waist-high dust clouds, trampling the little asters in clearings and sunny spots. But they were easily avoided,

and none of the human animals near the lodge appeared to have weapons or traps that he could see. Even so, he was never less than cautious near the lodge, even when he occasionally used the back wall along the outdoor swimming pool as a shortcut toward his pillar stone—he could leap from the pool wall into a line of towering pines and so save a long detour around the ski lift, a contraption he did not like and avoided whenever possible.

He used the pool wall this time, waiting patiently until the two women in the pool had retreated into the lodge, and he leapt up into the pines, energized by their sharp rude smell. He ran happily through the familiar trails in their canopies; the pines were close enough together in their procession that he easily slipped from one to the next. One person saw him flowing through the trees, quicker than a cat, more surefooted than a squirrel, utterly comfortable in his body and his milieu and the moment: the third chef, who happened to look out a window at just the instant Martin casually leapt from one tree to another, a chasm of about eight feet. A single instant in the unimaginably long history of the mountain and of marten and of men, but not one the chef ever forgot—and not because it was the one glimpse of a marten he would ever have in his relatively short life but because of the sheer confident wild soaring grace of the animal, the way it absolutely knew where it was and where it was going, the way it *belonged* there in a way no man or state or country claiming possession ever quite could. That imprinted itself mightily on the chef's mind, and curiously it was an image that came back to him often, especially when he was half-awake in the morning, not sure if he was dreaming. He would see the creature again suspended in the air, a splash of golden brown against the bright green pines and startling blue air and gleaming snowfield. Once or twice he even tried to paint what he had seen, but there was something missing, some verve and zest and almost humor—and besides, his mother made fun of his attempts, laughing in that awful wheezing cackle so that she could hardly get her cigarette going, laughing at him so bitterly that he crumpled up the paper and stuffed it in his pocket and slammed the door of the trailer behind him as he left.

63

MR. SHAPIRO, THIS TIME SUBBING for a teacher who was in the National Guard and had been suddenly sent abroad, is addressing his class. We have now spent a good deal of time on natural history, and I hope that one of the things you are discovering is that the very term *natural history* is essentially specious; all history is natural history, even what we would reasonably call unnatural; even the human pathology that results in massacre is in a sense natural as an aspect of the human animal, correct?

Unfortunately, said a student.

But that's our next month's work, the analysis of murder, excuses for murder, pathologies like religion and racism that lead to murder, possible correctives and therapies for such pathologies, said Mr. Shapiro. Today, I want to finish our natural history section by coming home, as it were—thinking about this place, this side of the mountain, this mountain, and all the ways we could consider the *natural history* of this place. Start with the orthodox.

Joel Palmer, logging, native history, said a student.

Native?

Native Americans.

Poor term. Specify. Most of us in this room are native.

American Indians.

Columbus's erroneous label, said Mr. Shapiro.

First Peoples.

Better. Klickitat, Molalla, Chinookan. Still labels, but.

Founding of the Zag.

Good.

Building of the lodge, visit by President Roosevelt.

Good.

Fish, mammals, insects, amphibians, reptiles, said a student.

Good, said Mr. Shapiro. Interesting, though, that it took us this long to get to what are undeniably the majority of the population in this place, by a factor of millions.

Trees, plants, bacteria, said a student.

Good. Also nematodes, microbes, fungi, and other life beneath the surface of the ground. A third of all life-forms are in soil.

Photons, rock, ice, water, quiescent lava, said a student.

More like incipient or patient lava, probably, said Mr. Shapiro. Very good. Note that it also took us this long to get to aspects of natural history that are not living beings. Do we have a species predilection or bias to living beings? Do we unconsciously rank them higher and consider them more important than other forms and aspects of the place we share? Is that just or fair? Or is that an evolutionary filter that developed because we have for so long ranked existence by what moves quickly and might be food? Worth thinking about. Anything else?

Music? Sounds? said a student.

Very good. Think, now—natural history means every conceivable aspect of this place, in every conceivable iteration.

Climatology, weather patterns, weather events, said a student.

Good.

Legendary events, said a student.

Very good. Such as?

Well, eruptions of the volcano that Indians . . . early people would remember.

Very good. This is the direction I wanted us to go for a

while. Doesn't natural history include story and legend, what we remember and what we tell of the place and what happened here? So that a map of this side of the mountain that shows only topography and roads and rivers and elevation and human settlements is a thin or shallow map, isn't it? A better map would also show layers of story and anecdote and memory. A better map would explore why certain places have certain names; names are the handles of story, aren't they? And each part of a place is not only a dell, a thicket, a bend on the river, a meadow, but a collection of the things that happened there over more years than we can count—and more things than just human things or living being things. Some things we know; here is the place where a man named Joel Palmer walked barefoot through the ice in 1845, for example. But what else happened there? Perhaps that is the place that wolverines cache elk calves. Perhaps this is the place where a woman ever so gently laid her infant and covered him with snow many years ago. Perhaps that is the place where ravens gather to ordain their holy ones. Perhaps that is the place where crabs gathered to give birth a million years ago when the mountain was the sea. Perhaps that is a place that rock born a billion years ago emerged again into the sunlight after an unimaginable stretch of darkness. You see what I am suggesting? That natural history is wider and deeper and thicker than we usually assume. So your homework assignment is only to consider that, briefly, in some thoughtful way. Take something of this place, your place, and *open* it for me. Due Monday. You can write an essay, draw a map, gather revelatory materials, record stories, record sonic revelations, write suitable music, carve or sculpt as you see fit. What is this place made of, composed of? What is the shape and nature of its flavor and endurance? Tell me in any way you like. I ask that you sit and think for a while before you do something. Dream first; do second. Yes, this will be graded, but I'll grade you on how much you thought about the assignment more than what you bring to class. A lot of a place is made up of voices. A lot of it is what happened in that air, on that water, in those woods. Most of a place is not what human beings think. Maybe we will be better human beings when we begin to see all the other things a place is besides all the things we think it is or wanted it to be.

64

WHAT ARE THE CHANCES, really, that a boy, aged fifteen, good in the woods but rattled by recent events and perhaps not paying full attention to safety concerns, and a marten, good in the woods but in an essentially reflective mood and so perhaps not quite as attentive to irregularities in pattern as he usually is, would both set forth from their dens, so to speak, on a lovely late afternoon

on the mountain and end up heading for the exact same spot—
and that spot a seemingly unremarkable pillar of rock that very
few creatures of any species frequented or even knew about,
anyway?

Not good, those chances, right? Infinitesimal, remote,
miniscule . . . yet that is exactly what just happened.

Dave was there first, having shinnied up for the view and for
a breather and perhaps at some level because the pillar looked so
remote and inaccessible—a good place to mourn, contemplate,
simmer, pout, ruminate, lacerate, grieve, ponder, reflect, recali-
brate, reboot his personal operating system. Once atop the tower,
he took his socks and sneakers off and guzzled some water and
finally took his shirt and jacket off. This might well be the last
brilliant day of summer's tail, and even this late in the afternoon,
the sun was sharp and warm on his pelt, although he knew the
mountain well enough to know that there would be a drop of
thirty degrees by midnight. First frost was a week or two away,
perhaps, and someone like Mr. Douglas, who knew the mountain
well, would say you could smell the ice growing more confident
of its time by the day.

Dave didn't fall asleep, exactly—there wasn't enough room on
the pillar for that, and it would have been too dangerous—but he
did zone out, semi-doze, enter what old folks like the Robinsons
would have called a brown study, so that when he heard a faint
scrabble of claws on the rock, it took him two seconds to be fully
attentive. And in those two seconds, Martin, equally unaware of
Dave's residency on his pillar, was over the edge and standing,
every muscle tensed, not four inches away from Dave's face.

Pause.

Did they recognize each other immediately?

Yes—Martin partly by Dave's scent and Dave partly by the
splash of white on Martin's chest.

Were either or both frightened?

Not *frightened*, no. Wariness squared, perhaps. Leery to the fourth power. Alert plus plus. Put it this way—neither Martin nor Dave thought that the other would injure him, but both were quite aware that the other was a muscled animal, capable of violence, unpredictable, especially if rattled, and both were also well aware that they were sharing a very small ledge on a naked rock high above unforgiving rock. A fall from the top of the pillar, whether by assault or accident, would be painful or worse.

Pause.

In a sense, this whole book has been working toward this moment, hasn't it? Two animals contemplating each other with the fullest and most piercing attention they could possibly bring to this moment. Two creatures, two beings, two unique consciousnesses unlike any that ever were or ever will be. Neither prey nor predator, hunter nor hunted, not mates or cousins, enemies, or teammates. So often we define beings by angle of relationship, by the nature of ostensible possession—my sister, my dog, your girlfriend, your rival. But here are two beings on a tiny ledge of rock on a vaulting mountain on a brilliant afternoon, and no labels apply. Each stares at the other. They apprehend, attend, absorb. Visually, certainly—the sheen of Martin's fur, the slight flutter of it in the wind, the flap of Dave's shirt around his waist, the scimitar scar on his calf, the muddle of his hair, the way Martin's thick neck slid gracefully into his sharp face. But something else. Curiosity? Yes. The heightened interest afforded by a slight familiarity? Yes. The heightened interest afforded by mystery? Yes. Made all the more so because they are of different tribes of being? Yes. The sure knowledge that no species will ever fully understand another, given the incontrovertible fact that we do not understand our own? Yes. Respect? Yes; each is aware that the other fits in its world and is deft at the things that it can do—or some of them. Reverence? Yes. Not religious, perhaps not spiritual; perhaps we do not have a word for the way that they see each other with something for which we can only use the word *reverence. Witness* or *savor,* perhaps? And perhaps each knows—in some private innermost bone—even now, already, in the few seconds they have shared the pillar and stared at each other, that this is a moment so rare that it will never be repeated, could never be repeated, though perhaps in a thousand years another boy will encounter another marten, inches away, and neither will think of flight or prey, capture or attack, subservience or even friendship.

Something else. How can we get all the way to this moment and run out of words? But *you* know, deep in your own bones, what they feel, though we cannot find the word. They *see* each other—and having seen and knowing the alp of the moment, each is . . . changed. Could it be that moments like this are windows through which we see the endless possibility of deeper moments? Could it be that moments like this are the greatest moments in a life? Could it be that moments like this are the moments that tilt the universe and make possible new ways and means and manners of being? Could it be that moments like that are why we invented religions and dream of peace in the bruised world and write books and music, trying to find the right sounds and stories for the thing we know but cannot say? If we ever succeed in naming it, would we be closer to achieving it? Is this why we write and read, in the end, in order to find new words for the things we feel but do not have words for?

Martin moved first; he sat down, although he kept his eyes on the boy. Dave, feeling the first hint of what would be a cold night, slowly put his shirt on but did not otherwise adjust his position. Martin watched as Dave put his shirt on, perhaps thinking about removable skins and pelts. They continued to look at each other for a while, and then there came another of those ordinary extraordinary moments that happen all the time, generally wholly unremarked; they each turned away from the other and faced into the sliding sun, and for nearly an hour, they sat together, half dozing, half alert to hawks and eagles and the skitter of pika and chipmunk in the rocks below. Once they both saw, at the same time, a large dark burly animal for an instant, between massive boulders; Dave thought it was a bear, but Martin knew it to be a badger. And once Martin smelled a fox, a scent that made the fur on his neck bristle. Finally, again eerily at nearly the same instant, they turned to look at each other again, and Martin silently and without ceremony vanished over the side of the pillar. A minute later Dave climbed down and walked home, trying to think of ways he could explain what had happened on the rock but not coming up with any good ideas. Supper was trout and huckleberry pie, and as Maria said that night before she fell asleep in the bear den, if there is anything in this world more delicious than huckleberry pie, it has not come to my attention, and I have been around for *years*.

★

Miss Moss chose a meadow. Mr. Douglas chose a trail to it that could be negotiated by the Unabled Lady, with cheerful assistance from Dave and the cross-country team. Miss Moss chose the food to be served after the unceremony. Mr. Shapiro did indeed provide excellent wines and ales and various delicious and savory ciders drawn from various species of apples harvested and pressed by a friend of his who lived in a yurt in an orchard. Dave's dad quietly arranged the use of the meadow with the Forest Service, and Moon's basketball coach arranged for folding chairs and tables to be conveyed to the meadow by members of the team in exchange for one day off from practice. Emma Jackson and Dave's mom brought shining redolent tablecloths and napkins from the lodge to be used at the unceremony and then presented to the beaming couple, courtesy of the lodge manager and staff. The morning waitress and the third chef conspired in the matter of pies, and there were pies of every hue and nature delivered to the meadow and laid end to end on tables, from which they released scents alluring and *redolentous*, as Cosmas said. Edwin patiently hauled, in this order, in consecutive trips to the meadow and back, a small piano, a cask of wine, a keg of ale, and four enormous sealed buckets of soup. Moon made fifty sandwiches of various kinds and carried them up the trail to the meadow himself, humming. Dave's coach, at Mr. Shapiro's request, helped his players submerge the keg of ale in an icy creek nearby. Cosmas rode his bicycle slowly up the trail with a basket of fresh tomatoes, each carefully wrapped in newspaper so as not to bruise or jostle along the way. There were thirty tomatoes, all small compared to the swollen nuclear tomatoes you can buy in stores, but each was a glorious berry of stunning appearance and taste; each was crammed with the essence of summerness and mountain air and the evanescent scents of fir and fern; and each had been persuaded by the Robinsons up through the tall green dream of its parent plant and out along the knobby fingers of its branch and out into the broad welcome of the sunlight and into Cosmas's fingers. Cosmas had picked each one gently and wrapped them gently in newspaper and tucked them in his bicycle basket as gently as you would handle new rabbits or thimbleberries or people.

65

THE DOG WHO HAD DECIDED to live with Mr. Shapiro, having survived by wit and skill and some startling luck in the deepest forests of North America, was tremendously sensitive to pattern, to the many things said without words, to the many signals issued without conscious intent. So it was that even before Mr. Shapiro blamed his old spectacles for his decaying vision and ordered one new pair after another to no avail, the dog saw his infinitesimal hesitation while reaching for things, and the way Mr. Shapiro now shuffled to be sure of his feet even in his own house and the way he leaned over the wheel and peered closely at the road at dusk and the way he occasionally peppered instead of salted, the dog silently inserted himself into Mr. Shapiro's days in so subtle a manner that Mr. Shapiro, for all his own vaulting intelligence and attentiveness, hardly noticed. When Mr. Shapiro rose from his reading chair, with its searingly bright new reading light, and shuffled down the hall to evening toilet and repose, there was the dog at his left side, at exactly the right height for Mr. Shapiro's hand to ostensibly be in affectionate caress, but more and more, as the weeks passed, to be laid upon the dog's spine for balance. More and more, the dog walked with Mr. Shapiro, and while the latter chaffed the former for clumsily bumping his legs here and there, the former might have called it guidance, or steering, or avoiding pitfalls, or assistance or affection, or slowly, shyly, learning to love.

This was no dog to retrieve sticks and newspapers or chase after slobbered balls and whirling bits of plastic or sit and sprawl on command or play the happy fool in exchange for bits of meat, and to Mr. Shapiro's credit, he never once entertained the idea that the dog was a pet or a servant or an amusing clown or a sort of replacement child. Also to Mr. Shapiro's credit, not a day went by that he did not express amazement and gratitude that the dog had chosen him, among all possible companions, and he never, even once, took the dog's residence for granted. Indeed, every morning, as part of his daily ablutions, he spoke directly to the dog, face-to-face over coffee, and said thanks. Every morning, he would also ask the dog his name—it was Mr. Shapiro's feeling that he had no right to impose a name on a being who had lived a life of his own and probably had several names already, names that would probably be remarkable and revelatory of his, the dog's, provenance and adventures—and every few days, usually in the evening as they sat in their chairs after dinner, Mr. Shapiro would ask gently if the dog would tell him something of his life. This is not to say that Mr. Shapiro expected a response in any language he knew; but he did think, as a historian and an appreciative student of journeys and voyages, that perhaps a way would become clear for him to understand what the dog had been through and how he had survived and what he had learned and what he had concluded in his long study of pattern and signals both conscious and unconscious.

You never know, as Mr. Shapiro said one day to Dave's dad at the high school. You just never know. I think it's less a matter of the dog not being able to communicate and more a matter of me not being sufficiently versed in his languages—many of which, of course, are not verbal but physical. As you know from your wife and children, perhaps. But one good thing about being a scholar is that you can concentrate wonderfully sharp when you are fascinated enough by something. And for me, it's a matter of professional pride too—how can I call myself a historian if I cannot piece out some of the history of someone I *live* with? Although perhaps that's the final frontier—maybe it's easier to understand things you don't love than things you do. The closer you are, the farther. That could be. I should be getting home, Jack—my regards to your lovely bride and to Dave and Maria. You might remind Dave that he has an exam on topography next Friday for which I am *sure* he has studied assiduously. From what I understand of your daughter, she could already teach that segment of the course herself. Remarkable child, I understand.

In very many ways, says Maria's dad with a smile. She's the kind of kid who makes you think you must have done something right to be chosen to be *that* kid's dad. She'll be governor someday, mark my words.

★

Edwin carried Miss Moss up to the meadow. Just before ten in the morning on October 4, she set out alone up the trail from the store where she had been since before dawn, staring into the fire, but when Edwin and Mr. Douglas arrived exactly at ten, as had been agreed by all parties so they could travel joyously nervously together, Edwin realized she had gone ahead, from pride or nerves or fury or fear, and he leapt up the trail, leaving Mr. Douglas gaping at the sight of Edwin moving with speed and alacrity.

Not only had I never *seen* him gallop or canter or trot or prance or sprint or any of the other paces horses are supposed to have in their toolboxes, but I had never even *imagined* him in a hurry, said Mr. Douglas to Dave later. It was unthinkable. He's the unhurriest creature you ever saw. But the unthinkable is thinkable, as the poet says. You wouldn't believe how fast he was, suddenly. Maybe it was just the once, but still. I decided you are right, by the way, and I am taking a year off from setting traps for marten. Marten on the mountain get a sabbatical year as a wedding present.

Miss Moss never explained that evening or ever after how it

was that Edwin persuaded her to board him or the nature of their meeting in the woods or who said what to whom about what; but when Mr. Douglas arrived at the edge of the meadow, there she was, sitting astride Edwin, smiling and weeping at once; and Mr. Douglas held out his hand and helped her down to the sinewy grass, and they went to stand together in the center of the circle of their friends; but as they did so, Mr. Douglas said something quietly to Edwin, and Edwin came with them into the center of the circle.

Dave was there, and Maria, and their mother and father; and Moon was there with his mother and father; and Emma Jackson was there, standing with the morning waitress, whose face was love and loss; and Mr. Shapiro was there, leaning on the dog with his left hand, for his back was aflame. In a larger circle outside this circle, there was Moon's basketball coach and Dave's running coach and various members of those teams, and the lodge master with one eye, and Cadence was there, and a few quiet men and women who turned out to be trappers and Forest Service staff and folks who trucked food to the store and a bent older man who brought fresh trout to Miss Moss in exchange for newspapers and spiritual advice.

And Cosmas was there, facing Miss Moss and Mr. Douglas and Edwin; and in the trees were silent birds, and high in a fir there were marten, and Maria said later she was sure she saw an elk for a moment, something big and brown and antlered. And there were dragonflies and damselflies and beetles unceasing; and in the forest there were grass mice and voles and snakes and uncountable infinitesimal beings of every species known and some not yet. All told in the meadow at noon, when the Unabled Lady began to play the music she had composed for the occasion, there were not thirty attendant souls but thousands—and this is not even to count those who flew by, curious, and those who knew from a distance, without having to see, that there was a gathering in the high meadow where the river went from trickle to rill, where the bobcats occasionally met in conference, where one day, many years before, a bearded barefoot man had stopped to rest after climbing over the holy mountain.

66

AT FIRST, when Miss Moss and Mr. Douglas had asked her to compose music for their unwedding unceremony, the Unabled Lady had thought she would compose something sinuous and serpentine, something that would gently suggest the wriggling growth of a love affair, its twists and turns, its ebb and flow, flood and stagger—something with the songs of the mountain in it too, the way the wind fingered and flickered through the fir trees in the Zag and environs, the piercing notes of hawks and osprey, the sift of snow, the suckle of mud. But then she began to experiment with a piece for voices. Initially, she sketched "A Composition for Two Finches to Sing Alternately and Together," but this proved too reedy for the deep throb of the occasion. Then there were days where she wrote sonatas for bears and bugling passages for elk and massive choral pieces for insects and an oratorio built around the trickle and murmur of the river. And then there were days when she concentrated on vegetative voices in concert with and contrast to wind and rock and even the weather, assuming that the day of the ceremony would be clear, so that the sun would be assigned something like a soft alto part, heard in the imagination more than the ear. One thing the Unabled Lady had learned in her composition work was to allow silence to speak; if you left space for silence, she had discovered, it served as a voice or a tone, shivering where a sound would be, a sort of yearning in the ear.

Finally, after many days and nights of work, she hit on a structure that involved all parties in the meadow that morning, from the whisper of the tall grass to the wheedle of chickadees to the one male voice she used as a tent pole to buttress the whole thing—a deep, sonorous sound with an earthy vibrato that shook your bones and made you feel for an instant that the mountain itself was humming or clearing its throat before issuing stern instruction and imprecation to its cousin peaks far away. Having found the shape of the music—the edge of the meadow, as it were—she wrote the music in headlong wild thrilled bursts, three or four hours at a time, writing furiously, hardly ever pausing to finger the piano or hum aloud to be sure of the key, only once pausing to play a snatch of Henryk Górecki just to be sure of an undertone, stopping only to nap for an hour or three, and then right back to the piano. She forgot to eat and made only teas, running through all the teabags in the canisters on the counter and then ransacking the kitchen for more—which is how she found, in a cabinet ordinarily too low for her quotidian use, a paper packet of teas made from every imaginable dried berry and savory plant on the mountain, with a note from Mrs. Simmons, in her perfect handwriting and awful spelling, saying, *mery christmis to you arial!* The Unabled Lady laughed aloud and thought, *she couldn't even spell my* name *right,* and then she burst into tears.

★

I used to think of writing darker music about life on the mountain, said the Unabled Lady to Emma Jackson later. They were sitting under a cedar tree at the edge of the meadow late in the afternoon of the Ceremony. Moon's mother was playing the piano—and beautifully too—and Moon was dancing cautiously carefully distantly with Cadence. I thought about writing "A Piece for Two Exploding Methamphetamine Labs" or "A Piece for Children Terrified of Weekend Custody Visits from Their Fathers" or "A Duet for Burglars of Vacation Cabins." Although now I think I should write those pieces, perhaps interspersed with pieces like "An Elegy for the Rough Grace of Single Mothers" or "Sonata for the All-Night Police Dispatcher." I could write "A Wy'east Symphony," all light and dark, with a slow, silvery passage in the middle for winter—a vaulting elevated mysterious piece with the rumble of logging trucks and the melting of glaciers and a volcanic undertone. I could do that, I bet.

You could do that, said Emma Jackson.

I'd better try before my head sinks down so far I can't see the keyboard anymore.

Good point.

Someone ought to try to write the music of the place, don't you think?

I agree wholly.

Because people have written *books* about the mountain, and God knows there are thousands of articles and scientific treatises and historical considerations and memoirs and political tracts and skiing tomes, but there are a *lot* of ways to tell stories, and what's a better way than music?

I couldn't agree more.

Plus with music you can hint at a lot of voices and tones that no other art can hint at quite the same way. Like finches and horses and hawks.

Or the patient mutter of the Robinsons' car.

The stringent insistence of huckleberries.

The way the river has one high tide a year, but it goes on for weeks.

What are you guys talking about? said Maria, who was wearing the finch in her hair. She reached up, and the finch walked out onto her hand, and Maria reached over and put the finch on the Unabled Lady's shoulder, and the finch sang a triplet of notes three times. The Unabled Lady laughed and said, really, in G? And she and the finch sang together for a moment, until Cosmas asked that the assemblage join him in a last toast to the happily unmarried couple.

★

Louis saw all this. Sure he did. He was ten feet deep in the fringe of the meadow. A new female elk was with him. She was five months old. She was his twentieth child and thirteenth daughter. They were very close. Usually elk calves born in spring stay with their mothers for a year until new calves are born, but in this case the daughter preferred the father and went where he went far more often than elk calves usually do with their fathers. They understood each other somehow. They were easy with each other. These things happen. Beyond the usual relationship, beyond the orthodox, beyond the normal, beyond the expected, beyond the necessary, sometimes there is an easiness, a friendliness, a connectiveness. You know what I mean. It happens in all sorts of relationships. There are the ways you are supposed to be in that relationship, and then sometimes there is something else. That is how it is with Louis and his daughter. Often he walks ahead, and she follows, learning things, but sometimes she walks ahead, and he follows with affection, learning things. What will we call her? She has several names, this little elk calf, twenty weeks old, three feet tall, spotted with white stars on her russet coat, eager and quick witted, bold and curious, silly and somber. Her mother has a sound to call her, her father also, and it may well be that many other beings in and around her residence have sounds or songs or whistles or signs by which they are referring to her among all other things. For us, here in this story, why don't we call her Kuleewit? A lovely word, sonorous, forest-like, as resonant as a thrush in a thicket. And indeed that word was spoken on this mountain once by a Nimi'ipuu man far from his home, traveling alone all the way to the sea for complex reasons, and on his journey, he passed over Wy'east, not far from the path later trod by Joel Palmer, and in a meadow not far from this one, he saw a young elk, and he called to her, *ta'c kuleewit!,* which means *good evening!* in his language, and she turned and nodded, which he accepted as a sign that he was in a good place and should continue his journey, which he did, but that is another story. But we will borrow his word and drape it on Louis' daughter, and this is apt, for she was born in the evening, just as swifts left the castles of their old trees and stitched new languages in the starry sky.

67

MISS MOSS ASKED DAVE'S MOTHER TO SPEAK, and she stood and said, No one can speak for all of us, but someone ought to try. We are gathered here with respect and affection for this man and this woman, who today, before all of us, go together deeper into mystery. Certainly, we are here to witness, we are here to support, we are here to celebrate, but we are also here as living testimony, each and every one of us, that when they need help, when they need attention and assistance against foul wind and dark tide, *we will be there.* When they are troubled, we will lend them ears. When they seek counsel, we will lend them what little wisdom we have. When they are helpless, we will lend them our hands and our hearts. When they are dark, we will endeavor to bring them light. When they are hungry, we will endeavor to bring them sustenance of whatever kind we can provide. That is what we do here. That is what we promise by our presence.

This ceremony is about all of us. We are bound each to each in this place even if we don't admit it except in times like this. We don't have to like each other, but we do have to attend to each other. We are graced and blessed to be here, and we are especially graced to be asked to witness and celebrate the love of two people we cherish. To be asked to be with them on the day they dive into life together, not knowing where it will take them, is a gift from them to us that no one can measure. We will savor this day, we will enjoy every moment of it, we will remember it for many years to come, but most of all, we will remember that on this brilliant day, Richard and Gina shared with us the joy and prayer of *their* love; and there is no greater gift than that. So let us thank them here together, with our hands and voices raised in blessing older and deeper than any religion, and say to them in one voice we celebrate you, we will carry you in our hearts as two made one, from this day forward!

And there rose among them at that moment a tumultuous shout all thrilled with joy, and there were tears also, many of them of many kinds, and among the voices raised were those of other species of beings for example equine and avian, but no one who heard that joyous noise could tell which voice was which, only that many voices were raised in salutation and laughter and unquantifiable uncategorizable prayer. The halls of the trees around the meadow rang as if they were bells that shimmered and echoed for a long time; and then there was such music and dancing and eating and drinking as could not be fully described were we to devote more books to them, and long books too.

*

It was important to Miss Moss that no man or woman was minister or celebrant at the Ceremony, except the principals; but she and Mr. Douglas did ask Cosmas to stand with them, as a sort of Prime Witness; mostly because we looked pretty cool against the mountainous glow of his orange jumpsuit, didn't we? said Mr. Douglas to Edwin later when they were standing at the edge of the meadow watching Miss Moss dance with Emma and Maria.

Well, one of us looked pretty cool, thought Edwin, but another one of us looked so nervous and tongue-tied that I thought for a moment I was going to have to say something when it was someone's turn to say *Yes, I will* to that lovely girl. That would have been an interesting moment, wouldn't it? Imagine the moral implications and emotional ramifications if she would have asked for your affirmation and you didn't say anything, and I was the one who had to say *Yes, you do*, or *Yes, I do*, or *Yes, we do*. Very confusing.

Cosmas came over bringing beer.

No beer for Edwin, said Mr. Douglas. He's driving.

Very generous of him. I will consider that I owe him a beer.

Thank you so much for being . . . what? The tallest witness?

An agent for Mr. and Mrs. Robinson, perhaps. They would be so delighted, Richard. I extend their most sincere and heartfelt congratulations.

Thanks.

Miss Moss came over, flushed from dancing.

May I offer a few words at this juncture? said Cosmas.

Up to ten, any length you like, said Miss Moss.

Well, then, said Cosmas, with a smile. Remember that we are here for you.

That's only nine words, thought Edwin. Throw in an adverb.

We will, said Miss Moss.

Not just the pleasure of the ceremony and its hurly-burly aftermath, said Cosmas, but every bit of this place. This is your place. Wherever you go from here, this was the place that brought you together. Its ratty old rusted mailboxes and the stop signs with bullet-hole punctuation. The trucks in the woods with trees growing through them. Beaver-barked trees. The whinnying of flickers and the chatter of kingfishers. Mud up to your knees in April. Maggots in deer carcasses. Cars from deep in the last century. Snarling tourists. Rude bald county officials. Clear-cuts. Huckleberry pies. Chaining up your tires in October for the next eight months at least. Cottonwood snow drifting and sifting everywhere against that incredible afternoon light sometimes. Remember that. That's all part of it. As we are. Strange as we are, suspicious, vulgar, selfish, grumpy, troubled. This is no paradise. This is no lovely sweet village in a novel. This is a crossroads notable only for the county's sand-truck depot and your store. But we throw together here as best we can. Sometimes we are actually a sort of village for a day. Like today. Remember that. Wherever you go, remember that. Today, you and Dickie made us a village. Tomorrow, we go back to being an obscure crossroad.

Hurly-burly, thought Edwin, is a very good word. Does a hyphenated word count as two words? If you hyphenated a whole paragraph, would it actually be one word?

*

Dave's dad is talking to Moon's dad. Beer is involved. Here's the greatest metaphor story *ever*, he says: One time I went to the funeral of a man who used to be a logger, and it was a great roaring funeral—he was Irish, and they have the roaringest funerals—and people got to drinking and dancing and courting, and a baby was conceived *on the coffin of the guy who died*. Hey? Is there a greater metaphorical story than that? Hey?

What's the metaphor?

I haven't the faintest idea, said Dave's dad. *What* a story, though, hey? I love that story.

I heard a story like that where a couple is getting married and the woman goes into labor *on the altar,* says Moon's dad. Now *there's* a metaphor for something or other. The way I heard the story, she said *I do* and then screamed with the first jolt of labor pain.

That's a great story. Can I borrow that story? That's a keeper of a story.

Is Miss Moss in labor? asks Maria, suddenly at his elbow.

I don't think so, said Maria's dad. She looks . . . serene. *Serene* is not a word I would use for a woman in labor. Your mother was anything but serene. I would use a word like *shrieking* if I were using one word for a woman in labor.

I hope she's pregnant, says Moon's dad. We have not had a new baby in the Zag for a while. Although I have been traveling and may have missed a few. Jack?

I think we should take up a petition and see if they can have triplets, said Maria's dad. Or at least twins. We are down two in population since the Robinsons. I wish they were here. He was the nicest guy ever, and she was nicer. They would be sitting right there under that tree holding hands if they were here. You never saw two people hold hands more than they held hands. They would sit quietly together on folding chairs at any and all events and hold hands. Let's put two chairs together under the cedar just in case they are here somehow and want to sit down. You don't want two people of that age to have to stand if they can sit, you know what I mean? And we'll get a little wine for them, and some berries. I'll be right back.

68

WERE THERE PRESENTS? Absolutely. Gobs and mobs and piles and towers, all of them cheerfully defiant of the bridal decree that there were to be *no presents whatsoever*, since there was no Wedding as regulated by any ostensible civic or religious authority. The presents were delicately stacked and balanced all over the chairs and the mantelpiece and the floor by the fireplace in the store so that when Miss Moss and Mr. Douglas walked into the store the next morning, they stepped into the mossy darkness and sensed some burly unfamiliar jumble where usually there were only the two lean old chairs by the fire, and Mr. Douglas flipped on the light, and they were startled and amazed for a second, and then Mr. Douglas laughed, realizing that Dave had engineered this surprise because Dave had the only other key to the store, but Miss Moss started to cry for reasons that remain murky. She went into the kitchen to warm the griddle and start the soup as Mr. Douglas picked his way through the gifts to start the fire, but when he heard a gasp from the kitchen, he ran to see if she was okay, and she showed him the gift certificate in the soup pot—a week in a cabin on the Oregon coast, all expenses for travel and meals and steelhead fishing trip paid. The place on the gift certificate where the donor's name was usually recorded was blank, but later, when Mr. Douglas asked Edwin if he knew anything about the gift or the donors, Edwin made a point of looking away and closely following the manic swoop of a kingfisher, and Mr. Douglas got the message and laughed and said okay, fine, I will just tell Ginny that it was you. Thanks. I have never been to the coast, isn't that ridiculous? Two hours away from the biggest ocean in the world, and I never once set foot in salt water. I don't believe that Ginny has, either. Have you? Don't answer that. Of all the horses in the world who would of course have a story to tell about being in the surf, you would be foremost. Of course you have been in the ocean. Foolish of me to even ask. I wouldn't be surprised if you have been on a ship. You have, haven't you? Is there anything you have not done in this life? Don't answer that.

Also, when Miss Moss went to the key rack to find the backup key for the deep freeze, she found the keys to Mr. and Mrs. Robinson's repaired Falcon hanging there, with a note from Cosmas saying, *from Mr. and Mrs. R. to the Happy Couple*, and she had to go sit on the front steps and stare for a while at the proud animals carved long ago into the old wooden railing posts.

*

And the dancing and drinking and eating. O sweet Jesus, the sausages and grilled trout and last corn roasted in its husk in the fire. The fire redolent with juniper and cherry and sage someone carried up the trail just for the brief pleasure of the scent of the smoke. Mr. Douglas dancing with Maria. Fiddle and pennywhistle and a clarinet. Miss Moss peers into the sifting dusk to see who is playing that lovely whirling clarinet, and to her surprise it is Dave's cross-country coach with his eyes closed and his knees bent. On the whistle is the morning waitress, trying not to laugh at how egregiously poorly she is playing the thing, and on the fiddle is one of Moon's basketball teammates, a pale boy with pimples all up the west side of his face. The first stars peering out of the sky going blue to black. How very many scatters of stars are named for animals, thinks Miss Moss. Eagle, swan, crab, bull, bear, fish, lion, goat, scorpion, horse. We see animals everywhere. We are animals. Or we used to be animals, and mostly now we forget how to be animals, which is why we look for them everywhere.

Speaking of which, she says to Edwin, are you enjoying yourself?

Very much so, thinks Edwin, although the prospect of picking our way down the trail again in the dark is not something I relish.

Mr. Douglas is suddenly there beside Edwin, smiling.

May I cut in?

It would be a pleasure, says Miss Moss.

I understand congratulations are in order, Miss.

This makes her laugh aloud. I suppose so, she says, although it seems to me I have probably simply volunteered for a much deeper wilderness.

It seems to me he is a very lucky man, says Mr. Douglas. I would guess that he too is a little rattled but thrilled at the possibilities for . . . depth.

Just kiss her, for heaven's sake, thinks Edwin. You two are always talking when you should be kissing and fencing when you should be wrestling. How human animals ever manage to reproduce is a mystery to me sometimes. So much chatter and jabber.

I'll convey your regards to, says Miss Moss, but she does not finish her sentence, because Mr. Douglas *is* kissing her with all his might in the flickering firelight, with Edwin behind them like a warm brown wall, and Miss Moss is kissing him deep and wild and thrilled, the kind of kiss where you just pour yourself into it without any thought or agenda or target or message, just complete furious trust and affection and joy, there's so much of that in you for this one soul in the world that you cannot speak except with your lips and your tongue and your arms and being pressed together like hands in prayer, and for a few seconds, almost a minute, you are lost and found. And you break apart, startled and electrified, and only then do you dimly hear everyone applauding, their faces flitting from light to dark to light as the fire fluctuates; and you bow, laughing, and somehow, that is the crescendo, the apex, the conclusion, the beginning of the end of your best day ever.

★

Can something be sad and happy at the same time? An event? A moment? Sure, thinks Dave, sitting on a log by the fire with Cadence and Moon. He likes Cadence and she likes him, but she does not love him and he does not love her, but they *like* each other in some other heartfelt, entertaining way. Why does it have to be love or not? Isn't like a form of love? Isn't like actually the crucial ingredient of love? It's easy to *fall* in love but not as easy to *stay* in love, and the only way to stay in love is to like, isn't that so? Because if you just depend on love, then when things change or people change, will you love the new person she is rather than just the person she used to be, the one you fell in love with?

You're losing me here, says Moon, and Dave almost falls off the log.

What?

You said before that this is a happy event, but it's also sort of sad. Why?

Because they're not actually married? says Cadence.

No, no, says Dave. That actually seems cool. It's their decision, and Miss Moss is real firm about how no other authority gets to tell them how they are related or committed or defined or whatever, and Dickie doesn't care what their status is called; he just wants to be with her. No, it's not that.

What then?

I don't know. Don't you guys feel it? An event like this is so great because it brings everything into focus; it's like a prism that bends all the light in one way. But after today, it'll be everything back to usual. Back to regular time, you know? Today is like an island where time doesn't apply. Today doesn't even end until we say so. But today also changes things. What if she sells the store and they move to Utah or something?

She'd never sell the store, says Moon. Where would the Lutheran dawn hikers eat? They'd starve, and that would be the end of the faith in America.

I know, says Dave. I just feel . . . weird. We hardly ever *are* a town, I guess, and it feels great to *be* one for a while, and then tomorrow, it's back to regular life where everyone lives apart, and here comes the snow, and soon we'll be in college or working or whatever, and I *like* living upstairs in our house with Maria, and soon I'll have to go away, and I don't *want* to. I love smelling bacon downstairs and running in the woods and talking to you guys and my dad making dumb jokes and then laughing for twenty minutes to himself. I *like* stepping in bear scat once a year. It's sad that it all changes so fast. Will we even *be* friends in a few years? Will we?

★

Sometimes we forget that we were all teenagers once, and we forget that teenagers are enormously sensitive, and for all their masks and disguises and japes and adopted personas and fear of being uncool and fear of being found out as only themselves, they are as sharply alert to the right time not to speak as any older seasoned bruised listener; and this was one of those times. So they sat there, the two boys and the girl, in the flicker of the fire, and not one of them spoke for a very long time.

The fire burned down as the stars lit up.

Here are Miss Moss and Mr. Douglas and Edwin at the far edge of the firelight, Miss Moss and Mr. Douglas with their heads together and Edwin behind them like a part of the forest himself; he is looking at them with some sort of spice in his eye—affection, surely, but isn't there something very like amusement? Yes?

The Unabled Lady wrapped in a shawl, laughing as Moon's

coach and teammates prepare to lift chair and Lady and all and carry her down the trail to where Moon's mom and dad rented a van to carry her home. Emma Jackson and Maria dancing one last dance, each swirling in place at the very edge of the meadow, and for an instant Maria vanishes into the oceanic dark under the trees but then pops out again laughing. Cosmas and Dave's dad and Dave's coach folding tables and chairs and carrying what little extra food there is to a spot under the trees to leave for the other Citizens & Residents, as Cosmas says. Dave's mom and the morning waitress in their autumn jackets waiting for the convoy to start down the trail. Mr. Shapiro and the dog and the finch leaning against trees at the edge of the clearing watching all this with mixed and complicated emotions. Nighthawks flit past and one small owl. The fire burns lower. Dave and Cadence and Moon stand and stretch, and Dave offers Cadence his jacket, and she declines courteously but smiles as she says no thanks, and Mr. Douglas says gently, I guess we'd better put out the fire, gentlemen. Miss Moss boards Edwin and everyone else starts down the trail slowly, carefully shuffling a bit, each and every one thankful for the rope banister set up by Dave's teammates for just this hour and purpose. Penultimate is Cosmas, who kneels to be absolutely sure of the fire's doused embers, and while he is on his knees he speaks very quietly to Mr. and Mrs. Robinson, and then he rises and says, Richard?

Mr. Douglas says right behind you, but as Cosmas vanishes into the dark, Mr. Douglas stands there and takes it all in—the broad circle of the sky stammering with stars; the dim soaring vault of the trees; the faint last scent of the bonfire; the fragrant bruised grass; the sharp faint call and whir of nighthawks. This was our chapel, he thinks. I'll always remember this. We'll always come here. Maybe when things are confusing, this will be the best place to be. It'll be all snow soon. We could build an igloo and visit in the winter. I'm scared. I'm thrilled. This is crazy. She's my kind of crazy, though. I don't believe it happened. It *did* happen, though, didn't it? It *did*. Didn't it? It certainly by god did, and he smiles and turns and vanishes into the trees, and there is the night meadow as it has been for a thousand years, as round and open as a mouth in song.

69

MARTIN SAW ALL THIS. Sure he did. He saw the whole thing from noon to moon. He saw the first arrivals in the meadow and the unpacking and the laying out of food and the building of the fire. He watched with interest. He saw the mice and voles scurrying out of the way of the feet of people and a horse. He saw the ouzel in the creek move disgruntled downhill to a lower pool. He explored the canopy along the trail and watched Edwin and Miss Moss have a meeting of the minds, and then she climbed onto the horse, and he carried her up to the meadow. He saw Dave climbing up, and he watched the boy he knew, holding hands with the girl who had been lost in the snow and took refuge in the hollow tree that the bobcat was going to poke into. That was long ago when Martin was young. Now he is seventeen months old and very nearly fully grown, and he has a companion, a mate, a partner who is with child. Two kits will be born in late April next year, two weeks after Martin is two years old. One will be female and the other male. The female will become a legend, but that is the story for another book. The male will very nearly drown but be saved from drowning by an amazing coincidence, but that is also the story for another book. We are still in *this* book, even though we are very nearly at the end of it.

Martin conducts his martenesque business all during the day of the Unwedding, but he returns again and again to the meadow, fascinated by the activity and curious about these animals in their riotous caperings. Once in the afternoon, he brings his companion, and they sit high in a fir tree on the uphill side of the meadow and watch. He sees Dave dancing with Miss Moss and with his mother and with Maria and once carefully, painfully, with Cadence. He sees the finch sitting on the piano as the Unabled Lady plays "A Tarantella for Eleven Dancers, One of Whom May Be Equine." He hears Cosmas explain his plans for a bicycle ramp an eighth of a mile long down a clear-cut with the exit point being thirty yards out over a small lake. What an attraction that would be for children from the city and environs!

Martin's companion returns to their den for a nap before the evening hunt, but Martin remains above the clearing and watches. He is there when the bonfire begins to burn down. He is there when the first meteorites whip through the sky so fast that before anyone can say *o my god shooting stars!* they are memories sharp against the sky. He is there when Cosmas says, Richard? and slips away into the darkness, and he is there when Mr. Douglas pauses at the edge of the meadow and thinks *this was our chapel*, and he is there watching when Mr. Douglas too slips into the darkness under the fringe of the trees, and nothing remains of the day but the gentle swaying of fir and fern where Mr. Douglas passed. For a long moment, Martin remains on the branch, high above the meadow, listening, aware of every rustle and thrum. And then, quicker than the eye could follow and quieter than any ear could catch, he vanishes; and you will have to dream the rest of his story yourself, perhaps as you walk in the woods or sprawl in a mountain meadow or lie abed early in the morning and stare out the window, sure that you just saw, just for an instant, a flash of golden brown against the long green splash of the trees.

THANKS & STUFF

My particular thanks to two attentive students of life in the Northwest woods: Sue Livingston of the U.S. Department of the Interior Fish and Wildlife Service in Oregon and Alan Dyck of the U.S. Forest Service in Oregon. Generous souls, open to any number of foolish questions, in my experience. You know, everyone wails and moans about The Government, but hardly ever do we stop and say, boy, are there a lot of expert, generous, brilliant people working for us. I say so here, now, and I mean it.

Also it seems to me that writers ought to admit here and there that many books and writers have seeped into their unconscious over the years and swirled and seethed mysteriously in their heads and hearts ("macerate your subject, let it boil slow, then take the lid off and look in—and there your stuff is, good or bad," as Robert Louis Stevenson wrote) and surely influenced and shaped their own work, and that is certainly true of me and *Martin Marten;* so I here thank and laud Jim Kjelgaard and Ernest Thompson Seton and Charles George Douglas Roberts and Barry Lopez and Cameron Langford and Henry Williamson and Marguerite Henry, whose *Cinnabar, the One O'Clock Fox* I must have read a hundred times when I was a small boy.

Also I have spent many hours with the wonderful series of books published by Arthur Robert Harding in the opening decades of the twentieth century, books I love dearly for their odd mixture of declarative fact and salty story. Harding, who started trapping for fox and mink at age nine, eventually started *Hunter-Trader-Trapper* and *Fur-Fish-Game* magazines (the latter still in print, with more than one hundred thousand subscribers), and among the many books he published are *Mink Trapping, Fox Trapping, Fifty Years a Hunter and Trapper,* and *Home Taxidermy for Pleasure and Profit.* Me, personally, I think Arthur Harding did a great deal to save and celebrate the beings he wrote and published books about, as he was an early and articulate voice for conservation.

Also I thank my family, who long ago concluded with a collective grin and sigh that I was a total nutcase about the mustelid family in North America (marten, fisher, otter, wolverine, badger, skunk, ferret, mink, and weasel), and especially our canine friend Ringo, a hunting hound who has taught me a great deal about attentiveness and patience and predation and alluring scent and angles of attack and how to dismember a mole in twelve seconds or less. You wouldn't believe how fast you can dismember a mole, even if you only have one fang, the other having been lost somewhere over the years, reportedly in a forest called the Dark Divide in Washington State, but that is a story for another day and a second glass.

My thanks also to the gracious souls at Timberline Lodge on Mount Hood, who have allowed me to wander widely in and around what amounts to the coolest old wooden mountain lodge in America, and especially to the McPhee family of Oregon, who lent me their mountain cabin on Wy'east, experiences which surely sparked this book; it is their cabin in which Dave and his family live. And finally a particular thanks to my son Joe, who one day, when he was fifteen, picked Cameron Langford's lovely *The Winter of the Fisher* off our bookshelf and read it with such pleasure, such empathy, such absorption, such amazement that there were such extraordinary beings in the world that something awoke again in me; and so let the final words in this book be gratitude to the late Cameron Langford, who was paralyzed in a car crash at age twenty-four but then threw himself into the study of the beings of his beloved northern Canadian woods and wrote his one great book before he died. Poor boy, trapped in his broken body, and dead even before his book was published—but what a spirit, what reverence and love for life, what courage to sing beautifully and humbly against the descending darkness!